Irate

Alexis Soleil

Published by Alexis Soleil, 2021.

This is a work of fiction. Similarities to real people, places, or events are entirely coincidental.

IRATE

First edition. September 24, 2021.

ISBN: 978-0578985619

Written by Alexis Soleil.

To my grandmother Zeldia Quick

RAMIRO'S PLAYLIST

"Orion" - Metallica

"Hallowed Be Thy Name"- Iron Maiden

"Raining Blood" - Slayer

"Disorder" - System Of A Down

"The Evil Woman" - The Electric Light Orchestra

"Come And See The Show" – Emerson, Lake, And Palmer

"I Don't Live Today" - Jimi Hendrix

"Raping Your Mind" - Mr. Bungle

"What Doesn't Die" – Anthrax

"People Are Strange" - The Doors

"The Spirit Of Radio" - Rush

"Get Up" – Van Halen

"It's Been Awhile" - Staind

"Midnight Carnival" – Mannheim Steamroller

"Voices In My Head" – The Police

("Don't Fear") The Reaper – The Blue Oyster Cult

"Bela Lugosi's Dead – Bauhaus

"Surfacing" – Slipknot

"Dittohead" – Slayer

"Hardwired" – Metallica

"Manteca" -Dizzy Gillespie

"The Children's Merry-Go-Round March" – Elvin Jones

"Sweating Bullets" - Megadeth

"Dragula" - Rob Zombie

"Children Of The Next Level" – Testament

"Evil Has No Boundaries" – Slayer

"Breathing Lightning" - Anthrax

"Message In A Bottle – The Police

"Synchronicity" 1 & 2 – The Police

"Wish Liszt (Toy Shop Madness)" – Trans Siberian Orchestra

"Limelight" - Rush

"Panama" – Van Halen
"Enter The Sandman" - Metallica
"The Call Of The Ktulu" - Metallica
"Carol Of Bells" – Trans-Siberian Orchestra

NOELLE'S PLAYLIST

"Rain" - Kerri Chandler

"Winter's Blessing"- Jerri Sydenham and Kerri Chandler

"Missing You"- Larry Heard

"Playground" - Schmoov

"Joy" - Robert Owens

"Mainline"- The Jason Load Experience

"Keep Looking" - Sade

"Christmas Time Is Here" – Ray Parker Jr.

"Twelve Days Of Christmas" - Frank Sinatra

"Gabriel's Message" - Sting

"Sleigh Ride" - Ella Fitzgerald

"Sleigh Ride" - Ella Fitzgerald, The Latin Project Remix

"The Other Side Of The World" - Luther Vandross

"Last Christmas" – Wham

"Winter Wonderland"- Annie Lennox

"Winter Wonderland" - Andy Williams

"Something Beautiful Remains"- Tina Turner

"Everything She Wants" - Wham

"Yo Mister"- Patti LaBelle

"Knocking On Heaven's Door" - Aretha Franklin

"Annette" - Dream 17

"Teardrops" - Womack and Womack

"Santa Forever" – featuring Mia Crosby by Dave Jay

"Butterflies" – Leon Vynehall

"Angel Of Mercy" – Metro

"What Is Love" - Haddaway

"Rescue Me" – Debbie Malone

"The Enigma" - Schmoov

"Stars" – Mr. Fingers

"The Machine" – Kerri Chandler

"Aether" – Mr. Fingers

"Take Me To The Sky" – Earth, Wind, and Fire
"Cold Cuts" – Marvin Dash
"Sing" – Travis
"Deck The Halls" – Mannheim Steamroller

CHAPTER ONE

"*Hallowed Be Thy Name*" by Iron Maiden blared from the headsets of twelve-year-old Ramiro Jose Espinoza while he relaxed in his full-sized bed with his eyes closed. The earphones wire connected to an MP3 player he borrowed from his friend Zack. A small Halloween Jack-o'-lantern and a rubber spider sat on his nightstand with a few pieces of candy. He opened his eyes, grabbing a strawberry Starburst, unwrapping it, and popping it into his mouth. *"I eat too much fuckin' candy. I hope I don't get a toothache. I've got to get to the dentist. I told my mom but she's got so much shit on her mind that she forgot to arrange an appointment. My Dad's been driving her crazy, which causes her to forget things. I have to remind her periodically,"* Ramiro chewed on the sweet, gummy treat. He again closed his eyes, visualizing a massive flock of screaming metal heads in a concert arena. He took center stage with his black bass guitar strapped over his shoulder. His two fellow lead guitarists stood alongside him. Ramiro glanced behind him as his drummer played. The first lead guitarist picked his guitar's string with its high-pitched, screeching sound echoing throughout the arena. He felt like a god on the stage in front of thousands of admirers. Whatever the band called themselves, they'd played one of their aggressive tunes. He headbanged while playing his bass guitar. The stage lights beamed on him as his fans rooted for him.

BACK TO REALITY, WHERE beaming headlights reflected on Ramiro's bedroom window with squealing car brakes. He didn't sense the ray of lights nor hear the vehicle parking. Long brunette tress, pretty, pink silk pajamas clad, Maritza, thirteen years old, crept down the hallway and barged in. She snatched her brother's headphones off. "What the fuck!" Ramiro sat upright in his bed while his lengthy hair draped on his shoulders. He widened his eyes, grabbing his earphones from his sister's hands. "Dad's home!" Maritza alerted her brother. His heart pounded in his chest, stashing the MP3 player under his pillow. Ramiro heard the car door slam as heavy footsteps crunching on dried leaves that have fallen from the bare trees. Keys jingled at the front door. Maritza dashed back to her bedroom, leaving her brother's door open. Ramiro closed his eyes, turning on his side towards the window. He then squinted, taking a deep breath, attempting to halt his rapid heartbeat. He saw leaves falling from the tree that stood by his bedroom window. He hated raking up the pile of accumulated brown, yellow, and red stuff on the ground.

"My father's going to get on my ass about those shitty leaves because it makes your home look like shit. Maybe, I can

  convince my sister to rake them for me. I'll see what I can do," Ramiro heard heavy footsteps ascending to the top of the staircase and panting. The man of the house stood at the top of the steps for a moment. Jorge Espinoza, who moved his family to Massapequa, New York, from San Martin, Peru. This black-framed glasses, late-forties, medium-build, brunette, gentleman noticed his son's opened door. Ramiro sensed his father standing there as if he had nothing else to do. *"Isn't he tired? He huffed and puffed coming up the stairs. Now, go to bed already,"* Ramiro shut his eyes, pretending to be asleep. Jorge stepped towards Ramiro's bedroom door with his monstrous shadowy figure in the doorway like *Krampus* coming to take bad kids to hell on Christmas Eve. Jorge stretched his hand out to the doorknob, shutting the door. His shadowy footsteps remained underneath the crack of the door for a second. Ramiro's father's hefty footsteps shuffled to the master bedroom down the hallway. The hinges of the door creaked as he slammed it hard causing the house to quiver.

WITHIN SECONDS, FEMININE cries echoed from outside Ramiro's bedroom door. His father always bitched about the house not being clean enough, or the wrinkles in his shirt not ironed, or anything that vexed him. Drawers, furniture, and objects rummaged from his parent's bedroom as if the house experienced an earthquake. Ramiro cringed at the chaotic disturbances with thuds and crashing. He clutched his pillow to his body in bed. Then Ramiro heard a smack and a crash to the wooden floor. His mother pleaded for her husband to stop his torture. Ramiro sprung from his bed, opening the door. His sister dashed down the hallway past him. Maritza pushed the master bedroom door open. "Get off my mother! Get off my mother!"

"When I become a big Rock star, I'm going to get my mother out of this hell. Why is this happening to my family? Why the fuck is my father such an asshole? No matter what my mother, my sister, or I do, we're always wrong!" Ramiro darted down the murky corridor towards his parent's bedroom. He kept running and running as the hallway got longer and longer. It felt as if he were in a nightmare that he couldn't wake up from because it was real. Not being able to get to that door fast enough. Ramiro picked up his pacing, kind of leaping, and finally hulked on his father's back. Jorge held the children's mother by her wrists on the bed. This young man kept a tight grip on his father's neck. The father and son then battled it out as if it were just the two of them. Ramiro hoped that this man would take his last breath, so he and his family could have some peace. Maritza attempted to pull her father off of her mother, crying. Jorge focused his attention on

this small-framed young man trying to take him out. Both of them fell to the floor as they both had each other by their necks. *"Please, someone make my father stop with his bullshit!"* Ramiro begged for someone or something to stop this crazy man from trying to snuff the life out of him. Their echoing voices subsided into the night. Then silence overwhelmed the Espinoza home until dawn.

THE NEXT MORNING, JORGE ate sausage and scrambled eggs at the table while his wife Anna Maria Espinoza, beautiful, poured his coffee in a mug with the Peruvian flag. Her long brunette tress almost touched the floor; she kept her hair in a tight-knit bun to keep it out of her way while doing her duties around the house. She scrambled to the stove, placing the coffee pot on the burner. Not once did Jorge glance at his wife, who dedicated her life to him and their children. He devoured his eggs like the issues in their home, but they mounted like mushrooms.

STANDING IN THE FULL-length mirror, Ramiro buckled his belt on his black jeans while dressed in his black long-sleeve undershirt and slipped on his Mr. Bungle black t-shirt. He hummed one of the band's tunes since no headphones were allowed in school. He noticed red marks on his neck. *"Holy shit! I can't allow my teachers or anyone to see the marks! My sister and I will be separated if the police are called! Hopefully, they'll go away!"* Ramiro doesn't even remember how the fight between his family even ended. There was so much constant battling with Jorge until none of them could recall how it started or ended. His backpack laid on his bed; he glanced at the one textbook, a binder, and a composition notebook. He hated heaving books to school, but Ramiro loved his composition notebook full of his song lyrics. During his lunch hour, he'd sit in the corner at a table alone and write. The students didn't dare interrupt him since Ramiro believed they feared him. He preferred it that way as if the lunch table had his name engraved on it. He combed his fingers through his shoulder-length brunette hair and was ready to start his day.

AT THE KITCHEN TABLE, Jorge glanced over his shoulders at the staircase, awaiting his son and daughter. Maritza strutted down the steps, skipping towards the kitchen table and plummeting into her chair. Her father glared at her without a smile or a morning greeting. "This isn't a playground, Maritza!"

"Sorry, Papi," Maritza whispered. Her mother set a plate of her eggs and sausage right before her eyes. Maritza poked the food with her fork and ate. Ramiro descended to the first floor; he swaggered to the table and sat in the chair. He didn't glance at his father, but Jorge eyed Ramiro. Anna Maria gave Ramiro his plate of eggs and sausage. Ramiro couldn't stand his father watching him like a hawk ready to devour its prey. He ignored the eyes watching him while he ate his breakfast. Due to the intense staring, Ramiro wished he could do something sinister to his father. He knew his father focused on his sinistered graphic t-shirt with the evil-looking rabbit and his long hair that he couldn't stand on men because it represented rebellion. Jorge grabbed his son's shoulder-length locks, "You need a haircut!" "What the fuck!" Ramiro sprung from his chair. He shoved his chair into the table, stormed away. He dashed upstairs to his bedroom as his father gave chase. "Who do you think you are, Ramiro!"

Jorge ran up the staircase as fast as he could to get a hold of his pig-headed son. He stormed into his son's bedroom, seeing Ramiro zipping his backpack. He threw the strap over his shoulder, coming face to face with his father, who stood at six-two. The pre-teen didn't let his father's towering height intimidate him. Jorge lunged at his son, crashing to the floor, missing him by inches. Ramiro scrambled out of his bedroom and hurried downstairs. His father rose to his feet, pursuing his son, and stumbled down the staircase to the first floor. Ramiro swung the heavy front door open, racing down the block with his schoolbag. "You're getting a haircut! Do you hear me! You're getting a haircut, Ramiro! And you better rake up those leaves too!" Jorge pumped his fist in the air. Then Ramiro gave his father the finger. Maritza rushed to catch up to her brother. Jorge turned fiery red in the face, slamming the door.

MINUTES LATER, RAMIRO strolled around his neighborhood before taking the shorter route to school. He noticed there was a school bus picking up kids, a man walking his dog, and a mother rushing her kids off to school by car. There were times when Ramiro wished his father had the time to drive him and Maritza to school, but he's busy being an asshole instead. Anyway, Ramiro had time to kill before the late bell rang. So, Ramiro wasted no time while he sauntered down the concrete sidewalk. He stumbled across an enormous home that towered over the other homes. Rumor has it that this home resembling a haunted house was called "Hell House." Ramiro didn't want to judge the people who occupied this home because he didn't want the same to be done to him. He passed slowly by the house with its three levels and an iron gate. His eyes fixed on the window at the top floor of the residence, wondering if someone was peeking through the curtains to figure out who he was. Maybe not.

"Ramiro!" a feminine voice echoed. He turned around, not seeing anyone behind him. And no one was.

"I'm over here!" the feminine voice alerted him.

"What the fuck are you doing across the street?" Ramiro noticed Maritza on the other side of the street.

"I was about to ask you the same thing!" Maritza walked slowly and then up her pace because she got the eerie feeling of "Hell House." Ramiro hurried across the street to his sister's side.

"Why are you walking this way? You're going to be late? And why are you walking by Hell house?" Maritza kept her fast pace.

"Why the fuck are you so afraid of this shit?" he hurried behind his sister.

"That's Hell house!" she shouted. Ramiro halted in his tracks, pissed with his sister for not realizing the real deal. He then took his strides again, picking up a quick pace.

"Do you know what fuckin' Hell house is!" he bellowed in her ear.

"You just saw it!" Maritza kept up her pace.

"We live in fuckin' Hell house! Fuck it! I live in a hell house! Mom lives in fuckin' Hell house! We don't know how those people are! The neighbors just want something to talk about! Our home is a Hell house! And you fuckin' know it!" he pointed in Maritza's face. He stormed ahead of his sister as she stopped in her tracks, shocked.

LATER THAT MORNING, an electric bass guitar strapped around Ramiro in music class, where he jammed along with the drummer and a guitarist. The trio did this jam session all the time during the fifth period. His teacher Mr. Oz allowed Ramiro to express his musical freedom because he saw promise in this twelve-year-old. A young guitarist, Aaron, and the drummer, Zachary McQuillan, thirteen years old, pounded on his drum kit playing an old seventies rock song. But Ramiro had a desire to play more aggressive rock. Female admirers sat up front, cheered for the trio. After class, Ramiro chatted with his music teacher, Mr. Oz, an African-American gentleman, early forties, sitting at his teacher's desk, advising this shining star's future. He wanted Ramiro to try expanding his musical horizons. Besides, listening to Heavy Metal, Ramiro also listened to jazz music. His musical appreciation came from Zack's father's vinyl collection of musicians from the forties to the present. Mr. Oz told him what if his Heavy Metal dreams didn't come true? There are opportunities in other genres, especially Pop music. Ramiro sighed at the idea, reluctant to hear his teacher out. He couldn't see himself on stage with some bubble gummy singer while he played bass. Ramiro grabbed his backpack, swaggering out of the classroom.

IN THE CAFETERIA, STUDENTS clamored over lunch as Pop music blaring from the speaker in the corners of the ceiling. Maritza and two friends sashayed to the two tables at the end of the lunchroom. She, Candace, and Fiona placed their book bags on the last table to save for Ramiro while they sat at the table in front. Three young men came in search of where to sit. They noticed the table, attempting to obtain it.

"That's reserved!" Maritza slapped her hand on the last table for her brother.

"No one's sitting here," the seventh-grader responded.

"Don't you see the schoolbags there?" Maritza glared at the boys. Ramiro hurried to the lunch table, throwing his backpack on top of the others. "What are you looking for?" he glared at three kids. The three young students scrambled away as Ramiro sat at the table. "What's up, Ramiro?" Candace greeted him with a smile.

"What's up, Candy?" Ramiro returned the greeting.

"Are you cool, Ram?" Maritza asked.

"Yeah," Ramiro pulled out his notebook and pen, writing more lyrics.

Maritza turned around in her seat, attending to her friends. Ramiro glanced around the cafeteria while holding his composition notebook in his hand, focusing on his work. Not his schoolwork, but writing song lyrics. He jotted down words of resentment on the blue-lined paper. Ramiro's heart pounded like a drummer on a Tama drum kit. He envisioned wrestling his father to the floor, overpowering him with punches to the face and head. Then Ramiro hurled a final blow to his father's temple. Ramiro stood over his father's body with a sneer. He wasn't sure this man was dead or alive. Ramiro swung open the basement door, descending the murky steps. Jorge squinted his eyes as rummaging came from the basement. He didn't have the strength to move or get to safety. He felt the excruciating pain in his head and murmured for help. Then an enormous blade manifested in his vision as Ramiro twirled a machete in his hand like a correctional officer with a billy club. He could see this man's face tremble and bulging eyes. "Are you afraid of me, Pop?" Ramiro continued to whirl the enlarged blade.

"Don't!" Jorge begged his son. *"Thou Shall Not Kill"* resonated in Ramiro's mindset. He whirled the machete. And with no thought, he slashed the blade along his father's neck. The bell rang due to the lunch period subsiding. Students exited the cafeteria, rushing to class. Ramiro snapped out of his vile fantasy and titled his dark, murderous song *"Thou Shall Kill."* He shoved the notebook in his backpack and headed to his next class.

THE AROMA OF HOMEMADE chicken soup boiled on the Espinoza kitchen's stove, where Anna Maria looked at the October calendar that afternoon. She noticed Ramiro made his way into the world on the thirtieth. Her forgetfulness seemed as if she had amnesia or Alzheimer's at an early age. Anna Maria recalled Ramiro's arrival on Devil's night. Her water broke during an argument with her husband Jorge. She believed the bad omen cursed her son. There was a knock on the front door; Anna Maria opened it. She greeted Ramiro with a kiss as he stepped in the door and rushed upstairs.

"Your birthday is tomorrow, Ramiro! You're going to be thirteen!" his mother stood at the foot of the staircase, watching him hurry to the second floor. Ramiro didn't give a shit about his birthday. He wanted to take a nap and didn't want to hear shit from anyone.

Ramiro dashed into his bedroom, noticing Zack's smashed Mp3 player, books scattered on the floor broken, smashed little pumpkin, crushed candy, and his mattress flipped over, etc. Ramiro stormed down the hallway towards his parents' master bedroom, where his father rested in a king-sized bed. He slugged his father in the face as blood dripped from his nose. "What the hell! Ramiro! Jorge sprung from his slumber.

"What the fuck!" Ramiro held up his fists, ready to take on his father as if they were the same age. "You think you can take me on! Try it! Come on! Coward!" Ramiro and Jorge fought like ruffians in the street. Anna Maria stormed into the room, trying to break them up. Her husband shoved her to the floor, luckily not hitting her head. "You pushed my mother!" Ramiro charged at his father, hurling fists. Maritza dashed upstairs. "Stop!' This fourteen-year-old dared enough to get in between her father and brother. "Maritza!" Anna Maria cried. Her daughter plummeted to the floor because of this fight that wouldn't end.

"I'll dial 911!" Maritza bellowed and burst into tears. Jorge pushed his son into the corner where Ramiro hit his back against the radiator. This young man endured agonizing pain and curled on the floor. The threat seized her father's attention.

"If you do that, you'll be in the system," her father crept towards her with piercing eyes.

"Just let Ramiro be!" Maritza tried to hold back her tears. Anna Maria embraced her daughter and wept. Jorge glanced at Ramiro with deep-seated hate. Ramiro hoped the neighbors didn't call the boys in blue. "*I'll lie my ass off to keep me and my sister from being separated,*" Ramiro strutted out of his parent's bedroom, hunched over in pain. *"What the fuck did this shithead do?"* While in his bedroom, minutes later, Ramiro was still in pain. He tossed the crushed candy and smashed Jack O'Latern in the can. But his rubber spider was in good condition. He put the phony insect on his dresser. He then struggled to place the mattress on its frame and did it successfully with the unbearable pain he experienced. He picked up the smashed MP3 player in his hand. *"What the fuck am I going to tell Zack? And his father? That's my fuckin' ass?"* Maritza and her mother struggled into Ramiro's bedroom. Ramiro placed the device on his table. He assisted his mother to rest in his bed. She inhaled as Ramiro fluffed some pillows under her head. His mother's warm hand caressing his face. Anna Maria didn't speak; she hid her feelings a lot. Ramiro sat on the edge of his bed while his mother held his hand. Maritza's jaw dropped, holding the crushed Mp3 player in her hand. "Ramiro, what the hell are you going to do? Zack's going to kill you!"

"I know I've got some explaining to do," Ramiro sighed. He took the music player from his sister's hand. Maritza swept her brother's bedroom floor. While his back killed him, Ramiro slapped the MP3 player on his side table and wanted to take the responsibility of straightening up his room. It exhausted him after grappling with his father. Then the front door of the Espinoza residence slammed. He released his hand from his mother, stepping towards the window. His father's car engine started up as it pulled out of the driveway. He gazed out at his father, hoping that his father would never return home. Ramiro then went back to his mother's side, holding her hand once again. He held his head down, feeling some back pain. He didn't bother to make eye contact with his mother. Anna Maria pictured Ramiro's life twenty years down the line. *"I would love for my son to become a judge on the supreme court or maybe a heart surgeon. But he loves his music and wants his rock star dream. I'm not too sure about it. What if it doesn't happen? I need for Ramiro to have something to fall back on,"* she stared at her son's shoulder-length ebony hair with his black t-shirt. God blessed Ramiro with the beautiful locks that Anna Maria loved running her hands through. She noticed how strong Ramiro bounced back from falling against the cast iron radiator. *And thank God, it wasn't hot.*

SILENCE GOVERNED RAMIRO'S bedroom while Anna Maria still grasped her son's hand. Ramiro woke up from the warmth of his mother's hand, from whatever brief nap he took, hoping to get rid of that pain in his back. He glanced at his mother as she slept. He cracked a smile and placed her hand over her chest. Anna Maria looked as if she died. Ramiro's eyes widen because God forbid if he were to lose his mother. More murderous thoughts of his father danced in his head, with devils encouraging him to take this man out. "Mom," Ramiro called to his mother. She slowly opened her eyes and smiled at him. Anna Maria rubbed his cheek. "Hey, baby." Ramiro grabbed his mother's hand. "Tomorrow is your birthday," she whispered.

"How could I forget?" he answered. Ramiro's birthday made his mother happy because she gave him life regardless of her circumstances.

THE FOLLOWING DAY, Ramiro's mother marched into her son's bedroom with thirteen glistening candles on an ice cream cake. "Happy birthday to you! Happy birthday to you! Happy birthday, dear Ramiro!" Maritza held a blue birthday bag in her hand. Ramiro sat upon the mattress as his mother presented the cake before his eyes. He blew out the candles, waving the smoke rising from the wicks of the candles.

"Happy birthday, Ramiro!" Maritza gave her brother a large gift bag. He pulled out an Anthrax t-shirt in his hand. In a full-length mirror, Ramiro slipped the metal band t-shirt on. He smiled at his mother and sister as their images reflected in the background. "Thanks, guys!" he embraced Maritza and his mother. Ramiro then grabbed a set of Apple earphones with a new MP3player from the gift bag. He inserted them into his ears, turning it on as he increased the volume that gave a crisp and bass sound. For a second, Ramiro indulged in his world as his mother tapped him on the shoulder, he pulled the headphones from his ear. "Hide them from your father." Ramiro nodded.

On this Halloween Eve, Ramiro celebrated his special day by watching the classic horror movie "Dracula" with his mother and Maritza. Ramiro lounged in his computer chair while his sister sat on the floor, eating popcorn in fear as his mother sat on her son's bed. *"Dracula is a joke! Why is Maritza scared of this shit? I can understand my mother because she's superstitious. I'm happy they're here with me. Fuck! My father's MIA. He worked overtime to avoid my birthday. It's because I was born on Devil's Night. Maybe if I were born on the first few days of November, my father would be here. He wouldn't see me as a threat."*

THE NEXT AFTERNOON, Maritza flipped through Glamour magazine as she waited along with her mother and Ramiro in the dentist's office. Anna Maria filled out the forms for Ramiro and sighed at the fact that she didn't know her son's social security number by heart. "Ramiro, I've got to get your SS number," she rummaged through her purse. "Dammit! It must be at home!"

Without hesitation, Ramiro spewed his social security number starting with a zero, then the double odd numbers, the two middle numbers with an odd and even number, and the last four digits. He then smiled at his mother.

"Are you sure that's it?" she lifted an eyebrow.

"Yes, I've got my SS number down packed," he leaned back in his chair.

MOMENTS LATER, RAMIRO laid in the dentist's chair as the dentist stuck a cotton swab in his upper lip to numb his mouth. The dentist's x-rays showed that he had seven cavities and needed fillings. He's been through this routine before and knew what to expect. Minutes later, the doctor gripped a large sharp needle in his hands, aimed towards Ramiro's mouth.

"Close your eyes, Ramiro. And take a deep breath."

"Holy shit! Here goes this shit again! Another needle!" Ramiro closed his eyes, inhaling and feeling a slight pinch of the needle deep into his mouth. The dentist removed the needle and walked out of the room.

"Now, I've got to wait until my mouth numbs up. Then I've got to go through all of this fuckin' drilling. I can't wait to get the fuck out of here!" he closed his eyes for a second. He drifted off into another world, taking a quick nap. Everything was pitch black and it was like he didn't know what was going on or what to dream of for a couple of minutes. He then heard light footsteps approaching the dentist's chair. His mother ran her hands through his hair, kissing him on the forehead. "Ramiro, this will be over before you know it. Just be the brave soul that you are. And don't allow your father to put fear in you. I'm proud of you for your bravery. Then light footsteps approached. "Wake up, Ramiro! Are we nice and numb yet?"

Ramiro halfway opened his eyes, ready to get his procedure on his teeth done.

THAT SATURDAY MORNING, Maritza raked up the leaves into a sizeable plastic garbage bag. She was willing to do her brother the favor. Their father was so tired from working until he forgot to re-mind Ramiro to do the job. Ramiro opened the side door and eyed Maritza. She peered up at her brother while proceeding to rake. "Good morning!"

"Good morning," Ramiro dropped his skateboard under his foot. And then he threw the rubber spider at his sister. "Someone else wants to give you a morning greeting!" he cackled.

Maritza dropped the rake as the black rubbery toy flung her way. "What the hell, Ramiro! Get that thing out of here!"

"It's a fake spider! It's not real! Women!" he continued to guffaw. Then he stopped poking fun at his sister. "I'm sorry."

"Going to hang?" Maritza picked up the rake, pulling the garbage can closer to her.

"Yeah. Thanks, Maritza," he rolled the skateboard back and forth underneath his foot. "Thanks for what?" she placed the hefty bag in the can.

"For doing the job for me," Ramiro then flipped the skateboard's tail end with his foot.

"No problem. How does your mouth feel?" Maritza put more leaves in the can.

"It's cool. See you later," he skateboarded down the street to Zack's house. His friend lived a few blocks away, close to the water, where boats docked at the pier along with residential homes like parked cars in the driveways. Drums echoed in the distance while he skateboarded faster and faster, getting closer and closer to Zack's house. Ramiro skateboarded past pretty, early-forties, Mrs. Stein, who sported old denim, a button-down shirt, work gloves, a scarf on her head, watering roses in her front yard. The sound of Ramiro's skateboard racing along the concrete sidewalk was just as annoying as the pounding drums down the street. "Dammit!" she thrust the small shovel into the soil. The drumming got louder and louder in his ears like headphones at a high volume. Ramiro hopped off his skateboard in front of his friend's residence, noticing the opened garage. Zack thumping away on his Tama drum kit. Ramiro heaved his skateboard under his arm towards the widened garage. Zack halted his playing, giving Ramiro a hi-five.

"What's up, dude?" Zack greeted.

"Fuckin' fierce sound," Ramiro threw his skateboard on the ground, wheeling it back and forth with his foot.

"Thanks. How was your birthday?" Zack asked.

"Quiet. Just me, my mom, and Maritza," he shrugged.

Further, into the garage, Zack's father, Neil McQuillan, mid-forties, shuffled from a heap of rusted junk with a couple of bikes from the early days, roller skates, chains, links, tools, and some more modern days' things such as Zack's dirt bike, first kiddie drum kit, and now his Tama kit, which took up a lot of space. Neil's lit cigarette burnt every time he inhaled. He extended his hand to Ramiro, blowing smoke into the air. "Happy belated birthday, rock star? How's it going?"

"Same shit! Different fuckin' day! Thanks!" Ramiro threw his hands up in the air.

"Your old man on your ass?" Neil scoffed.

"No one else but him," he exhaled.

"Kick the shit out of him!" Zack twirled his drumstick in his hand.

"Watch your mouth, you little shit!" Neil showing poor parenting skills. He waltzed behind the heap of the junk pile in the garage. Ramiro eyed the detail of his friend's drum kit. From the floor bass drum to the tom-toms with five glistening cymbals on each side. He envied Zack because his father spent a pretty penny on his drum set. "*Shit! I wish my father believed in my dream. Neil's cool and hip, while my father is an old-fashioned fuck. I don't know how I'm going to deal with him. I have no other choice. He's the breadwinner. Holy fuck! I'm still going to get my haircut! Fuck! Fuck! I hope Zack doesn't ask about the Mp3 player,"* he gazed at his friend's fascinating instrument. Zack drummed fast, striking the tom-toms, snares, and cymbals. The loud, pounding drums grabbed Mrs. Stein's attention, who marched down the street. She's strutted on the McQuillan's property with her fingers plugged in her ears and soiled clothing. Zack didn't feel his neighbor's presence while he dwelled in his musical world. She snatched one drumstick from Zack's hand, smiling. Zack halted his playing.

"Why did you do that, Mrs. Stein?" this young drummer tried to grab his drumstick from his neighbor's hand.

"You're disturbing the peace, young man!" Mrs. Stein placed her hands on her hips.

"Dad! Mrs. Stein is here! And she is a real...," his neighbor cut Zack off before he could complete his insults.

"Watch your filthy mouth, Zack!" Mrs. Stein attempted to snatch the other drumstick from his hand, but no luck. Neil waltzed from behind the pile of junk, taking the last puff of his cigarette, and mashing it in the ashtray. Neil rushed to his son's drum kit, attempting to reason with this old widow who might have poisoned her husband in favoritism of her cats. Ramiro watched the drama unfold as Neil, Zack, and their neighbor exchanged ugly words. She threatened to call the authorities or report them to the neighborhood board for noise pollution. Neil grabbed his son's drumsticks from Mrs. Stein's hands, and then Zack snatched them from his father's hand. He drummed, drummed, and drummed, getting on his neighbor's nerves.

"Dammit! That does it! I'm going to report you!" Mrs. Stein bellowed at the top of her lungs.

Neil grabbed his son's hands to seize him from drumming. Ramiro and Zack glanced at each other, snickering. Then Zack rose from his drum seat and swaggered into the house. His father and their neighbor continued to exchange harsh words.

MINUTES LATER, THE boys looked through Zack's father's record collection in the living room as Jazz music played from his stereo. Neil had various musical tastes in his vinyl collection, such as Miles Davis, the Doobie Brothers, Earth, Wind and Fire, Kiss, Jimi Hendrix, and countless others. Zack liked Jazz because of the drum solos; that's one reason he played. And then his love for Heavy Metal as well. Ramiro enjoyed the Jazz genre as well due to it being an art. Neil stepped into the living room noticing his son, and Ramiro listening and discussing his variety of music. He knew these two had promise and took them somewhere they'd love.

LATER THAT AFTERNOON, electric, bass, and acoustic guitars hung on the wall like paintings in a museum very colorful, shiny, and intriguing to music lovers in this local music store. "Manic Depression" by Jimi Hendrix blasted from the speaker in the ceiling corner. Salespeople assisted customers with the instruments that captivated their interest. The boys hurried into the establishment as Neil lagged, puffing on his cigarette. Ramiro stood in the middle of the floor, looking at the bass guitars on the wall. Zack dashed further to the back towards the drum section.

"You like what you see, Ramiro?" Neil approached him from behind.

"There's no smoking in here, sir?" a long pony-tailed, blond rocker, sporting his awesome 3D biomechanical forearm tattoos on both arms, early-thirties, sales associate advised.

"What's up, Matt?" Neil gave his friend a hi-five. Then he swung the entrance door open, throwing away his cigarette.

"What's up, Neil? I haven't seen you in a while!" Matt embraced his friend.

"I've been busy," Neil blew the last mist of smoke from his mouth. Ramiro smelt the nicotine emerging from Zack's father's pores. Loud, fast, pounding drums materialized from the back of the store. Ramiro, Neil, and Matt heard Zack showing off his talents. He did this wherever he went. Neil eyed Ramiro and introduced him to Matt. Ramiro smiled at this 3D tattooed rocker, admiring the art on his forearms. He then focused on his purpose which was the colorful guitar pedals that alternate the sound of a player's instrument. Matt followed this thirteen-year-old and could tell he knew what interested him. "What kind of guitar are you looking for, Ramiro?" Matt strutted from behind the glass counter. Ramiro focused his eyes on the black basses; he wasn't interested in any other color.

"I heard the Sterling bass is good," he eyed the black basses.

"You're right," Matt grabbed the Sterling bass, presenting it before Ramiro.

MOMENTS LATER, RAMIRO and Zack jammed out in the store's rear, where they attracted a small audience. A mother and her three daughters held books on playing clarinet, a slender gentleman in his sixties, who looked like he was in a blues band. These kids played an old rock tune from the sixties as the mini audience, then grew with a few more spectators. Ramiro attempted to envision playing before thousands of metalheads, but he kept his mind on the audience in front of him. "That's Zack on drums and Ramiro on bass guitar," Matt informed the small group of admirers. While Ramiro played, again a woman's little girl smiled at him as if she had a crush. Then it hit him: he was going to learn to sing. *"What the fuck! How am I going to pull this shit off? It's not like I'm James Hetfield,"* he told himself. The young musicians concluded the song as the small crowd applauded. Ramiro felt as if he were walking on air, even though there were a few spectators. The sixty-something gentleman named

Earl shook Ramiro's hand and Zack's. Matt and Neil gave them hi-fives.

THAT NIGHT, RAMIRO wrote more song lyrics in his notebook as he sat up in bed. Maritza danced and sang to the House song "Rain" by Kerri Chandler from her brother's headphones. Ramiro kept his concentration on his lyrical content as her singing annoyed him. He couldn't stand House music because the people were annoying. His sister didn't have a spectacular voice or was even passable. Maritza wouldn't be qualified to sing for any type of music. She peered over her brother's shoulder while he wrote a song with repetitious f words. She lifted an eyebrow. "Are you going to sing, Ramiro?" Maritza removed the headphones from her ears, scratching her head.

"What do you think?" he stopped doodling in his composition book. "Can I have my headphones back?"

Maritza gasped at the shocking words that her brother thought about their father. She slowly gave Ramiro back his headphones. "Here you go." Then her eyes popped out of her head. "Holy crap, Ramiro!"

Then beaming headlights brightened Ramiro's bedroom window. "Good night, Maritza," he pointed to the door. Without saying a word, Maritza sprinted out of her brother's bedroom, closing the door. His father's car engine shut down as the gravel under Senor Espinoza's feet crunched. Ramiro stashed his earphones and composition notebook into his school bag. *"Here comes this shit again! Are we going to tear the fuckin' house up again? Oh, did my mother dust the furniture, mop the floor, cook his dinner? He's such an asshole."* Ramiro faced his closed bedroom door while keys rattled at the front door from downstairs. The top lock clicked as the hinges on the front door creaked. He would not pretend to be asleep and dared his father to challenge him. The front door squealed closing back as Senor Espinoza entered. He sighed as his keys jingled in his hand. Then Ramiro's father ascended the carpeted stairs to the second floor with heavy steps. *"What the fuck is wrong with this fuckin' fuck! He comes up the steps like an exhausted, overweight fuck!"*

His father got to the top of the staircase, looking at his son's closed bedroom door, and stood there for a second. While Ramiro lay in his bed, he didn't move a muscle. Ramiro figured his father would check on him. He kept his eyes open, facing his challenge. His cardiac muscle pounded in his chest. Jorge walked towards his bedroom door and thrust it open, seeing his son glaring directly at him. Ramiro and his father were like two cowboys at a showdown with their egregious looks. "Why are you still awake, Ramiro?" his father's shadowy figure stood in the hallway as if it were a demon. Ramiro had plenty of those that he didn't reveal yet. In time, he'll show them. For now, it was he and his father's battle.

"Ramiro! I asked you a question?" Senor Espinoza repeated himself.

"I'll fall asleep," Ramiro gazed at his father.

"Are you disrespecting me?"

"No, I'll fall asleep soon," Ramiro kind of raised his voice.

"Who the hell do you think you are! I'm the breadwinner around here!" Senor Espinoza bitched and bitched as the world slept. Jorge wanted to lie down and forget about his rebellious son. This thirteen-year-old iconoclast didn't want to put his mother through any trouble. So he laid on his side, giving his father his back, shutting his eyes, and trying to force himself to go to sleep. Ramiro closed his eyes even tighter, hoping to drift off into his little world away from his father's bitching that didn't stop. Ramiro cringed at every word his father uttered. He couldn't help but hear him, and then his bedroom door shut. Most of his father's talk was gibberish, but the only thing Ramiro made out was a trip to the barbershop in the morning. His father's bitching had Ramiro fired up. He then gave the finger as the door shut.

"A haircut? I dread this shit!" Ramiro eyed the ceiling, erasing the thought from his mind, and fell asleep.

CHAPTER TWO

That Sunday morning, Dr. Charles Stanley played on the Espinoza's television in the master bedroom. Anna Maria ironed her husband's dress shirt, making sure that it was wrinkle-free. Jorge was glued to the screen listening to this preacher give his sermon about non-believers. All sorts of thoughts and beliefs entered Jorge's mind. He knew his stubborn son always rejected God. As he kept his eyes glued to the television, Jorge stood to his feet ready to challenge the boy who rebelled against his morals. Then Maritza entered her parents' bedroom, holding two dresses in her hands. "Which one should I wear Mommy?"

Jorge glared at his daughter. "You're not going to a fashion show, Maritza? You're going to church! Go wake up your lazy brother."

MEANWHILE, RAMIRO LAID on his back in bed and could slightly hear the television coming from his parents' master bedroom down the hallway. He tossed and turned. And then he turned his back towards the bedroom door, inhaling the cold air through his nostrils. It felt as if he had a stuffy head. He squinted his eyes, aware that it was the Lord's day. Ramiro hoped that he didn't have a cold. It was probably allergies due to the autumn weather. His father loved keeping the house cold. He didn't turn the temperature up until later in the day. Then his bedroom door widened. He figured it was his father.

"Are you awake, Ramiro! You have to get ready for church," Maritza held the stylish dresses in her arms. she then closed his door back.

"Why did Maritza have to do his dirty work? She had to tell me to get ready for church? I'm not going. I'm not feeling well. I think I've got a cold coming on," Ramiro continued to toss in his full-sized bed. He closed his eyes. The clock read: 8:34 a.m. Minutes went by and then an hour.

HEAVY FOOTSTEPS STOMPED towards Ramiro's bedroom as Jorge stormed into his bedroom. "Get the hell up out of that bed, Ramiro! You were supposed to be ready an hour ago!"

Ramiro cringed hearing his father bitch him out. He squinted his eyes, seeing his window with a bare tree before it. "I wish I could climb out of this window and down the tree to get away from my father. I never tried it I guess it's because I faced my father," Ramiro still laid on his side. His father rushed over to his son's bed, snatching the blanket off him.

"What the fuck!" Ramiro jumped to his feet.

"You're getting that haircut!" his father waved both fists in the air.

"No!" hollered Ramiro

"You demon!" Jorge gestured strangling his son.

"Well, I guess I am!" Ramiro said proudly.

Maritza and her mother stood in the doorway, hoping there wasn't another altercation between the father and son.

"I can't stand that long hair! You look like a girl!" Jorge bellowed.

"That's too fuckin' bad!" Ramiro ran his fingers roughly through his hair.

Jorge glared at him, shocked by his son standing his ground. "You're not my son. You're not my responsibility anymore," his father stormed out of the bedroom.

Ramiro saw that his mother and sister witnessed him and his father going at it again. There were no fists hurled, pushes, chokeholds, just an exchange of words. Ramiro swaggered to the other side of his bed, staring out of the window. He didn't mean to give his mother and Maritza his back, but he did. Ramiro wanted to lay down and try to sleep his stuffy head away.

LATER THAT MORNING, Ramiro arrived at Zack's house, noticing how quiet the surroundings were, and how no birds sang. *"Why the fuck is it so quiet? Shit! This place feels like a ghost town!"* Ramiro rang the bell at the McQuillan's front door. Then a bird landed on the porch, chirping. "Are you the only sole survivor?" he murmured. Then the front door clicked, unlocking as it widened. Zack's face lit up, seeing Ramiro before him. He could tell he had another fight with his father. Ramiro mumbled to himself and marched into the house. Seconds later, Ramiro dropped his ass in the recliner and rocked in it of the McQuillan's living room. "Are you supposed to be at church?" Zack sat on the couch.

"Nope!" Ramiro focused his eyes on the cartoons on television.

"How did you manage to get out of that?"

"I cursed him the fuck out and told him to fuck off," Ramiro shouted.

"Okay, calm down Ramiro! Shit!" Zack laid on the couch.

"You don't have a Jesus freak father," Ramiro rocked in the recliner. He felt as if he were dishing out his problems to a therapist. He ran his fingers through his hair, smiling. Grateful that he didn't get a haircut.

"You stood up to that fucker! Good job, Ramiro," Zack stood to his feet. "Do you want to see something?"

RAINDROPS DRIPPED ON the window of Zack's bedroom minutes later as the radio blasted "Sweating Bullets" by Megadeath and cartoons on television at the same time. Zack twirled his drumsticks as he stretched in his full-sized bed. Ramiro held a male Mexican red-legged tarantula in the palm of his hand. Ramiro smirked at the obscure, creepy insect with its eight legs tickling his skin. The spider didn't scare Ramiro not one bit. But he knew it would scare the crap out of his mother and sister. A fiendish smiled emerged on his face. *"This creepy-crawly would make my father shit his pants or give him a heart attack. I could see balls of sweat cascading down his face, trembling in fear."*

"Ramiro!" Zack snapped his fingers in the air. Ramiro stared and stared at the tarantula, fascinated with this creature that triggered ideas in his head. Zack placed his drumsticks on his bed. "I'll take him now," he reached for his pet from Ramiro's hands. The spider crawled into Zack's hand. He placed the arachnoid in a tank that he created with rocks, sand, tiny artificial plants making the setting comfortable for the bug. "What does he eat?" Ramiro couldn't keep his eyes off of the insect.

"Mice, rats, or whatever he can consume," Zack shrugged his shoulders, closing the top of the tank.

"That's fuckin' cool," Ramiro grabbed a loose-leaf paper with a pen. He focused on the blue-lined paper and wrote some song lyrics. The spider crawled on the side glass tank in the line of sight. Ramiro glanced at this bug again as if it spoke to him. He knew the creature saw through the tank with the eight eyes as it had legs. Ramiro had an obsession with the creature and wanted to ask Zack if he could take it home. But, he would probably say "No."

Instead, Ramiro focused on writing music. The first song where the title spoke for Ramiro's life.

"FROM HELL"

"My father, the son of Beelzebub, cast down from above, he isn't human, the darkness within his path, by his snarling teeth, he'll grab your soul needing total control of my every move....," Ramiro jotted down lyrics of his creation as he wrote with a vengeance. He wasn't lost for words because the spider that he befriended probably understood him better than Zack. Once again, he and the spider made eye contact. The only thing Ramiro thought about his father not being human and that he was a demon in human form. His father married his mother and had two children to make their lives hell. As evil as his father was, Ramiro believed he would become an abusive man himself. *What could he do to avoid being like his father?*

Ramiro focused his attention from the tank, noticing Zack twirling his drumsticks between his fingers again, gazing at the cartoons on television. Ramiro shoved the loose-leaf paper in his face as he snapped out of his gaze from the t.v. "What do you think, dude?"

Zack read the first couple of lines and shook his head. Astonished by the lyrics, he lifted an eyebrow. "Are you serious?"

"What do you expect? Happy shit!" Ramiro bellowed.

"Is this how you view him?" Zack asked.

"Yes," Ramiro smiled at the spider. He grabbed the loose-leaf paper from Zack's hand. He jotted down more insane lyrics. He didn't care if the songs were explicit or bizarre. He wanted to write about mutilation and bondage.

"Severed heads, chopped limbs, blood splattered everywhere. Fuck with me, and I'll have your body shoved in the freezer. Fuck with me, and I'll place your head on a serving platter to your family at Thanksgiving dinner. I'll feed your heart to the dog; I'll chop your ass from head to toe, serving the scraps to rats...," Ramiro wrote this grotesque song. He pictured his father's chopped head in a freezer. His mother

opening the icebox and screaming at the top of her lungs at the hor-
rifying discovery of her husband's hacked head. She fainted, plummeting to the floor from the horror. Ramiro would feel the guilt of
putting his mother through such anguish. But, shit! Look at the hell
his father put her through along with him and Maritza. The thought
of killing his father would spare his mother's life. Ramiro snapped
out of his obscure fantasy and brought up singing. There was no
way anyone else was going to be the front man of the band. Zack
advised him to discuss that with their vocal teacher, Mrs. Lance.
Ramiro waved his fists in the air and disagreed. What would this older woman know about singing Heavy Metal? She only knew about
mainstream Popstars. Ramiro doubted this music teacher's musical
knowledge. He had to figure something out or do something on
his own. Neil stormed into Zack's bedroom eavesdropping on the
boys' conversation and adding his two cents. He advised never to
underestimate anyone's knowledge of anything, especially if they're
in that field. Ramiro remembered imitating the cookie Monster's
raspy voice and couldn't speak for an entire week. He'll never do
that again. Some Heavy Metal singers sang like that or a demon.
Ramiro relinquished the thought and wrote whatever crazy lyrics
came to mind. Neil wanted to take Zack and Ramiro to see Ravens
and Crows in concert at Nassau coliseum. Ravens and Crows, a famous thrash Heavy Metal band formed in the late-nineties. Neil
wanted Ramiro to ask his parents for permission. Anna Maria would
let Ramiro go and now his father doesn't care. He could do whatever
he pleased. Also, Ramiro had dirty thoughts on his mind, he couldn't
wait to fuck. *"Women throwing themselves at those rock musicians
backstage at your concerts. That's the life I want to lead,"* he thought.
Neil encouraged the young men to focus on their craft. Ramiro
sucked his teeth, changing the subject to the women because that's
where Ramiro's mind was. Zack glanced back and forth at his father
and Ramiro discussing groupies. Neil, of course, had his man-to-man

talk about the birds and the bees with Zack. Senor Espinoza didn't talk about sex; he wanted his son to be pure until marriage, which wasn't reality. But Ramiro learned about sex on his own.

THAT NIGHT AT DINNER, Ramiro's family bowed their heads at the table as Jorge gave the blessing without Ramiro present. An empty chair was right next to Jorge. He knew Ramiro hated sitting next to him at suppertime discussing God repeatedly. Ramiro didn't even cross his father's mind. Jorge concluded the blessing, shoving a piece of roast beef in his mouth. Anna Maria scooped mashed potatoes on her fork, eating. She glanced at Maritza chowing down on her dinner. Anna Maria chewed her food slowly, noticing the empty chair. This was the first family dinner without Ramiro present. And probably after that, family gatherings wouldn't be the same. Even though the Espinoza had their share of issues. Maybe, it would be better if Ramiro wasn't at the table so there could be some peace. And of course, Anna Maria fixed a plate for her son. Then there was a knock at the door, Maritza hopped from her seat and knew her brother's knock. His mother closed her eyes praying to Thank God that her son made it home safely. Her son didn't attend church with them that morning. Ramiro entered the home, dashing upstairs without saying a word. He slammed his bedroom door.

LATER, RAMIRO STRETCHED in his bed listening to Exodus through his headsets. His mother barged in Ramiro's bedroom, holding a plate of food. She greeted her son with an angelic smile, placing the roast beef dinner in Ramiro's lap. He sat upright, devouring his meal without greeting his mother. She sat on the edge of her son's bed and didn't mind if Ramiro didn't say "Hello". All Anna Maria wanted was for him to eat, sleep and be well. Ramiro didn't give off the impression that his mother was disturbing him. He kept his eyes on his plate and ate. Anna Maria stood up from the edge of the bed where she sat. She headed towards the door. From the corner of her eye, Ramiro raised his head from his plate. "What's wrong, Mom?"

His mother turned to him with a smile. "Nothing."

"You can stay," he proceeded to chew his food. His mother turned back and sat down on the edge of her son's bed. Anna Maria heard Ramiro's chewing in her ear. She looked at him enjoying his food as he usually did. "You didn't come to church with us this morning. And you didn't get your haircut."

"The chemicals in the barbershop give me a migraine. Plus, I'm not a kid anymore."

"Where were you then?"

Ramiro swallowed his food and looked at his mother. He saw that she wasn't angry, but concerned. "I was at Zack's house."

"Did you enjoy yourself?" Anna Maria held her son's hand.

"Yeah," he shoved a scooped of mashed potatoes in his mouth.

"Ramiro!" Jorge stood in the doorway of his son's bedroom. He didn't bother to step further inside as if it inhabited demonic spirits.

Ramiro gawked at his father, easily swallowing the mashed potatoes. "*What does this fuck want?*"

"I'm too old to be running after you! You're going to be on your own in a few years," Jorge cleared his throat.

"*Holy shit! This fucker's going to kick me out! I can't wait to get the fuck away from this fuck!*" he shoved significant pieces of meat in his mouth. His father didn't say a word about Maritza leaving. Who was going to protect his mother and Maritza? They would have to deal with this crazy man on their own. Jorge would allow Ramiro to dig his own grave. Anna Maria feared for her son's well-being. Her eyes widened as she pictured Ramiro homeless or an inmate. Her husband lectured Ramiro about making plans for his future.

"On your seventeenth birthday, you're shipping out," Jorge stormed out of the doorway. When Ramiro heard his father's repulsive words as his heart dropped like glass to the floor. He saw his mother trembling, sensing that her heart thumped in her chest. He sat his plate on the side table. Ramiro clutched his mother's hand. She glared at her son, stroking his cheek.

"Don't worry, Ramiro. I'm going to make sure that you don't wind up in a bad situation. I'll always be here for you and you've got your sister," Anna Maria kissed her son's hand. They looked and saw Maritza leaning in the doorway. She invited herself in with her eyes fixed on her brother. Maritza sat Indian-styled on the wooden floor. "He can't kick you out!" Maritza whispered, looking up at Ramiro. Maritza didn't know what to say to her brother, but someone had to start the conversation. She frowned at Ramiro as he turned to her.

"What's up, Maritza?" he wiped the last tear from her eye.

"Nothing. Did Zack ask about his Mp3 player?"

"Not yet. Most likely he should forget because he's got so many electronics," he shrugged.

"What are you going to do if Dad kicks you out?" Maritza asked.

"I don't know," Ramiro said.

"What if he were to do it now?"

"Then your father would have to kick us all out?" his mother squinted her eyes while she laid in her son's bed. She rested her hands on her chest.

"I'll figure it out when the time comes," Ramiro exhaled. He had to have a plan before this shit happens to him. "I have to learn how to sing," he scoffed. He asked Maritza about the chorus teacher, Mrs. Lance. She never took chorus class and felt her brother didn't need to waste his time on that. Heavy Metal doesn't require good singing; just growl and snarl like a creature. Ramiro knew one thing he wanted to sing in an aggressive tone. He's pissed about a lot of shit.

THAT MONDAY MORNING, Maritza and Candace strolled down the street with their pink and purple schoolbags, dressed in the latest fashion for young women while babbling about the exciting high school years that awaited them. Ramiro took strides down the street, looking straight ahead of him. He constantly daydreamed of being a vocalist/bassist playing for thousands of cheering fans, pack-stadiums, photographers taking pictures, traveling the world, and the women never faded. *"I would love to have my picture plastered on a lovestruck girl's bedroom wall. Now, am I going to speak to Mrs. Lance or maybe, I should leave it alone. I'll figure it out!"* he heard the clamoring playground of his junior high school. He felt good because he still had his shoulder-length hair that he fought good and hard to keep. By Ramiro being the rebel that he was, he felt confident about his Heavy Metal dreams. Whether he sang or not.

DURING THE FIFTH PERIOD in school, Candace, Maritza's friend, sang in Mrs. Lance's chorus class. The large group sang "Memories" from the play Cats. *"Shit! They sound like they're dying! Or bored!"* Ramiro sneered. He grasped the hall pass in his hand while peering through the glass door of the classroom. *"Why didn't Maritza tell me that Candace was in the choir?"* Ramiro was going to give his sister a piece of his mind at lunch. He headed back to his science class down the hall. He marched into the classroom, dropping the pass on the teacher's desk. He took his seat right in front of Zack.

"So?" Zack leaned close to Ramiro.

"What do you mean, so?" Ramiro whispered as he faced forward, jotting down the science notes from the blackboard in his binder.

"Did you find anything out?" he whispered from behind Ramiro, doing his classwork.

"Candace is in Mrs. Lance's chorus class," Ramiro copied the science notes from the blackboard into his notebook.

"Shit! Why didn't Maritza say anything? I'd kick her ass if I were you," Zack scoffed.

"Shut the fuck up! That's my sister!" Ramiro reminded him.

"I'm just saying, dude. My bad!" Zack leaned back in his chair, finishing his classwork. If anyone were going to confront someone in his family, it would be Ramiro, not an outsider.

AN HOUR LATER DURING the sixth period, Ramiro swaggered into a crowded cafeteria with Zack behind. He seemed pissed at Zack as he heaved his bookbag over his shoulder a few feet ahead of him. Zack didn't give a shit about Ramiro's feelings. Ramiro hurried to the last two tables, throwing his backpack on it to holding for Maritza and her friends. Then Zack placed his school bag on the first table also and sat at the last table in front of Ramiro. Ramiro folded his arms with a frown on his face, looking straight ahead.

"Are you still pissed, Ramiro?" Zack exhaled.

"Fuck it. I'm over it," Ramiro shrugged. In the distance, he noticed Maritza and her friends rushing to the table. They placed their bags on it and sat down.

"Maritza!" Ramiro cried to his sister.

"What's up?" she bumped her hip against Zack to move over at the table.

"Why didn't you tell me that Candace was in Mrs. Lance's class?" he turned red in the face.

"I figured you would find your voice. I thought it would be no big deal," she sighed.

"Shit! It is a big deal," he unfolded his arms.

Zack attempted to add his two cents into the conversation but kept his mouth shut. Ramiro had the expression of *"Don't try it."*

"Do you want me to get you a tray, dude?" Zack asked before leaving the table.

"Yeah, cheeseburger and fries," Ramiro sat like a king on his throne. Maritza made eye contact with her brother, noticing his pompous attitude. Her brother glanced in the other direction.

"Sorry, Ramiro," his sister gave him puppy dog eyes.

"I'll figure something out," he shrugged and sighed.

"Am I in your good graces again?" Maritza asked.

"You're always in my good graces," he slightly smiled. That put a big Kool-aid smile on Maritza's face because she's off the hook.

"Come on, Maritza. We've got to get some grub!" Fiona scrambled from the adjacent table. Maritza gave chase.

Across the cafeteria, an African-American girl kept glancing at Ramiro, a couple of tables ahead of him. As this myelinated-skinned female stared at him, it didn't break him out of his gaze. Ramiro then caught this young lady's eye. The seventh-grade girl smiled at Ramiro as he returned the friendly gesture. Zack rushed to the table, placing the two trays of lunch on the table. Ramiro broke from his stare at the girl and took a bite out of his cheeseburger. Food does the trick; it woke Ramiro up and kicked him off his throne.

THAT FOLLOWING WEEKEND, the rock bassist of the metal band "Ravens and Crows" played solo on a dark-brown wooden electric bass guitar with psychedelic lighting on a round stage surrounded by seats in the arena. Then the drums and the two electric guitars emerged into the musical number. The rock musicians convulsed their heads. The thrash heavy metal band formed in the fall of 1997 in San Jose, California. The band sang about malevolent tales about things that went bump in the night that captivated listeners everywhere. Ramiro admired the lead guitarist/vocalist, Perry Viola, who experienced hardships in his life. Ramiro, Zack, Neil, and Matt sat in the balcony rows, cheering for their metal heroes. Down below, fans took part in a massive mosh pit where they crashed into each other, plummeting to the floor. Then the band's drummer, Alex Michaelson, played a fierce drum solo. Zack and Ramiro smiled at each other in delight with the stroke of the drumming, piercing sound. As the performance proceeded, Ramiro's mind raced with ideas. *"How could Perry Viola incorporate unique sounds into his music?"* he had no time to think about his musical endeavors. For now, just enjoy the show.

AFTER THE TWO-AND-A-half-hour recital, Ramiro and Zack swaggered out of the concert arena, making plans as if they already had their band established. They were kids living out their dreams after seeing their favorite band. Neil and Matt followed suit, noticing the boys acted as if the adults weren't there. Neil whistled between his two fingers. "Boys! Snap out of it!" he beckoned Zack and Ramiro.

The kids dashed back to Neil and Matt's side.

"You guys are in your world!" Matt cackled.

"So, where do you guys want to eat?" Neil asked as they strolled through the parking lot towards his vehicle.

IN A CROWDED THEMED restaurant, pop music blared from the ceiling speakers while servers served customers meals and drinks. The smokey bar guests puffed on cigarettes releasing nicotine smoke that clouded the air. Neil, Zack, Ramiro, and Matt ate at a booth where most families ate. The hopeful musicians poked their forks into each other's plates of fries, shrimp, shredded chicken, steak, and veggies while bellowed to each other due to the loud music in the establishment.

"The show was great, right, Ramiro?" Zack stuck his fork into his friend's steak, shoving it in his mouth. "What the fuck, dude!"

"You're not eating it!" Ramiro spoke with his mouth full.

"So what!" Zack poked his fork in Ramiro's plate, shoving French fries in his mouth.

"Can you kids stop!" Neil chugged down his beer.

"Can you take Ram and me to more rock concerts?" Zack asked with his mouth full.

"You're not in the zoo, Zack!" Neil slammed his glass on the table.

"Are you guys, alright?" a server sashayed to the table, smiling.

"We're fine. Are you guys cool?" Neil held his beer mug in his hand.

"I'm cool," Ramiro stuffed his mouth with French fries while Zack munched on his burger.

"Thank you, madam. We're fine," Neil proceeded to chug down his beer.

He picked the kids' brains about their future since they were so enthused about the show. *Their ideas. What would they name their band? How many members would there be?* Neil loved to hear the kids talk. Ramiro had song lyrics, but he didn't find his voice. He still needed to speak to Mrs. Lance about singing. Matt advised him not to wait too long. Ramiro's bass playing impressed Matt and he already knew about Zack's drumming style. Ramiro didn't have a bass guitar like Zack had his drum kit. He told Matt about his Jesus-freak father, who believed Heavy Metal, Blues, Jazz, House, Pop, and other genres were the devil's music. He wasn't allowed to practice bass at home because of his father. This young musician only played in music class. As he narrated his unhealthy relationship with his father and then a smile surfaced on Neil's face.

LATER, SPECTATORS ENCIRCLED Ramiro playing "Purple Haze" on an Ibanez GSR series black bass guitar in the music store where Matt worked. Zack cheered for his friend. On the other side of the establishment, Neil inserted his Visa Debit card into the credit card machine; it beeped: reading APPROVED. He removed it. The store manager handed Neil the receipts. Ramiro noticed Neil at the register. *"I wish I could have this thing. It's just right,"* he proceeded to play. Neil rushed to Ramiro, handing him the receipt that read: Happy belated birthday, Ramiro!" Ramiro embraced his best friend's father as if Neil were his biological father. "Thanks, Neil!"

"No problem, kid!" Neil hugged Ramiro along with Zack as if he had two sons. The crowd applauded the young musicians.

THAT NIGHT, THE IBANEZ GSR black bass guitar stood proudly on its stand like a sculpture in a museum. Ramiro glared at the instrument while he laid on his side. Maritza barged in as usual. She gasped at the beautiful guitar and sat right before it. Maritza admired it along with her brother. "Oh my God! It's beautiful!" she caressed the four-stringed bass.

"I still can't believe Zack's father brought it for me," Ramiro turned over and laid on his back. He looked at the ceiling and closed his eyes.

"What about dad? Oh, no!" Maritza's jaw dropped.

"What the fuck about him?" Ramiro's face alternated from his beige complexion to red. "That Jesus freak said, that I could do whatever I wanted. It's my life. So, if he challenges me about my guitar I'll have to go to fuckin' battle with him again," then he heard the hinges of his bedroom door squeak. He lifted his body, seeing his mother tiptoeing into his bedroom unannounced. She saw his prized possession in the corner. She laid a kiss on her son's forehead. Ramiro felt relieved, laying back down. He drifted off as his eyes became heavy.

Then headlights reflected on Ramiro's bedroom window along with screeching brakes and a low-running engine. Anna Maria and Maritza raced out of Ramiro's bedroom. "Got to go!" Anna Maria closed her son's bedroom door "Sweet dreams, son!"

"Sweet dreams! Oh, well. Mom still sees me as the baby. Because of the shit, I've been through along with her and my sister. This mad man never smiled, and even laughed. He never told a joke or watched a sitcom on tv? It was all about Jesus. I'm pretty sure Jesus would love to have a good laugh and loosen up!" Ramiro squinted his eyes and didn't move a muscle. The car motor shut off.

"Fuck! This fucker better not try it!" Keys rattled at the front door as Jorge entered, slamming the door. His heavy feet ascended to the second floor. Ramiro set his eyes on the bottom of the door where he saw his father's silhouette. "He had another fuckin' bad day at work again. Someone probably insulted his religious beliefs. God would probably tell him about himself!" he closed his eyes. Then his bedroom door swung open while his father stood in the doorway. Jorge's eyes scanned the room, spotting the bass guitar standing majestically beside his son's bed. He marched over, eyeing the instrument from top to bottom. He sneered at it as if it were dog feces on the sidewalk. Jorge then reached into his jacket, dousing the brand-new guitar with lighter fluid. Ramiro sniffed the air. He smelled a gas-like aroma. Ramiro rose from his slumber.

"What the fuck!" he saw his father directly in front of his bass. Jorge struck a match, throwing it on the instrument. Ramiro's gift from his friends was engulfed in flames.

"Fuck no!" Ramiro sat up in his bed, panting. He looked in the corner at his bass still resting on its stand. Untouched. He wiped the sweat from his forehead, exhaled, and fell back to sleep.

CHAPTER THREE

F our years later, a crowd of party guests/rockers gestured the "Sign of The Horns in the air. "Happy birthday, Ramiro!" they cheered at his seventeenth birthday celebration. Ramiro played an old eighties rock tune on his Ibanez GSR bass guitar strapped over his shoulder. And since it was Devil's Night (Halloween Eve), a tall skeleton dressed in a tuxedo and a top hat, a scary Zombie girl dummy, and some jack-o'-lanterns surrounded Ramiro from every angles just the way he liked it. A small audience of neighborhood kids and fans of Heavy Metal came from a few miles to hear this local bassist play. The crowd headbanged while others took part in a small mosh pit. Ramiro grew taller, along with a mustache, goatee, light sideburns, and his twenty-two-inch long-brunette hair signified his *"Fuck you!"* attitude to anyone who turned their nose up at him. His mother, Maritza, Neil, and Emmy (Zack's mom), watched the show while seated behind Zack as he played on his drum kit. They felt like they were at a rock concert, rooting for their kids backstage. Plenty of girls cheered Ramiro on, especially Kim, a gorgeous long-haired blond-bombshell, blue-eyed female, seventeen years of age, who caught Ramiro's eye. She sported black spandex pants, a pink sweater cropped top, and a cropped black MC jacket with rocker pins. She had groupie vibes to her, not by the way she dressed or listening to the latest bands. She had the attitude of getting any rocker she wanted even if he were an actual famous musician. Ramiro headbanged as his hair flew in every direction. *"Damn, I've seen this blond around school, but she never noticed me until she found out that I played bass.*

I'll have to admit. I noticed her around school as well. The guys flocked around her like bees to honey. I could see that she loves the way I play," Ramiro thought to himself. He saw from the corner of his eye this hottie fanned herself. *"She's getting hot. Maybe, I'll get lucky tonight. It is my birthday,"* he proceeded to play his bass.

"HAPPY BIRTHDAY TO YOU! Happy birthday, dear Ramiro!" the guests sang. Neil presented a rectangular ice cream cake with seventeen glistening candles before Ramiro's eyes as Kim grasped his arm along with his family, friends, and followers by his side. Maritza noticed this loosely dressed young woman who held her brother tight for what he was about to become. Kim wasn't the type of girl you would take home to your parents. Maritza wanted to warn her brother about this girl but allowed Ramiro to find out for himself if she was a match for him. As for his mother, she didn't judge Kim. The only thing Anna Maria wanted was for her son to be successful in every area of his life. Ramiro blew out the candles and didn't make a wish.

MOMENTS LATER, RAMIRO and Kim kissed, breathed heavily while stripping off their garments in a spare bedroom on the second floor of the McQuillian's home. Ramiro didn't even think about him being disrespectful to his best friend's parents. Within minutes, balls of sweat poured down the nude bodies of these two lovers who didn't think about getting caught. In the hallway, Maritza and Zack crept to the second floor and heard the moaning and groaning from the bedroom. Maritza's eyes widen, knowing Ramiro and Kim were in the middle of getting hot and heavy. Zack snickered and did his best to keep quiet as he and Maritza snuck back downstairs to the party.

LATER THAT EVENING, Ramiro mingled with friends and other neighborhood kids about different bass guitars, music, and future goals. Maritza glared at Ramiro while she stood in the corner by her mother. She saw Kim flirting with another guy, which angered her. But still, Maritza didn't interfere in Ramiro's business. Let him handle it like a man. Ramiro could fight his battles, but girls like Kim can break a man. Again, Maritza proceeded to keep her mouth shut.

THAT NIGHT, A CLOCK ticked as it read: two, fifty-seven a.m. Maritza tossed and turned in her bed, laying on her back. She didn't blame her brother for celebrating his birthday like hell because he was a year older. Anna Maria slept well in the master bedroom down the hall and put her son's future in God's hands. Jorge didn't attend Ramiro's birthday celebration. He didn't purchase him a gift or even say "Happy Birthday" to his son. *How cruel was that?* Jorge snored inhaling bubbling mucus sounds as he slept. The disgusting sound echoed down the hallway. Maritza couldn't stand that nasty sound. Keys rattled at the front door as she sat up in her bed. The front door's hinges squealed that irritated anyone's ears as it slammed shut. Maritza crept to her bedroom door, peeking into the hallway. She saw Ramiro lumbered into his bedroom, closing the door. She noticed Ramiro's resemblance to his father, he entered the house just like his father. No matter how much Jorge wants to disregard Ramiro, that's his son. Ramiro was just like him in every way.

Grunting, sighing, and taking off his sneakers, Ramiro sat on the edge of his bed in his darkened bedroom. He partied all night with people who loved him. The only person missing was his father, but everyone else present made things right. He stripped off his pants and took off his t-shirt, leaving only his boxers. He yawned, throwing the comforter on himself. Ramiro closed his eyes, hearing a tap at the door.

"What?" he mumbled from under the thick comforter.

Maritza made her way in, closing the door back with ease. "It's me, Ramiro."

"Why are you so late! I know it's your birthday! But shit Ramiro!" she placed her hand on her hips.

"Who are you! My mother!" Ramiro peered from under the comforter, squinting his eyes. He then turned his back on Maritza.

"Did you enjoy yourself?" she asked.

"What do you think? It's all about me!" Ramiro mumbled. He pulled the heavy blanket over his head.

"I'm not crazy about that girl!" she stomped her foot on the floor.

Ramiro sat up in bed, pulled the comforter off his head. "She's not bothering you! Can you please let me sleep!" He laid back down, continuing to give Maritza his back.

"It's your life!" she sashayed out of her brother's bedroom, closing the door.

THAT FOLLOWING WEEKEND, Ramiro and Zack strolled around a crowded shopping mall trying to figure out what to spend. And of course, for Ramiro, he received lots of money from admirers on his birthday and knew what he wanted. A tattoo parlor advertised dozens of ink art in its window. Ramiro swaggered into the establishment with his best friend behind him. He eyed the 3D tattoos as his jaw dropped at how realistic they looked. There were art creations of cartoon characters, horror imagery, flesh, and bloody gore, photos of people, insects, etc. Speaking of insects, the red kneed tarantula tattoo fascinated Ramiro which would scare the shit out of anyone. A fiendish smile surfaced on his face as he addressed an overwhelmingly tattooed gentleman with lots of body piercings. He wanted to know how long this work would take and how much? The sales associate then noticed Ramiro and heard about his local reputation as a bassist. On top of that, the tattoo artist knew about Zack's drumming style. He managed to give these two young upcoming artists a discount on any type of artwork.

ABOUT AN HOUR LATER, the ink gun spewed ink into the flesh of Ramiro's skin creating the detailed art of the arachnoid on his shoulder. He had to cope with the needle that poked him repeatedly. The tattoo needle felt worse than getting that needle at the dentist's office. The artist engraved the dark-colored body of the spider with the orange patches on the joints of its legs. And then the tattoo artist added a touch of red coloring making the artwork pop. Some blood surfaced on Ramiro's shoulder as the artist wiped it away as the needle continued its duty.

And then WALLAH, a beautiful large Mexican red-knee tarantula 3D tattoo on his shoulder.

"Holy shit!" Zack's eyes bulged out of his head. "It looks like my tarantula right on your shoulder!"

"This is fuckin' awesome! I hope I don't scare my mother and sister. I'll use it to keep my father out of my fuckin' way!"

"And he just might kick you out!"

"Fuck it! He's not kicking me out!" Ramiro sucked his teeth. The tattoo artist placed a bandage on his shoulder.

"You have to wait twenty-four hours before removing the bandaged," the artist advised.

"Okay," Ramiro agreed.

TWENTY-FOUR HOURS LATER, that morning Ramiro stood in the bathroom mirror applying Vaseline ointment on the shoulder of his enormous tarantula tattoo. A devilish smile surfaced on his face due to things that he could use this tattoo for.

"Oh My God! Ramiro, get that thing out of here!" his mother gasped noticing the tattoo on her son's shoulder in the mirror's reflection.

"Mom, it's not real! It's my new tattoo!"

"Tattoo! There's a spider on you! Have you lost your mind!" Anna Maria screamed to the high heavens.

"Yes, it is on me! It's my tattoo! I'm trying to explain to you!" Ramiro proceeded to apply the ointment.

"What's going on!" Maritza dashed into the bathroom. Her eyes widened. "What the hell, Ramiro! Are you out of your freakin' mind!" she slapped her hand in the doorway.

"I'm telling you it's my tattoo! Shit!" Ramiro touched the artwork on his shoulder, showing his sister.

"What!" Maritza took a step closer with her head tilted.

"You see!" Ramiro moved closer as Maritza took some steps back. "Come on! See!" he touched his tattoo again. His sister was relieved that her brother wasn't crazy enough to bring a real eight-legged creature into their home.

"Mom, it's a 3D tattoo!" Maritza beckoned her mother. Anna Maria crept into the bathroom, where Ramiro applied ointment on his shoulder. His mother held her hand over her chest.

"You almost gave me a heart attack, Ramiro!"

"I'm sorry, Mom"

"Why a tarantula?" Maritza placed her hands on her hips.

"Because I plan on getting one," he placed the top back on the ointment tube.

"Getting one!" Maritza bellowed.

"Where are you going to keep it! Don't bring a spider into this house! Ramiro, no!" Anna Maria stormed away. Ramiro smirked at his sister. Maritza stormed away as well. He exhaled.

"Now, why the fuck would I use a tarantula to scare my family. But as I said before using something eerie like this would make my father shit his pants. Fuck it! I'm glad I got this tat on my shoulder. It's cool.

A COUPLE OF MONTHS later, a December chill filled Ramiro's bedroom while a blue comforter covered his entire body from head to toe. He tossed and turned in his full-sized bed as his body shivered, but the cold still made its way underneath. Ramiro heard his mother clamoring in the kitchen downstairs. Maritza marched up and down the hallway, passing his bedroom door. Minutes later, she stood in the bathroom mirror, brushing her very, very long brunette hair, creating a ponytail. She braided it to the end, placing an elastic band on the end, and twirled it into a bun, pinning it and then leaving some leftover braid to hang over her shoulder. Ramiro changed his position to his side and then rolled on his back again. He snatched the comforter from his head, brushing his long brunette hair from his face. He pulled the blanket from his body, exposing his 3D tarantula tattoo on his shoulder, his bare chest with two nipple rings, and his sideburns that have thickened on his face. Ramiro refused to shave it off. One thing is for sure, he attracted the ladies in school. And he was known for his tarantula tattoo which made them curious.

"Maritza! Are you finished in there yet?" Ramiro sat on the edge of his bed wearing his black boxers. He yawned and wanted to lay back down. He dreaded school, reading pointless books about people from the early twentieth century. His music kept him going to school because he and Zack jammed out, giving students free shows.

He didn't find his voice yet, but they played lots of instrumentals. Maritza opened her brother's bedroom door, "It's all yours."

MINUTES LATER, STEAMY, hot water spewed from a shower-head as Ramiro stood under it, allowing the water to work its wonder through his long hair; he had both ears pierced with three holes. He poured the shower gel in the palm of his hand, washing his body from head to toe. He thought of his schoolwork and needed help from someone. There's a smart girl who can do the work for him. Ramiro acknowledged how lazy he was when it came to education. Zack wasn't doing so hot in school, either. He passed with sixty-five to seventy in his classes. He had too much pride to ask for help. Ramiro attempted to take shortcuts in school. But there are no shortcuts in life. He rinsed off the soapy lather from his body, turning the water off, and wrapped the terry towel halfway around his body. Ramiro stormed into his bedroom, resting his drenched head in bed. His pillow became soaked with moisture. He didn't care if he got sick. Then he sat up erect in his bed as he smiled. "Noelle!" he murmured. The water dripped from his long hair like a faucet that someone hasn't turned off. He twisted the ends of his tress, getting his bed wet, which didn't bother him.

AN HOUR LATER, RAMIRO put on his black jeans, black shirt, black construction boots, and wore his men's cologne in its black bottle. "I'm pretty sure Noelle wouldn't mind helping me out! Or would she? Noelle would probably tell me to fuck off!" Ramiro brushed his long hair in a full-length mirror. Since the semester began, he has always pictured Noelle's face in his mind. He did not know why she was so prevalent? This African-American myelinated-toned female, with a feminine mannerism, was the reason for

Ramiro's mind to have kept photograph proofs of her beautiful face? He threw his bass guitar carrier over his shoulder and his school bag, heading out the door. He trotted down the stairs as his mother stirred around in the kitchen.

"Ramiro! Eat before your food gets cold!" his mother set Ramiro's plate on the table.

"I'm not hungry!" he stormed out of the front door, slamming it shut.

"Alright!" Anna Maria tossed the plate on the counter.

IN A MATTER OF NO TIME, Ramiro stumbled upon the grounds of Massapequa high school, weaving his way through the subgroups of students such as the geeks, the cool kids, the outcasts, and loners. These kids had their musical preferences as well. And, of course, Ramiro and Zack were in the metal scene of aspiring guitarists, drummers, and fond fans of the genre. Both young men approached, giving each other hi-fives and embracing. The large circle of rockers greeted Ramiro. Especially the girls. Kim spotted Ramiro as she wore hot pink spandex pants, a low-cut rock band shirt, and a black MC jacket. She ran her fingers on Ramiro's chest. He cracked a fake smile because he couldn't forget the gift she gave him for his birthday. That took him away from his worries. Ramiro had a feeling that his father would give him the boot soon enough. Kim laid a kiss on Ramiro's lips. Then the school bell rang as the students were ready to start the school day.

IN ALGEBRA CLASS, THE instructor Mr. Cicero, a skinny gentleman, mid-fifties, sat in a wooden chair at his desk, rubbing his eyes and yawning. "Guys, I'm drained. Who would you like to teach the class today?"

Ramiro and his classmates looked around, trying to pick out the smartest person amongst the pupils. Ramiro rose his hand.

"Yes, Ramiro," Mr. Cicero rubbed his eyes.

"Noelle should teach the class," he eyed this pretty, young lady of fifteen years of age, seated in the last row, the second seat next to the window.

"Yeah, Noelle!" a student in the classroom's rear agreed.

"Noelle, you go, girl! Teach that Algebra, girl! Hey!" three girls in the middle row encouraged. The entire class erupted into laughter and applause, including Ramiro, who kept a big smile on his face. Some classmates could tell Ramiro had a thing for her, but they focused on their work.

"Noelle! Noelle! Noelle! Noelle!" the class cheered.

Noelle blushed beyond her mahogany complexion. Ramiro noticed the redness surfacing on her face. Her presence was easy on the eyes and a pleasure to see.

"Thank you, guys!" she rose from her desk, holding her notes in hand, giving the lesson for the day.

"Open your textbooks to page, one-fourteen," Noelle instructed.

Ramiro had no problem obeying everything she commanded. She copied down some math examples on the board and challenged her fellow students. Noelle paced back and forth and then she stood on the side of the blackboard. She glanced around at the students, figuring out the mathematical questions. Ramiro couldn't concentrate on the math problem; he waited for someone to answer. Also, he couldn't keep his eyes off Noelle. He cracked a smile as he caught her eye. She smiled in return.

"Do you understand it?" Noelle mouthed to him. Ramiro nodded. Some students noticed Ramiro and Noelle gesturing to communicate. One girl in the middle rows noticed and snickered. Mr. Cicero sat at his desk and watched Noelle's teachings play out.

"I wonder if she has a boyfriend? I would love to have her as a girlfriend. Noelle would turn me down. I'll try to see what happens," Ramiro then snapped out of his mindset, realizing the school bell rang.

"Shit! That was fast!" Ramiro mumbled. He grabbed his book and his bass guitar, blocking Noelle's path. "Noelle?"

"Yes?" she had a look of love in her eyes. Ramiro noticed it.

"You're an excellent teacher. You ever thought about going into teaching?" Ramiro asked, looking around and scratching his head.

"No," Noelle answered.

"You did well up there. I'll see you in music," Ramiro swaggered away. Noelle glanced, noticing him bolt out of the classroom like a bullet.

"What the fuck was that shit! Has she ever thought about teaching? Why the fuck didn't I get her phone number! I'm such a fuckin' dick!" Ramiro weaved in and out through the packed hallway. *"Noelle's going to attend some prestigious university and become a big-time success. She wouldn't want a dreamer like me. That's what I am. A fuckin' dreamer. What if my goal of becoming a musician doesn't happen? If it doesn't happen, then I'm fucked!"* Ramiro made his way to his music class.

DURING MUSIC CLASS, Ramiro and Zack played the classic rock song "Break On Through" by the Doors. Ramiro still didn't discover his voice, so the entire musical piece was instrumental even though there are lyrics. The class gathered around, jumping around them as if they were at a concert. They took videos with their cellphones and snapped pictures. The two young musicians' performance captivated a few students who strolled in the class. Mr. Oz observed Ramiro's showmanship headbanging while his long hair flew in every direction. Zack's excellent coordination on his drum kit.

He had a good handle on the school's two-decade-old instrument, even with its horrible condition. While Ramiro and Zack played, Noelle, with her friend, Cathy, applauded and enjoyed the rock performance. She couldn't keep her eyes off Ramiro as his dark, long hair hung down to the middle of his chest. *"I wonder about Ramiro. Boy, he can play that bass. He's good."*

SOON AFTER, A TALENTED, sixteen-year-old pianist played the black and white keys of an old grand piano as Noelle stood before it, releasing a vivid, melodious voice of "Ave Maria." Noelle captured her fellow students' attention, especially Ramiro, whose eyes locked right on this beautiful songstress. Kim noticed Noelle's presence right in her boyfriend's sight. Kim turned red in the face, nudging Ramiro. "Earth to Ramiro. Earth to Ramiro"

"What the fuck is your problem!" Ramiro inched his chair from Kim.

After class, students commended Noelle for her voice, especially around the holiday season. The rockers, especially the female admirers, praised Ramiro's bass playing. Ramiro peered over his shoulder, noticing Noelle had fans as well. He kept his eye locked on Noelle until he caught her eye. She then smiled at him in return. Debbie, a pretty red-head, rocker chick, black mini-skirt, t-shirt, hugged and kissed Ramiro on the cheek. He focused his attention on Debbie and her friend Vivian, who took pictures with a cellphone. Another girl took shots and captured a video from her Apple tablet of Ramiro and Zack.

"Have you thought about singing, Ramiro?" Vivian then videotaped him with her cell.

"I don't fuckin' know," Ramiro responded.

"I think Ramiro would be good. He'd have to find his voice," Zack added.

Kimberly watched the females hover over Ramiro in the background, cradling her books in her hands. She could tell that Ramiro enjoyed his fame. He then recognized Kim shaking her head. She also witnessed Ramiro peering at Noelle while she loved her few minutes of fame.

"What the fuck is she so pissed about? Kim needs to fuckin' relax," Ramiro departed from his high school fans and swaggered to Kim. He kissed her on the cheek. *"It's too soon to tell if she's going to throw a shit fit every time I come in contact with another female,"* Ramiro then kissed her on the lips and expunged the notion of his girlfriend's insecurities.

"So, what's up, babe?" Kimberly gazed into Ramiro's eyes.

"Nothing much," Ramiro threw his bass guitar case on his shoulder.

"Later, Ramiro," Zack gave him a hi-five, exiting the classroom.

"Let's go to my place. We'll have the entire house to ourselves," Kim placed her pelvis on Ramiro and engaged in a wet kiss.

A SLOW ROCK SONG BLARED from Kimberly's desktop computer while she and Ramiro got hot and heavy once again, moaning and groaning with pleasure. Sweat emerged from Ramiro's hairline, chest, back, and entire body. The lovers achieved their climaxes, exhaling and tired from the fast bodywork. Ramiro rolled off Kimberly, lying beside her. Kim fondled the details of Ramiro's tarantula tattoo plastered on his muscular shoulder and then she worked her way up to his nipple ringed chest. He eyed the ceiling and drifted into another world. Somewhere else was where he wanted to be. Ramiro closed his eyes.

"Dreaming of me?" Kimberly whispered in his ear.

Ramiro nodded, lying his ass off. Noelle came to mind while he smirked. *"I wonder what Noelle is doing? I believe she's studying for finals. She's a winner,*" he pictured Noelle studying in her bedroom with its exotic red painted walls, full-sized bed with red bedding with fuchsia, and pink stuffed animals and dolls adorning the room. Girly wall décor hung on the walls with floral imagery and pictures of herself. Then Ramiro envisioned Noelle graduating high school, then attending a prestigious university not only where she earned her degree, but where she would meet her future husband who shared the same goals. Noelle stood at the altar, dressed in her wedding gown with a long train, exchanging their vows with that man. He then opened his eyes and heard "The Wish Liszt (Toy Shop Madness)" by Trans-Siberian Orchestra blasting from the kitchen. Pots and pans, dishware, utensils clamored as loud as the holiday rock song. Ramiro rose in the bed and noticed Kim wasn't there. He waltzed into the kitchen as Kim pranced in her panties and her cut-off AC/DC t-shirt, tossing a hamburger patty in the frying pan. The hot oil from the pan popped as Kim jumped out of the way. Ramiro caught Kim in his arms. "Hey, baby! I'm making burgers for us, okay?" she kissed him.

A LEFTOVER JUICY BURGER half-eaten laid on Ramiro's plate, a couple of french fries, and a half-glass of soda. Kim stuffed French fries in her mouth, caressed Ramiro's thigh. Ramiro didn't utter a word the entire time. He was still tired. Sometimes Ramiro didn't get enough sleep. And when he was asleep, it was time for school. Ramiro's cellphone vibrated on the kitchen table. He realized he got several text messages. Neil sent pictures, messages, and a video.

"What the fuck!" Ramiro opened the first picture message. An enormous crowd of metalheads packed Zack's driveway to the street. Then he played the video, where spectators cheered for Zack playing drum solos.

"Ramiro, you got to get down here! Bring your bass!" Neil plugged his finger in his ear. Kim's face lit up when she saw the cheering rockers while Zack drummed on his Tama kit. Ramiro noticed the excitement in his girlfriend's face for other guys. He was convinced that Kim wasn't the one for him. "This enormous crowd is waiting for you! Come on and jam, Ramiro!" Neil encouraged this young bass player.

IN NO TIME, RAMIRO played his black bass guitar strapped over his shoulder. He headbanged while his long black hair flowed and swayed. The cold did not bother him because of his blood pumping through his veins. The duo played rock instrumentals while the crowd headbanged their heads to the music. Local spectators captured videos and pictures, posting them on the internet.

MEANWHILE, MARITZA did some job hunting on the web in her bedroom at the Espinoza residence. She looked up at her Facebook icon with notifications and messages. Out of curiosity, she clicked the LIVE social media page icon and notifications. She gasped, seeing her brother strumming his bass guitar with enormous spectators and Zack drumming in the background. "Mom! Mom! Mom, come quick!" Maritza turned up the volume on her computer. The local rock musicians' edgy sound blared through her speakers.

Anna Maria dashed upstairs to the second floor from the kitchen with a wooden spoon in her hand. She rushed into her daughter's bedroom, out of breath. "What's the emergency?"

"Your son! Look!" Maritza pointed at her computer monitor.

Anna Maria inched towards the twenty-seven- inch computer monitor, squinting her eyes. Ramiro maneuvered his fingers along the neck of his bass with his long hair covering his entire face. He then threw his head back, flipping his long tress and proceeding to play.

"My baby! Look at him!" Tears streamed down Anna Maria's cheeks. Maritza embraced her mother as she sobbed at Ramiro playing his bass like a professional.

"He looks so handsome up there! I hope he doesn't get sick! He's only got a t-shirt. It's twenty-four degrees out there! I know the girls are going to be after him!" Anna Maria said.

"They are!" Maritza said.

"What about singing? Doesn't Ramiro want to sing?" his mother shrugged her shoulders.

"He'll get around to it, somehow," Maritza answered.

"Wow! He's a real heartthrob!" Anna Maria placed her hand on her heart while more tears cascaded down her cheeks.

AT THE NEIGHBORHOOD concert, Ramiro and Zack played a Heavy Metal version, "Sleigh Ride, making this holiday song their own. Adoring fans applauded. While Ramiro played, he scanned the body of onlookers, guys, with a few feminine faces in the crowd. *"I wish Noelle could see me. She probably doesn't like this type of music. I don't know what she likes. What her favorite color is? Her favorite place to go? Was Christmas her favorite holiday? What were her favorite things?"* Ramiro concluded the Christmas classic. Blue and red flashing lights with sirens of police cars made their way to the scene. The cops exited a stretch of police vehicles, maneuvering their way through the crowd. Neil did the same, weaving his way through the rockers approaching the Officers. "Good evening, Officer?"

"Good evening, do you know that you're disturbing the peace?" an officer placed his hands on his hip.

"It's over now," Neil said.

Mrs. Stein stormed between Neil and the boys in blue, shivering in her wool coat.

"What took you so long, Officer? I should've filed a complaint against you and the little drummer boy from the beginning!" Mrs. Stein pointed in Neil's face.

"Don't point in my face, Mrs. Stein!" Neil smiled.

"Get your finger out of my father's face!" Zack shouted, approaching his father's side.

"Watch yourself, young man!" the Officer addressed Zack. Neil stood in front of his son. Ramiro weaved his way through the crowd as Kim held his arm. He recognized Mrs. Stein, Zack's neighbor, who couldn't stand the noise they created, drove her insane. "I can't take this noise that you call music! I've lived in this community for years before you got here!" Mrs. Stein pumped her fists in the air. The spectators observed the dispute and added their two cents.

"Use some earplugs if the music bothers you!" a short-haired, rocker male, late teens, bellowed in her ear.

"Neil, I know you don't have a permit!" Mrs. Stein continued to pump her fists in the air. Zack screamed in this older woman's face.

"Fuckin' go home if you didn't like it! Use fuckin' earplugs like he suggested, bitch!" Zack pumped his fist in the air as well. Zack, Ramiro, the neighborhood kids, and Mrs. Stein participated in a screaming match.

CHAPTER FOUR

A red Christmas bulb glistened from the branch of a seven-foot Fraser fir live tree with its perfumed pine smell. "Jingle Bell Rock" by Brenda Lee blared from the radio in the living room. Maritza always decorated while her mother and grandmother cooked the holiday Peruvian Christmas dishes. Jorge strung up holiday lights on the exterior of the home and showered only his wife and Maritza with gifts. Except for Ramiro. His father shunned him on every occasion, and force-fed Ramiro bible verses. He used to cry about his father not loving him the way a father should. When his family had get-togethers, Ramiro either slept or hung out with friends. His father gradually backed off with his abuse towards his son. Maritza trimmed the tree with red and gold ornaments, along with penguins and polar bears figurines. *"Ramiro hasn't been home for almost a week. Where is he? Every time I call him, he never answers the phone. I know mom's worried to death about him,"* Maritza glanced at the picture of her and Ramiro's baby photos. Then her brother's childhood photos in five by seven and eight by ten frames. Anna Maria seasoned the turkey with Peruvian spices as her mother, seventy-something, Rebecca Flores, whipped up cake batter, adding vanilla flavoring and mixing it in a bowl. She reminisced when Ramiro was eight years old and how he always wanted her to leave a little batter in the bowl. Kids and some adults love dipping their fingers in the cake batter. Ramiro wished for a real electric guitar at the tender age of eight. He begged his grandmother for a guitar, but she said he was too young to handle such a cumbersome instrument. Rebecca promised him when he got older; she'd buy him a professional bass guitar. Even though, she knows he already has one. Ramiro will have two basses. Her husband, Salvador Flores, died of a heart attack when Ramiro and Maritza were toddlers. They didn't get the chance to know their grandfather, but Rebecca compensated for that for their grandchildren.

THAT EVENING, MARITZA, Anna Maria, and Rebecca entered through the automatic double doors a music store with a wall décor of different colors and styles of guitars on it. A ten-foot-high Christmas tree stood in the establishment's center, decorated with multicolored ornaments of different shapes and sizes. The customers packed the stores, purchasing gifts for passionate music-loving family members. "Carol of the Bells" by The Trans-Siberian Orchestra blared from corner speakers. Rebecca focused her eyes right on the black speaker that hung in the corner. She listened to the holiday rock music "This is the music Ramiro wants to play? Am I right, Maritza?" Rebecca held her granddaughter's hand.

"Yes. The music is thrash metal. You can say it's Christmas thrash metal. He wants to play thrash Metal," Maritza explained.

"What is trash?" Rebecca raised an eyebrow, frowning.

"Mama, you would consider it crazy music. It's pronounced, thrash music, Mama," Anna Maria further explained to her mother.

"Thrash music. Thrash music is crazy? Everything is crazy. The television people, walking down the streets, even I'm crazy," Rebecca shrugged her shoulders.

"What kind of guitar are we looking for, Maritza?" Anna Maria eyed the guitars along the wall.

Maritza did not know what brand of bass guitar to get for Ramiro. But, she knew to get it in a nice black. A long-haired rocker, mid-twenties, dressed in blue jeans and a black t-shirt with tattoos blanketing his arms, wiped the glass counter with Windex. "Can I help you with something, ma'am?" the rocker employee put his cleaning products behind the counter, approaching Maritza and her family. Maritza smiled from ear to ear because this young man resembled her brother. The rocker employee gawked at Maritza as if he wanted more than helping her with whatever she needed. "Hello, we're looking for a bass guitar," Maritza sighed.

"For my son," Anna Maria added.

"For my grandson," Rebecca added her two cents with a smile.

"What kind of bass?" the rocker employee folded his arms.

"A rock bass guitar," Maritza shrugged her shoulders.

"A nice bass," Anna Maria said.

"The best," Rebecca nodded with a big smile.

"We've got the Spector five-string bass in black," the rocker employee handled the instrument with caution. Maritza saw his name tag that read: JOSHUA. She addressed Joshua, this younger rocker, about the same age as her brother as he strapped the bass guitar over his shoulder, and played a couple of familiar tunes. The high volume didn't startle Rebecca as Anna Maria clutched her. Rebecca nuzzled her daughter away and mouthed, "I'm fine." Joshua put on a show for this family. He usually did this in case he bumped into a producer in the music industry. This young man played an old eighties rock tune. Maritza smiled at this talented and bound-for stardom guitarist similar to Ramiro. He played the guitar as if Maritza, her family, and the customers were at a private rock concert. Rebecca took a couple of steps back because of the ear-piercing bass guitar. She turned her nose up to this young bass player. Rebecca couldn't wait to see her grandson put on a show. Later, Maritza, her mother, and grandmother debated over getting the first bass guitar that the salesman demonstrated. Maritza checked out the other bass guitars, but they went with their first choice. She didn't want Joshua showing her every bass guitar. The black matte Spector bass is priced at three-thousand-four hundred. Anna Maria made a money transfer from her savings to her checking on her cell. Maritza had twelve hundred dollars on her Master debit card as for Rebecca; she had eight hundred dollars cash.

"Do you have a gift box?" Maritza asked.

THAT NIGHT ON CHRISTMAS Eve, the three women wrapped the cumbersome bass gift box with gold Christmas paper. The soothing sound of "Silent Night" by Nat King Cole played from the desktop computer. The three women enjoyed taping the fancy paper on the corners of the oversized box. After wrapping Ramiro's gift, Anna Maria added an enormous black bow, and then Maritza slapped on the gift tag, and Rebecca wrote her grandson's name on it. Then they clanked the mugs filled with eggnog and drank up the holiday beverage. Keys rattled at the door as the front door opened with the frigid air sweeping throughout the living room. Maritza noticed her father marching inside with loads of gifts in his arms. She welcomed him home with open arms. "Merry Christmas, Papi!"

"Feliz Navidad, baby!" Anna Maria laid a kiss upon her husband's cheek.

Rebecca applauded seeing her son-in-law coming home from a hard day's work. Jorge places a kiss upon his mother-in-law's cheek. "Merry Christmas, Mama!"

"Feliz Navidad, Jorge!" Rebecca embraced him.

Jorge rushed over to the seven-and-a-half foot Christmas tree with lots of presents under the tree. He noticed the large gold-wrapped gift with a black bow with Ramiro's name on the tag. Jorge rolled his eyes and frowned, knowing what was inside. He wanted to ask Maritza what it was but didn't bother. Jorge strolled into the kitchen, where his wife added frosting on a cake. A roast chicken baked in the oven along with stuffing and other holiday dishes.

"Merry Christmas, honey!" Jorge presented a small gift box, kissing her on the cheek. Anna Maria placed the frosted covered knife down on the counter, opening her gift. She gasped at the 10mm pearl earrings. "They're beautiful!"

"What did you get, Mom?" Maritza rushed to her mother's side, seeing the fancy earrings.

"Earrings," Anna Maria showed the opened box of jewels.

"Those are nice," Maritza's jaw dropped.

Jorge opened the refrigerator door, pouring some eggnog in a cup. He eyed his wife, Maritza, and then his mother-in-law's unbalanced stride into the kitchen. He heard that Ramiro and Zack had a fan base. Jorge paced towards the kitchen glass door and turned to his family with a dead-hard stare. Anna Maria tried on the earrings as her daughter and mother admired the jewelry. Then Maritza felt eyes dead-set on her; she saw her father standing there like a madman from a slasher movie. Anna and Rebecca caught on to Jorge's gaping eyes. "What's wrong, Jorge? Are you feeling okay?" Anna Maria's heart pumped hard in her chest as she grabbed her mother's hand. Rebecca returned a stare of her own to let him know not to overstep his boundaries. He then snapped out of the fixed look on his family and smiled as if nothing happened. "When do we eat?"

"Now?" Anna Maria slipped her oven mittens on, grabbing a roasted chicken and stuffing from the oven. She knew her husband saw Ramiro's gift in the large box with the gold wrapping and wasn't too crazy about her and the rest of the family getting him anything. But Anna Maria didn't care what he thought because Ramiro was her only son and wanted him to have this beautiful gift. "Jingle Bells" rang from Maritza's cellphone loudly, which echoed from the living room. She rushed to answer it. Anna Maria prayed her son would come home for Christmas. "Ramiro! When are you coming home!" Maritza hollered.

"My son! Ramiro!" Anna Maria snatched off her oven mittens. Maritza rushed into the kitchen to her mother's side. "Talk to your son!"

"Ramiro, baby! When are you coming home?" Anna Maria sobbed.

"I'll be over for Christmas!" Ramiro laid on a full-sized bed in a guest bedroom at Zack's house. Cartoons played on television.

"Ramiro, how long are you going to stay at Zack's house?" Anna Maria asked.

"I don't know," Ramiro answered.

"You know you're going to get a job," his mother added.

"Yes," Ramiro answered.

Anna Maria pleaded with Ramiro not to be a deadbeat on anyone. He had to find employment and try to get himself a place to live. He sure and hell didn't want to come back home. His father didn't kick him out; yet. Ramiro had to get away from home for a while. He asked his mother if he could bring Kim to dinner. Anna Maria didn't mind because of the food she cooked and knew it wouldn't go to waste. She yapped about Ramiro taking responsibility, going to college, and pursuing whatever field he wanted. As for now, he went to school, jammed out, fuck, ate, and slept. Neil had talks with his son and Ramiro about getting jobs. He wouldn't think of kicking his son out in the cold, unlike Ramiro's father anticipated doing. Anna Maria gave the cellphone to her mother. Rebecca greeted her grandson in Spanish. She loved and missed Ramiro, hoping that he'd come home. Rebecca had a big surprise waiting for him. It's been a long time since Ramiro has seen his grandmother.

ABOUT AN HOUR LATER, Ramiro and Zack jammed out in the garage, playing, creating noise: his throbbing Ibanez bass and pounding Tama drums. They didn't give a fuck if the neighbors called the cops. They'd do it again and again. Ramiro loved to irritate people who hated the noisy music he desired to play. He disregarded the status quo and embraced his creative musical freedom. *"If you don't like my music then cover your fuckin' ears! I'm not a follower. So fuck everyone!!!"* Ramiro bitched in his head. He continued to play his bass with chaotic headbanging with his long, brunette hair swinging around. Ramiro expected a knock on the front door which he couldn't hear because of the cringing playing. The boys in blue would have their guns drawn, confronting the young musicians who disturbed the peace. Neil trotted down the basement steps, signaling Ramiro and Zack to subside their band practice. The young men halted their tunes, obeying Neil's demands.

Before dinner, Zack and Ramiro peered through the glass tarantula tank where a female spider was added to the mix. The female tarantula kept watch over her eighteen eggs. Ramiro smirked, gazing into the eight eyes of this insect. The soon-to-be arachnid mother sat on her eggs, sensing a threat. *"These eggs will hatch soon, I want one. Or maybe two or three. Or all eighteen of these eight-legged fucks. And then I'll terrorize the world. Ah, I'm just talking shit! I would like to have at least three. I don't know,"* Ramiro proceeded with his glare with the spider. He sensed Zack taking a couple of steps back from the tank. Zack allowed his best friend and his pets to bond.

"You're sure in love with my spiders. Shit!" Zack exhaled.

"Exactly when are her eggs going to launch?" Ramiro smiled at the spider even more.

"Soon," Zack sat on the edge of his bed.

"Are you going to keep all of them?" Ramiro lightly tapped on the glass tank.

"No. I don't know how many of the babies I'm going to keep. The others I'll sell to a pet shop," Zack answered.

"Give me two of them," Ramiro demanded.

"Alright. You got it," Zack said.

"Great! I'll have these pets like a dog or a cat and allow them to crawl around the house. It would scare the shit out of anyone who dared to fuck with me," Ramiro snickered.

DURING DINNER, THE aroma of tomato sauce, sausage, and meatballs filled the McQuillian home due to Emmy slaving over a stove all afternoon. She and Neil didn't mind having another mouth to feed. They always wanted two sons. They gathered at a black cherry table with matching chairs, devouring their dinner. A seven-foot white artificial tree stood in the corner decorated with black, red, and gold ornaments. A red velvet tree skirt had a load of gifts surrounding the tree, and gold reindeer figurines added to the holiday décor. Trans- Siberian Orchestra Christmas music blared from the computer speakers. Ramiro never felt so good about Christmas because he didn't have to deal with his father. Zack and his parents projected love and happiness over this home-cooked meal, which wasn't the case for Ramiro. Ramiro enjoyed Neil's stories about his past life as a teen in high school and the girls he hit on. Neil remembered one girl who was quiet and who said little. He wanted to get to know her, but he was too shy. His high school crush is now the president of a fortune five-hundred company. Emmy gave Neil the side-eye, sucking her teeth. He ensured Emmy she was the best thing that ever happened to him. Noelle came to Ramiro's mind as if a brick hit him in the temple. He didn't have the balls to ask Noelle out on a date. Ramiro would have to take baby steps to win her heart. After graduation, he'd never see Noelle again. Ramiro wondered about her plans with her family for the holidays. He attempted to erase Noelle from his mind, but he couldn't even if he tried. Ramiro pictured Noelle being his wife because there's something about her that drew him. Noelle's angelic spirit captured his darkness. He noticed the way Noelle dressed, which was the opposite. She wore colors like red, fuchsias, pinks, white, and yellow. Her fragrance always struck Ramiro below the belt. He got that reaction when he laid his eyes on her hourglass-shaped figure. Her body parts triggered his every desire. Zack snapped his fingers in front of Ramiro's face. Ramiro blinked and focused on the conversation at the table. Zack snickered, knowing who Ramiro had his eyes set on. Neil and Emmy had that feeling as well.

CHAPTER FIVE

Christmas morning, Ramiro rested in the full-sized bed of the guest bedroom in Zack's home, where the cold gave him a migraine headache. He knew it wasn't his loud music; it was the weather. The pain felt like a construction worker pounded his temple with a sledgehammer. He leaned over his bed, checking the clock that read 6:13 a.m. It was dark outside because of the fallback time that Ramiro loved. He enjoyed short days, long dreary nights, frigid temperatures, blizzards, frozen branches on trees, and icy lakes in the winter. Goosebumps surfaced on his abdominal area, arms, and legs because of the chill. Bizarre things made up Ramiro's persona. He couldn't wait for those tarantula eggs to hatch. He anticipated befriending a creature that was feared by most. Ramiro sat up in his slumber, checking his cellphone for text messages and voicemails from his family and Kim. His mother invited them over for Christmas dinner, so he wanted to be there bright and early. Ramiro laid back down, staring at the ceiling as Noelle came to mind. He pictured her dark-brown skinned complexioned thighs wrapped around his waist while he thrusts away as she reverberated sensual moans. The blood vessels and veins caused Ramiro to have an enormous bulged in his boxers. *"Shit! Noelle turns me on like that! I have to make my move! And my migraine is gone!"*

MEANWHILE AT THE ESPINOZA home, "Feliz Navidad" by Jose Feliciano blared from the radio later that day as Anna Maria opened up a gorgeous holiday gift box, pulling out a bottle of Chanel No. 5 fragrance. Jorge laid a kiss on her lips. Rebecca unwrapped a large red box and held up a red sweater. Maritza pulled an ugly Christmas sweater from her gift bag, putting it on as her father took a snapshot of her with his cellphone. The family continued opening presents, taking pictures, and laughing. Anna Maria smiled at her family, interacting right before her eyes. Her smile turned upside down, and she glanced at the clock on top of the fireplace that read: 9:19 a.m.

"Ramiro, where are you?" Anna Maria murmured to herself. She stormed away from her family's sight in the living room to the kitchen. All she thought about was her son on this holiday. Yes, she wanted Ramiro home, but her son and husband's relationship was in turmoil. Anna Maria preheated the oven at four-hundred, fifty degrees, and then she set the pre-seasoned turkey on the counter. Almost she placed the stuffing in the oven, which was too soon for that. The thought of her son not coming home felt like death. Anna Maria held her head down and wept. She attempted to keep her composure because she wanted to scream to the high heavens. *"Ramiro never got in trouble with the law; he never did drugs and took part in reckless behavior. He learned to play bass guitar, creating his style all his own, and maybe someday he would rock crowded stadiums all over the globe,"* she engaged in her line of thought and continued to weep. She buried her head in her chest with her back turned.

"Mom!" a masculine voice called her. Anna Maria didn't hear the call because of the blared holiday music and her mindset on her son's destiny.

"Mom!" the masculine voice then shouted.

Her eyes widened as she turned, noticing her baby boy standing in the doorway. Ramiro looked as handsome as ever with his long brunette tress almost the same length as hers. She rushed to Ramiro with open arms and kissed him as if he were a toddler. His cheeks became rosy red, and he laughed at the affection his mother gave him. From the corner of his eye, Kim stood in the doorway snickering.

"Come and meet my mother, Kim," Ramiro beckoned his love interest. She crept to his side, smiling and extending her hand to his mother's.

"How are you, Mrs. Espinoza? Merry Christmas!" Kim greeted her with a kiss.

"Merry Christmas, young lady!" Anna Maria embraced Kim.

MOMENTS LATER, RAMIRO unwrapped the gold gift wrapping paper, removing the lid, tissue paper and pulled out the Spector matte black bass guitar. He held the instrument in one hand, as some rock musicians do. His mother, sister, Kim, and grandmother applauded like admiring fans.

AT THE ELLIS RESIDENCE, a burgundy gift box with a gold ribbon sat on Noelle's lap. She removed the top and pulled out a fancy box of perfume. Her eyes bulged at one of her presents given by her parents being their only child along with additional family members. Enwreathe with dozens of offerings, Noelle received a Fuschia sweater, pajamas, shower gels. Body lotions, more perfume, a new coat, etc. A seven-and-a-half-foot green Christmas tree decorated with red and silver ornaments and clear lights gleamed in the living room corner. "Noelle, smile!" her father snapped a photo from his cellphone. He took another picture of Noelle singing "Sleigh Ride" as she embraced her mother in front of the Christmas tree. Then the sparkling holiday lights from the tree later alternated into sixteen birthday candles glistening on the cake. It read: Happy Birthday, Noelle," her family and friends sang. Within seconds, she closed her eyes and blew out the candles as everyone applauded.

BACK AT THE ESPINOZA home, Jorge kneeled on the side of his bed, holding the Bible in hand. Like a priest living in the rectory, he prayed to God about how to get rid of Ramiro's sinful lifestyle. A rocker's life had demonic influences that would turn anyone into a ticking time bomb. Ramiro probably would never get married or even have kids. He'd participate in fornication with multiple women and drug use that some musical artists consume to where they lose their minds, looks, and even lose their careers. If Jorge could, he would shoot his son point-blank in the head, but he had to put it in God's hands. He would not preach to Ramiro or throw the Bible at him. Jorge did the cross's sign and stood to his feet, hearing his family downstairs enjoying the festive gathering. He wondered about the enlarged box with the gold wrapping with a black bow. The family cheering for Ramiro calling him a "Rock star." Ramiro's Christmas gift must be a guitar. Jorge placed his Bible on the pillow where he laid his head. The holiday clamor became louder and louder. He covered his ears, but the sound became deafening. Jorge believed that Ramiro taunted him. He wanted Ramiro out now. He's seventeen and it's time to go. Jorge's hesitation overwhelmed him, and he couldn't face the evil. Jorge feared Ramiro. He rose from the bed, inched to the bedroom door. The clamoring downstairs sounded like demons laughing and enjoying a hellish gathering. Jorge shook his head, knowing the eerie noise couldn't be real. He bowed his head, praying to God for strength. He inhaled and took his time going downstairs. As Jorge got to the bottom of the staircase, his family embraced Ramiro as he had his black matte bass guitar strapped around him. Maritza took a photo of Ramiro and Kim with his new bass. Jorge froze in his tracks and didn't know what to think. He stared and stared as his heart pounded in his chest. Jorge wanted to march upstairs, close the door, and pray the demon away. But he didn't and headed to the kitchen.

Ramiro's father breezed into the kitchen, ignoring Ramiro. He didn't allow his father's negative ways to affect him. He received kisses and a hug from his grandmother, who spoke to him in her native language. While his grandmother did this, he peered at Kim because it's rude to speak in another language in front of them. Kim didn't seem bothered. Rebecca realized what she did and greeted Kim with a "Merry Christmas" in English and continued to speak in English. Rebecca heard about her son-in-law's abuse towards her grandchildren, and her daughter Anna Maria. Rebecca tolerated Jorge because of Anna Maria's so-called happiness and hiding the family secrets. She feared Anna Maria marrying Jorge because of his domineering persona and used the Bible to justify his views. That's why Ramiro had negative feelings towards God. He explained to his grandmother if God loves us so much, why would he allow abuse of children, neglect, hatred, war, sickness, and other sins in the world to happen? "All the sin in the world is the fault of man. Not God!" his grandmother responded. Ramiro shook his head, refusing to believe it. His father had no reason for being hard on him for playing loud guitar music and wallowing in the rocker lifestyle. "Shit! Why can't he see that I'm creative! Fuck it!" Ramiro raised his voice. He then realized his use of foul language and apologized to his grandmother. Rebecca nodded and smiled at her grandson, letting him know that she understood. Anna Maria scrambled into the kitchen while Maritza set the dining room table with Christmas dishware, utensils, glasses, and a fancy holiday table cloth. Three large "North Pole" candled jars from Yankee Candle sat in the middle of the table with wintry candle holders. The candles released a pepper-minty scent into the air.

AT DINNER, RAMIRO AND his family held hands, praying to the Lord, giving their blessings for seeing another holiday, and looking forward to the New Year. Jorge sat at the head of the table as

Anna Maria sat on the other end. Ramiro sat by his father, though tension lingered. Everyone took different servings of side dishes and placed slices of ham and turkey on their plates. Christmas music blasted throughout the house. Maritza cracked jokes at the table, trying to ease the tension that she sensed. Kim's eyes shifted from left to right and felt something wasn't right. Ramiro grabbed her hand, clutching it. He peered at Kim, scooping the fork of stuffing in her mouth. He didn't discuss his family affairs with Kim because he believed she didn't give a shit about him. Maritza cracked more and more jokes, which got the family laughing up a storm. "You should've been a comedian, Maritza! You're a liberal arts major!" Ramiro smirked.

"Have you figure out what else you are going to major in, Ramiro?" Anna Maria chewed her food.

"I didn't apply to any schools yet," her son answered.

"You better get right on it?" Jorge sipped wine from a tall glass.

Ramiro gave his father a dead-hard stare. He wished he had a gun, so he could aim it right at his father's forehead and pull the trigger. His father's lifeless body dropped to the wooden floor as blood splattered everywhere. Ramiro wouldn't want to traumatize his family. If he committed such a crime, they probably would never forgive him. "You don't have a clue about what college to attend? You want to be some hot-shot rock star. It's time for you to create a roof of your own," his father placed the wineglass down hard on the table. The father and son glared at one another. Anna Maria's heart pounded in her chest, *"This can't be happening on Christmas Day."* The family and guest gasped as Jorge lectured Ramiro about making a life for himself and whoever else was in it. Anna Maria dropped her fork on her plate with watery eyes. "No, you can't, Jorge. It's Christmas."

"Fuck it! I'm out!" Ramiro rushed away from the table as Kim gave chase. He ran upstairs with pounded feet on the carpeted staircase.

"Are you kicking him out, Dad! Not on Christmas!" Maritza stood from the table.

"Where is he going to go?" his grandmother cried.

UPSTAIRS IN RAMIRO'S bedroom, he scurried around, shoving his clothes into a backpack. He grabbed two bottles of colognes; he rummaged through his drawers to see if there was some cash in a drawer. Anna Maria dashed to the second floor, peering into her son's bedroom. "Son, I've got some money for you!" Anna Maria dashed to the master bedroom, searching through a jar of money she saved for a rainy day. There were tens, twenties, and a few fifty-dollar bills. She grabbed the dollar bills and rushed back to Ramiro's bedroom. He still scrambled around, gathering his things. His mother gave him about two hundred dollars. But Ramiro didn't want to take it because she would probably need it. Anna Maria insisted that he take the money. Ramiro kissed his mother on the cheek, grabbing his old bass guitar, and stormed out of the bedroom. Kim helped him with his things. He rushed into the living room and also grabbed his new bass guitar. Ramiro embraced his grandmother with two bass guitars on his shoulders.

"I love you, Ramiro! Please, take care of yourself!" Rebecca spoke in her native tongue.

Maritza embraced her brother. "If you need anything, call, please. Don't forget!"

"Thanks," Ramiro smiled.

He swung the front door open with Kim behind him while Maritza held the front door open. Ramiro knew there's no need to say anything to the man who gave him the boot. As he and Kim stepped outside, the frigid cold swept under his clothes. Ramiro didn't have enough layers on. They headed down the street and didn't say a word about what took place in the house where he grew up.

WITHIN A FEW HOURS, Ramiro laid in the guest bedroom's full-sized bed at Zack's house; he held his composition notebook in his hand and wrote lyrics about his religious father meeting his demise. The song contained gruesome and vulgar words, which he didn't care about the fruitful use of the f word. Rock music played in the background at a low volume. He glanced at the clock on the nightstand that was thirty-four minutes past one in the morning. Ramiro continued writing lyrics. Song entitled:

"MEET YOUR DEMISE"

"Struck over the head with a metal bat, your body collapses to the floor for dead. But the air you breathe from your lungs remains after taking that plunge. The shit you put me through for being an individual, I could never appease you. God cursed me; he hates me, and so do you. His messenger to make my life a living hell as I dwell in the father's house who brought me life. Like my father, you brought me into this world, and, as your son, I'll take you out...." Ramiro continued writing his song about his father's death.

He glanced at the clock which read, one, fifty, one. Ramiro turned to a clean page in his composition notebook and jotted down more lyrics. He couldn't figure out what to write next; he already envisioned a killing on paper. "I'll write religions that claim to do God's works, but they only do it to benefit themselves. The news stories about the Catholic church and accusations of sexual abuse towards minors. And what about the Jehovah's witnesses, who are the ultimate evil? They're known for preaching the Bible about sins that man commits, and then they turn around to commit those same sins. Ramiro tapped his pen against the blue-lined paper. Then he jotted down the title of a song on the top of the page:

"RELIGIOUS FUCKERY"

*"Who do you serve? God, Lucifer, or yourself? Looking for
a way to rip off an old woman who looks to living in one of
those Many Mansions in the sky, pretty soon after it's said
and done, she kissed her life goodbye. Altar boys assisting
priests during Sunday Mass, only to give up the ass, being
robbed of their innocence. For years keeping his guilt and
shame and blamed himself.*

*Jehovah God, an odd religious practice, no Christmas, no
Thanksgiving, no birthdays or Allegiance to the Stars and
stripes. What the fuck is your gripe?*

*Fuck your religion! It's nothing but fuckery! Religious fuck-
ery!"*

Ramiro's ideas rolled off his brain onto the paper. He made creative progress and concluded this song with more offensive content.
These sacrilegious words would hurt his mother and grandmother.
They always kept Ramiro in prayer so that God would protect him.
As for Maritza, she understood her brother's prolific talents and
wanted Ramiro to keep her posted on his musical journey. Then the
clock read, two, thirty, eight. Ramiro's eyes weren't heavy at all. His
eyes wandered around the bedroom, from the ceilings to the floor
and the walls in between. He had another piece of lyrical content,
but it had nothing to do with his poor relationship with his father.
Then there was a knock on the door.

"Who is it?" Ramiro sat up in bed.

Zack stormed into the bedroom. "They hatched!"

A TINY BABY TARANTULA crawled in Ramiro's hand as he gently petted the insect. The other fifteen spiders crawled on the inside of the glass tank. The adult spiders kept an eye on their young as two baby spiders crept their way up Zack's arm. "Wait until Kim sees this?" Ramiro chuckled. "So, what's going to happen to the little ones?"

"Dad! The spider eggs hatched!" Zack cried from his bedroom. Then heavy footsteps pounded down the hallway towards his bedroom as his father stormed in. Neil stepped towards the glass tank and saw the itsy-bitsy spiders.

"Holy shit! Look at them!" Neil got a closer look.

"Are we going to take them to the pet shop?"

"of course, son!" Neil yawned.

"I want to keep two of them," Ramiro smirked.

"Do you know how to take care of spiders?" Neil asked.

"I'll learn," Ramiro focused on the tiny insect in his hand.

"You got it!" Neil nodded.

"I can't stop gazing into those tiny eight eyes that amaze me. Spider's eyes freak most people out, but I dig it. Maybe, I could write a song about the creepy crawly bugs that would scare the shit out of everyone. I can't think of any lyrics right now, but it'll come to me in time. As for now, I've got the world's greatest pet," Ramiro lightly stroked the small spider.

CHAPTER SIX

O n New Year's Eve, Zack struck his drumsticks on his drum kit while Ramiro zipped his fingers along the fingerboard of his Spector bass guitar with another loud metal sound in the garage. It was heavy and fast, the way Ramiro wanted it. Music notes were laid on the side table and his composition notebook with song lyrics he wrote. He knew to put it to use because his life was on the line. Ramiro better sing or else? Kim straddled on a stool with her legs wide open with star-struck eyes. She kept Ramiro's presence in the line of sight. As he headbanged with his hair swishing, he saw glimpses of her sexy attire that left nothing to the imagination. Kim wore black spandex pants with a camel toe between her legs while the imprint of her perky nipples on her pillows in her low-cut band t-shirt. She sported the outfit to turn Ramiro on. The aspiring musicians didn't discuss getting a lead guitarist or thought about it. They wallowed into their music as Neil and Emmy tiptoed into the garage. These two young rockers played, raising hell. Neil embraced his wife, proud parents of their son, and best friend's talents. Emmy noticed Kim sitting with her legs apart, smirking. Zack's mother saw this hot in-the-pants young woman who had eyes for her son. But Kim was supposed to be Ramiro's girlfriend. Emmy frowned, and just like Maritza, she didn't get involved in any drama.

"TEN, NINE, EIGHT, SEVEN, six, five, four, three, two, one, Happy New Year!" Ramiro, Zack, and his family and friends clanked holiday cups of eggnog. "People are Strange" by The Doors blasted from the radio. The young kids lounged around while Zack's parents stayed upstairs in the living room. Zack grabbed a bottle of Tequila hidden behind a cabinet. He poured the alcoholic beverage into a paper cup, offering it to Kim with a seductive smile. She took the cup, smiling in return. Ramiro noticed the interaction between his best friend and his so-called girlfriend. He didn't get uptight about it because he had eyes for someone else. Kim reached out to hug him. Ramiro didn't reciprocate the affection; he held his hands to his side. "What's wrong, babe?" she asked with puppy dog eyes.

"I'm tired of playing," Ramiro yawned.

"Loosen up, Ram! Stage lights are burning bright on our future!" Zack poured Ramiro some liquor in the paper cup. Ramiro bumped his paper cup with his best friend and Kim. They gulped down their Tequila. Zack and Kim released enormous burps. Ramiro sneered, noticing Zack and his girlfriend having eyes for one another, on their way to becoming stoned drunk. Ramiro wanted to go upstairs, but he didn't want to be a party pooper. Kim pecked him on the lips. Still, he didn't return any affection. He glared at this young woman whom he didn't trust. Thirteen minutes after two in the morning the clock read. "I'm fuckin' tired," Ramiro crumpled the paper cup in his hand, tossing it in the trash can.

"See you in the morning, dude," Zack lifted his paper cup in the air.

"I'll be up in a minute, babe," Kim blew a kiss to him.

Ramiro shrugged, marching upstairs as he ascended from the garage to the first floor.

"She'll come to bed in a minute? Hopefully." he stomped his heavy feet up the carpeted steps to the second floor. He remembered Zack's parents welcomed him to stay with them until further notice, so he had to show respect. He ascended the staircase with a lighter weight on his feet. Moans and groans came from Zack's parent's master bed-

room down the hallway. *"Shit! OMG! His parents still fuck!"* Ramiro
cringed as he headed into the guest bedroom. He closed the door
with ease, leaving it cracked. Kim's flirtatious ways and possibly getting it on with different dudes was a reality. But he had to see it,
to believe it. The three baby tarantulas didn't crawl around in the
small tank much. They seemed to be tired from whatever activities
they participated in. Ramiro got a closer look at the insects. Zack
and Neil helped Ramiro to create a natural habitat for the spiders,
so they would feel comfortable. He smirked at the bugs, hoping they
crawled on the glass. But they got some rest just like Ramiro needed. He yawned and erased his creepy pets from his thought. He took
off his construction boots, jeans, t-shirt, and undershirt, only leaving
his boxers. Throwing the down comforter over his body, Ramiro was
grateful that he'd get some shut-eye. He glared at the covers over his
head, only seeing the blue-colored fabric that compensated the ceiling he usually focused on. Ramiro closed his eyes, staring into complete darkness.

A FEW HOURS PASSED into dawn, Ramiro squinted his eyes,
where he stared into the blue comforter with a splash of white light.
He snatched the covers from his head as his vision became vivid. The
first thing, he witnessed was the white ceiling above him. The bed
Ramiro stretched out in felt empty. He noticed Kim wasn't there.
"Where the fuck is she?" he murmured. The clock read: five forty-
three a.m. He sat up in bed, raising an eyebrow, and got up from the
bed. His baby spiders were up and about crawling around in their
tank. "Good morning, creepies. I'm sorry that I have to refer to you
like that. But I'm going to seek beautiful names for you. I promise,"
Ramiro smirked as it alternated into a sour expression. He threw on
his jeans, t-shirts, and boots. He opened the door with caution so
he wouldn't disturb anyone. Down the dimmed hallway, Zack's par-

ent's door remained closed and quiet as church mice. Ramiro crept to Zack's bedroom door and opened it with ease. His bed remained tidy along with everything else in the bedroom. Ramiro balled his hands into fists, stormed downstairs.

AS RAMIRO CREPT DOWN to the basement, looking toward the garage door where an old rock tune played from the radio. He maneuvered to the heavy door as he heard a female moaning. Ramiro inched his hand to the doorknob, cracking the door open. Kim bounced on top of Zack butt-naked while sweat trickled down their bodies. Ramiro kept his eye peering through the crack as it enlarged in its socket. His heart pounded, balling his hand into a fist. Ramiro didn't know whether to beat the shit out of his best friend or Kim. He sure and hell didn't want to get kicked out of Zack's parent's house or land in jail. He turned fiery red in the face, storming into the garage. "I knew your whore ass was up to something!"

Kim covered her breasts with a t-shirt, jumping off of Zack. His best friend held his hand over his crotch.

"Good morning, babe?" she greeted with a phony smile.

"What! That's why you didn't come to bed last night, so you could fuck him!" Ramiro grabbed the empty Tequila bottle, ready to throw it.

"Don't fuckin' do it, Ram! What the fuck!" Zack cringed to protect himself.

"Baby, I'm so sorry!" Kim put on her panties and other garments.

Zack then put on his jeans as his parents rushed into the garage. Neil had on an old t-shirt and jogging pants. His mother wrapped her robe around her body, rubbing her eyes.

"What the fuck!" Neil noticed Zack and Kim rushing to get dressed while Ramiro stood there with the glass bottle in his hand.

Emmy sneered at Kim and knew this loose girl had tricks up her sleeve.

"Holy shit! Zack, this is your best friend!" Neil threw his hands up in the air.

Ramiro placed the glass bottle on the table, storming out of the garage.

"Ramiro! Please listen to me!" Kim pleaded with tears in her eyes as she gave chase. He exited the front door of his friend's house, marching down the block. His face was fiery-red with both hands clutched into fists. He wished he could beat the shit out of Kim, but he had to calm down. He had to get the thought of doing physical damage to this woman, even though she did him wrong. He stormed past a frozen lake with the frigid air that caused goosebumps on his arms because he only wore a t-shirt. He didn't care if he got pneumonia on this New Year's Day. It was better than having the woman you trusted to fuck your best friend and bandmate.

"Now, what the fuck is my band's future if I don't have Zack as my drummer! I wouldn't do anything to betray my best friend! Fuck it! He can have her! But I must care. I'm dealing with Kim. I'm not sure about the woman that I wanted!" he paced the icy cold pavement and then planted his ass on the cold bench. He didn't feel the 2-degree temperature because he was so hot temperature and temperament-wise. Kim sat beside Ramiro, placing her hand on his shoulder. He pushed her hand away.

"Don't fuckin' touch me! Slut!" he insulted with deep-seated hate in his eyes. Ramiro trembled in the face, continuing to clench his fist.

"Babe! I was drunk!" she attempted to hold back tears.

He then held his head in the palm of his hands and wanted to call it quits. But he kept his trap shut while Kim wept about wanting to work it out. Her words went through Ramiro's ears and out of the other. He owed Zack's parents an apology for the disturbance and had to get back to the house before he caught pneumonia. He marched back to Zack's house without looking back to see if this two-faced broad trailed him.

MINUTES LATER, RAMIRO marched up to the second floor of his best friend's home. He entered his bedroom, where Zack sat in the chair. "Ramiro, let me explain!"

Ramiro leaned in the doorway, raising an eyebrow.

"She came on to me, dude! I noticed the way Kim looked at me when we were jamming out! When my mom came into the garage, she noticed Kim gawking at me!" he explained. Ramiro scoffed after hearing that his best friend's mother saw Kim giving Zack seductive looks. And no one said a word. He had no other choice than to believe it. The proof was right in the pudding. And he didn't want to end his friendship over a female when they've got big plans.

"Brothers?" Zack extended his hand out to Ramiro to receive a hi-five.

"Brothers!" he reciprocated his friend's hi-five. And then the two young men embraced.

LATER THAT DAY, RAMIRO sang his heart out as he played his bass guitar. He had no other choice. He better sing or else. So, Ramiro had to use his rocker vocals the best way he could to reach his goal. Zack played the beat on his drum set of the famous sixties song "Light My Fire." He knew Ramiro would come around with his vocals and he was pretty good. The thing that Ramiro didn't have was a microphone. He sang as loud as he could, mastering the lyrics. Neil pushed the heavy garage door open, yawning. He grabbed a stool, taking a front-row seat as if he were a fan at one of Ramiro's concerts and, of course, his son's. Emmy then stormed through the door and saw Ramiro singing her favorite song. Zack always entertained his mother with old rock songs on drums. She loved Elvis Presley, Jimi Hendrix, Black Sabbath, Rush, Metal Church, The Killer Dwarfs, and other rock bands. Neil played lead guitar in a high school band, but he never attempted to popularize their music. He focused on the future with his wife and raising his son.

THE WINTRY MONTH OF January brought more fierce winds, cold with dropping temperatures. The whistling of the wind kept Ramiro up as he sat in his slumber, writing more obscure and offensive lyrics. As he wrote more grotesque words, he glanced at the spiders in their tank, crawling on the rocks and the sand under their eight legs. "You can't sleep either can you?" Ramiro spoke to the insects in his mind as if these creatures would respond. He focused on his work while the frigid nights proceeded to motivate him. He thought about writing an eerie song about winter. Something about Christmas or Frosty the Snowman. Sinister lyrics like a murder or a person haunted by a vile spirit during the holiday. *"Fuck, I hope I can keep that idea in mind."* On a half-written page, he conjured up the idea of a fallen musician that came to mind.

Now, why would he be writing about a fallen rocker? Ramiro's father kicked him out, now crashing at his best friend's house; his girlfriend slept with his best friend; he doesn't have a job and not a penny in his pocket. As the wind whistled, a tree branch tapped at the window. It seemed as if the tree wanted to tell him something. Maybe about his future? Ramiro turned to the window. The tree got on his nerves while the tapping continued. He ignored it and kept writing. "Was Ramiro going to be some washed-up rock star? Not a pot to piss in or a window to throw it out of? Or some fucked up lifestyle," As more ideas came to Ramiro, he wrote even faster. Staying up all night long, working hard, and paying their dues, where

Ramiro could lead his best friend and another fellow guitarist to fame and fortune. He finally found his voice. Ramiro just let it out, like regurgitating. He might as well vomit lyrics out due to his broken family. Ramiro needed to focus more on his vocals and seeking a lead guitarist. He had to put a lot of thought into it, but he called it a night. Ramiro closed his composition notebook, placed it on his nightstand, and turned the lights off. He turned on his side while the spider tank glowed throughout the darkened bedroom.

IT WAS THE WEEK OF final exams in late January, where Ramiro took his last test for his algebra class. The final exam comprised of fifty questions; he peered at Noelle. Ramiro knew she would ace this test. He couldn't keep his eyes off her, but he had to because the instructor would get suspicious. Ramiro wondered what she was doing this afternoon? Maybe this would be an excellent opportunity to pursue her. Noelle rose from her desk, throwing her schoolbag over her shoulder with her test paper in her hand. She hurried to Mr. Cicero's desk, handing her exam in, and headed out of the classroom. Ramiro's heart raced in his chest as his hands quivered. *"Stop shaking, Ram! Stop acting like a bitch! All you have to do is get her, and you'll be fine! Finish your exam!"* he told himself.

SECONDS LATER, RAMIRO stormed out of the classroom, noticing the girl he desired heading down the staircase. "Noelle!" he cried. He dashed down the steps behind Noelle to get up close and personal as if he wanted to kiss her. Ramiro kept his composure and was lost for words.

"Hello, Ramiro. How are you?" Noelle held her tight grip on her school bag.

"I'm cool," Ramiro exhaled.

"How do you think you did?" she asked.

Ramiro shrugged. "I hope I passed. I know you passed."

"Are you sure about that?" she chuckled.

"You're smart. And you're beautiful too," Ramiro complimented.

"Thank you. So are you?" Noelle returned the compliment.

"I don't know about that. So, what are you doing after this?" he gazed into this young woman's brown eyes.

"I've got another exam. English," she replied. As they exchanged small talk, Kimberly made her way up the stairs; she stopped on the third step on the bottom. Kimberly noticed Ramiro being overly friendly with this girl who could be from an impoverished neighborhood, raised by a single mother, and who didn't know her father. She probably has a brother in jail for drug dealing or murder. Every negative stereotype about her crossed Kimberly's mind. Ramiro and Noelle exchange numbers as they said their goodbyes. Ramiro bumped into Kimberly as he descended the stairs. She turned red in the face as she stood at the foot of the staircase with her schoolbag. Ramiro sneered at Kim as well, keeping his pace without slowing down. "Did you exchange numbers with her?"

"And what the fuck is it to you?" Ramiro sneered.

"I know I was wrong, but I still care about you," Kim blocked Ram's path.

"You showed me how much you cared when you were fucking Zack," he bellowed.

"Why would you want a girl like that! When you've got me!" Kimberly clenched her teeth.

"What the fuck do you mean, a girl like that? And I've got you? Fuck no!" Ramiro reversed the question.

"Some black guys in my class told me that black girls have attitudes, wear bad hair extensions, and live in Blackistan," she insulted.

"What the fuck! Black guys! What fuckin' black guys! They live in Blackistan as well! And what the fuck were you doing while listening to these fuckin' Tyroaches!" he rose an eyebrow.

"No. No fuckin' way would I do anything with those niggers," she turned red in the face.

"I bet you fuckin' would.... or you fuckin' did! Some robust thug from the projects rode your ass into the sunset pulling you by your long, silk hair! Cocksucking bitch! Get the fuck out of my face!" Ramiro stormed away.

CHAPTER SEVEN

Four years later, red, yellow, and brown leaves fell to the concrete grounds of a college campus in Long Island, New York, as Ramiro hauled his bass guitar case on his shoulder. He majored in music, hoping to get a Bachelor's degree. It wouldn't guarantee him a career as a professional musician, but he could teach music in junior high school or even senior high. He had to keep his job options open after he graduated college because he needed an income. The music building was a structure of dreams where musicians hoped to play at Carnegie Hall or before thousands of screaming fans at packed concert arenas around the world. A bifocal-wearing, twenty-something young man, heaving a Cello case, struggled through the door as Ramiro held the door for the classical musician. "Thanks, man," the nerdy artist nodded.

"No problem," Ramiro cracked a smile.

The marble hallways of the building, similar to Lincoln center, inspired students to achieve greatness. Colorful photos of former students who accomplished their dreams in Jazz and Classical music hung on the walls. Ramiro passed through the corridors every day; he acknowledged two pics but overlooked the rest. Noelle came to mind when he saw these photos of female singers who possibly sang jazz such as Bille Holiday or Ella Fitzgerald. All he knew was that Noelle had a beautiful voice. On top of that, there were no rockers on the wall, but he didn't let that bother him. Ramiro set his mind on his priorities as he took the elevator to the sub-basement. He glared at the enormous steel double doors while he descended in this steel box to the lowest floor of the building. He still hasn't contacted Noelle because he didn't want to get into another confrontation with his best friend over a woman again. Ramiro had her phone number stored on his SIM card. He hoped that her number would still be in service. On the other hand, he focused on looking for a lead guitarist, hoping to start a band. The elevator stopped as the heavy doors widened. He stepped off and entered into a brick corridor, well-lit ceilings, and more photos of well-known musicians on the wall.

RAMIRO APPROACHED SOME soundproof music booths, noticing a variety of unique artists practicing their craft. He slowed down his pace, seeing a long brunette tress woman, early twenties, stroking her bow on the cello strings. On the other side, four violinists practiced in another booth. Towards the back, a small band played in a larger booth with a trumpeter, bass player, pianist, and drummer in a booth on the other side. Ramiro assumed they were a Jazz band. Then in a lonely corner, a long-black-haired Caucasian male, mid-twenties, black clothing, headbanging while hastening his finger along the fingerboard of his ESP black electric guitar in a small booth. Ramiro watched this crazed guitarist with hair longer than his, playing tunes he couldn't hear but had incredible showmanship. Then the rocker subsided his session, brushing his hair from his face. He blinked at Ramiro, who stood outside of the glass booth. They looked like long-lost brothers separated at birth now reunited. Ramiro cracked a smile as he took a couple of steps away. The booth door swung opened, as the young guitarist gawked at Ramiro.

"You play the guitar?"

"Bass," Ramiro smirked.

"I play drums as well. I'm Danny," he extended his hand to Ramiro.

"I'm Ramiro," he exhaled.

"Where are you from?" Danny wondered.

"Massapequa. And you?" Ramiro asked.

"Smithtown," Danny replied.

IN NO TIME, THESE TWO rockers exchanged ideas over lunch in a nearby diner off-campus. Daniel O'Connor grew up in a single-parent household, where his father raised him and his two younger brothers after his mother died of heart disease. His father didn't want Danny to become a guitarist and traveling on the road from state to state or internationally. Being a rock musician was a thing of the past because there's no more vinyl or CDs where listeners could purchase the music so the musicians can make a living. Danny knew that technology affected the music industry and didn't allow that to stop him. Another thing, Danny's father, wasn't a Jesus freak like Ramiro's father. So, his father allowed him musical freedom as a child. Zack swaggered through the entrance as bells chimed of the restaurant above his head. He rushed towards the booth where Ramiro and Danny sat.

"I'm Zack," he extended his hand to Danny.

"The drummer right?" Danny cackled. "I play lead guitar."

"Cool," Zack added.

A SHORT TIME LATER, the three musicians got more acquainted, they discussed what bands inspired them and admired; how often they would practice if anyone wrote lyrics, and whoever wanted to do so and wanted to create a business out of it. A thin server sashayed towards their booth with a notepad and pen in her hand, ready to take their order.

"Are you guys starving?"

"We're starving artists," Danny laughed.

"What will it be?" the server jotted their orders on the pad.

ABOUT AN HOUR LATER, the trio clanked their bottles of beer and drank to a promising future over scraps of waffles, a burger, French fries with ketchup, a half-chewed pickle, a steak, and a salad left on their plates. Danny wanted to jam out in the booth, but Zack needed a drum set. They had to see if the school building had one for him to play.

Ramiro beckoned the waitress to the booth. She smiled at him as he placed his Discover credit card on the table.

AT BAND PRACTICE, IN a sizeable soundproof booth later, Zack pumped his feet on the bass drum pedals and hit the snare and tom-toms with drumsticks on a Pearl drum kit. Ramiro and Danny watched him and could tell it displeased him. Zack paused. "This drum kit fuckin' sucks!"

"Just play, dude!" Danny clapped his hands with encouragement. He wanted to see Zack's drumming style. Zack pumped the bass drum pedals as best he could, hitting the tom-toms and snares with his drumsticks, showing off his talent. Ramiro saw Zack struggling with this thirty-year-old drum kit. All of the good drum kits were used by other students. The old beat-down Pearl drum set was available and Zack had no other choice than to deal with it. Sweat trickled down Zack's face, panting while he played and played, and then he turned fiery red in the face. This worn-down instrument had a mind of its own. It was dead. Zack then pounded and pounded as he became frustrated. His playing turned into a bunch of noise. He seized his playing as Ramiro and Danny applauded his determination with this problematic drum set. Ramiro reached into his backpack and showed the musical notes for the song he created, "Religious Fuckery" to Zack. Zack nodded and knew he could drum up an aggressive sound. Ramiro gave Danny the same music notes. Danny inserted the plug of his electric guitar into the speaker and zigzagged his fingers on the guitar strings creating a distorted sound. Ramiro did the same with his bass guitar.

"Let's do it."

Zack played wicked drumming as Ramiro, and Danny added in their guitars into collaboration. While playing the music, Ramiro sang "Religious Fuckery" and drifted off into another world. He stood center stage of a packed stadium, blaring out lyrics and playing along with his bandmates before thousands of roaring fans. Headbangers participated in the mosh pit while other's body surfed. He envisioned Noelle relaxing in a comfortable skybox watching him from above.

MEANWHILE, IN A HOT pink painted bedroom, Noelle lounged in a chair with headphones with a built-in mic, listening to an instrumental house track that contained deep bass and synthesized sounds. Girly and music décor wall art adorned the atmosphere with a full-sized bed with a rosy red comforter and decorative pillows along with antique dolls. She closed her eyes and envisioned taking baby steps into a rose garden. "I am love and devotion; the familiar fragrance I used to seduce your mind, body, and soul that devours you whole; it's out of your control," she recited over the dance track. Her notebook laid on the side table filled with poems about love, hate, and worldviews. This reserved young woman had a poetic talent along with singing. Her parents trusted her tastes and knew she was going down the right path. Being an only child had its benefits; Noelle's father spoiled her like hell. During Noelle's poetic session, she pictured Ramiro clutching her as they sailed along the Caribbean sea on a cruise ship. Noelle danced while proceeding to spew the words from her heart, keeping a clear picture of Ramiro in her mind.

MEANWHILE, AT RAMIRO'S band practice, he and his bandmates continued with their belligerent performance in the booth. Two Caucasian gentlemen, early forties, ear piercings, tattoos, dressed with professionalism in a dress shirt, tie, blazers, and jeans waltzed by the booth and halted. They noticed the showmanship of these three young men, headbanging with their long hair. Douglas Berghoff and Stanley Mitch were music managers searching for the next hot metal act. They hit the nail right on the head because they had connections to A&R executives at Ominous records that promoted Heavy Metal bands with edgy, dark, aggressive styles. The metal trio didn't realize they had some important eyes on them, which could make or break them. The band concluded their aggressive piece as Ramiro noticed these two men applauding. He opened the glass door of the booth with his bass guitar strapped to him.

"Can I help you dudes?"

"Yes, dude! You can start by showing us your work and tell us about yourselves," Douglas smirked as he glanced at Stanley.

"And of course, we couldn't hear because of the booth. We can tell your sound must be amazing just by your showmanship," Stanley added.

The band glimpsed at each other, shrugged, and performed an old rock cover song from the sixties.

BACK AT THE DINER AGAIN later, Ramiro, his bandmates, the managers, lounged at a bigger booth with only two half-eaten plates of a chicken wrap, waffle fries, a shrimp salad with ranch dressing, and half-empty beer bottles. The soon-to-be rockers already stuffed their stomachs a couple of hours earlier. The same server who served them did it again, along with these two music managers. Douglas focused on developing the band's sound, image, and fan base. His ideas were on the right path, but Ramiro didn't want Douglas to alternate them into something that would make the public feel comfortable. He wanted to do the opposite and tear shit up. Stanley understood the trio's style and wanted them to be true to who they were: thrash metal musicians. Ominous records had three thrash metal acts on the label, Shitload, Night Of Demise, and Reckless. These three musicians glared at these two gentlemen with doubt. The one thing Ramiro wanted was to make a business out of their career so they can make a good living. He didn't want to play music in concert venues worldwide and get ripped off. Ramiro and Zack didn't discuss that with Danny yet because they just met. But he was pretty sure Danny wanted to make some cash off his music as well. Zack tapped his foot on the floor. "When do we record some music?"

"You could make some sample tracks. We'll put our heads together and come up with something and whatever else you may already have," Stanley drank from his glass.

"Cool," Zack nodded. He glanced at Ramiro, who looked unsure about the situation. Ramiro felt this offer from these music managers seemed fraudulent. The trio only had one band practice, but his bandmates assured him to take a chance with these gentlemen who could pull some strings. Ramiro hoped his bandmates were right about these two guys. Still, there was no mention of another guitarist. He believed they could pull it off. Stanley and Douglas said nothing. But when the issue comes up, Ramiro will be ready.

THAT NIGHT, A DIGITAL clock read ten, fourteen p.m. on Ramiro's computer monitor at his apartment not too far away from campus. His three pet tarantulas grew some but not quite full adults but they were on their way. The insects crawled along the sand in the large glass tank. Ramiro slumbered in his full-sized bed, watching "The Night of the Living Dead". His cellphone laid on a pillow next to him as if it were a woman. He had Noelle in mind, but he was tired from jamming out with his bandmates. He squinted his eyes with a blurry vision of his bedroom. He heard a woman screaming from the television because of a zombie chasing her. "What time is it? I've got to call Noelle," he widened his eyes and grabbed his cellphone. He dialed Noelle's number. His cellphone made a connection as it rang and then....

"Hello," a feminine voice answered.

"Noelle! How are you?" Ramiro mumbled.

"Ramiro, how are you? Where have you been?" Noelle lounged in her full-sized bed with Fushia bedding with her cellphone to her ear, wearing leopard print pajamas. On the other end of the phone, Ramiro apologized for not calling sooner. *What kept this guy from calling me for four years? He'd better come up with a good reason; why?* she waited for more of an explanation. Noelle sat upright in her bed as soon as he uttered his reason. Her heart pounded in her chest because of this guy who shared the same similarities. He explained more about his ambitions of becoming a professional musician and he wanted Noelle to check him out. She told Ramiro that she wrote poetry and sang House music. On the other end of the phone, Ramiro rested his head against his pillow and cracked a smile. "That's good," he responded. He wasn't too crazy about House or Pop music or whatever the fuck annoyed him. He wanted to see her as soon as possible. Noelle wanted to see him as well. If they ever got together, Ramiro would not let Noelle go.

CHAPTER EIGHT

About a week later, in a small music recording studio, Ramiro screamed in the microphone with headphones, playing his bass guitar. Danny ran his fingers along the strings on the fingerboard of his electric guitar while Zack played a double bass drumming using the foot pedals and striking the tom-tom with his sticks on a Tama drum kit. He was now very pleased with this set of drums. The collaboration of these three musical instruments gave a fast, aggressive, and irritating sound. The guys recorded their first song, "Meet Your Demise." Ramiro spewed out the angry lyrics as he imagined his father standing right before him. This father and son took part in a staring match as the music became more aggressive. Jorge stood his ground while Ramiro played a warmongering tune with his bandmates. The sound engineer adjusted the tone levels of the music while Stanley and Douglas watched the trio give not only an aggressive sound but also their zealous showmanship. Noelle relaxed in a chair, smiling from ear to ear and seeing Ramiro play. She felt as if she were at a concert watching him.

NOELLE HAD TIME TO check out Ramiro's jam session that early afternoon. She attended college in Westbury, majoring in Liberal arts and Business administration. Noelle didn't care for her business classes that much because it wasn't her thing. She listened to Ramiro blare out another song "Religious Fuckery" as her eyes bulged, hearing the horror spewing from his mouth. As Ramiro kept singing, the music became somewhat uneasy. Noelle believed in God, but she wasn't a fanatic. She hoped Ramiro wasn't an atheist, but chances are he was. He has profane written content, dresses in black with no sign of light within his persona. But Ramiro was a badass bassist. The band's managers applauded as the recording session subsided. Ramiro swaggered out of the booth with his bass guitar strapped around him. He laid a kiss on Noelle's lips. Her heart raced for this rebel with a cause.

ABOUT AN HOUR LATER, Ramiro, his bandmates, and management sat in a semi-circle discussing more music to upload to the internet. Ramiro's composition notebook was full of ideas as more in his head. Danny had some ideas as well. Ramiro didn't care; he had more. The music had to keep coming. Noelle paced the hallway outside of the music studio. So much crap went through her mind and more. *"What will Ramiro and I make of this? I know what I'm desiring, but I've to keep my panties in a notch. I can't give it up to him on the first day. That's not a good move. So, I have to focus my mind on getting to know him. I hope Ramiro's not a creep. Maybe, this was a big mistake by me coming to see him. I should go home. Or maybe, I'm paranoid,"* she sat down on the small bench. Ramiro stormed out of the studio in the hallway, rushing to Noelle. He grasped her hand as she rose from the bench and strolled out of the building.

THAT LATE AFTERNOON, an orangey glowing sunset sat over a small beach as the seagulls screeched in the air. A lighthouse stood in the middle of the sands, with a few people strolling along the shore. Ramiro stopped short with the brakes squealing of his second-handed black Dodge Durango that he purchased with the help of his scholarships, his mother and grandmother, who had the money for him. Ramiro and Noelle dawdled along the boardwalk that led to the beach. Next to it was tall dried grass with deer attempting to camouflage themselves from humans. Noelle noticed a fawn glaring at her. The deer within the tall grass resembled a painting on someone's living room wall.

"Look at the deer," she chuckled.

"They've got plenty of them around these parts," Ramiro clutched Noelle's hand and proceeded towards the water.

"So, what do you think about my music?" he asked.

"It's interesting! Somewhat weird," Noelle kissed him on the cheek.

"My bandmates and I are going to be signed to this label. And we'll go on tour and see the world," he said. And then he thought about Noelle. What about her? If she was going to be an important part of his life, shouldn't she be included? He knew she had to finish school and get her life going.

"Do you have any siblings?" Noelle stroked his hand.

"I have a sister. And you?" he cleared his throat.

"I'm an only child," she smiled.

"Wow! You've got everything to yourself!" the cool October breeze blew Ramiro's long hair exposing his three pierced earrings. He wore a small silver hoop and two studs; when Noelle saw that, she smiled. It turned her on. Ramiro caught Noelle's smile and didn't bother to ask why she smiled at him from ear to ear. "When is your birthday?"

"Christmas Day," she grasped Ramiro's hand. "And yours?

"Next week. On the thirtieth," he laughed.

"Devil's Night?" she scratched her brow.

He could tell Noelle felt uneasy as she focused her eyes on the sand. They strolled upon some vast rocks on the edge of the beach. The waves didn't cause a threat to anyone who wanted to lounge on these enormous solid materials formed from the earth. Noelle climbed onto the largest one and placed her buttocks down. Ramiro stood alongside her on the smaller rock. He hoped Noelle didn't fear him.

"Do you like the ocean, Ramiro?"

"It's cool," he eyed the calm waters. Ramiro moved close to Noelle and smiled. They clutched hands. Noelle wasn't afraid of him because of the day that he was born. That's something Ramiro couldn't help.

"It would be exciting to see you on an enormous stage. You've got a magnificent stage presence," Noelle smiled. Ramiro loved the fact that she would watch him from backstage while he performed in cities and countries worldwide. The lovers glared into each other's eyes as if they could tell what the other was feeling. The couple engaged in a passionate kiss. He grabbed Noelle around the waist, pulling her close to him. Of course, Ramiro couldn't lay Noelle down because rocks weren't the best place to make love. He reached his hands from Noelle's waist to her breasts. She didn't resist Ramiro touching her.

THAT EVENING IN RAMIRO'S darkened bedroom, he and Noelle engaged in passionate body movements between black satin sheets halfway wrapped around their unclothed bodies. His dresser mirror captured their reflections in his black-painted apartment. He glared into her eyes, knowing he had total control of her mind, body, and soul. She moaned, almost as if she cried not of pain but pleasure. He cracked a devilish smile as they both achieved their climaxes. Ramiro kissed Noelle on the lips with sweat cascading from his face. She wiped the moisture with the back of her hand.

He rolled off Noelle to the other side of the bed. He had to catch his breath after a loving workout. He then kissed her on the forehead and peered at the skeleton head clock on his nightstand that read eleven, thirty-eight p.m.

"What the fuck! The night is still young!" he gazed at Noelle while she rested on the other side of the bed without a care in the world. His flat panel television hung on the wall before his king-sized bed with a blue night light behind it. Ramiro wanted to turn on the box but didn't want to disturb Noelle. He gave her that respect as he eased himself out of bed, slipping on his boxers. He stuck his face close to the tarantula tank, assuming his pets were hungry. He grabbed some dead flies from the jar on the side of the glass tank. Ramiro slid open the lid, dropped the decaying insects for the spiders to feast. Luckily, she didn't recognize the spider tank when they entered his bedroom because they were in the heat of passion and his bedroom was dark. And she didn't even recognize his enormous tarantula tattoo. He wondered if she was afraid of spiders. He'll introduce her to his creepy pets soon enough and hopefully, his body art won't freak her out. Ramiro crept out of his bedroom and headed down the dim hallway of his college apartment. It resembled his childhood home where he grew up. He shuffled to the bathroom in complete darkness, shutting the door. He stared at the toilet and didn't have to take a leak, but he needed to meditate. He pulled his boxers down anyway and sat on the porcelain as if he had to take a shit. He thought about jotting down lyrics involving his sexual encounter with Noelle. Some x-rated shit describing Noelle's voluptuous breasts, her juicy thunder thighs wrapped around his waist as he's pounding away. Noelle wouldn't want their sexual relationship publicized. So, Ramiro changed his mind, trying to conjure up something else. His mind was blank, only instrumentals. He stood up from the toilet, wiping his ass, and flushed the cleaned piece of toilet paper. And, of course, Ramiro washed his hands. He would not touch his bass with filthy hands. Hypothetically speaking.

IN THE LIVING ROOM'S corner, Ramiro's black matte Spectator bass guitar rested on a mahogany wooden stand at an angle, and on the other side was his first Ibanez black bass guitar given to him from Zack and his parents on his thirteenth birthday. The instruments were surrounded by an abundance of skeletal décor such as a large silver floor skull on the side of an artificial coal-black fireplace with a skeleton with a top hat, creepy clown figurines sat on the ledge, and an eerie clown canvas on the wall. Ramiro strapped his Spector bass guitar around his waist and sat in his recliner. The picture of the clown gazed at Ramiro as if he knew about him. Ramiro inserted the plug of his bass guitar into the speaker and then his headsets. He wanted to write more lyrics but couldn't come up with any ideas. "What could I write this time? I want to write something crazy. A song that'll scare the shit out of everyone!" he gazed at the clown canvas. He grabbed his composition notebook, turning to a blank page with its blue lines, and made eye contact with the clown again. Ramiro felt as if this creature knew his thoughts and hinted at him.

"Holy shit! I know!" he snapped out of the gaze with the picture. Then Ramiro jotted down the title of a song.

"KLOWN"

"The world loves a Klown, at the circus or carnival, with whiffs of Popcorn and cotton candy in the air, with floating balloons everywhere.

The world also fears a Klown, an evil being from beneath the earth, tormenting and terrorizing....." he wrote the insane lyrics about symbols that are supposed to bring happiness. But he reversed the feeling and turned it into a musical horror movie. A clown leaned forward in a recliner, smiling at him and nodding. This circus performer grinned at Ramiro, giving him the "Go" to create the sickest, most fiendish lyrics that would make people cringe. He and his bandmates would have to come up with a fast, aggressive, circus-like, creepy tune. For now, he continued to write the repulsive lyrics. Ramiro eyed the clown who wore a black velvet-like suit with large white buttons, enormous white floppy shoes, his face painted skeleton-white like in the movie "Dead Presidents."

"Am I seeing this clown before my eyes? Or is it my bullshit imagination? It's my fuckin' imagination. I know I'm not out of my mind and don't fuck with drugs," he focused his eyes on the composition notebook.

".....stalks you in your dreams, from the top of your lungs you'll scream,

for this monster to be gone, hold your bible tight and pray to God that you make it

through the night, this Klown is right in plain sight....," he wrote on and on with the eerie piece. He rose his head from his notebook and noticed the recliner was empty. His eyes shifted all around his living room that he had adorned with such malevolent décor. Ramiro's heart pounded in his chest.

"Why is my heart racing? Am I afraid of what I'm writing? Is my creativity scaring me? Bullshit!" Ramiro's hand trembled while holding a pen. Then a hand touched his shoulder as he hopped off the seat. "What the fuck!"

"Oh! I'm sorry, baby!" Noelle flinched. She placed her hand over her chest.

Ramiro exhaled as he clutched Noelle like a child who woke up from a scary dream. She had a top sheet wrapped around her nude body with it trailing on the floor. She pressed her body close to him as they engaged in a passionate kiss. He was ready for round two with another bulge in his boxers. Noelle locked her legs around his waist as she noticed his 3D tarantula tattoo.

"Oh my God! There's a tarantula on you, Ramiro!" Noelle backed into a corner with the sheet around her body.

"I know it's my tattoo. It's not real. It's 3D," he explained. Ramiro saw that Noelle wasn't comfortable with his body art. He extended his hand to her.

"Baby, it's alright," Ramiro rubbed his hand along his spider tattoo.

"Oh, boy," Noelle looked confused.

"Do you want to go home?" he asked.

"No, I don't. I came here to be with you, Ramiro," Noelle said.

"I don't want to make you feel uncomfortable. I want to make things as pleasant for you as possible. Do you trust me?" he reached his hand out to Noelle again. She took baby steps towards him due to his tattoo being so realistic. As she got closer to Ramiro, she gently touched the tarantula artwork and saw that it was just a tattoo. Noelle patted the enlarged arachnoid on Ramiro's shoulder.

"How long did it take to complete this?" she asked.

"Five hours," Ramiro wrapped his arms around Noelle's waist, pulling her close to him. He laid a passionate kiss on her lips. He fondled every part of her body, trying to put her mind at ease.

Ramiro laid Noelle on her back as she locked her thighs around his waist as they went for round two.

MOMENTS LATER, NOELLE slept on the sofa with the bedsheets wrapped around her nude body. Ramiro crept into the living room with both of his hands cupped together. He approached the sofa where Noelle laid peacefully. Then she slowly opened her eyes, feeling Ramiro hovering over her.

"What's up, baby?" she moaned.

"I want you to see something. Now, be very calm," Ramiro kneeled next to the sofa.

"What is it?" Noelle's eyes widened as she leaned back.

Ramiro slowly opened his hands with the tarantula moving a bit. It cowered in its owner's hands.

"Holy crap!" she scurried away from the couch and cringed in the chair on the other side of the living room. "You own a real tarantula? Oh my God!"

"I've got a total of three. The other two are in the tank," he lightly petted his spider. "Do you want to hold it? Ramiro moved towards her with the creepy insect in his hand.

"No, Ramiro! Get it away!" she scurried away from the chair and into the kitchen.

"She's harmless," Ramiro laughed as he stroked his hairy pet in his hand.

"Please put it away," Noelle begged.

"Alright," Ramiro returned the spider to its tank.

MINUTES LATER, RAMIRO closed the lid on the tarantula tank. Noelle crept into the master bedroom to see if her would-be lover had a fascination with an insect that most women feared. Snakes, spiders, and other insects that were related freaked people out and it did a job on Noelle. She inhaled and took strides to Ramiro's side while he hovered over the glass tank. "Three tarantulas? Why not a dog or a cat?"

"Maybe later I'll get a dog," Ramiro turned to Noelle. He kissed her upon her cheek. "Let's eat."

AN HOUR LATER, RAMIRO cooked waffles on an iron pan on the kitchen stove. He didn't use a toaster because they didn't hold the heat that well. His mother always cooked his waffles this way. "Noelle," he swaggered into the living room with the plate of three buttery waffles and syrup. She slept on the sofa in a long band t-shirt and didn't respond.

"Noelle!" he rose his voice. She tossed and turned, sitting up drowsy.

"Here you go," Ramiro placed the waffles on her lap. He kissed Noelle on the lips.

"Thank you, babe! How are you?" Noelle smiled.

"I'm good. I'm very good," he smiled. Noelle lifted an eyebrow, seeing him stick his chest out. Which most men do. She poked the fork in the piece of waffle and shoved it in her mouth. Bite after bite, Ramiro kept staring at Noelle. She caught this fiendish grinning rocker glaring at her. "I know Ramiro's proud that he pleased me. Yes, he did," Noelle returned the vile grin. She didn't know what to say. The only thing that spoke were her eyes, which showed him. "Ramiro, I want you. My attraction is strong, and I hope you feel the same," Noelle fed a piece of waffle to him. Ramiro chewed the breakfast food with ease. Her attraction to Ramiro was so strong that she forgot about the tarantulas that he had. He kept his eyes set on Noelle, then another fork of waffles aimed at his mouth. Then his glare became far-reaching as he gulped down the last piece of waffle. Ramiro laid another passionate kiss on Noelle again.

"Ready for round three?" Ramiro gazed into Noelle's eyes with a straight face.

FIVE MINUTES LATER, Ramiro had Noelle on her back in the lounge chair while they engaged in rhythmic body movements. Her alluring moans directly in his ear, her nude body exposed in the line of sight with her thighs surrounding him from every angle. Balls of sweat trickled down his body as he did his duty. He worked up more of a sweat than he did when he played his bass. Noelle would play a paramount role in his life. Pretty soon, he'd have to meet her relatives. What would they think of this long-haired White-Latino male with tattoos who plays rock music, especially her mother? She would be the first to voice her opinion about this rocker who wasn't fit for her daughter's future. He'd have to see how things play out.

THAT AFTERNOON, RAMIRO'S Dodge Durango parked in front of Noelle's Bethpage, Long Island home. Noelle exited from the passenger's side of the vehicle as Ramiro hopped out of the driver's side. He rushed to assist her, but she slammed the passenger door of his vehicle. He wrapped his arms around Noelle, escorting her to the door of her residence. Late-forties, Fuschia jogging outfit wearing Samantha Ellis, Noelle's mother, sported old sneakers, holding a broom in her hand while opening the front door with her eyes fixed on this long-tress stranger embracing Noelle. Samantha didn't know what to think, but she thought her daughter had fallen for someone of the same gender. But as the young couple got closer, Samantha realized this was a guy with long hair, very long hair. Noelle kissed her mother on the cheek as she entered the house with Ramiro following. Right away, Noelle introduced her new lover to her mother, who held the front door opened as she smiled at him. Of course, Ramiro returned the friendly gesture, extending his hand. "How are you, Mrs. Ellis?" he shied.

"I'm fine. How are you?" Samantha backed away.

"I'm cool," Ramiro could see that this woman possibly feared him.

They entered the living room with the standard set up with a couch, a recliner, a coffee table, a lamp, a side table, a lighted ceiling fan, household décor on the wall, figurines, and photos of Noelle from a baby to the present day. Ramiro plopped his butt on the end of the couch, where a five by seven framed photo of Noelle eight years old sat on the table. In the picture, she wore a jazz tap outfit with a hat and cane.

"Would you like something to drink, Ramiro?" Noelle asked as she and her mother sashayed away into the kitchen.

"Yes, thanks," he replied. While Noelle and her mother clamored in the kitchen, Ramiro browsed through the photos of her family. He smiled at her baby and childhood pictures to more recent photos. Then he noticed photos of her mother and a gentleman, which could've been her father. Then there are other similar pictures of this gentleman and Samantha at their wedding. So, then it was Noelle's father. Noelle and Samantha were quiet in the kitchen. Ramiro knew he was the topic of conversation. *"I could sense that Noelle's family will not approve of me. I wonder what they're saying?"* he continued to check out the Ellis family photos.

Water poured from the kitchen sink while Samantha washed pots and pans so she could cook dinner. Noelle grabbed a two-liter bottle of Sprite from the refrigerator and poured the beverage into two clear glasses. The mother and daughter didn't exchange any words, but Samantha kept peering over her shoulder at Noelle. Noelle didn't notice her mother acting awkward about her new love interest. But as she was about to strut out of the kitchen with the two glasses in her hand.

"Noelle?" Samantha placed the pan on the stove, turning the sink off. Without hesitation, Noelle waltzed to her mother's side. "Yes," she responded.

"Where did you meet Ramiro?" Samantha wiped the pot dry with a dishtowel.

"In school, of course," Noelle answered.

"Did you guys have a lot of classes together?" her mother questioned.

"Only music and algebra," she smiled.

"And what does he do for a living? I don't mean to ask so many questions, but....,"

"But, what Mom?" Noelle cracked a smile.

"I want you to be with a man who has a promising future," Samantha dried a pan, placing it on the stove.

"Ramiro's a musician," Noelle answered.

"A musician? What kind of music?" Samantha asked.

"Heavy Metal," Noelle exited the kitchen.

That told Samantha her daughter's new lover's future was questionable. The music industry was full of temptation. And what made Noelle believe she would be Ramiro's long-term girlfriend while dozens of women threw themselves at him. Noelle heard about these musicians and the groupies that stormed backstage. Not for an autograph. She expunged the thought from her mind about the enthused female fans who wanted a sexual encounter with a musician. She and Ramiro seemed serious, and then she thought maybe they should take it one step at a time. But you never know what may happen in the long run. Noelle entered the living room holding the two glasses; Ramiro stood at the wall, admiring her family photos. She offered the glass of soda to Ramiro and grinned.

"Thanks," Ramiro sipped the cold beverage.

Keys rattled at the front door as a tall, fair-skinned, Dorel Ellis, an African-American male, early fifties, entered, snatching his keys out of the lock of the door.

"Hello, daddy!" Noelle addressed the man of the house.

Ramiro felt the kind-hearted gentleman who smiled at him and extended his hand. Without hesitation, Ramiro reciprocated the friendly gesture of this man who seemed very down to earth. Noelle told her father a little about Ramiro as he gave off a non-judgmental and welcoming persona. Dorel didn't bombard this musician with questions; he chatted with him about his job as a paralegal in the court system. He went on and on about how he couldn't wait for his retirement. The stress of courts dealing with cases. Noelle's father asked Ramiro about his educational level and ambitions. He didn't feel negative about this older gentleman's affable talks. Dorel rose an eyebrow, impressed with Ramiro's musical aspirations.

"With God all things are possible," the bible verse spewed from Noelle's father's mouth. Dorel shook Ramiro's hand and headed into the kitchen. Ramiro's eyes shifted from left to right, not knowing what to think about Dorel. While Ramiro's father was a Jesus freak, Noelle's father was fond of Christ. Still, Ramiro didn't believe in the Almighty, but maybe someday he will. Noelle laid a kiss upon Ramiro's lips. She had a good feeling Ramiro and her father would get along fine, like two peas in a pod.

THAT NIGHT, RAMIRO'S Dodge Durango parked in a lover's lane as the stars glowed in the dark blue sky. In the passenger's seat of the vehicle, Noelle wallowed in the leather seat as Ramiro, of course, took charge in the driver's seat. He wanted to introduce Noelle to his mother, sister, and grandmother. These three women meant so much to him, and with Noelle in his life, she'd be the fourth. Noelle cracked a smile as she eyed his sideburns with his ear piercings. He then brought up his cultural upbringing, whatever he knew of Peruvian culture because most of his life he was in America. And of course, he couldn't forget his grandmother, Rebecca, and how much he loved her. Ramiro couldn't get into the long history of his family, but he told her all she needed to know. And his sister Maritza who he has a tight bond. His father shunned him as a kid and through his teen years until he got the boot on that Christmas day. Ramiro got lucky and had his best friend's family to back him up. Now, he's making a life for himself and hoped to gain more resources along the way. As for Noelle, she had her House music to fall back on.

"Tears, tears, due to all my fears, Love me, love me not

My passion's hot, the sweat from my brow. We make love the night away, hoping to make you stay, day and night, our love in flight...," she recited one of her poems.

Noelle ran her fingers along with his thick facial hairs. Ramiro wanted to go for another round by getting hot and heavy in a car as the windows got fogged. He got turned on by her caressing his sideburns. Ramiro laid a big passionate kiss and would go for the fourth time. Then his cellphone vibrated as the caller ID read Zack.

"What's up, Zack?" Ramiro clutched Noelle's hand and pressed it against his chest. Letting her know that she's got his undivided attention. He gazed into Noelle's eyes again and cracked a smile. She could hear Zack's voice muffled from the cellphone.

"Are you fuckin' serious? Stop bullshitting me!" Ramiro sat upright in the parked driver's seat while pressing Noelle's hand against his chest harder. Regardless of who Ramiro talked to, he still gave Noelle his undying attention. His eyes widen as Zack's voice muffled from the cellphone. Noelle could tell it had something to do with his music. She had a positive feeling about Ramiro's career. Then negative thoughts crossed Noelle's mind, *"What if Ramiro becomes the next big Heavy Metal sensation. OMG, he'd drop me like a hot potato. Maybe, I should take Ramiro's so-called love with a grain of salt."* She kept smiling.

"Alright, bet!" Ramiro disconnected his call. He gazed at Noelle and kissed her.

Babe, that was Zack, and we've got more band practices, meetings with important people hoping to get a deal," Ramiro smiled at Noelle as he took a deep breath. Her heart raced in her chest and embraced him.

"I'm so happy. Good Luck with that!"

"Thanks," he laid one last kiss upon her lips again.

"I know you're going to do well," the two lovers embraced. He hoped this was a promising one.

CHAPTER NINE

A week later, on the arm of Ramiro's Spector bass guitar, a Snark ST-8 bass guitar tuner captured the vibration of each of the strings while he tightened and loosened to achieve the right sound. He and his bandmates prepared to record another track, "Klown." Their managers, Stanley and Douglas supported them but had concerns after reading the lyrics. They were eager to ask Ramiro what troubled him? He told them, who would be on the road to his success, that yes, the earlier recording of "Meet Your Demise" was about murdering his father. He went into detail about the guts and bloodshed of the man who judged him for the first time he listened to "Come and See The Show" by the rock band Emerson, Lake, and Palmer from the seventies. From there, Ramiro listened to Jimi Hendrix with such songs as "Manic Depression, When the Wind Cries, Mary, and Hey Joe. Then Black Sabbath, Rush, and as the rock progress into Heavy Metal, it drove his father insane, which he threw the bible in Ramiro's face every day. Ramiro stopped telling Stanley and Douglas about his life and wanted to express his feelings through his music.

"Can we get this show on the road!" Ramiro cradled his bass guitar in his arms like a baby. His long, straight hair draped elbow length with a glare of a serious musician who didn't like to waste time, not because of studio time, which is money, but of creativity. The managers invested lots of money in the studio and took this young bassist's advice who was ahead of the game.

IN NO TIME AT ALL, the sound engineer adjusted the sound on the enormous soundboard as Ramiro and his bandmates recorded the song "Klown." The band's sound hopefully intrigued fans as their audience would grow. Then an audience materialized in Ramiro's sight, with mostly young white males jumping around, crashing into one another in a giant mosh pit, wearing various and eerie clown masks. Ramiro delivered an aggressive and malevolent carnival-like tune for those to enjoy. He saw the enthused fans continuing to collide into one another, getting nose bleeds, busted mouths, bumps, and bruises in the pit. Young women took part in this brutality, possibly getting injured. One thing for sure, he wouldn't want his sister or his girlfriend to engage in this barbaric dance. Ramiro wanted them to sit down and look pretty. He headbanged with his hair flying all over the place while he strummed his bass guitar fast.

Danny delivered a lead guitar solo with a screeching sound. Zack pounded on his drum kit to bring the foundation that gave a hard-hitting sound. The band's managers and sound engineer bopped their heads to the song and loved this trio's sound. "Klown" concluded with a grand finale of pounding drums, lead guitar, and bass combined. The sound engineer then lowered the soundboard levels because of Ramiro and his bandmates finishing their performance.

AN HOUR LATER, RAMIRO and his bandmates listened to these gentlemen plotting their future at a big round wooden table with dimmed lighting. Ramiro rocked in a chair, proceeding to have his ears open to Stanley and Douglas's ideas. Plot means to conspire, which means to harm, harm to Ramiro, and his band financially. He sat upright in his chair, reaching across to Douglas who shuffled some papers.

"What are you doing, Douglas?" Ramiro grabbed his hand to see what he was doing.

"I'm preparing your mini contract!"

"Mini Contract?" Ramiro lifted an eyebrow.

"Yes, Ramiro. That's a part of the business," Douglas shrugged.

"I wanted to make sure that we're not getting ripped off," he held an even tighter grip on Douglas's hand.

"I'm very aware of that," Douglas snatched his hand from this salty bassist's grip. Ramiro's eyes shifted over to Zack, who looked dumbfounded, and Danny seemed to be in another world.

"Snap the fuck out of it, you two!" Ramiro pounded his fist on the wooden table.

"Sorry, dude!" Danny blinked his eyes and focused on Douglas and Stanley.

"What's the problem, Ramiro? Don't burn your bridges," his manager advised.

"I don't want to get ripped off," he leaned in his chair, rocking back and forth.

"After we finish your mini contract. You can consult an attorney," Douglas suggested.

"I'll do that, Stan," Ramiro nodded his head. He rocked in the chair, faster.

"What the hell! Ramiro, you don't trust us?" Stanley asked.

"Attorneys are a lot of money, Ram! I'm broke!" Zack said.

"The same here, dude," Danny added to the conversation.

The managers appointed an attorney to Ramiro and his bandmates associated with Ominous records.

"You didn't come up with a name for your band, Ramiro?" Stanley eyed him. Then he glared at Danny and Zack, shrugging their shoulders.

Ramiro leaned in his chair, bitching about getting ripped off. He didn't have a band name, wishing to invent a unique name like

"Metallica or Megadeth." Something strong and unique. Maybe it could be something affecting his life, like when he's writing song lyrics. Ramiro would have to sleep on it. Danny wasn't any help; he hung out with his enormous entourage that was cool. Danny and his cronies all wanted to hang out that night because their favorite bassist's birthday was the next day. This lead guitarist's friends admired him as much as they did Ramiro. The guitarists' tight-knit fan base wanted to hang out as soon as the clock struck twelve, celebrating Ramiro's birthday who would bring their band success. They didn't cause any issues, but Ramiro needed Danny's feedback and participation in their future. But Ramiro passed on their offer and needed some rest.

THAT NIGHT, RAMIRO gawked at the ceiling in his bedroom, with the television glowing as the 1930's horror movie "White Zombie" played with its creepy music, adding a touch of ambiguity to his apartment. He usually indulged in classic horror movies, but he had things to figure out. He placed his hand on his tarantula tattoo, wearing black boxers stretching in his king-sized mattress. He checked his cellphone. Noelle didn't call him, but they did text back and forth during his recording sessions and his meeting with A&R executives. Ramiro figured she was probably asleep. They planned on meeting up later that day for his birthday. All Ramiro wanted was Noelle. As far as gifts were concerned, she was his gift. She's busy trying to finish college, so they could be together. He hinted to Noelle that if his career took off, she would go on tour with him. Ramiro guessed Noelle would say yes. He'll bring it up to her again, later on. The most important thing was figuring out a name for his band. It had to be something that he and his fellow bandmates agreed on. Still, Danny and Zack's minds were elsewhere. Ramiro had to do all the thinking.

"What kind of fuckin' bandmates are these? A bunch of lazy shits!" Ramiro stroked his chest and shook his head. His cellphone vibrated on his nightstand with the photo of his sister, Maritza. Ramiro remained in his slumber, not responding to the call. "That's probably Noelle. I'll talk to her tomorrow," he thought, not bothering to see who the caller is. Ramiro then laid on his stomach. He grabbed the television remote, turning off the box. Maybe, if he got a good night's rest, he'd come up with something catchy. He shut his eyes as his vibrating cellphone stopped. Then, thirty seconds later, his cellphone vibrated again. Ramiro ignored the call, giving his cellphone his back. The cell stopped vibrating and then did it again.

"Who the fuck is this!" he sat up in his bed and grabbed his cell, noticing his sister's photo on the caller ID.

"Maritza, what's up!" Ramiro answered.

His eyes widened as the terror in his sister's voice made him leap to his feet. Ramiro rushed to put his jeans, shirts, and sneakers on. He couldn't get dressed and listen to what she had to tell him at the same time, so he put his sister on speakerphone.

"Abuelita is in the hospital!"

A HALF-HOUR LATER, in a not-so-crowded emergency room of buzzing phones, muffled voices bellowing from the loudspeakers through the atmosphere while nurses and doctors assisted patients, Ramiro stormed through the automatic double doors. He stopped at the nurse's desk, where there was no one around. Then he heard murmuring of an elderly man stretched out in a hospital bed. Ramiro glared at the helpless, poor man who reached his hand to him as if he was a doctor or angel coming to take him from his suffering. This dying man needed everything in the world to cure him. Ramiro's heart throbbed in his chest. "Holy shit! Did my grandmother have a stroke or fall?" He took long strides down the hallway with blinking eyes, trying to find his relatives like going through a thick fog.

"Ramiro!" a feminine voice cried out.

Ramiro trotted to his mother and sister, embracing them. He noticed his grandmother, Rebecca, laying in the hospital bed with her eyes shut. She looked peaceful as if she were on burial grounds in her native land. "What the fuck happened?" Ramiro tried to control his temper. He clutched his mother and sister close while tears streamed down his face. "What the fuck happened?"

His mother nor did Maritza respond to his question. Ramiro had a tight grip on his mother's sweater and tugged at it hard.

"Fuckin' answer me!"

Anna Maria slowly looked into her son's eyes as he glared into hers, demanding answers. Then he had a feeling that there was something wrong.

"Tell me!" Ramiro grasped his mother's sweater tighter.

"I wanted to give you some money for your birthday! But your father had a fit when I withdrew funds from our joint account!" Mama got in the way! Trying to protect me...." Anna Maria sobbed in Ramiro's arms.

"What the fuck!" Ramiro demanded a straight answer. His mother cried.

"All I know is when I came downstairs. Abuelita was unconscious on the floor," Maritza cried.

"He fuckin' pushed her?" Ramiro eyed both his mother and sister. Anna Maria sobbed some more.

Then the heart rate machine beeped constantly. A medical team trampled towards Ramiro's grandmother's hospital bed.

"What's happening?" Anna Maria panicked. A nurse gently pushed her away as Ramiro and Maritza consoled their mother.

"Our Father, Who Art in Heaven, Hallowed would be thy name..." Anna Maria recited the Father's Prayer, clutching her two grown children in her arms. Even though Ramiro didn't believe in God, he hoped God would spare his grandmother's life. Then the heart rate constantly beeped and beeped. Doctors and nurses clamored over Rebecca, trying to revive her, but the heart rate machine flatlined with a long beeping sound.

"Holy fuck! It can't be! Abuelita!" he stormed away from his mother and sister's arms. He rushed down the hallway with tears streaming down his face and crying like a baby. He felt like one as he bumped into the medical staff, not giving a shit.

LATE THAT NIGHT, SILENCE surrounded the Espinoza residence; along with three police vehicles guarding the premises. The stars twinkled in the dark autumn sky as a light cold breeze swept through the neighborhood. Halloween décor on every doorstep made the setting obscure with death in the air. Screeching tires cut the block's corner as Ramiro sped towards his childhood home in his black Dodge Durango. The truck halted at the front door with squealing brakes. Ramiro stormed out of his vehicle, slamming the truck door. He paid no attention to the police vehicles. "You fuck! I'm going to rip your fuckin' head off!

"Where the fuck are you!" Ramiro dashed into his childhood home and fled to the second floor. A couple of officers sat in the living room and noticed this menacing young man with long hair acting boisterously.

"Excuse me! Who are you!" the officer followed Ramiro to the second floor. He dashed down the hallway and opened Maritza's bedroom door. His sister's room was in excellent condition. A team of officers confronted Ramiro. "Excuse me! Who are you?" an officer confronted him. "I'm Ramiro Espinoza. This was my childhood home before I got the fuckin' boot!" Ramiro brushed past the officer and then toyed with the doorknob of his former bedroom. He kicked it open. "What the fuck! He got rid of everything! Even me!" his voice echoed as the hinges of the door screeched throughout the bare and unoccupied space. His bed, dresser, and other pieces of furniture were gone. He swung open the closet, where he saw nothing but hangers. His father probably threw his clothes out. Only the blue walls remained.

"Can I talk to you? You're Ramiro?" the officer beckoned. Ramiro stood before the Officer with tears in his eyes.

"Yes, I'm Ramiro. And who are you to the victim?"

"Rebecca Flores was my grandmother? Officer, what exactly happened?

MOMENTS LATER, ON THE first floor in the dining room, Ramiro noticed a fallen table, a broken vase with its pieces all over the floor with a splash of red coloring on the wall. As hard as Ramiro could, he attempted to fight back the tears. But he couldn't help it as he sobbed. The first officer gave his condolences.

"I can't believe this! She's dead on my birthday!" Ramiro continued to cry as he plummeted himself in a chair.

The Officers glanced at each other and shook their heads.

"All we know there was an altercation with your mother, father, and grandmother...over money," the officer gave the bigger picture.

"Where the fuck is he! I'll fuckin' kill him!" Ramiro stood from his chair. Officers blocked him from leaving the house, trying to calm him down.

"Mr. Espinoza, please! I can understand that you're upset," the Officer empathized.

"How would you understand! My grandmother was snuffed out on Devil's night. And on my birthday which makes things even worse," he plopped himself on the sofa and wept. He placed both hands over his face because he didn't want anyone to see him.

"Fuck! On my birthday, my grandmother's gone! This is going to bring me lots of hell for fuckin' sure!"

"Ramiro, you're going to be fine. Happy birthday!" Maritza entered through the opened front door. She rushed to her brother's arms as they regressed to helpless kids crying. Their mother took baby steps through the entrance of their home. Anna Maria gazed without blinking an eye, but they were watery. She heard her children crying like babies, but she remained dumbfounded by her mother's transition. His mother planted herself in a chair and did her sobbing.

"I don't think I want to comfort my mother right now. Maritza needs me. Abuelita would still be alive if my mother left my father when my sister and I were small, but like most women, she wanted to work it out. I think that was fuckin' selfish. Maritza and I should have been her main priority," he glared at his mother who shed tears in the chair from over his sister's shoulder. He didn't know what to think of her at this time.

CHAPTER TEN

The scintillating sun beamed on Saint Peter's Catholic Church in Lima, Peru, as mourners from far and near entered the house of worship to pay their respects to Senora Rebecca Flores. They came with flowers, rosaries, tears, and tissues in hand to a very beloved, respected, and active woman in the church. The magnificent historic interior with its high, well-crafted ceilings and walls with religious imagery set the tone for tranquility. Flowers adorned before the front row, where Ramiro, Maritza, and Anna Maria sat. Distant relatives from Rebecca's side of the family, and her in-laws, which were Ramiro's grandfather's family, sat in a moment of silence for the woman they loved. The sweet, soft-spoken woman with a heart of gold laid in her casket embedded with roses. Ramiro sat between his mother and sister, giving them his shoulders to cry. He grasped both of their hands as they huddled as if they stood in cold weather.

"I can't believe this! I can't believe this happened! I swore she was going to make it to one-hundred years old," Ramiro shut his eyes, trying to hold back tears. He then opened them as more tears flowed down his cheeks. He tried to be tough, but he couldn't.

"She loved you and your sister so much," Anna Maria rubbed her son's face and kissed him. A minister approached the altar accompanied by two altar boys, giving the eulogy.

"In the Name Of The Father, And The Son, And the Holy Spirit," the priest crossed himself as the congregation did the same.

"Amen," the mourners concluded.

MOMENTS LATER, A MID-fifties, chubby gentleman, Julio Diaz, stood at the podium, speaking into the microphone about his older sister's life, how they grew up, and had families of their own and getting to know his great-niece and nephew, Ramiro and Maritza. Julio got choked up and fought back his tears. He glared at Anna Maria as she sat in the front row with her two grown children by her side. She leaned on her son's shoulder, shedding tears. Ramiro noticed his great uncle eyeing his mother for his sister's death. Julio wasn't too crazy about the man Anna Maria married. Ramiro then returned the dirty look to his Great Uncle, who he met for the first time to back off. Rebecca's family feuding would appall her at a time like this. Julio proceeded with his sister's eulogy, bursting into tears. He stepped away from the podium and took a seat in the front row across from Anna Maria. It seemed as if they were blaming Anna for her own mother's demise. By her family sitting on the other side, it was clear as day.

Soon after, Ramiro and Maritza stood at the podium, introducing themselves as Rebecca Flores's grandchildren. Maritza spoke into the microphone with a trembling voice about her love for this woman she recently got reacquainted. As she spoke about whatever knowledge she had of her grandmother, Ramiro stood by Maritza's side and glared at the mourners. It felt like he got stage fright. He didn't hear a word his sister uttered; just gibberish. Ramiro blinked his eyes, hearing Maritza sobbing. He embraced his sister while becoming watery-eyed himself. Ramiro inched his way towards the microphone. "I'm Ramiro. Rebecca Flores' Nieto (grandson). Like my sister said, we became reacquainted with our Abuela (grandmother) after so many years. At least, we got to know more about her and her family. She believed in my dream of becoming a musician and brought me a professional bass guitar with what cash she had. She wanted to know about thrash metal music. My grandmother listened to some of my stuff and she never judged me. Mi Abuela always kept an open mind for different things. I miss her already. And especially Christmas. Te amo Abuela (I love you, Grandma)," Ramiro's eyes watered while his voice quivered.

"Te amo Abuela," Maritza's voice trembled. They stepped away from the podium as complete silence proceeded throughout the church. Ramiro glared at his grandmother, laying in her casket with roses. He kissed her on the forehead.

At the home of Ramiro's Tio Julio, he and Maritza sat on the couch while all the family sat around and talked about their grandmother. The family surrounded Anna Maria, showing photographs of Rebecca, Julio, and their relatives. Maritza was curious about her grandmother's photos but didn't bother to see them. Ramiro swaggered out of the house, leaving the front door open. Maritza gave chase.

Under a moriche palm tree, Ramiro leaned his back against the trunk as the wind swept through the air. He placed one of his hands over his face, sliding his back against the tree. His rear end hit the ground. His mind was full of nothing. What could he think of at a time like this? His grandmother has gone to a better place. But the way she transitioned wasn't good. He felt a light wind blow through his long hair. He forgot about his birthday because that wasn't important to him. It was all about his grandmother. He spoke to Noelle on the phone and told her what occurred. She was devastated as Ramiro sobbed in her ear. Ramiro's grandmother's passing brought Noelle to tears as well. He could hear Noelle's quivering voice in his head as it brought him to more tears.

"Ramiro," a feminine voice called his name.

"What," he sniffled, wiping his eyes.

"I wanted to see if you were ok?" Maritza leaned against the tree.

"I'm not okay? Abuelita is dead. And who's responsible? Dad!" he glared at Maritza with fury. "The police ruled Abuelita's fall an accident. "Was it?"

Maritza was lost for words, and she didn't know what to believe. Ramiro's blood boiled, causing him to lash out at Maritza. He had to get back to New York and catch up with his bandmates to get a head start on their careers. Under these circumstances, he still didn't think about the name of his band. Maritza patted him on the shoulder.

"I'm sorry, Ram," she sighed.

Their mother stood a few feet away while Ramiro and Maritza stood under the exotic tree on their uncle's property like kids daydreaming. Anna Maria had red eyes from all the tears, some wrinkles formed on her face from the lack of sleep and the years of chaos from her husband. She took baby steps towards her children.

"Maritza," Anna Maria called. Maritza turned to her mother, rushing into her arms, crying.

"You can stop crying now. Abuelita is in a better place," Ramiro glared at his mother and looked away into the distance.

He wanted to lay a guilt trip on his mother because she should've left their father from the beginning. Ramiro had no remorse for his mother for being so weak and so in love. She tried to fix someone that couldn't be fixed.

"I'm filing for divorce!" his mother cried.

"It's too late for that," Ramiro still glared into the distance. Anna Maria burst into tears as her daughter embraced her.

"And he walked! No charges! I've got a flight to catch," he stood to his feet, kissed his mother and sister, storming away.

BACK AT A NEW YORK recording studio, a couple of days later, Ramiro and his bandmates created some more music right off the top of their heads. The collaboration of the lead guitar, bass, and drums was noise, lots of noise. He could've written lyrics to this instrumental piece, but he and his bandmates improvised. Stanley, Douglas, and the sound engineer watched these three young men perform, especially Ramiro. The managers lifted an eyebrow as Ramiro played his bass guitar as if he were killing someone. They heard about his grandmother's death and gave their condolences. His grandmother's demise intensified Ramiro's showmanship. He played the fuck out of his bass guitar, showing no mercy on the strings. Sweat trickled down his face. Zack beat the shit out of his drum kit while sweat dripped from his head. The excessive moisture emerged from Danny's head as if he got out of the shower.

After the band's instrumental performance, Ramiro sat on a stool, tired. He inhaled some mucus, releasing it on the studio floor. He didn't give a shit at this point.

"Ramiro, what the hell!" Stanley threw his fist in the air. "Are you out of your mind!"

He dared his management to challenge him, but he had to back off because this was the start of his career. He apologized for his stupidity, cradling his bass guitar. With his grandmother's death and music endeavors overwhelming him, Ramiro forgot all about Noelle. He reached for his cell phone, dialing her number. He tapped his foot on the floor, hoping she'd pick up.

"Ramiro!" the sweet feminine voice muffled on the cell.

"Yes, baby! It's me!" he stood up from the stool while holding his bass guitar by the arm and the cellphone to his ear.

"Why didn't you call me! I was thinking..." Noelle whined.

"Whatever negative thoughts you have, get it out of your head," Ramiro cut her off.

IN NOELLE'S GIRLY BEDROOM, she rested her head on her pillow in her full-sized bed. She turned on her side, exhaling. Ramiro spoke his truth to Noelle about his grandmother's death and his music. But, from Noelle's point of view, "Why didn't he send a quick text message, but she kept her mouth shut and was receptive to the circumstances? He wanted to see Noelle, but he didn't want to result in breaking objects, cursing, and causing havoc around her. By Ramiro spitting on the floor that was the start, and if given the opportunity, he'd probably set the recording studio ablaze. He'd be kicking himself in the ass. Crazy shit ran through his mind like water running out of a faucet. Maybe he shouldn't see her right now.

"Noelle, maybe I'll see you some other time. I'm going through a lot of shit right now," Ramiro scratched his head. He paced back and forth along the small dark corridor.

"I miss you, babe," she sucked her teeth.

"Same here. I've got to go, babe," he hung up the phone without giving Noelle a chance to get her last words in.

THEN A SKELETAL CLOCK on Ramiro's apartment read 1:18 a.m. in Ramiro's gloomy flat. His bass guitar resided on its stand in the living's corner room with the black lounge chair and side table with the Clown figurine. He added more skeletal décor to adorn the living room and down the murky hallway towards his master bedroom with photos of skeletons, images of death on the walls. Ramiro dozed on and off in his bed while his flat panel television played the movie "Predator 2." His eyes widened when he heard the screams of the voodoo priest whose head was severed by the humanoid creature in the alleyway.

Then the front door buzzed. Ramiro sprung from his bed, wearing his clothes. He peered through the peephole and swung the door open. He pulled Noelle into his arms, engaging in the most extended kiss. He closed the front door with his foot.

A MINUTE LATER, RAMIRO laid Noelle down on his king-sized bed, engaging in a passionate kiss. She moaned and groaned as Ramiro worked his hands up her sweater squeezing on her breasts. But, he couldn't at a time like this because he was in mourning. His eyes began to water while he had them shut. He didn't open them because the tears would trickle down on her face. How would Noelle react to seeing him cry like a baby or a bitch as some would call it? But Noelle sensed his pain as she nuzzled Ramiro's face from hers. He widened his eyes as they were red, watery, and a tear streamed down his cheek. Noelle wiped the watered droplet with her hand and kissed him.

"Baby, I'm so sorry," she wiped more tears from Ramiro's face. He rolled off Noelle, laying beside her, and glaring at the ceiling.

Ramiro didn't give her the details of what happened to his grandmother. All he knew was he had a fucked-up birthday. Someone dying on your birthday is fucked up. But what's even worse is when it's someone you love dearly. To get his mind off things, he had to move on with his life, focusing on his music career, and building a life with Noelle. She wanted to know about his relationship with his grandmother. The good things. She wanted to know about Peru and learn more Spanish. The only thing she knew how to say was, "Good Morning," "How are you?" And what's your name?"

Ramiro smirked at the beautiful face that he always had pictured in his mind.

"Why do you want to learn Spanish?"

"What kind of question is that, Ramiro?" Noelle sucked her teeth. "Because it's good to learn another language?" she responded, sitting up, looking down at him. Ramiro gawked at Noelle as she spoke about traveling, learning different languages, trying new foods, and cultural music. Her nonpartisan mentality came from her upbringing and her being a House Songstress/poet. Noelle wrote tons of poetry and song lyrics for world issues and love, similar to Pop music. She went into detail about House music and how she would love to play keyboards with synthesizers. But reading and writing music was Noelle's burden. Ramiro threw it up in her face about how he could read and write music.

"Would you teach me? Or I forgot that's not your type of music?" Noelle wiped the extra moisture from his eyes, though his crying ceased.

Ramiro shrugged his shoulders and sucked his teeth. He had no time to play instructor to Noelle. She has to figure that out on her own. The lovebirds went from talking about music to their lives together in the future. Ramiro dreamt of relocating to the San Francisco Bay Area, where some rock musicians lived. The Bay area has a New York feel to it, so Ramiro would feel right at home. Noelle loved palm trees, all four seasons, holidays, people, and was thankful to be alive. She reached for her Unique Homes magazine from her bag. She flipped through the periodical to the section of the real estate properties on the West coast. Noelle flashed the mansion in Sausalito, California, priced at nine million. Ramiro eyed the colorful pages of the property and another home on the next page located in Tiburon which was in the Bay area as well, priced at two million.

"Could you see yourself living in one of these homes?"

"Yes, I could see us living in one of these homes," Ramiro smirked, clutched her hand.

Within this moment, he forgot all about his sorrows and anger. Being in Noelle's presence was comforting and an escape. He wanted her to be there for him always. In good times and bad, like now. He had to introduce his mother and sister to Noelle because he believed she was the one. Ramiro spoke of his mother, who he loved dearly and didn't judge his musical tastes, and when he was twelve years of age, that's when his hair started getting long. She refused to cut Ramiro's hair because it was his way of expressing himself. He wasn't harming anyone. His father, on the opposite end of the spectrum, disagreed. Ramiro refused to talk about his father as his face turned fiery red due to his grandmother's death. He took a deep breath and focused his mind elsewhere.

As for his sister Maritza, they were a year apart; she was the eldest. Ramiro wished he had some brothers, at least one, so they could talk about man shit. He was proud of Maritza, who works as an accountant in a lawyer's office. Ramiro gave no more details about his sister. He avoided discussing his family because his grandmother would become the topic of conversation and more hellbent on his father. Noelle respected his wishes and kissed him on the lips, resting her head on his chest.

"Baby, it's going to be alright!" she caressed her hand on his chest.

"I hope so," he shut his eyes, experiencing nothing but darkness. A murky mist hovered over Ramiro that wouldn't let up. She was the light at the end of the tunnel. Then his cellphone vibrated on the nightstand. He ignored it and lip-locked with Noelle. He rolled on top of her as if they were about to make love again. His cell continued to vibrate while kissing Noelle. He reached for his cellphone as it fell on the floor.

"Fuck!" Ramiro rolled off Noelle, reaching his hand on the floor, grabbing his cell. It continued to vibrate, and the caller ID read: Stanley.

"What's up, Stan?" he greeted. Noelle laid in his king-sized bed and could hear a man's muffled voice over the cellphone.

"How's everything going?" Stanley asked.

"I'm cool. I'm home now,"

"Okay, have you thought of a name yet?" he asked.

"Not yet," Ramiro said.

"Do you guys want this or what? I can't upload the music without your band's name. And you didn't even sign your contract," Stanley's voice intensified.

"I had a death in my family! Can you cut me some slack! Fuck, man!" Ramiro argued as Noelle touched him on the shoulder from behind.

"I'm sorry about your grandmother," Stanley spoke in a softer tone.

"I'll come up with a name," Ramiro hung up.

"What's up, Ramiro!" she asked.

"My manager's on my case about naming the band," Ramiro dialed Zacks' phone number. It rang and rang with no answer. He hung up.

"Where the fuck is Zack?" he redialed his number. It made a connection again, ringing and ringing. Zack still didn't pick up. Ramiro disconnected the call and dialed Danny's number.

"Hello," Danny answered on the first ring and in a sleepy voice.

"Danny, what's up?

"Nothing much! Sorry about your grandmother!" he gave his condolences.

"Thanks. Have you thought of a band name yet?" Ramiro asked, kissing Noelle on the lips.

"No, I was waiting on you," Danny sucked his teeth.

"Collaborate with me here. I can't fuckin' do everything," he bellowed.

"Ramiro, I'll do some thinking," Danny yawned.

"Please, fuckin' do!" Ramiro disconnected the call. He stared into Noelle's eyes without saying a word. For a minute, they gazed into each other's eyes.

"What?" Noelle ran her fingers through his straight hair.

Ramiro kissed her on the lips. "That's what."

He laid on his back, closing his eyes as Noelle sat up. She felt lonely for a moment but then understood that he needed some alone time. "Are you going to go to sleep now?

"Babe, yes," Ramiro mumbled.

"Was that your manager? Sorry if I'm being nosy?" she stroked Ramiro's hair.

"That's okay?" he yawned, stretching in his bed. Still, his eyes remained closed.

"Have you thought of a band name yet?" Noelle exhaled.

"No," Ramiro answered abruptly.

"I'll leave you alone because I know you're grieving right now. At a time like this, it would make anyone irate," Noelle expressed. She laid down next to Ramiro and closed her eyes.

Then Ramiro's eyes opened, widening as he sat upright in his bed. "Noelle!" he whispered.

"What baby?" she mumbled.

"Irate!" Ramiro climbed on top of her.

"What do you mean, Irate?" she frowned.

"My band's name! Irate!" he laid dozens of kisses on Noelle. She giggled like a kid. Ramiro was wide-eyed, recalling the shit in his life. His father's abusive ways towards him, and his family. Jorge followed up when he kicked Ramiro out of the house at seventeen and by him getting away with murder. Ramiro turned red in the face and nodded his head.

"You're a genius, Noelle. I love you," he kissed and embraced her.

"The name Irate for your band?" Noelle asked.

"Irate! Yes!" Ramiro exclaimed.

THE NEXT MORNING, THE black Dodge Durango pulled up to an apartment complex with its screeching brakes. Ramiro shut the engine down and exited the vehicle, swaggering to the property. He rang the doorbell of Zack's apartment. No one answered. He peeked through the window as no one responded. He then rapped on the screen door. "Zack, open up!"

Then a pretty brunette, Caucasian female, early twenties, swung the door open, only wearing a short lingerie gown.

"Yes," the pretty girl yawned.

Ramiro barged right into the apartment without a morning greeting. He marched into Zack's master bedroom; the shades were pulled down that caused a gloom, with garments scattered all over the place. There were used soiled condoms on the floor, opened beer cans, the smell of marijuana, and the potent aroma of sex in the air. He held his nose.

"Zack! What the fuck!" Ramiro opened up the shades, snatching the comforter off the king-sized bed as two nude white females leaped from the bed. They grabbed their clothing to cover their important parts, hustling out of the bedroom. Zack rubbed his eyes, yawning and disoriented. "Who the fuck is that!"

"This is what you're doing! Fuckin' up a storm, Zack!" Ramiro threw the beer bottle against the wall.

"Alright! Don't throw things around!" Zack struggled to his feet from his bed, putting on his boxers.

"Did you think of a name for our band?" he pounded his fist on the dresser.

"No! I'm sorry!" Zack putting on his jeans.

"Look, I'm going through a family crisis, and I got back from Peru as soon as I could! And you're fuckin' around!" he stormed out of the master bedroom as Zack gave chase.

In the kitchen, Ramiro cracked open a beer can from the refrigerator, slamming the door. He gulped down the alcoholic beverage. Zack entered, putting his t-shirt on as Ramiro gave him the death stare. Ramiro threw the can at him. Zack quickly ducked. "What the fuck!" The aluminum can hit the wall.

"I've got to do all the thinking!" Ramiro waved his arms in the air.

"Let me go see Stanley! I'll think of a name along the way!" Zack headed back to his bedroom to finish getting dressed.

"My girlfriend beat you to it!" Ramiro stormed out of the apartment.

LATER THAT MORNING, in a boardroom at Ominous records, a long-pony-tailed, body-inked, mid-fifties, Caucasian male, sporting black jeans, dress shirt, Chad Ryan, the president of this successful company, rocked back and forth in his recliner. He listened to "Klown" blaring from the speakers with its aggressive instrumental tunes. This Heavy Metal music mogul handled successful acts such as Cyclops, Pandemonium, and Turmoil. The rock executive loved the antagonistic sound that never got old, and he promoted it to a new generation of listeners. Ramiro, his bandmates, and management glared at this edgy music professional while seated at a long wooden table. Ramiro balled his fists and wanted to punch someone. But he kept his composure. Danny headbanged, imitating his guitar playing. Zack did the same as if he were on his drum kit.

"This is some fuckin' shit!" Ramiro murmured. He swirled his recliner in the other direction, giving them his back.

Chad turned off the music with the remote control, turning to these three rockers with an enormous smile. He noticed Ramiro's chair faced in the other direction, totally disconnected from the meeting. Stanley felt embarrassed because of this rocker's behavior.

"Ramiro!" Stanley called his name. Ramiro was still disconnected from the present world.

"Ramiro!" his manager pounded his fist on the wooden table.

The recliner slowly turned towards them as Ramiro had an expression that he wanted to kill.

"What!"

"Ramiro, you guys have two singles that we can upload to the internet. All we need is a band name," Stanley waited for an answer.

"I have a graphic artist who can come up with something quick," Chad added. All eyes were on Ramiro; he was the leader of this band.

"Irate!" Ramiro rocked in his recliner.

"Irate!" What?" Stanley cocked his head, confused.

"Irate? Is it because of your personal life?" Chad asked.

"Yes. I felt like this most of my life," he answered.

Chad shook his head in agreement. "Sounds great to me!"

"Cool!" Danny chuckled.

"Are you sure, Ramiro?" Douglas straightened his glasses on his face.

"Yes, my girlfriend is," Ramiro swirled his recliner, giving his back to everyone at the table.

CHAPTER ELEVEN

A month and a half later, lights flared down on Ramiro as he growled in the microphone to the song "Religious Fuckery" with his bass guitar. Danny headbanged with his lead guitar as Zack kept the fast, aggressive rhythmic foundation on his Tama drum kit. The band performed at a small venue in Los Angeles, California. Ramiro's music career was on a roll, and he had to rock this platform with enthused headbangers loving the sound. Irate's fan base is males, from teens to adults, with a small fraction of women. Their managers stood backstage, accompanied by Chad Ryan who cheered them on. While Ramiro sang these warlike lyrics, he eyed the audience. He didn't want to leave a stone unturned for acknowledging a fan who headbanged. As Ramiro continued to spew his monstrous lyrics, he wondered how many admirers stood before him. There could've been well over three hundred attendees. He'll find out later. Noelle came to mind as he wondered what she was doing at the same time.

THROBBING BASS BEAT blared through the headphones over Noelle's head as she sang into a microphone connected to the computer. She recited one of her poems about love and, this time, about Ramiro. By her being his girlfriend, it gave her more ideas.

"Love, Love, Love, Love like a dove that spreads its wings to elevate us high above the earth. Nine months later I give birth," Noelle recited the poem she wrote that came from her heart. Ramiro crossed her mind because she missed him already. She had to face that there were going to be other women throwing themselves at him. Doubt crossed her mind about a future with Ramiro. Noelle stopped in the middle of her poem, lowered the volume, snatching her headphones off, and turned off the computer. Her cellphone sat in a red shoe cellphone holder with no sign of any calls, voicemails, or text messages from him. Still, she checked her text messages, there was nothing. She checked the voicemail, but they were old. Noelle plopped her head on the pillow in her bed, sliding her cell under it. She didn't call or send a text because Ramiro was very busy with his music. "California, wow! I traveled there three times, and I never got sick of it! Ramiro's in the City of Angels, and afterward, some actor would invite him to a Hollywood party. Or he's probably up in the Bay Area," then Noelle closed her eyes.

SEAGULLS SOARED ACROSS the sunny skies of San Francisco, the Golden Gate Bridge, and the entire bay area as the rumbling engine of a black matte Mustang drove on the winding streets of Tiburon/Belvedere island. The northern California winds swept through the front seat as Noelle occupied the passenger's seat and Ramiro dominating the driver's side. The gusty air caused Noelle to shiver as goosebumps surfaced on her skin. The cool breeze didn't bother Ramiro at all. She pressed the window button, closing it. The Mustang proceeded up the curvy road that led to a property that looked like a Villa somewhere in the Mediterranean.

The muscle car slowly entered through the opened gate where a female real estate agent awaited them. Ramiro shut down the engine of his fast car, stepping out from the driver's side. Noelle couldn't believe her eyes with the beautiful estate right before her as she exited the passenger's side of the car. A slender, Caucasian female, mid-thirties, shook Ramiro and Noelle's hands, giving them a tour of their soon-to-be home. The real estate entrepreneur inserted the key in the lock and pushed the heavy wooden brown door open. The couple stepped into the foyer hand in hand. A fancy light fixture from the high ceiling was surrounded by windows that gave lots of light. Noelle pulled Ramiro gently behind, still clasping hands to the living room. And, of course, the home was unfurnished, but Noelle had ideas in mind on what to do. The real estate agent escorted the couple into the formal dining room with a massive chandelier in the ceiling. Noelle continued through the home as she stumbled upon the family room with a fireplace and another light fixture above. She strolled into the kitchen where an enormous island table in the center, two sinks, a stove with eight burners, an oven, microwave, and lots of cabinet space. Noelle envisioned herself over the hot stove cooking food for Ramiro. A vast bay window gave more light to the breakfast room, where she pictured a cat sleeping. Ramiro crept up behind Noelle, wrapping his arms around her waist and laying a kiss on her cheek. Double doors of a master suite opened as the realtor continued with the tour of the residence. In the master bedroom, a fancy ceiling fan, a bed platform, and a sitting area had a balcony that captured panoramic views of Northern California. Noelle opened the double glass door, stepping onto the terrace with downtown San Francisco, the Golden Gate Bridge, and the bay area in the line of sight. A twenty-five-foot swimming pool with a jacuzzi, patio, and an outdoor kitchen was in the home's rear.

"Do you want it, babe?" Ramiro strolling on the balcony.

"Yes," Noelle kissing him on the lips and then on the cheek repeatedly. Then they engaged in a passionate kiss that wouldn't end.

Noelle's cellphone vibrated rigorously, where she opened her eyes and grabbed it. She noticed the caller ID read: Ramiro.

"Ramiro, hey!" she answered in an exhausted tone.

"Hey, Noelle! How are you doing?" Ramiro smiled because of hearing her voice.

"Tired," she sat up in her slumber with her eyes half-closed.

"You were asleep?" Ramiro paced the sidewalk along Hollywood Boulevard along with palm trees, right insight, and the sunny sky.

"Yes. How's LA?" Noelle mumbled.

"It's cool. So, were you dreaming about me?" Ramiro asked.

"Yes, I was," she chuckled.

"You're shitting me," he continued to pace, trying not to bump into the public garbage cans along the Hollywood Boulevard sidewalk. "I love you," Noelle's voice muffled in his ear as she told this rocker who stopped in his tracks.

"You do?" he asked.

"Yes, baby," Noelle answered.

Ramiro didn't know what to say. It got quiet for a second.

"Hello," Noelle cried.

"Yes, I'm here," he then paced again.

"How's your music going?" Noelle stretched in her bed.

"It's cool. My bandmates and I are going to record a full album tomorrow," Ramiro replied.

"That's good. I'm proud of you," she praised.

"Thanks," he noticed Zack, Danny, and the executives exiting the building. "Babe, I've got to go. I love you too," Ramiro added and disconnected his call. He stood there in a daze for a second. Ramiro never thought he'd hear Noelle tell him she loved him. The only woman who Ramiro thought loved him was his mother. He didn't care if Maritza said it or not.

"Ramiro, snap out of it!" Danny snapped his fingers in his face. Ramiro blinked, coming to his senses. He headed towards an RV parked in front of the club while roadies loaded their instruments in the rear. The low rumbling engine started up on the RV as he sprinted on with pretty, short, glasses-clad Nancy, a Caucasian female, behind him, roadies, and the trio's management. Stanley stood at the entrance of the bus, making sure everyone was on board.

"Are we ready to go?" Stanley shouted. He stepped into the trailer as the door closed. The tour bus drove off with the Uhaul trailing it.

Irate's management booked some small gigs for them at some venues in Fresno, San Jose, San Francisco, and Santa Rosa. Ramiro, his band, and his team cracked open beer cans celebrating their first show during a three-and-a-half-hour ride from Los Angeles to Fresno during the middle of the night. The band's new song "Noise Pollution" blasted from the stereo that vibrated the motorcoach. The dimmed fancy black marble interior of this RV was a rocker's pad on the road with a gourmet kitchen, a sink, stove, microwave, oven, and the refrigerator and cabinets filled to the capacity. A small bathroom next to the kitchen had a marble sink, shower, and toilet. Down the narrow corridor, nine bunk beds with their shudders for privacy, and across was an oversized bathroom and changing room. Finally, the lounge room had leather seating, a long wooden table, a flat panel television, and the stereo in the RV's rear. "We did it!" Zack smashed their beer cans together. Ramiro gulped down the foamy, bubbling alcoholic beverage. Nancy rushed to Ramiro's side and wrapped her arms around him. He showed the same affection, not thinking anything of it. She laid a kiss on his cheek with sparkles in her eyes. Her hand caressed the middle of Ramiro's back and then lowered close to his buttocks. Ramiro didn't bother to push her hand away; he let it slide.

MOMENTS LATER, RAMIRO lounged in a recliner in the bus's front that put him to sleep. He needed every ounce of energy for his next show. The smooth ride of the tour bus put this rocker to sleep as if he were a baby in a cradle.

"Ramiro," a gentle feminine voice called his name. He squinted with a blur in his vision, getting a whiff of MFK (Marcus Francis Kh) 540 rouge perfume in the air.

"Noelle," Ramiro awakened from his mini dream while in the recliner. Nancy exposed her porcelain white breasts with its pink nipples, hovering over him.

"Who's Noelle? she asked with a disgusted expression on her face.

"What are you doing?" Ramiro shoved her away.

"Relax. Whoever Noelle is, she doesn't exist," the secretary climbed on top of Ramiro. He continued to push this woman off him.

Stanley crept into the sitting area and stopped in his tracks, witnessing his secretary misbehaving.

"Nancy! What the hell are you doing!" he noticed Ramiro trying to avoid the situation. Ramiro then snatched his hands off the secretary. Nancy buttoned up her blouse, climbed off him, and strutted to the lounge room.

"What the fuck is going on, Ramiro!" Stanley stepped closer to the recliner with his hands on his hips. Ramiro sat up in the recliner.

"She threw herself on me!" he explained.

Stanley didn't say a word to his client, patting him on the shoulder. He nodded to Ramiro, gesturing that" He'll take care of the situation."

THE NEXT NIGHT, A FOGGY mist emerged on a medium-sized darkened stage at a venue in Fresno, California, with the band's logo that was a sketch of Ramiro's Mexican kneed tarantula. Then a bright creepy light brightened the platform as the audience cheered. Ramiro bellowed the lyrics for the song "Klown" while playing his bass. Danny hastened his fingers along the fingerboard of his electric guitar while Zack kept the fast monstrous rhythm that shook the entire place. An enormous mosh pit started from the first row to the middle rows of male fans between the ages of seventeen to mid-forties, colliding like cars in a massive motor accident. And on top of that, they wore creepy clown masks. The fans screamed their heads off, excited because of the in-your-face sound. Ramiro got his dream, fans right before his eyes, giving him the thumbs up on his performance as they sported "IRATE" t-shirts. He earned admiration from this small audience, which meant a lot to him. He made it his mission to follow up with a full album with more unheard tracks. The band's management monitored their clients' every move to make sure they wouldn't become dehydrated or any ordeals that could occur. As Ramiro continued to play, sweat trickled down his face because of the stage lights that gave off heat. They felt like the sun beaming down on him in the desert. He sported the band's t-shirt with the band's logo of his pet spider, long black shorts, and sneakers. By Ramiro wearing black clothing, of course, it absorbed lots of heat, causing him to work up a sweat. Zack's t-shirt was drenched in sweat from head to toe. He only wore shorts and a tank top because of the stage being hot while on his drum platform. Danny sported his favorite jersey; he wanted to show it off even though he worked up a sweat. "Noise Pollution!" Ramiro screamed into the microphone. The audience cheered and slammed into each other in the mosh pit.

AFTER THE SHOW, A LARGE crowd of groupies flocked around the band. A beautiful Asian female, mid-twenties, wrapped her arms around Ramiro's waist. He returned the affection. Her friend snapped shots with their cellphone cameras. Ramiro signed an autograph photo in black and white for a young thirteen-year-old boy with long hair. The young kid reminded Ramiro of himself; he wanted to learn to play the bass. This kid complained about how difficult it is to learn music. Ramiro already influencing the youth to learn the craft. Maybe one day he'll give lessons on guitar playing. Zack grabbed a groupie by the arm towards the parked RV while two more girls followed. Stanley blocked the entrance of the bus and shook his head.

"No!"

"What's the problem?" Zack cackled.

"I'll explain later!" Stanley said.

A blond female fan approached Ramiro with a smile, kissing him, and whispered in his ear. He autographed his name on her breasts and kissed her. "Thanks for listening."

DURING THE BUS RIDE to San Francisco, Stanley paced the floor before the band about sexual harassment. He had to fire Nancy even though she was Irate's secretary. She acted just like a groupie. The band's manager knew how groupies operated. These females are after money, and most aren't sincere. Stanley wasn't crazy about Ramiro signing that girl's breasts because she could accuse him of sexual harassment. He had to save the band's ass to avoid any issues in the future. They had no secretary to take care of their business affairs. One of Stanley's business colleagues would have to take on those tasks. The band's manager set his mind on the next show at a bigger concert venue. Ramiro lounged in a recliner, turning it towards the window. He heard his manager's complaints and understood while drifting off into his world.

BACKSTAGE AT A BAY area concert venue, Ramiro tuned his bass quickly, Danny strapped his electric guitar over his shoulder, and Zack tapped the wooden dresser with his drumsticks ready for the show. Stanley and Irate's management team were surrounded by security with static radios to alert the band when to get on stage. Ramiro finished tuning his bass guitar, he then tilted his head and frowned. He swaggered to the dressing room door, hearing the loud echoing audience. Sweat trickled down the side of Ramiro's face. He stopped pacing and felt the droplets on the side of his cheek. *"Why the fuck am I so nervous? Maybe, because my success is moving quickly and becoming huge,"* Ramiro dialed Noelle's number on his cell. The phone rang and rang, but there was no answer. He paced faster and faster, and still no response.

"Fuckin' shit!" Ramiro disconnected his call.

"Ramiro! Let's go!" Stanley clapped his hands. Ramiro gave his cellphone to his manager.

He abruptly opened the dressing room door and dashed up the stairs. As he got closer and closer to the stage, he could tell that the crowd was more significant than the last. Zack's drum kit waited to bring the show to life for impatient fans. Ramiro scrambled to the platform where thunderous fans cheered. "Ramiro! Ramiro!" the audience applauded, whistled, and cheered his name. Ramiro felt a rush seeing the enormous crowd. And he was right. It was bigger. The music venue held over six hundred people with double balconies on both sides of the stage. The spotlight beamed on him as the stage darkened. The fans rooted for this bassist, ready to showcase. Zack hopped on his drum kit platform as the stage light gleamed on him. He began a drum solo while the fans cheered. Danny cradled his guitar in his hand on the stage by Ramiro's side.

"Are you ready for some shit! Are you ready for shit!" Ramiro interacted with the audience. They cheered.

"Noise Pollution!" Ramiro bellowed on the microphone.

When the aggressive music started, the fans collided with each other. They received bloody noses, mouths, and other injuries. Ramiro, Danny juddered their heads, playing their guitars. Stanley and his management stood backstage with towels and bottled water for their clients. They cheered for the rockers.

TWO HOURS AFTER THE band's performance, Ramiro and his bandmates took photos with some fans outside where their tour bus was ready to go. Tons of women approached the rockers, dressed half-naked. One brunette Latina, who wore a black lace ruffled blouse with no bra and very short black miniskirt, embraced Ramiro and wouldn't let go. This female admirer placed her pelvis against Ramiro's, trying to give him a hard-on. Stanley shook his head, watching Ramiro enjoy himself with the ladies.

"Ramiro, how are you? Are you single?" the female fan sighed, running her hands through his straight hair.

"Yes, I have someone," he responded with a smile.

"I can make you change your mind about her," the Latina fan stuck her tongue in Ramiro's mouth, giving him the most extended kiss. "Babe, I've got to go," he pushed the Latina fan off him.

"Ramiro!" Stanley stood by the RV entrance.

Danny and Zack had a sea of female fans waiting to get an autograph and take pictures.

"Oh, Ramiro! Take me with you," the Latina admirer hugged Ramiro, smothering him with dozens of kisses. Once again, he got the crazed over-sexed fan off him. He swaggered towards his manager waiting at the RV. Ramiro didn't make eye contact with Stanley and hopped on the bus.

"Hurry up, the rest of you!" the band's manager stomped his foot on the concrete. Danny and Zack trotted up the RV steps as management rushed on the bus with its doors closing. It pulled away.

MINUTES LATER, RAMIRO relaxed in the recliner, which was his spot. Stanley approached this rocker with caution. "You need to be careful, Ramiro!" he sat on the sofa across from the recliner.

"I know, Stan! I know! Noelle's not here!" Ramiro focused his eyes on the window.

"Be careful, please! Ramiro, come on!" Stanley rushed to the rear of the bus.

AN HOUR LATER, IRATE'S tour bus drove along the Pacific Coast Highway back to Los Angeles. Beyond the views of the Pacific ocean, hills, and mountains, Ramiro and Stanley had an exchange of words, including Douglas now amid the drama. Lounging in the recreation room, Zack and Danny eavesdropped on their managers bitching Ramiro out. Zack beckoned Danny to turn down the volume of the stereo. When Danny did so, the bickering from the bus's front was as loud as the stereo.

"I can't waste fuckin' time! Right!" Ramiro grabbed a beer from the frigid in the kitchen. He then lounged in the recliner.

"Dammit! Ramiro, wait until someone instructs you to get on the stage," Douglas said in a gentle tone.

"Everything was ready! We were ready!" Ramiro popped the cork off the bottle, guzzling down the beverage.

"The owner felt disrespected when you waltzed on the stage like you were a god!" Douglas shook his head.

"A god? I am a god! Shit! Let me talk to the owner!" Ramiro reached for his manager's cellphone. He attempted to dial a number. "What's the number, Stan!"

"Are you fuckin' kidding me, Ramiro!" Stanley wrestled his cellphone from Ramiro. Then he finally snatched his device from Ramiro. Douglas intervened between the two men.

"Ramiro, please! We want what's best for you! Shit, Ramiro!" Douglas stomped his foot on the floor.

"I fuckin' heard you, Doug! There's no fuckin' need to shout!" he sat up in the recliner, pounding his fist on the recliner's arm.

"Ramiro, wait for instructions! What if something went wrong!" Douglas pounded his fist in return.

"But nothing went wrong! So, can you and Stan drop it!" this bassist lounged in the recliner. "I apologized to you and Stanley because if it weren't for you, I'd be an unknown bassist."

"Don't blow your chances, please! Irate's name is circulating," Douglas had the last word.

"I need a new cellphone," Ramiro added.

"What's wrong with yours?" Douglas asked.

"It's old," he mumbled with his eyes shut.

"Alright! What brand?" Douglas smiled.

"I don't know. An LG or a Samsung. Whatever," Ramiro answered.

"Done," Douglas stormed to the back of the bus.

Ramiro guzzled down his beer and shut his eyes. "I told my manager right. I am a god. I won't allow anyone to stop me from doing what I want. Because if I take everyone's advice I'll never achieve my goals," he told himself. "I'll just stay focus and do what I feel is best for me."

CHAPTER TWELVE

D own a murky corridor of a recording studio, Ramiro sang another disturbing song dealing with so-called false Christianity in a booth. Zack and Danny played their part in the music. The band's managers and the recording studio engineer watched the thrash metal band perform from behind soundproof glass. Stanley shook his head, pleased with Ramiro's hard work even though he could be a shithead. But Ramiro's management overlooked the flaws that he carried. While the lead singer of this band spewed more lyrics about the church's corruption, he eyed his manager, who watched from the other side. Ramiro was aware of his arrogance and smirked every time he thought about it. *"I will not change for anyone,"* he continued to sing and wasn't about to conform to anyone's beliefs.

LATER THAT DAY, A ROLLING Stone magazine photographer snapped multiple photo shots of the band members, wearing lots of black gear, very handsome but menacing. The trio stood alongside each other with their hair draped over their shoulders; Ramiro wore a black long-sleeved shirt with a skull on the front, black jeans, and sneakers. Danny sported a black jersey, dark blue denim, with black construction boots, and Zack had on a sleeveless t-shirt which had the band's name and logo: Irate with Ramiro's pet red kneed tarantula. Then the photographer took another shot with Ramiro on the side, Zack in the middle, and Danny on the right, still glaring at the camera. The cameraman snapped more pictures of the group and then individually. Danny posed for his separate pics with his electric guitar. Zack holding his drumsticks and Ramiro with his bass guitar. Ramiro watched from behind the scenes as Douglas crept into the photo session, beckoning Ramiro. His co-manager pulled Ramiro to the side and gave him a cellphone brand new in the box.

"Your sim card is in the phone!" Douglas patted his client on the shoulder.

"Thanks, Doug! I apologize for acting like an ass!" Ramiro opened the cellphone box.

"Don't worry about it!" Douglas shrugged.

Ramiro grabbed his old cellphone, taking the SIM card out of it, and inserting it into the new one. He checked his phone records, which were the same. Noelle's number remained. He figured that she probably called. "Excuse me, Stan. I've got to call my girlfriend," he hurried outside of the building, dialing Noelle's number. He swaggered down the bottom of the staircase as a drowsy feminine voice greeted him. "Hello, baby."

"Hey, Noelle. Are you sleeping?"

"Yes,"

"Why are you so tired all the time? Are you pregnant?" he teased.

"I'm not!" she rose her voice.

"How do you know?" Ramiro chuckled, pacing the cemented ground.

"I took the pregnancy test, and it came negative," she responded.

"What if it came out positive?" Ramiro stopped pacing.

Noelle laid in her full-sized fuschia-colored bedding, wearing her red silk pajamas as she turned on her side, not responding to him.

"Hello," Ramiro called to her on the cellphone.

"I don't know. Let me ask you that question. What if it came positive?" Noelle asked a question with a question.

"We'll keep it and get married," he responded.

"You mean that?" Her face lit up with a smile.

"Why are you asking me a question like that?" Ramiro scoffed.

Noelle sighed as she turned on her back. Her eyes fixed on the ceiling while she sank into the bed. "Noelle, I don't know when I'll be back in New York," his voice muffled in her ear. He exhaled.

She sat upright in her bed, hearing the disheartening news. Her heart raced in her chest, sensing there was someone else that caught Ramiro's eye. The words between Ramiro and Noelle fell silent for a moment.

"Who is she?"

"She who?"

"Some groupie or some actress. You are in Hollywood," Noelle poked jabs at him, trying to get him to be honest.

"Since you want to go there! Who are you seeing," Ramiro returned the question?

"I'm not seeing anyone. I've got my heart set on you, Ramiro," Noelle tossed in her bed.

Ramiro's blood boiled, clutching his fist. He couldn't believe Noelle would accuse him of cheating. Now, some men didn't give a shit about cheating. But he did.

"I've got to go, "Ramiro disconnected the call.

"Hello, Ramiro! Ramiro!" Noelle held the cell close to her chest after he hung up. She didn't know if this was the end or what.

ON A SUNNY SATURDAY afternoon, Noelle strutted down a Greenwich Village sidewalk gawking at an old warehouse building. She sported black dress pants, a red sweater, wearing black shoes, a trench coat with her handbag. Noelle approached the steel bolted door and rang the buzzer. Ramiro moved on with his life; he's got his music career, so she did the same. A stocky, middle-aged, jeans and t-shirt clad, white male, widened the door. She took a couple of steps back from this intimidating giant. The only thing to get to this monstrous creature's soft spot was to smile. "Hello. I'm Noelle, the singer. I applied for the position," she explained in a gentle tone. Her girly persona got to this monster to smile and offered her to enter. Noelle wasn't sure if she wanted to go into this old, strange building. She hesitated to go. The guard noticed Noelle was timid and refusal to go with him.

"What is your name?"

"Noelle Ellis,"

"I'll get the boss. Wait here," the bouncer closed the door behind him.

Noelle exhaled, relieved she didn't have to enter this facility with this obscure man. She paced the ground with her eyes focused on the Manhattan sidewalk. Noelle always dreamed of living in the city, whether it be New York or San Francisco. She'd have to be with her boyfriend, whoever that would be. As for Ramiro, it seemed as if they weren't on good terms now. He'll marry some blond from the latest Hollywood blockbuster film or a porn star. She convinced herself to forget about him and move on.

SECONDS LATER, CLUB owner, Terry, a high-pitched voiced Caucasian male, skinny, late-forties, wearing the Paradise club logo shirt, approached Noelle. He shook her hand while he held her CD.

"I listened to your demo, and it's terrific. How long have you been singing?" Terry asked

"All my life," Noelle rocked while she stood in one spot.

"Are you nervous?" he lifted an eyebrow.

"No. I apologize," she halted her rocking.

"That's okay," Terry chuckled.

"Who are your favorite DJs or house artists?" Terry asked with a friendly smile.

"Tony Humphries, Ja Big, Kerri Chandler, and Larry Heard," she smiled proudly.

"You're a die-hard house fan," he laughed.

"Yes, I am!" Noelle said.

"Step inside," he held the door open for Noelle. She eased inside with caution. And then Noelle's eyes widened as she gazed up at the five-leveled House venue with its Cathedral ceilings, colorful lights, balconies on the sides, where people watched performances from a bird's-eye view, and beyond them were lounges and dining areas. Noelle felt the podium calling her like a mother to her child. She ascended the staircase on the side of the stage, standing in the middle, and gazed at the enormous wooden glossy dance floor. Throbbing bass with synthesizing keyboards sounded in her head. Noelle smiled, closing her eyes, and opened them as the Paradise Club came to life. The dancers grooved to the deep underground house sound that made anyone want to party. They dressed in regular outfits, nothing extravagant as their minds were set on the beat. Noelle saw a lonesome, beautiful African-American girl her age, sporting a curly afro with breathtaking ebony eyes, waiting to be swept off by some handsome stranger. A slick-haired, skinny, white young man, early twenties glared across the dance floor. the young female character's love interest stormed towards her. This assertive guy grabbed this girl in his arms, dancing the night away. The synthesizing clamor intensified as the dancers around the lovers disappeared one by one. Would this be someone's love story of some sort? Of course, this girl and guy were probably from different backgrounds and their love of music brought their hearts together. That's a good tale anyone could relate to.

"Noelle!" a voice echoed in the distance. She widened her eyes, snapping out of her fantasy.

"Yes, Terry," she made her way off the stage.

"That's alright, Noelle! You look good up there!"

"Really!"

"Sure! You're a star. Aren't you?" Terry complimented.

Within a matter of minutes, Noelle recited her poem entitled: "ROSES" over a professional bass house beat with the synthesizing keyboards. Her feminine and sexy voice made the owner sensually eye her. Noelle didn't notice Terry gawking at her in this manner; she indulged in the sounds of the music. Her body moved like a graceful swimmer in the middle of the ocean. Noelle had a slender frame, which would make most men have a hard-on for days. Terry pictured this young woman with her sexy voice, dressed in a tight alluring outfit as she danced amongst the crowd in his venue.

MILES AWAY ON THE WEST coast, Irate recorded one of their tracks on their upcoming album entitled: "DON'T F*** WITH ME!" in a recording studio. Ramiro bellowed offensive lyrics on the microphone, playing his bass guitar. Danny headbanged, strumming his lead guitar, and Zack drummed up an aggressive beat. The words to the song "You Get The Finger" were about Ramiro's issues in his life. Also, he wanted to speak to fans who had similar situations with their strict parents or were pissed with society who judge them for their lifestyle. As he got deeper and deeper into the song, the instrumentals got louder. He rocked in the time with the monstrous sound.

RETURNING TO THE PARADISE club on the East Coast, Noelle went from reciting her poetry to singing it over loud electronic harmonies with a proceeding bass. She could see the owner eyeing her, but Noelle didn't feel awkward about swaying her hips. *I know good and well that Ramiro wouldn't like this. Who cares? He's a figment of my past,* she then went on a high note.

BACK IN THE RECORDING booth in Los Angeles, Ramiro also hit a high note at the end of the song. The band's management and sound engineer applauded the band's session. Ramiro stomped out of the booth, taking his bass guitar off him. He stormed down the dark hallway with his cellphone in hand. Ramiro pushed opened the handle of the entrance and trotted down the stone steps. He dialed Noelle's number, pacing the ground.

BACK IN NEW YORK, NOELLE exited the Paradise club with an enormous smile on her face as Terry opened the door. "We'll work on some new tracks and get some gigs for you," he waved, shutting the door. Noelle strutted down the street as "Spring La Primavera" by Vivaldi played from her cellphone. She rummaged through her purse and grabbed it. The caller ID read: Ramiro.

"Yes, Ramiro," she answered.

"What's your problem!" Ramiro paced the West Coast cemented grounds.

"Nothing," she sighed.

"Who is he!" Ramiro threw the question back at Noelle.

"He who? There's no one!" she argued on her cellphone.

"There better not be! You're not getting away from me!" Ramiro threatened. The two became silent for a minute. "Hello!"

"I'm still here, Ramiro. When are you coming home?" her voice muffled from the cellphone.

"When I finish my music! Shit, Noelle!" he stomped his foot on the concrete. "Why didn't you even bother to call me?" Noelle hung up.

"Hello! What the fuck!" Ramiro dialed her phone number back. His call rang and rang, and then went to voice mail.

"Hello, this is Noelle. Leave your name and number, and I'll get back to you as soon as possible," the voicemail beeped. The recording began, Ramiro couldn't utter any words.

"Noelle, I'll be home soon. Bye," Ramiro ended his voice message.

BACK IN THE MURKY RECORDING booth with an eerie atmosphere, Ramiro's fingers swiftly slid along the fretboard of his bass. He didn't need the aid of the electric guitar or drums. He produced whatever riffs can to mind with aggression that spoke louder than words. While he brought out the monster from his instrument, the entity was in him. For some odd reason, Noelle vexed him. He didn't know why but he'll soon find out. Maybe, there was another guy. He hoped not because he wasn't excited about the different women that rushed backstage to get a fuck out of him. Ramiro's distant relationship drove him crazy, but he had to keep his cool. Because of his career, he and Noelle would have difficulties spending time on their birthdays, holidays, family, and so forth. Ramiro was going to make it his business to introduce Noelle to his mother and sister. His managers, bandmates, and the studio engineers watched this fierce bassist play with their jaws dropped to the floor. He performed an insane solo, convulsing his head in time with the riffs. Zack had full knowledge of his friend's talents, but never the depths of his bass playing. His eyes got wider and wider as the vocalist/bassist of their new band brought ear-splitting bass lines. A migraine started in the middle of Ramiro's head as if someone hammered a nail in it. The headache intensified more and more, and then he concluded his musical session. Ramiro dazed at his bandmates and management through the glass. Sweat trickled down the sides of his face. Everyone gawked at one another due to his brilliant performance.

Ramiro inhaled through his nostrils, spitting mucus on the floor as the studio faded into darkness.

CHAPTER THIRTEEN

S omewhere in America, a jet-blacked, greasy-haired, young man, late teens, sat before a brightly lit computer screen with a murky background. This metalhead logged on to a music website. Discovering Irate's music, he checked out photos of the trio and their history. Then this troubled young man clicked on Ramiro's bass solo, listening to the track. He nodded his head to the sound of the bass line. And then he listened to the rest of Irate's album.

"DON'T FUCK WITH ME"

1. Klown
2. Migraine
3. Noise Pollution
4. "Darkness"
5. "Meet Your Demise"
6. You Get The Finger
7. "No God"

Then in a small American town, a young Asian barmaid turned up the volume of a stereo in a dimmed bar with bikers chugging down beers at the bar. One rocker slammed down his mug, causing a mess. "Hey, babe. Who's that?"

"They're a new thrash metal band: Irate," the barmaid wiped up the beer with a dampened cloth.

"Fuckin' cool. I'm going to check these guys out!" the rocker gulped down his brew.

IN A CROWDED SHOPPING mall at the Hot Topic boutique store, Irate's music blared from the speakers in every corner of the establishment. Three gothic-looking chicks, sporting black, unpleasant clothing, and dark make-up waltzed into the store. "It's that new band, Irate! It's their song, "Meet Your Demise! It's so cool," she held up the band shirt with the logo of Ramiro screaming with clutched fists.

"The lead singer is so cute!" the second girl held an Irate sweatshirt close to her heart.

"His name is Ramiro Espinoza, and he can play the fuck out of his bass," the third gothic girl sighed. A stock boy hauling a box of extra Irate band t-shirts interjected into the girls' conversation. "You're Irate fans?" the stock boy filled up the shelves with Irate clothing.

"Yeah, I would love to see them in concert," the first gothic girl lightly stomped her foot.

"They've got a show coming up at the Bowery Ballroom! Check it out!" the stock boy proceeded, to packing the shelves with band t-shirts. The enthused Irate fans darted to the register with the band gear.

ON A COLD JANUARY SATURDAY night, a long line of Irate fans waited outside of the Bowery ballroom on Delancy Street to see the band's live performance. Mostly, white and Latinos males with long hair, dressed in band t-shirts, short MC jackets, and jeans freezing their asses off, and as for the females, provocatively dressed regardless of the low temperature. A bouncer removed the velvet rope, taking tickets of the fans as they headed into the venue. The admirers made weird creepy noises, noticing the murky arena with the light-ly lit stage before them. The platform looked like something out of a horror movie. Two guys swaggered up to the front row, hollering the band's name.

BACKSTAGE, RAMIRO PACED the floor while on the phone with his mother. He was going to call Noelle but changed his mind. "I'm sorry I didn't tell you and Maritza earlier. This whole scheduling of tour is crazy," he explained.

"It's not your fault, Ramiro. Just do what you have to do, and we'll see when we see you," Anna Maria poured some rice in a pot of boiling water. She placed her hand over the cell. "Maritza, hurry your brother's on the phone!"

Maritza dashed to her mother's side. Her mother gave her the cell. "Ramiro! How are you?"

"I'm cool. Backstage waiting for the go," he proceeded to pace the floor.

"Do you have a groupie girlfriend? I feel sorry for you. She's probably similar to the other one you had," Maritza sighed.

"Why would you say that? I have an actual girlfriend," he took offense.

"Oh, what's her name?" Maritza beckoned her mother to eaves-drop on the conversation from the cell. Anna Maria put her ear to the phone.

"Noelle!"

"Noelle huh? Where's she from?" his sister giggled.

"She's from Bethpage. Right on Long Island? "Where else," Ramiro irritated by Maritza doubting him. He sucked his teeth.

"I thought you'd get one of those blond Hollywood groupies or an actress," she teased.

"Why does everyone think like that?"

"That's what happens when you make it to the big time, Ramiro," Maritza held her mother close to the phone. He described Noelle, where they met, and that she introduced him to her family. His nosy body sister drilled him with questions about her persona. Ramiro asked if she wanted to meet Noelle without Ramiro present. Maritza didn't want to introduce herself to a stranger, making the situation awkward.

"No, Ramiro. She might think I'm a lesbian stalker!"

Anna Maria couldn't help- but release her laughter as she waltzed to the stove.

"Is that Mom!" Ramiro sucked his teeth.

"A lesbian stalker!" his mother's chuckle echoed from the background as she stirred the pot of rice with a wooden spoon.

MEANWHILE, DANNY HELD his electric guitar leaning against the wall, smoking his cigarette as the ashes fell to the floor. He mashed it with his foot to avoid any serious fire outbreaks. Zack tapped his drumsticks on the dressing table, on Stanley's head, and along the walls. The management team and security wore static radios on their hips to keep everyone aware of showtime.

Five hundred sixty-two clamoring metalheads packed the auditorium, becoming impatient.

"Irate! Irate! Irate!" fans whistled, clapping their hands.

A drum solo started the show as the stage was still dark, and a bluish light beamed on Zack playing. Ramiro contributed his bass line while aggressively shaking his head with his long, brunette hair flowing. Then the electric lead guitar joined the instruments. Ramiro hurried to the microphone and spewed the lyrics for "You Get The Finger."

Fans rammed into each other in the mosh pit, screaming, and enjoying the show. "I listen to whatever I want. If you don't like my music cover your ears, I've always wanted to play this so-called noise in my younger years, turn away because I'll beat your ass out of the way, and then you can get the finger. Rather than closing my ears to whatever your criticism. You can get the finger...," he hollered the song on the microphone. This grotesque song would offend the average person who didn't care for this crazed music.

ON A ROSE-ADORNED STAGE at the Paradise Club in Greenwich Village, Noelle carefully made her way down a short set of steps, wearing a red gown, red pumps, and hair styled with roses. She recited her poem while looked out into the audience, with the groovy bass line collaborated with synthesizing keyboards. A long-haired brunette guy, Italian or Latino, mid-twenties, danced with a girl who couldn't dance if her life depended on it. Noelle was captivated by this young man who resembled Ramiro and liked House music. She and this young man made eye contact as she recited her poem. No way would Noelle want a carbon copy of the man that she loves. While flirtatious eyes proceeded between Noelle and this Xerox of Ramiro, she focused her eyes on other audience members. Her song thrilled the audience as they shook their rear ends.

BACK AT THE BOWERY Ballroom, Irate concluded the show with a grand finale by Ramiro headbanging on bass, Danny on lead guitar, and Zack drumming like an animal on his Tama drum kit. "Did you guys like the show! Or love this shit!" he screamed on the microphone. "We love this shit!" the fans responded, clamoring. They applauded and whistled as Irate stood before them on the enormous stage and bowed.

"Thank you, New York! We'll see you in Long Island!" Ramiro gave his last word and exited the stage, holding his bass by the arm.

MINUTES LATER, IRATE'S tour bus parked on the venue's rear, groupies awaited the rockers. Security stood by the rear double steel doors, making sure the musical trio wouldn't run into any danger. The girls wore sheer leggings and light garments where anyone could see their important parts, tops with the imprint of their nipples, and short skirts. Some girls weren't wearing panties. The entrance door of the tour bus opened, three groupies saw an opportunity and got on it. One red-tressed groupie slid herself into one of the lower bunks, pulling the drapes back while a brunette slid under the kitchen table, and the second brunette girl got in a closet by the bunk area, closing the door. The nine security guards stormed the RV, searching for these women.

"There better not be anyone on this bus!" a male guard hollered. He heard a noise from the kitchen area.

"You young ladies can't do this!" the guard grabbed one brunette girl by the arm from under the table.

"Come on! Give me a break!" the brunette groupie pleaded.

"You're hurting me!" another guard snatched the red-headed girl out of the bunk.

"Let's go, young lady!" the second guard escorted her off the bus. A few more guards searched further towards the rear of the RV. "I think there's one more back here!"

Security eased their way between the bunks and a closet. "Stop fooling around!" the third guard opened the closet door, pulling the second brunette girl by the arm.

All nine security guards successfully escorted the three out-of-control young ladies off the tour bus. "If it weren't for me, Irate wouldn't be shit! Fuckin' amateurs!" the red-headed girl fought with guards who had a grip of her arms.

The band made their way to the bus, while security at the door shielded them from every angle. Ramiro felt his cellphone vibrate. He read the caller ID: Noelle.

"Noelle?" Ramiro greeted his girlfriend. He sneered because of the loud House music in the background.

"Hey, baby! How are you?" Noelle plugged her finger in her ear so that she can hear Ramiro.

"I'm cool. My band and I just wrapped up a show," Ramiro arrogantly.

"That's great! How did it go?" she paced the floor backstage of the Paradise club.

"It was great. Wild as shit!" he chuckled.

"Where was it held?" Noelle wondered.

"At the Bowery Ballroom," he answered, stepping on the bus.

"The Bowery Ballroom?" Noelle excused herself from the circle of admirers.

"Why? What happened?" Ramiro relaxed in the recliner on the tour bus.

"I'm right down the street, baby," she maneuvered her way through the crowd of people with the music blasting. Ramiro sat upright in his recliner. He looked over both shoulders for his manager. "Stanley! Come here!"

"What, Ramiro?" his manager strolled to the recliner.

"Tell the driver to drive up the block to the Paradise club," Ramiro stood to his feet.

"Ramiro, we're on a schedule here. We don't have the time," Stanley glanced at his watch on his wrist.

"The Paradise Club is two blocks up," he said.

"We've got shows," Stanley shook his head.

"Bullshit! The club is right there!" this bassist shouted.

The tour bus pulled off and headed down the block in the opposite direction. Stanley went to the rear of the bus. Ramiro's face turned fiery red.

"I've got to do something. I've got to see Noelle's beautiful face because I'm going to be on tour for fuckin' six months. I know we've had a spat. Doesn't every couple? Think quick. What the fuck!" Ramiro thought. *"Grab something before you miss out on this last opportunity to see Noelle!"* Seconds later, a shiny blade of a butcher's knife glistened as Ramiro smirked. The RV halted at a red light and then switched on the opposite lane.

MINUTES LATER, NOELLE stood in front of the disco venue, noticing a black and silver bus pulling to the curb. "Ramiro, Ramiro, Ramiro," she murmured, keeping her eyes focused on the bus's entrance. The bus driver brought the RV to a full stop with its screeching brakes. Ramiro threw the large blade on the dashboard as the door swung opened and he exited. Ramiro inhaled some mucus, releasing it to the ground.

"Why the hell are we stopping!" the managers raced to the front. They noticed Ramiro embracing a young lady in his arms like lost lovers.

"Why did you stop?" Douglas questioned the driver. The bus operator touched his neck, noticing blood on his fingers.

"He threatened you?" Stanley grabbed the blade. "Fuck, Ramiro!"

Ramiro and Noelle engaged in an endless kiss, forgetting about the spat they had over the phone. Stanley stood at the bus entrance, bellowing. Ramiro heard his manager bitching about his behavior.

"Give me a minute, Stanley," Ramiro suggested. As he turned back to Noelle, he gazed into her eyes. She couldn't help but notice that large bus over his shoulder. *"Oh, no! Ramiro's music career is hap-*

pening. He'll be touring all over the world, and he sure and hell will meet lots of women. I don't fit into his Thrash Metal world," she received constant kisses from Ramiro upon her lips. "I'll be home in six months, and we'll pick up where we left off. You're not getting away from me," he threatened in a somewhat loving tone. Noelle noticed the deep-seated glare that he gave her. It scared her for a moment, but she let it go as they kissed one last time.

"She's the one for me. And like I said, Noelle's not getting away from me. And I'll make sure of it!" Ramiro hopped back on the RV as Stanley followed behind, closing the door. As Ramiro's tour bus pulled away, Noelle's eyes became watery.

"That's it. Ramiro will forget about me. Move on," a tear streamed down her cheek.

CHAPTER FOURTEEN

"No way, no light, no hope, no invisible man in the sky, the church preaches lies, no cure for the sick, no sight for the blind, no sound for the deaf, no resurrection for the dead; it's bullshit instead...," Ramiro bellowed a new track titled "NO GOD" on the microphone while strumming his bass guitar. Fans engaged in a brutal mosh pit, which took place at all the band's shows. He stepped away from the mic, performing his bass solo with only drums as Danny subsided his lead guitar. Sweat trickled down the sides of Ramiro's face and causing his hair to have an oily look. He brutally shook his head, playing his bass guitar. He then withdrew his bass from the musical piece while Zack played his drum solo. Ramiro ran backstage, Stanley handed him bottled water. Ramiro gulped the water, causing the plastic bottle to deflate like a balloon. "I'm fuckin' tired," he sat down on a large trunk.

"Catch your breath," Stanley encouraged as he kept watch on Zack playing drums. Then Danny grabbed a bottle of water from Stanley. Danny gulped the H2o and rushed back on stage. He added his guitar with the drums having a screeching, treble sound.

"Where's my cellphone?" Ramiro glanced over his shoulders. Stanley gave Ramiro his cell. He noticed the caller ID: Noelle.

Ramiro swaggered further away from the stage as business colleagues, roadies, and beautiful groupies hung out. The female admirers smiled and waved at him. He returned the polite gesture to the women. He didn't want to be rude or anything. Ramiro dialed Noelle's number and on one ring, she answered.

"Baby, how are you? How's your show going?" she elevated her voice due to the hubbub audience in the background.

"It's cool. How's everything on your end?" Ramiro plugged his finger in his ear, walking further backstage to hear Noelle better.

"Everything's ok," she replied.

"Are you still writing your poems?"

"Yes," Noelle stirred a pot of soup on the hot stove. She placed the wooden spoon on the counter. Ramiro praised her talents. He didn't care for House music, but he supported Noelle's craft like she supported him being a rock musician. He wished that Noelle could tour with him. And then it hit him. Maybe next time, he could have Noelle tag along. Stanley snapped his fingers in the air, getting Ramiro's attention. "Ramiro! You've got to get back on stage!"

"Noelle, I've got to go," he marched from the back to the stage. "I love you!"

"Love you too!" Noelle replied. They both hung up.

Ramiro trotted with his bass guitar on stage, adding his bass line to the music. The audience bounced up and down, where it looked like a wave. "Noise Pollution", Ramiro shouted on the microphone. He and his band played the instrumental piece. The mosh pit became bigger, going from the front to the rear. The security tried their best to keep the crowd under control since the mosh pit made its way to the stage. Ramiro eyed the audience, hoping that the first three rows of fans didn't get any ideas. Danny didn't recognize the unruly fans, but Ramiro did. His heart pounded in his rib cage as he rushed to conclude the song. The loud, piercing, screeching guitars and pounding drums caused the crowd to erupt into a deafening cheer.

"Thank you, Asbury Park, New Jersey!" Ramiro screamed into the microphone. He, Danny, and Zack took a bow, leaving the stage.

ON ANOTHER STAGE IN Connecticut, Irate performed their songs from the "Don't Fuck With Me" album. The crowd engaged in the same scenario, mosh pits and lots of headbanging. Ramiro hoped no one got hurt. He didn't want that on his conscience. As he and Danny played their guitars side by side, they moved about the stage, engaging with fans. Danny noticed the pit stretched from the first row to the last. "Holy shit!" Danny mouthed while playing his guitar. Then they concluded the show with a musical finale. "Thank you, Hartford, Connecticut!" Ramiro, Danny, and Zack bowed.

NIGHT AFTER NIGHT, mostly on weekends, Irate performed before sold-out audiences in every American city. They gave their gratitude to American metalheads across the land.

"Fuckin' thank you, Burlington!" Ramiro shouted. The fans cheered.

"We'll fuckin' see you next time, Boston!" Ramiro engaged with fans.

"Thanks, Toledo!"

"Fuckin' thanks, Philadelphia!"

"You've been fuckin' great, Detroit!"

"Fuckin' thanks to the Windy City!"

"You've been fuckin' great, San Antonio!"

"Dallas, fuckin' good night!"

"Good night, Houston! Keep fuckin' rocking!"

The roars of fans continued throughout the United States and back to California, performing for a second time. Los Angeles, San Francisco, San Diego, San Jose, etc.

SIX MONTHS LATER, RAYS of sunshine beamed on Ramiro's face from an airplane window as he sat in first class on a United Airlines flight. His eyes were heavy, but Ramiro fought to keep them open. From his bird's-eye view, the enormous earth's natural green tones, brown, and yellow looked like a map in every school classroom. The low roar of the plane's engine kept Ramiro from sleeping. *"I played so many shows, meeting so many people, including fellow rockers. My bass and I rocked every night for enthusiastic fans, especially in the mosh pits. Tons and tons of groupies pursuing me and my band,"* he glanced at his manager resting in the aisle seat next to him. Stanley seemed to be in a deep sleep. He had the blanket covering him from head to toe. Ramiro didn't give a fuck about disturbing him from his peaceful nap.

"Stan! Stan, wake up!"

"What! Are we about to land at Kennedy yet?" Stanley snatched the blanket from his face, squinting his eyes as he stretched in his seat.

"We've got another two hours. Since we don't have a secretary, maybe Noelle could handle the job," Ramiro exhaled.

"Was that the girl you were hugging in front of the paradise club?" Stanley looked at him.

"Yes, Ramiro answered. "This way I can avoid issues," Ramiro leaned his head in the headrest.

"How long have you been with her?" Stanley asked.

"A while," Ramiro responded.

"Sounds good. I'm going to encourage Danny and Zack to get steady girlfriends," Stanley pulled the blanket over his face as his voice muffled.

"Thanks, man," Ramiro grinned.

"No problem," his manager yawned.

Ramiro shut his eyes with a smirk. *"Holy shit! That was easy. Now, I could have Noelle with me. So, we don't have to worry if the other one's cheating. During this entire tour, Stanley kept the groupies at bay. I kept myself under control with self-gratification. To me, that's not a bad thing. If sexual harassment wasn't an issue, I'd probably fuck these groupies and take part in threesomes,"* he admitted. *"And if I ever cheated on Noelle, I wouldn't blame her if she hated the shit out of me. Or just call it quits.*

THAT NIGHT, BASS LINE House music blasted from giant speakers of the Paradise club, where dancers packed the dance floor. Noelle and a young male dancer grooved to the rhythm. A smile always surfaced on her face because of the fascinating sounds of the beat. The moment felt like something out of a romance novel, but the cute guy named Jeremy, mid-twenties had a thing for Noelle. He's the one guy who was in the audience when Noelle performed her song "Roses." Jeremy was a regular at the Paradise club. He came from an Italian family who lived in Sheepshead Bay, Brooklyn. He worked as a UPS deliveryman Monday through Friday, and on the weekends, he'd help his father in his restaurant in Little Italy and then danced the night away in his spare time. In the romance department, Jeremy wanted to find the right person, but he took his time with the ladies because he wanted to live a little. Of course, that was no problem at all because Noelle loved Ramiro very much. She told Jeremy about Ramiro and his rock band gaining popularity. Jeremy's brother listened to Heavy metal and was familiar with Irate. She loved Ramiro so much that's who had her heart. He was her number one. When Jeremy partied at the venue, he danced with Noelle first. Jeremy grabbed Noelle by the waist, pulling her close to him. Noelle nuzzled him away, keeping a space between them. For some strange reason, she sensed a set of eyes upon her. Jeremy respected Noelle's feelings and knew she loved Ramiro.

"You can leave now!" Ramiro rudely cut between the couple.

"Ramiro! Baby!" Ramiro kissed her on the lips. Jeremy slowly backed off, maneuvering his way through the crowd.

"Who the fuck is that!" Ramiro frowned.

"He's just a guess here at the club," she added. Noelle laid more kisses on Ramiro's cheek.

"Or is he your guess!" Ramiro glared into Noelle's eyes. He kissed Noelle, squeezing his arms around her waist. The House music released another throbbing low bass and synthesizing sounds of electric keyboards.

DURING THE WITCHING hour that night, Ramiro and Noelle got hot and heavy between the black satin sheets in his bed. Balls of sweat surfaced on their nude bodies while Noelle moaned as if she were singing. Ramiro had a vile grin on his face that alternated into a death stare. *"What the fuck, Noelle! We both accused one another of seeing other people. I kept my dick in my pants and I jerked off for months while on tour. And I come home and you've got some guy dry fuckin' you!"* he proceeded his duty as a man while he gazed into Noelle's eyes. She loved Ramiro's every stroke that he laid upon her body. She didn't realize that he wasn't pleased with Jeremy. Ramiro wanted to ask her if she fucked him. Then their climaxes arrived on the scene while Noelle's panting got louder. This Songstress performance was similar to the House music she sang. He didn't mind Noelle having her passion for her music, but not for anyone else.

"Ramiro, what's wrong?" she touched his chest.

"Nothing," Ramiro closed her legs. He turned his back, sitting on the edge of his bed. He slipped on his boxers.

"I don't mean to give Noelle my back, but she fuckin' pissed me off. She knew what she did. I'm going to ask Noelle to tour with me. If she says "No," then she's fuckin' around for sure. And I'll scare the shit out of her with my tarantula. If she says "Yes," then she loves me," he thought. Noelle covered her essential parts with the bedsheet sitting behind him.

"I'm so happy you're home. I missed the hell out of you!" she kissed Ramiro's neck.

"How much did you miss me?" he asked.

"Can't you tell, Ramiro?" Noelle responded in a seductive tone. She pecked Ramiro on the lips. The clock on the nightstand read 6:34 a.m. Ramiro chuckled.

LATER THAT MORNING, sun rays brightened Ramiro's obscure apartment an hour later, as "CNN" blared from the flat panel television in the living room. Noelle opened the windows breathing in the fresh air, wearing an Irate t-shirt and some of Ramiro's old jogging pants. The apartment didn't have that creepy ambiance, making it more cheerful despite his horror décor. Ramiro lounged in his recliner, dosing off. Noelle waltzed over, kissing him.

"Sleepy?" she climbed into the chair with him, resting her head on his chest.

"Yes. Where the fuck is the food! Shit! We should've gone out!" Ramiro mumbled, squinting his eyes.

Then his apartment buzzer buzzed. Noelle hopped up as Ramiro gave chase. "Fuck! That food better be hot!" he stomped his feet on the wooden floor.

Noelle opened the door as a short gentleman stood on the other side of the screen door.

"Delivery!"

"No shit, Sherlock!" Ramiro held some cash in his hand.

"Be nice, Ramiro!" Noelle gently slapped him on the arm.

"Thirty-Two, forty-four," the delivery man said. Ramiro handed him thirty-seven dollars.

"Here you go! Thanks!"

"I'm a big Irate fan! My favorite song is "Meet Your Demise." My brother and his friends went to see one of your shows," this fan kept nagging Ramiro. He tried nicely to brush this obsessed fan off but couldn't get rid of him.

"Thanks for being a fan," Ramiro tried to close the door, but the delivery man kept talking. He then gave him another tip. He was pretty sure that's what this gig worker wanted—or even needed.

"Thank you, Ramiro! I can't wait to see you in concert again!" the deliveryman waved.

"Have a good day!" Ramiro politely closed the door. "Does he think money grows on trees!" he leaned his back against the wall.

"Ramiro, you're a walking dollar sign!" Noelle grabbed the bag of food from his hand.

DURING SO-CALLED BREAKFAST, Ramiro didn't eat the traditional morning dishes while lounging in his recliner. He took a massive bite out of a double cheeseburger as ketchup and melted cheese dripped down the corner of his mouth. Noelle sneered at her burger, tossing it in the tin pan. "I said no cheese! Why don't these people learn to take orders! You can have it, Ramiro!" she pushed the extra cheeseburger towards this starving musician.

"So, you're going to starve," Ramiro swallowed his food. He gulped down his water from the plastic bottle.

"I'll figure something out," Noelle shrugged, leaning back in her chair. Then Ramiro's apartment buzzer buzzed once again. "Stay there and finish eating," she hopped out of her seat, rushing to the door. She abruptly opened it, noticing that no one was around. "Good morning," the mailman waved, delivering letters to the residents next door.

"Good morning! Thank you!" Noelle grabbed the stack of letters from Ramiro's mailbox. She slammed the door.

Ramiro shoved a ketchup-dipped French fry into his mouth. He looked like a total pig, grunting and not giving a shit who saw him in such an embarrassing moment. Noelle stomped into the living room, stopping in her tracks and witnessing him devouring the saturated cheesy double beef sandwich like an animal.

"Ramiro, what's wrong with you? You're a mess!" she placed the stack of letters on the end table next to him. She stretched her body in the long recliner in the opposite direction, facing the television. "I've been on tour, and there's no food for you to cook for me," he spoke with his mouth full.

"We can go to Shoprite later," Noelle smiled. She glanced at Ramiro, taking the last bite of his sloppy cheeseburger.

Ramiro wiped his mouth with the napkin, hearing that Noelle would cook for him. He'd have fresh food packed in his freezer, so she could whip up any dish that he desired. Ramiro was curious about her culinary skills. Noelle focused her eyes back on the television. He then released an enormous burp from the sandwich that he gobbled up. It sat heavily in his gut and would take hours to digest. Ramiro shuffled through the stack of mail of past cellphone bills he knew he already paid, college tuition bills, and then a couple of extra letters. He opened up the letter regarding a Macy's credit card bill for over nine thousand dollars. "What the fuck is this shit!" Noelle turned and sat up. "Ramiro, what happened?"

"I've got a credit card bill close to ten-thousand dollars. I don't shop at Macy's! "Ramiro ripped the notice up. Then he opened up another letter for a MasterCard in his name for seven-thousand, three hundred dollars.

"What the fuck is going on here? Who the fuck is using my name to open up credit cards!"

"Are you sure?" Noelle leaped from the recliner to his side. She looked over his shoulders at the bills in his hands.

"Yes, Noelle. I'm sure! What the fuck! Maritza!" Ramiro turned red in the face as he crumbled up the credit card bill.

THAT AFTERNOON, A SMALL, tidy home sat on a suburban
street in Syosset, Long Island, where Anna Maria moved to her new
residence after the courts completed her divorce. She and Maritza
lived there, and of course, there was room for Ramiro if things didn't
work out for him. As for Ramiro's father, God only knows where the
hell he's living. His black Dodge Durango pulled in front of the residence with its screeching brakes. The engine shut down as Ramiro
hopped out of the driver's seat, closing the door with his rattling
keys. Noelle exited the passenger's side, slamming the door on this
huge monster truck. The birds chirped as the sun beamed its rays as
a small dog barked from across the street, still a considerably quiet
area. Ramiro grabbed Noelle's hand, strolling to the front door. The
wind chimes at the entrance chimed through the air.

"Ramiro, say nothing until you know for sure," Noelle pleaded.

"I'm sure," he rang the doorbell.

The young couple could hear Pop music from inside the comfortable residence; Ramiro knew it was New York's 106.7 Lite FM.
His mother always listened to that station. The lock clicked as his
mother opened the front door. Her jaw dropped, seeing her handsome son with his long brunette hair almost as long as hers. Anna
Maria hasn't seen him in a while.

"Ramiro! Ramiro!" she kissed her son as if he were still a baby.
"Oh, my God! How was your tour?" Anna Maria noticed this pretty
African-American young lady from over her son's shoulder. His
mother smiled at Noelle and assumed she was Ramiro's love interest.

"Hello. How are you?" Anna Maria's eyes widened. Noelle's
myelinated-complexion, her wavy hair with its medium to long
length, and her size five body mesmerized Ramiro's mother.

"Hi, I'm Noelle," she smiled and shook Ramiro's mother's hand.
Anna Maria escorted them inside as they strolled into the beautifully
furnished living room, with extra lovely pieces and younger pictures

of Ramiro and Maritza and other family photos. Noelle glared at Ramiro's baby pictures. "Ramiro, is that you?" she sighed.

"Yeah, that's me," Ramiro replied with a sneer. He approached Noelle from behind.

"That's Ramiro when he was almost two years old," his mother answered while her voice faded in the distance towards the kitchen.

"You're so cute!" Noelle's heart melted.

"I'm cute?" Ramiro lifted a brow and shaking his head.

"You still are!" Noelle complemented as Ramiro wrapped his arms around her waist.

"Hey! You two come in here!" his mother bellowed.

Ramiro grabbed Noelle by the hand, navigating their way through the dining room to the kitchen.

"Mom, you did a good job of fixing the house up!" he praised.

"Thanks to your sister!" Anna Maria said. A light bulb went off in Ramiro's head as he started thinking about Maritza. He glared at Noelle. She could tell by the expression on her boyfriend's face what he was thinking. She shook her head, giving him a sign not to make any accusations.

"Where is Maritza, by the way?" he wondered.

"She should be home shortly," Anna Maria lowered the flames on the stove.

Noelle and Ramiro sat at the kitchen table. They both sniffed the air of tomato sauce cooking.

"What's that in the pot?" Ramiro stormed from the table. He lifted the lid from the pot on the stove.

"Tomato sauce with sausage, ziti. I'm too lazy to cook," Anna Maria chuckled.

ABOUT AN HOUR LATER, they ate dinner at the kitchen table while Anna Maria did most of the talking as Noelle and Ramiro devoured their meals. He kept his ear pierce to his mother's words as she praised her daughter for decorating their new home. Ramiro chewed his food slowly, wondering if his mother had a hand in using his name for purchases and credit card bills. He then deleted the notion from his head. *"I doubt my mother would do this. But that bitch sister of mine has to be behind it,"* Ramiro continued eating. His mother also told Ramiro they had a spare bedroom for him. She avoided the conversation about her x-husband (Ramiro's father) and why he wasn't in the picture. Instead, Anna Maria remained on topic about their home with its bedrooms and cheerful ambiance. And how would it have been easier if Ramiro was there to help? His mother understood that Ramiro had a career to pursue and live his life. But she and Maritza made it work. Ramiro could tell his mother avoided discussing his father at every angle of the conversation. After hearing that, Ramiro felt guilty about not being there for his family. "What if that asshole tried to do something to them? I would never forgive myself for it?" Ramiro chewed his food while his mother kept chatting, sipping her tea. Keys jingled at the front door as it swung open. "Mom, I'm home!" Maritza is out of breath with a Bloomingdale's bag.

"I'm in the kitchen. Hurry!" Anna Maria shouted.

Ramiro placed his fork on the plate, wiping his hands with his napkin.

"Don't!" Noelle mouthed. She clutched Ramiro's hand and shook her head. Then Maritza sashayed in, noticing her baby brother leaned in the chair as he got up and embraced her. She tossed the department store bag in the chair. "Oh my goodness, Ramiro! How was your tour?"

"It was cool," Ramiro embraced his sister. He noticed the Bloomingdale's bag with its large lettering and logo.

Why didn't you call?"

"I had no time. We're continually performing, signing autographs, interviews, photo sessions, and shit.

"Did you meet anyone along the way?" Maritza nudged her brother.

As soon as Noelle heard his sister say that, her smile dropped like a hot potato. She wiped her mouth with the napkin.

"No. I had someone all along," Ramiro walked to Noelle, clutching her hand and pulling her out of her chair. "Maritza, this is Noelle. My girlfriend. This is my sister, Maritza," Ramiro introduced.

"Wow, she's beautiful," Maritza complimented, shaking Noelle's hand.

"Thank you," Noelle smiled.

"Are you still staying at the college apartment?" Maritza placed her purse on the table.

"I'm going to move out of their next week," Ramiro pulled Noelle close to him. He raised an eyebrow at Maritza, recognizing her fancy sweater, pants, and boots. He got a whiff of her beautiful fragrance that perfumed the air. Ramiro and Noelle glanced at each other. His heart pounded in his chest. He wanted to roar at Maritza. But he respected Noelle's wishes and didn't want to upset her or his mother. He backed off until he figured it out.

"Meanwhile, you can stay here," Maritza took a seat at the table.

A FEW MINUTES LATER, Maritza pushed open a bedroom door of a blue blanketed painted wall, a full-sized bed with black bedding, horror figurines, heavy metal posters of Irate, and other metal bands plastered on the walls, etc. Ramiro stepped into this room that he would never occupy because he's going to be on his own. His mother and sister fixed up the bedroom for him if his living situation got rough. Ramiro guided Noelle behind him into the bedroom. He plopped on his foamed mattress. "The bed is suitable." Noelle noticed the posters of her boyfriend's band on the wall. She has the same ones plastered on her wall as well. Ramiro crept to Noelle, hugging her from behind. You like it?" he asked her.

"Question is, do you like it?" Noelle wrapped her arms around him.

"It's doable," Ramiro shrug.

"I'll leave you two alone. I'll be downstairs," his sister smiled as she left the bedroom door cracked.

Like a rebellious teenager, Ramiro laid Noelle on the foamed bed with heartfelt kissing, reaching his hand up her shirt, and attempting to remove her bra. Then there was a knock at the door; Ramiro abruptly removed his hand from Noelle's shirt. Anna Maria glimpsed at what they were doing and jumped back. "Ramiro and Noelle, your food is going to get cold!"

"Alright! We'll be down in a minute!" he answered. His mother went back downstairs to the kitchen.

Ramiro kissed Noelle on the lips "We'll continue this later."

He laid his head close to Noelle's, glaring at the ceiling, thinking about his childhood bedroom, similar to this room that Maritza decorated. He knew he'd never feel comfortable in this bed, where he and Noelle laid. He was moving up in the world and wanted to provide for Noelle. He wasn't sure what type of home he wanted for them, whether it be an apartment or a house. Either on the east or west coast. Comfort was all that mattered to Ramiro, and he shared his thoughts on a home for them. And of course, he didn't forget that Unique Homes magazine that Noelle showed him. Picking a home from that periodical would make things easier.

"Are you serious, Ramiro?" Noelle sat up in the bed as her eyes popped out of her head.

"We have plans to get hitched, right?" he clutched Noelle's hand and kissed it.

"Yes, baby," she laid beside him. These two spoke about their future, laughing and lovey-dovey as if they didn't have a care in the world. Ramiro closed his eyes, looking forward to the future.

IN A SOMEWHAT CROWDED supermarket that night, Noelle pushed the shopping cart filled with steaks, chicken, sausage, canned goods, milk, soda, and beer. Ramiro dropped cookies, candies, potato chips in the shopping cart like a child.

"You're a baby, Ramiro," Noelle steered the cart down the frozen aisle.

"I'm going to get some ice cream," Ramiro opened up the rectangular freezer door as the cold mist blew into his face. He grabbed two gallons of ice cream and loaded it into the cart. He loved his junk food over veggies like most kids. Ramiro also craved other sweets as well. He focused on her beautiful face while she pushed the shopping cart further in the frozen aisle. "I could see Noelle navigating a cart of food through the aisles of a supermarket for our family in a few years. She even suggested that I eat better. Just like a wife or mother would," Ramiro and Noelle stood in line, waiting to have their groceries rung up at the checkout.

"Since we have all this food, what do you want me to cook?" Noelle looked at the food.

"It doesn't matter to me, babe," he kissed her on the lips, opening up the package of Oreos, shoving a cookie in his mouth.

THAT NIGHT, RAMIRO and Noelle ate two rib-eyed steaks broiled in the oven, broccoli steamed in the pot, and a tossed salad at a small table. Two wine glasses sat on the sides of their plates, Irate's music played in the background. The aggressive tunes made this romantic setting awkward for Noelle. She smiled at Ramiro as he shoved a piece of the steak in his mouth, grunting. She could tell he enjoyed his food. He overate that evening and didn't stop. Before Ramiro ate this Rib-eye dinner, he devoured half of the cookies with a half-gallon of Edy's ice cream and a corned beef sandwich. He's fully aware of his eating habits, junk foods, along with healthy stuff, but he knew he could still gain the weight.

"Do you want dessert?" Noelle placed her wineglass on the table. Ramiro halted his eating, giving her a seductive look.

"I would love dessert," Ramiro pinched Noelle's leg from under the table.

"Stop, Ram!" I'm talking about red velvet cake," Noelle released an enormous laugh.

"I'm full now," Ramiro placed his fork back on the plate. He wiped his mouth with the napkin and leaned in his chair. He suddenly became quiet, looking in the other direction as if something vexed him. Noelle knew those credit card bills worried him, but he probably clean up his credit in no time at all. "Earth to Ramiro," she snapped her fingers before his eyes. He blinked and grabbed Noelle's hand, kissing it. He was thankful that she took him from his worries. A smirk surfaced on Ramiro's face as he jumped from the table. "What! Not now honey! Not on a full stomach!" Noelle knew by her lover's smile what he was thinking about. He grabbed Noelle from the table, spinning her around like a little doll in his arms. Ramiro and Noelle were well on their way to building a life together.

THREE WEEKS LATER, two moving men hauled a black sofa from the rear of a moving truck into a studio apartment in Greenwich Village, Manhattan. Ramiro dictated the arrangement of his furnishings. "Place the sofa right here!" Ramiro pointed to the center of the wooden living room floor. He gave further instructions on furniture arrangements like his coffee table, side tables, recliner, small rugs, framed posters, pictures, figurines, etc.

Then the moving men carried in the boxed spring and top mattress into a large bedroom. His dresser, nightstand, small lounge chair, and other décor added to the setting.

For the kitchen, Noelle unboxed Ramiro's pots, pans, dishes, glassware, utensils, etc. She stacked the black plates in the cabinets, the glasses, and the mugs in the cupboard. Noelle sneered at the slightly bent fork, sucking her teeth, and threw it in the drawer. "You need new utensils, Ramiro." Then Ramiro placed a large glass jar with his two tarantulas crawling around in it on the counter. She jumped back as her heart pounded in her chest.

"Are you talking to yourself, babe?" he smirked.

"Yes, honey. You need new utensils," Noelle nodded. "What are you going to do with these things?"

"Noelle, please could you stop being so paranoid. How do you like our new place?" he began kissing all over Noelle.

"Our new place? I thought this was yours!" she said.

"No, it's for us," Ramiro said with a straight face.

"For real?" Noelle's eyes lit up.

"Yes," Ramiro nodded.

There were a few things Noelle didn't like about the apartment. She hated that it was closed-in with no elbow room. When she looked outside of her bedroom window, a brick wall was right in her face from an adjacent building. Additional apartment buildings were surrounding the area had fire escapes. Noelle would have a hard time getting used to this because she loved Long Island. She'd wake up in the morning as the birds sang, the ruffling leaves in the trees while the wind blew. The scent of fresh-cut grass in spring and summer. Yellow, brown, and red leaves falling to the ground in autumn, and snow fall in the winter. In their new apartment, it had a tiny porch that only had room for one chair and nothing else. "Boy, this sucks!" Noelle noticed the seat as she and Ramiro gave themselves a tour of their new residence.

"Baby, it's only for a little while. We won't even be here. You'll be traveling with me," Ramiro hugged Noelle.

"Traveling with you?" she asked.

"Yes. I need you, Noelle," Ramiro kissed her on the neck.

"I've got my college classes, and I've got my job at the Paradise club," she turned away from him.

"You can take classes online? And you can do your House shit later!" Ramiro insulted.

"How could you say that? I never put down your music," she marched to the master bedroom.

As she entered, Noelle noticed that she couldn't lie down because the king-sized bed wasn't made. She placed the fitted bedsheets on the mattress, then the cover sheet, and inserted the pillows in the pillowcases. Ramiro stood in the doorway, watching Noelle take care of their home.

"Do you need some help?" he smirked.

"Don't worry. I've got it!" Noelle threw the comforter on the bed. She continued to straighten up the bedroom while Ramiro watched.

"She's not making any eye contact with me. Noelle's pissed because of my tarantulas for sure. These mother fuckers are harmless. She probably watches too many horror movies. I'm the one experiencing the horror. I'm experiencing identity theft. I still said nothing to my sister about this shit. But, if I get any more notifications concerning credit card bills, I'm going to confront Maritza," Ramiro swaggered out of the bedroom doorway. Noelle then noticed that he left. She grabbed Ramiro's clothes from the suitcase, seeing that he had a lot of bands and horror t-shirts. He had lots of black and navy-blue jeans.

"How the hell could Ramiro belittle me. House isn't music! What!" Noelle threw his garments in the drawer. She hung up his sweaters, jackets, and coats on the hangers roughly in the closet, slammed the door. Noelle stomped to the other side of the bedroom where she treated her clothing the same way. She threw her panties and bras in the drawers.

"I'm going to get some food?" Ramiro kissed her on the cheek.

"Alright," Noelle slammed the drawer back.

TWO BLACK CANDLESTICKS burned on the small dark wood table, matching chairs on opposite ends in their new apartment. Ramiro and Noelle ate Chinese takeout. She had to toss the groceries away they purchased a couple of weeks earlier. Ramiro finished eating the junk food, half of the meats because the rest would spoil. A new track by Ramiro's band played from the computer while the screensaver displayed photos of Noelle and Ramiro as a couple, individual pictures, and his band Irate. Ramiro devoured chicken with fried rice; he wouldn't slow down for anything. He didn't bother to look at Noelle to see if she was eating. "My goodness! Look at the way he's eating. He hasn't stopped for days. He better watch his weight because I will not tolerate an overweight bassist," Ramiro snaps his fingers in front of her face.

"Why are you so quiet?" Ramiro swallowed the rest of his food.

Noelle remained quiet, staring at him. She shoved a spoon of rice in her mouth without taking her eyes off him. The disrespect Ramiro showed Noelle because of her musical tastes other than his own was a slap in the face. She wanted to throw some food in his face.

"Are you upset because of what I said to you?"

"Yes, Ramiro!" Noelle threw her fork on the plate.

"My manager is going to stop by and talk to you?"

"About what?"

"I want you to be my secretary," Ramiro answered.

"I am your girlfriend, so I might as well be your secretary," she folded her arms. "You didn't even give me details. Ramiro, you're laying down the law. It is what it is!"

"Whatever, Noelle! I want you to go!" he drank from a can of soda.

"You've got it!" she ate another spoon of rice.

"So, that's a yes!" he gazed her right in the eye. Noelle continued to eat.

Ramiro sipped some soda, slammed the tin can hard on the table. "Fuckin' talk!"

"I said, you got it! Yes!" Noelle threw her fork down, storming away from the table. Ramiro gave chase, grabbing Noelle by the waist and kissing her.

"Ramiro, let go!" Noelle stomped her foot on the floor.

"No!" Ramiro lay kisses on Noelle.

Then the doorbell rang.

"Baby, I need you. You're coming on tour with me, "Ramiro released his grip from Noelle's waist. She dashed to the bathroom. "That's Stanely. I'll make sure that you get paid," he shouted as Noelle closed the door. The doorbell rang again.

"I'll be right there!" Ramiro approached the door. He unlocked the door and opened it.

"What's up, Stan?" he shouted from the front door. Noelle peered through the crack of the bathroom door, holding it halfway open. His managers headed inside, embracing Ramiro and making their way to the living room. Noelle closed the bathroom door with ease.

LATER, RAMIRO AND HIS managers ordered more takeout from a local diner with a half-eaten chicken sandwich, a small soup, with half-empty beer bottles in the dining room. Ramiro popped the top off a beer bottle, chugging it down along with Douglas. Stanley took the last bite out of his chicken sandwich. Noelle still hasn't made her presence known. Ramiro engaged in deep conversation with his management which made him forget about his girlfriend. He glanced over his shoulder, noticing she was out of sight. He wiped his mouth with his napkin, gulping down his beer.

"Noelle!" Ramiro cried. There was no response from his girlfriend. "Excuse me, gentlemen!"

He swaggered to the master bedroom and opened the door. Noelle stretched out in bed, sleeping. "Noelle," Ramiro called her name. She didn't respond. He eased into the bedroom, strolling to her side of the bed. She looked so peaceful that he didn't want to wake her. *"My managers wanted to meet her, and she's knocked out. She's tired. Shit, so am I, but I'm still talking business with my manager. By Noelle meeting with Stanley and Douglas, this would be her job interview. She won't get hired. Fuck! Maybe tomorrow they could meet her. I'll tell them Noelle's sick,"* Ramiro rubbed the back of his hand along Noelle's face. He smiled and exited the bedroom, closing the door halfway.

CHAPTER FIFTEEN

"For Fuck's Sakes," the newly titled album from Irate, uploaded to the internet for listeners to continue to get more of the band's distorted sound. The trio collaborated on eleven tracks. Danny wrote the lyrics to "Sickness of the Mind" and Polluted Politics," Zack wrote, "I hate Everyone" and "Hell On Earth. Ramiro wrote the rest of the seven tracks entitled: "Six Feet Under," Everyone Sees Death," I Hate Life," You're Not Getting Away from Me," "Dark Romance, "I'll Kill You If I Have To," and "For Fuck's Sakes. Ramiro wrote lyrics in his spare time between shows on his first tour, spending time away from everyone. The song "Six Feet Under" targeted his father where it read:

> "Eighty-six years of her life snatched away by an evil being in the night, taking flight on this wholesome soul, who wanted more than to stop the chaos, but lose the battle from a demon who felt no remorse for striking her down like a lightning bolt from the sky, why? I'm going to confront you everything you have done, you miserable fuck....," the song played from a computer of a twenty-eight-year-old, Caucasian man who turned up the volume.

Ramiro had another person who could be a target for his songs.
"You're Not Getting Away From Me,"
"I can't stand to see you with anyone else, I can't let you out of my sight, I can't let go, You're Not Getting Away From Me, I provide, pro-

tect, I give good fuckin' sex, I give you my all, shit! You're Not Getting Away from Me," the song blasted through a teen-rocker girl's headsets on her way to school, dressed in black attire and make-up, carrying her backpack. Irate's most popular song on the band's second album was Dark Romance. The track contained disturbing, offensive words to any woman in love with a man only to find that his soul is foul, wanting to harm or perhaps kill his bride. Ramiro seemed to operate the same way because he displayed similar patterns. Like putting down Noelle's goals and wanting her to do what he wanted her to do. Like father, like son. In his mind, some people would say there's no excuse for abusive behavior. He didn't realize he was becoming controlling. He didn't do this to Kim. Ramiro sat in a recliner in a studio where a rock music news reporter interviewed him about the band's album. Logan Spelling, a short, bald, tattooed, pierced young man, early thirties, sat in a chair across from him. Since Ramiro was Irate's front man, he had to do lots of interviews.

"What's up, guys? Welcome to the Metal Forum. I'm sitting here with front man Ramiro Espinoza of the thrash metal band "Irate." How are you, Ramiro?" Logan shook his guest's hand. Ramiro relaxed on the cushioned chair while Logan peppered him with questions.

Logan admired his bass solo Ramiro performed in a poorly lit recording studio. And he agreed Irate fans loved Ramiro's bass playing, influencing kids in high school and younger to play bass guitar. He had a tight schedule to where he didn't have time to look at social media. Ramiro wrote lyrics, studio time, photo sessions, Noelle, and other things on his list. Noelle, Stanley, Douglas, and the rest of the band stood behind the scenes while Ramiro did his interview. Noelle's heart melted when Ramiro mentioned her being an essential part of his life. She believed the future seemed bright for the two of them.

"What are your musical influences?" Logan squirmed in his chair, leaning forward.

"A lot of different genres of metal. Thrash mainly, death, speed, black, punk. And I listen to a lot of Jazz as well.

"Jazz is cool. I wanted to ask you about the lyrics. They're very dark and your music is aggressive, which causes a person listening to look over their shoulder," Logan laughed.

"There's no reason to glance over your shoulder unless someone is after you," Ramiro laughed it off.

"We've got that cleared up. Some of your fans would like to know about the lyrics for "Six Feet Under," Logan smirked.

That question hit Ramiro like a ton of bricks, and the song was about his father responsible for his grandmother's death. And Ramiro hoped to bury him six feet beneath the earth. His eyes watered and avoided the question.

"Don't ask me that question," he stared at the interviewer with tears in his eyes.

"Next question," Stanley shouted from behind the scenes. Noelle saw Ramiro's eyes water. Ramiro still kept his future wife in the dark about his grandmother's death.

"I apologize. Are you alright, Ramiro," Logan shook his hand.

"I'm cool," Ramiro fought back his tears.

"Let's talk about your upcoming tour. I know you're pleased with that?"

"I'm happy. I'm going to give my fans the best show ever.

ON DEVIL'S NIGHT, RAMIRO and Noelle strolled hand in hand down the Halloween-decorated streets of Greenwich Village. Enormous skeletons, witches, ghosts, black cats, and other Halloween décor adorned storefronts. The city people got into the spooky spirit, dressing as zombies, Freddy Kruger, Chuckie, Jason, Michael Myers, and other horror characters. The lovers chuckled as the Halloween goers tried to give them a scare. Plus, it was Ramiro's birthday, he didn't think about it because of his grandmother's demise on that day. He avoided thinking about getting that phone call from his sister about his grandmother. There were times when he'd cry privately. But he knew she was in a better place and watched over him. A twenty-something dark-haired young man with Zombie make-up and ragged clothing lumbered towards Ramiro and Noelle, groaning, playing in his character. He halted in his tracks and came out of character, "Ramiro Espinoza!"

"That's me!" Ramiro poked out his chest.

"I'm such a huge fan! I went to your show in Jersey," the Zombie fan shook Ramiro's hand.

"Thanks," Ramiro said. The Zombie fan noticed Noelle as she shied away. He greeted her as she returned his polite gesture. Noelle turned away again because this was Ramiro's time. He's the famous one, and people would recognize him wherever he went. She recalled her mother telling her that this is inevitable, especially the women. Noelle didn't have a problem when other guys approached Ramiro, but the women were the ones that vexed her. She had to try her best not to show any jealousy. The Zombie fan and Ramiro shook hands as the Metalhead lumbered down the street, getting back into character. Ramiro and Noelle proceeded down the block; the air had a chill with a breeze that gave Noelle goosebumps on her arms of an orange sleeveless turtleneck sweater, blue jeans, and combats she wore. On the opposite end of the spectrum, Ramiro felt hot sporting his black leather MC jacket. While he had his arms wrapped around Noelle, not only did he feel her bumpy skin, but her shivering. Without saying a word, Ramiro took off his jacket and placed it on Noelle. "Thank you," Noelle felt the warmth of her lover's body temperature within the jacket. She got a whiff of his cologne and whatever deodorant he wore. A kitty-Kat make-up, Kat suit-wearing woman, gave out candy from the plastic pumpkin bucket. "Happy Halloween!" she gave a mini Hershey candy bar to Ramiro.

"Here you go, baby," he handed the candy to Noelle.

"Thank you," Noelle unwrapped the chocolate and fed it to Ramiro. He bit off half of the candy, and then Noelle ate the other half.

"Do you want to go to the haunted house?" he chewed the chocolate.

"Alright," Noelle shook her head.

MOMENTS LATER, A LINE of people wrapped around the block, dressed in Halloween costumes waiting to experience the Haunted Manor as Ramiro and Noelle stood behind a group of teens dressed in clown outfits and make-up. A clown young man aimed his horn in the air and honked it in the air. Everyone burst into laughter. Ramiro covered his ear because of the loud honk. "What the fuck!"

"Not that loud," Noelle slapped Ramiro on the shoulder and laughed.

Security guards in black shirts, static radios, and guns from their holster on their hips eye the premises from the rooftop to the ground—a bald, ginger-beard young white man, early twenties, dressed in black who stood behind them.

"Ramiro Espinoza!" the red beard fan shook Ramiro's hand.

"That's me," Ramiro stuck his chest out again.

Noelle didn't shy away because she saw these three white females, dressed in sexy maid uniforms. Their long brunette hair draped down their backs, wearing gorgeous make-up; they seemed nice but smiled at Ramiro. Noelle exhaled and watched Ramiro interacting with his fans.

"I got plummeted in the middle of the mosh pit! Your shows are awesome!"

"Ramiro Espinoza!" another twenty-something white male, a security guard, approached from the side, recognizing the rocker off-stage. Ramiro turned to another one of his fans. The security guard shook his hand.

"What are you doing here!"

"I'm having a good time with my girlfriend like everyone else," Ramiro held Noelle's hand.

"How are you, darling?" the guard greeted Noelle. "You don't have to stand on this long line! Come on, I'll get you inside!" the haunted house security guard (fan) escorted Ramiro and Noelle.

The ginger beard fan and Ramiro shook hands.

"Thanks for listening!" Ramiro wrapped his arms around Noelle and into the haunted house they went.

Errrrr! A cutting edge sound of a chainsaw echoed in the distance as the crazed man with his eyeball falling out of its socket chased Ramiro and Noelle around the house. Noelle ran around bumping into another young lady about the same age. "Sorry!" the young lady held her hand to her chest.

"That's okay," Noelle catching her breath. Then two Zombies dressed in tuxedos lumbered towards the ladies. "Will you marry me?"

"I'm sorry. I have a boyfriend," Noelle sprung to her feet, dashing around the haunted manor with the young lady behind. More Zombies chased guests around.

WHILE OUTSIDE OF THE Greenwich Village Haunted Manor, fans surrounded Ramiro, snapping photos and taking videos with their cellphones. By him being the well-known rock bassist, Ramiro's admirers knew everything about him. They knew it was his big day as they sang "Happy Birthday" to him. Ramiro loved Halloween so much that he would forget about his birthday. And even Noelle slipped his mind while continuing to take pictures with fans. Noelle exited the haunted house. She wasn't pleased, placing her hands on her hips. Every curse word known to man crossed Noelle's mind. "What if this had been an actual situation?" Noelle watched one girl in the sexy maid outfit with her hands all over Ramiro. Noelle couldn't help but feel some way. Her heart raced in her chest as she made eye contact with Ramiro. She sucked her teeth and stormed down the street.

"It was nice meeting you guys! Thanks for listening!" Ramiro stormed away, waving to his fans.

"Happy birthday, Ramiro!" the crowd cheered.

Noelle took enormous strides along the concrete sidewalk, maneuvering around the pedestrians dressed in their Halloween costumes. "Halloween's not until tomorrow!" Noelle shouted at a man dressed up like Uncle Sam. She felt Ramiro's presence running behind her. Ramiro blocked her path.

"What's wrong with you, Noelle!"

"You left me in a Haunted house!" she pushed Ramiro out of her way and continued down the street. Ramiro turned red in the face. He trotted behind Noelle, grabbing her by the wrist.

"Ramiro, you're hurting me," Noelle wrestled out of Ramiro's grip.

"Stop acting so fuckin' dramatic! What is your problem!" Ramiro raised his voice and lowered it a bit, still gazing into her eyes.

"You left me in a Haunted house!"

"Noelle, you're not making any sense right now. It's not fuckin' real," he took a couple of steps back, staring at Noelle. Ramiro sensed that she was scared. She turned away, not saying a word. *That's the reason she doesn't like the apartment because it's eerie or maybe it's because of my tarantulas. She loves light, joy, and happiness. Noelle's musical tastes differ from mine. I'm from the darkness and she's from light.*

Opposites attract. I love Noelle for tolerating my dark ways. At least, she likes my music," Ramiro stroked her hair.

"It's your birthday. We should be celebrating. I love you," Noelle wrapped her arms around Ramiro.

LATER THAT NIGHT, A small birthday cake read, "Happy birthday, Ramiro" sat on the table. Two small paper plates with cake half-eaten with a bottle of soda and water. Burning candles brightened Ramiro's apartment, making it a little more comfortable for Noelle even though they were black. They lit up the entire living room, kitchen, corridor that led to the master bedroom. Ramiro and Noelle sat face to face on his bed, as she sang "Happy birthday to Ramiro in her most melodious voice. "Her beautiful voice always made me smile. Shit. I didn't mean to tell her that her craft wasn't music. I'm sorry," Ramiro continued to smile. He thought of his mother and sister who were probably trying to call him several times because of his special day. He hoped that his mother didn't buy him anything because he wasn't expecting anything. "Happy birthday, baby! This is your mother! If I don't see or hear from you. Enjoy your day!" Anna Maria greeted from voicemail. And as far as his bandmates, he received some calls from his management on his day. They understood he wanted to spend his day with his girlfriend. They sent birthday wishes through text messages and voice mail.

"Happy birthday, Ram! Enjoy your day! I'll check you out later!" Stanley ended his voicemail.

"Happy birthday, Ramiro! You're getting old. Enjoy!" Zack greeted from the voice message.

ON THANKSGIVING, A sparkling seven-and-a-half-foot flocked Christmas tree stood in the living's corner room already decorated.

As always, Maritza and Anna Maria decorated their home early and did that every year. They made the best of their new lives, looking forward to the future. Maritza's love life was blurry because she kept her guard up at all times with men. She'll date, but refused to allow a man to get her heart and crush it. Her two best friends, Fiona and Candace from Junior high school, who kept tight friendships over the years, spent the holidays with her and her mother. They'd bring their boyfriends with lots of presents and a gift for Maritza, which is a single guy. She didn't like her friends playing matchmaker. She'll decide when a guy is the one. Anna Maria, Maritza, and her friends sat at the table. The turkey sat in the middle of the table, ready to eat. Anna Maria was seated at the head of the table with folded hands, ready to say the blessing, but then they realized that there were two empty seats for Ramiro and Noelle.

Anna Maria slammed her hand on the table.

"Where's Ramiro?"

"Let me call him," Maritza got up from the table to get her cellphone. Then the doorbell rang.

"That's probably him!"

The front door squeaked as she opened it. "Ramiro, we've you been! Hello, Noelle! How are you?" Maritza kissed, embraced her brother and Noelle.

Ramiro and Noelle hurried into the dining room; Anna Maria stood while her son rushed into her arms. "We were about to start without you! Hello, Noelle!"

"Happy Thanksgiving, Mrs. Espinoza. How are you?"

Candace and Fiona hugged and kissed Ramiro because he's this excellent Heavy metal bassist with his long, brunette hair, built body, facial hair, and his girlfriend that came along with the territory. Candace shook her head, blinking her eyes at this African-American female. Ramiro introduced Noelle.

"This is my girlfriend, Noelle."

"Happy Thanksgiving, everyone," Noelle greeted.

Candace greeted Noelle with a smile and shook her hand. "It's nice to meet you."

"Hello, I'm Fiona. How are you? We went to school with Ramiro since junior high, and now everything is going well for him."

"Are you going to get married, Ram?" Candace asked.

Not only did Noelle catch the catty behavior, but Ramiro witnessed it as well. He wrapped his arms around her waist, escorting Noelle to the table. "What the fuck is your problem!" Ramiro insulted Candace. Fiona punched her in the arm while Maritza frowned, gesturing, slapping Candace. Then Ramiro's family took their places at the table, bowing their heads. Anna Maria gave the blessing for another holiday.

AFTER DINNER, RAMIRO held Noelle's hand, keeping her close to him. He didn't like Candace's attitude towards Noelle and on top of that, he couldn't stand the sight of Candace's pretty boy boyfriends, who probably spent more time in the mirror than they did.

"Noelle, I heard you sing and you write poetry," Maritza asked.

"Noelle sings House music, and Ramiro is a Heavy Metal bassist! Isn't that great!" Anna Maria applauded.

"We all listen to House, Noelle! That's good!" Candace shouted.

Ramiro squeezed Noelle's hand tight as his family and friends interacted with her about House music, the creators, and the DJs. They made a big deal out of Noelle's craft, making Ramiro less important.

Fiona's boyfriend, Mario, a jet-black hair, slim, well-dressed guy, mid-twenties, took part in some flirtatious chat with Noelle, "What club do you sing at?"

"The Paradise club—,"

"And she won't be singing there anymore. She'll be touring with me. Right, baby," Ramiro cut Noelle off.

Everyone became quiet, sensing that something could be going on between Ramiro and Noelle that wasn't right. Maritza reminisced about the rocky, abusive relationship her parents had when she and her brother witnessed as kids. She hoped to God that Ramiro wasn't doing anything to Noelle. History repeating itself.

By the end of the evening, Maritza's friends went home as her mother wanted to have some alone time with Ramiro. Maritza and Noelle took a drive to the store to do a little Christmas shopping. Ramiro ate a large piece of red velvet cake without making eye contact with his mother while his mother ate a slice of Lemon Meringue pie.

"What's bothering you, Ramiro?" Anna Maria asked.

"Nothing," he gulped his soda from the glass.

"Is everything going okay between you and Noelle?"

"We're perfect," he smiled.

His mother wasn't too sure about that. When an abuser says things are good in their relationship, it's the opposite. She prayed to God Ramiro wouldn't turn out like his father. Or maybe it's too late.

"Ramiro, be honest with me. Are you bullying, Noelle?" his mother touched his hand. Ramiro looked at his mother and shook his head.

Anna Maria had to be honest about her son's possibility of afflicting pain on his girlfriend, "I want you to be happy with the woman you love."

"I am happy. I love Noelle," Ramiro said.

"If you guys have any problems, there's counseling," Anna Maria removed her hand from her son's hand and continued eating.

"My mother and Maritza know that I'm probably doing shit to Noelle. Fuck! I've got to do something about this shit! Maybe a therapist would help prevent any issues in the future," Ramiro didn't touch his cake, staring at his plate.

IN A HALFWAY CROWDED shopping mall, Maritza and Noelle stormed out of Macy's with a couple of gifts in their hands. The two new friends headed into the nearby Ruby Tuesday restaurant to eat. "Holly Jolly Christmas" by Burl Ives played from the speakers while they looked over the menu. Noelle slammed it on the table.

"Maritza, we had Thanksgiving dinner!"

"It's the holidays. Eat, drink, and be merry," Maritza laughed.

"Thanksgiving doesn't even have its own space without Christmas infiltrating it," Noelle looked over the menu again.

"I know, right," Maritza peered up at Noelle from her menu, exhaled. "Noelle, I don't mean to ask you this, but are you and Ramiro having any issues?"

"No. We're happy," Noelle laughed it off.

"Are you sure?" Maritza rested her back against her seat.

"Yes. I love Ramiro. I love him very much,"

"You probably wonder where our father is. My mother divorced our father because he constantly put his hands on her and she had enough," Maritza spilled the beans, holding the menu. She gazed into Noelle's eyes. "What did he tell you, Noelle?"

"Ramiro mentioned nothing to me," Noelle took a deep breath.

"If you have any problems with Ramiro, you can call me," Maritza said.

"What makes you think that?" Noelle placed her menu down.

"I saw how he cut you off when Mario asked you about the Paradise club," Maritza flipped through the menu.

"He's not too crazy about House music," Noelle shrugged.

"That's no excuse, Noelle," Maritza said.

LATE THAT NIGHT, RAMIRO drove his black Dodge Durango from Long Island back to Manhattan on the Long Island Expressway while Noelle wallowed in the passenger's seat. She felt something vexed Ramiro; Noelle looked at him. Not once did Ramiro glanced at her. Ramiro kept his eyes on the road, not uttering a word. Noelle focused on the passenger's side window, where the Long Island landscape made her eyes heavy. Ramiro then shifted his eyes on Noelle and cleared his throat.

"It's funny how you flirt with guys right before me. And I caught you at the club dancing with another guy," Ramiro shook his head.

"Alright, Ramiro! Who is she?" Noelle slammed her hand on the dashboard.

"That she is you! You are the only one,"

"Yeah, right! You're the one who had those girls all over you at the haunted manor! And touring for six months! God only knows what you were doing!" Noelle bellowed.

"Nothing, Noelle!" Ramiro slammed his hands on the steering wheel. The Dodge Durango switched lanes, cutting off other vehicles. He slowed down because he didn't want the highway patrol to stop him.

"Are we going to be together on Christmas? Not only Christmas, my birthday?" Noelle gave Ramiro puppy dog eyes.

"What do you think?" Ramiro shifted his eyes on Noelle and the road.

"That's a yes," Noelle smiled from ear to ear.

"I've got to keep my eyes on the road here. What the fuck else does Noelle want from me? Shit!" Ramiro gave Noelle the silent treatment, swerving into the next lane.

"So, what are you going to get me?"

"I said. I'm going to tour with you. Don't you remember?"

"I remember. But still," Ramiro continued to chuckle. Ramiro stroked her thigh, but then focused his eyes on the road.

"I'll be there on your birthday," Ramiro added.

A LIVE GREEN FRASER fir Christmas tree stood at six and a half feet, with red and gold ornaments glistening with eight-hundred warm lights in Ramiro and Noelle's living room. Ramiro spent time with Noelle on her special day. For the first time, Noelle didn't spend Christmas Day with her parents. Ramiro gave her the leeway to decorate the place the way she wanted. Instead of an eerie horror/Halloween feel, Noelle added a more cheerful Christmas touch. But Ramiro preferred the weird sense of Christmas, something like "A Christmas Carol." Noelle refused to do so because it was her birthday as well. She didn't want any darkness on her day. She wanted to be happy on this holiday, which was the twenty-fifth of December and her birthday. Ramiro knew how to get Noelle's mind off the creepy things that vexed her. Since it was just the two of them, Noelle cooked something for him. A small turkey breast roasted in the oven, Broccoli Rabe, white rice, stuffing, candied yams, and toasted rolls. Holiday dishware with candle lights adorned the table for the two of them. With a small carved bird and only five dishes, they enjoyed their holiday together. Ramiro stuffed a slice of turkey in his mouth, grunting like a pig.

"Slow down, Ramiro," Noelle spoke with her mouth full.

"This is good," he complimented, chewing the dry white meat. He swallowed his food, sipping wine from a tall glass and clearing his throat. "Yes, babe. I love your cooking".

"Thank you," Noelle ate rice from her fork.

Ramiro glared at his future wife for a second. "I wonder if Noelle will give it up tonight. She probably won't because it's sacrilegious. I'll see if I can get her legs open and hopefully forget that it's Christmas and just another day. But, of course, Noelle will remember her birthday," he ate.

LATER, A SMALL RED velvet cheesecake with two and one numeral-shaped candles for her age, twenty-one, glistened as Ramiro presented before her. He kissed her on the cheek. "Happy birthday, babe," he continued to kiss her.

"Thank you, Ramiro! That's so sweet," she blew out the candles.

"Not as sweet as you, Noelle," Ramiro gazed with seductive eyes. He then engaged in a passionate kiss, inching his hand up her red sweater, unfastening the strap of her bra. Ramiro got Noelle in the mood. For a second, she forgot it was Christmas and even her birthday. She snapped out of it, blinking, and pushed Ramiro away.

"I can't do this, Ramiro," she took sharp breaths.

Ramiro held his head down, turning fiery red in the face. His heart pounded in his chest. He exhales, raises his head, kissing her on the forehead. The bulged in his crotch decreased because of the blood flow. "Alright, I respect that. At twelve o one tonight, you're mine!"

"Yes, babe. I'm yours," Noelle kisses him on the lips.

TWELVE O FOUR MIDNIGHT, the twenty-sixth of December, Noelle laid on her back in the long leather chair while Ramiro stroked his love upon her. No man forgets about laying it on his girlfriend. He loved seeing and hearing Noelle gaze into his eyes, moaning while being in their world. Her thighs wrapped around his waist—sweat balls surfacing on their nude bodies giving a shimmery tone. And for fuckin' sure, Ramiro would bend Noelle like a pretzel while on tour.

CHAPTER SIXTEEN

A roaring crowd of Irate fans packed the Felt Forum at Madison Square Garden that held approximately over five thousand people. Successfully, the band sold out tickets within two days. The clamoring audience reverberated all the way upstairs to the dressing rooms, where Zack tapped his drumsticks on his legs. He sported his shorts and the group's logo on a tank shirt. Danny tightened the strings of his guitar to make sure he got the proper sound. Ramiro sat on the wooden bench, clutching Noelle in his arms. His bass guitar in the other. Noelle quit her job at the Paradise club to tour with Ramiro around the world. After the band finishes the rounds in the United States, they'll be traveling overseas.

Noelle always wanted to go to Paris, and that's where Irate would be playing. Ramiro tried to see if he could do something romantic for her while their time in France would be short. *"London, Paris, Milan, Copenhagen, Stockholm, and other European cities that I dreamt of as a kid, and it's happening with the man I love,"* Noelle rubbed the back of her hand against Ramiro's cheek. She laid a kiss upon it and rested her head on his shoulder. She listened to his heartbeat, saying that Ramiro loved her, and they would spend their lives together. *"I believe Ramiro loves me, and I love him. I would love to live in a house with an enormous backyard where our kids can play. I'd cook dinner in the kitchen while Ramiro relaxed in the recliner of his man cave, watching television,"* she envisioned her future with this metal bassist. Then Stanley clapped his hands, alerting Ramiro and his bandmates that it was showtime. Noelle snapped out of her fantasy, springing from her lover's grip to her feet. Ramiro grabbed his bass guitar and acted accordingly. He led his way out of the dressing room and dashed up three flights of concrete steps with Danny and Zack trailing him. Noelle couldn't keep up with Ramiro, who bolted like lightning. Ramiro must've forgotten to kiss her. He wasn't thinking about Noelle now. Ramiro had to get his ass on stage and give the fans his all. She trotted up the flights of stairs along with Stanley, Douglas, and the management team behind.

"I'll Kill You If I Have To!" Ramiro's voice echoed on the microphone throughout the arena. His voice sounded something out of a horror film. His malevolent tone frightened Noelle for a moment. Her heart pounded in her chest. The Tama drum kit trembled the stage with its bass drum, snares, and the cymbals' splashes. Ramiro and Danny collaborated on their guitars along with the foundation of the song. Noelle rushed to the side stage, where she saw Ramiro blaring into the microphone. Some song about taking someone's life if given the reason. Noelle noticed thousands of fans screaming their heads off, colliding in the mosh pit. The pit started in the middle of the audience and worked its way to the front row. She smiled, seeing the people admiring Ramiro, screaming his name, and enjoying the show. As the girlfriend of a musician, Noelle felt like a love-struck female fan.

"Everyone Sees Death!" Ramiro bellowed to the audience. The fans crashed into each other in the mosh pit as they helped each other up to their feet and continued the disorderly dance. Noelle eyed Ramiro's hair, draping down the middle of his back. He performed on stage in his regular clothes: his black jeans, sleeveless skull t-shirt, and construction boots.

She held bottled water and a towel in her hands. She knew Ramiro got hot from performing under those stage lights. They gave off heat like the sun in mid-July in which would give anyone a migraine. Ramiro wrote a song, "Migraine" because he suffered from the pain since he was little. He held his father accountable for his headaches. Ramiro's pain came from all of the screaming and yelling, shoving and pushing, slaps and punches his father afflicted on his family. Just thinking about it at times, gave Ramiro a headache. Surprisingly, Zack's drumming didn't bother him because it was their music that was an escape for him. Zack played his drum solo; the fans went berserk. Ramiro rushed backstage, kissing Noelle upon the lips as sweat trickled down his face. She patted the salty moisture dry with a towel that dripped from his sideburns. Noelle held the towel on the side of his face to soak up the sweat.

"Drink up, babe!" she offered him the water.

Ramiro opened it and gulped the H2O down while the plastic bottle deflated.

"You got more!" he threw the plastic bottle to the floor.

"Ramiro! Don't do that! More water!" Noelle glanced over her shoulder. Douglas gave the water to Noelle.

"Here, baby!" Noelle shouted over the loud drumming. Again, Ramiro opened the top, gulping down the water. She reached for the plastic container before he tossed it to the floor. "I'll take that!"

Then they engaged in a passionate kiss; he tried pressing his body close to Noelle's but had no luck because his bass guitar hung at his pelvis.

"Your bass is coming between us!" Noelle smiled.

"She's jealous right now," he cackled.

"You need to tell her, I'm your one and only," Noelle snickered. Ramiro laid a kiss upon her cheek, scurrying on stage.

"Dark Romance!" Ramiro's voice echoed on the microphone throughout the concert arena. The audience clamored with applause and held the sign of the horns in the air. Some fans ran around in the mosh pit in a circular motion. It looked like a whirlpool in the middle of the ocean.

"A candlelight dinner on a cloudy night, a bouquet of black roses in the center of the table, tarantulas crawling on the walls, a python slithers on the floor and the table. You screamed your head off in terror at the creepy crawlers; you're in my presence, you're mine, you're at my mercy," Ramiro sang into the microphone. Noelle bopped her head to the music's rhythm. She lifted an eyebrow at the lyrics he recited. She planned on looking up the song lyrics because it seemed abusive towards a woman.

"Is Ramiro talking about me? I know he probably wrote the song because he wanted to dominate the woman who was a part of his life. Holy crap! Maybe, I made a mistake by touring with him," Noelle's hands trembled. Ramiro headbanged to the music. *Does he love me?* She wanted to dash back to the trailer and cry her eyes out. Noelle couldn't let Stanley see her watery eyes, but the tears still rolled down her cheeks. She quickly strutted down the steps and headed to the ladies room. Hopefully, no one was in there to hear her cry. *"Is Ramiro going to do something terrible to me?"* Noelle entered the stall, locking it.

The fear and anxiety overwhelmed her mind, body, and soul. *"What am I going to do? I love Ramiro. I heard about abusive relationships that escalate from pushes to slaps to punches, etc. Maritza told me her father beat her mother severely, where there were visible scars. Maritza feared that Ramiro and I might have a copycat relationship,"* she wiped her eyes, took a deep breath. Noelle heard Ramiro bellowing on the microphone again as the crowd whooped. *"I better get backstage before Ramiro has a fit if I'm not there,"* she opened the stall, grabbed a tissue, wiping her eyes, exiting the ladies' room.

AFTER THE FELT FORUM show, Ramiro, Noelle, bandmates, and management hopped aboard the RV. Ramiro lounged in the recliner as always, but Noelle tried to avoid him as she breezed by him.

He grabbed her wrist, glaring. "Where do you think you're going? Sit here, Noelle," she obeyed Ramiro's command. Noelle sat on the end of the leather couch next to the recliner. He stared and stared, not uttering a word. Tired from a long show, Ramiro needed as much rest as possible. The RV engine started up, pulling out of the parking lot. The band's next destination was the concert arena in Sayreville, New Jersey. They would be there in no time. While Ramiro continued to glare at Noelle, she could tell something vexed him. She attempted to ask him but avoided the question.

"Where were you?" Ramiro kept the grip on Noelle's wrist.

"I went to the bathroom," she replied.

"Okay. Are you feeling alright?" he glared deep into Noelle's eyes.

"I'm fine," she turned away from him. Ramiro grabbed her chin towards him. He kissed her on the lips, releasing his grip from her wrist. He slipped his hands under her t-shirt and wanted to pound Noelle on the recliner. But he didn't want anyone seeing Noelle's voluptuous breasts, juicy thighs, and other parts of her body and hearing her moans that were for his ears only. He wanted their privacy.

So, he pulled his hands from under her t-shirt and kissed her on the forehead. He lounged in the recliner and closed his eyes. Noelle strutted over to the bunk area and climbed into hers which was right above Ramiro's. He made sure to keep his love close to him. He didn't bother to see what Noelle was doing. The smooth ride of the tour bus put Ramiro to sleep fast. Irate's tour bus zoomed along the FDR drive and into the brightly lit Holland tunnel.

DURING THE LATE-NIGHT hours, the band's tour bus pulled into a parking space in the back of a Jersey concert arena with its rumbling engine. The driver then shut the motor of the RV down.

Its doors swung open as Stanley and Douglas exited the bus, meeting the arena's managers. Silence overwhelmed the bus as soon as the motor turned off. Ramiro sensed the bus still and extremely quiet. He could hear his managers bullshitting outside. He squirmed in his recliner, squinting his eyes. Usually, he would sleep in his bunk with Noelle but he didn't bother. Then the night alternated into the early morning, where the sun peeked from the horizon and birds chirped. Danny and Zack clamored in the recreation room with "Light my Fire" by The Doors playing from the bus's rear. Noelle waltzed by the recliner, fully dressed as Ramiro grabbed her by the wrist again.

"Where are you going, Noelle?" he tightened his grip.

"Ramiro, I'm your secretary, remember?" she wrestled her wrist from Ramiro's grip.

"I almost forgot," Ramiro squinted his eyes.

"I've got to get to work," Noelle stormed away.

Ramiro widened his eyes, sitting upright in his chair and noticing the RV parked at their destination. He stood up stretching and yawning. He marched out of the trailer. For some strange reason, his heart pounded in his chest, balling his hands into fists and turning fiery red. Noelle told Ramiro where she was going to be. So why the anger? Ramiro must've felt some insecurity whenever she interacted with others? Or was it because he wanted Noelle right by his side? In the distance, Ramiro saw Noelle and his management team gathered in a circle with the owners of the arena chatting. And of course, Ramiro was the topic of conversation. He released his fists, slowing down his rapid heartbeat as the fiery red coloring in his face turned to normal. *"Was I going to put my hands on Noelle more in the future? As for the present, it's too late. I already have! What the fuck! I can't control my fuckin' self! I don't want to be like my father! She's discussing her secretarial duties with Stanley and Doug,"* he thought as he got closer and closer to his team. Noelle smiled at him.

"Baby, we were talking about you," Noelle wrapped her arms around Ramiro. He reciprocated the affection as he kissed her on the forehead.

"How are you doing?" Ramiro sleepy-eyed.

"I'm good. Check out the stage, okay," Stanley placed his hand on Ramiro's shoulder.

MINUTES LATER, RAMIRO stood center stage, glaring at the empty seats that will be filled with admiring fans. The roadies assembled Zack's drum kit, amplifiers, testing guitars, and other duties in the background. Ramiro focused his eyes front and center, feeling gentle arms wrap around his waist with a whisper in his ear. He leaned over his shoulder while Noelle greeted him with a kiss.

"Anticipating your show?" she whispered.

"Yeah," he replied.

In the background, Zack swaggered towards his drum kit, noticing Ramiro and Noelle in one another's arms. Zack remembered Ramiro and Kim being an item in high school. But Ramiro said he didn't care if they didn't work out. Kim threw herself on Zack. His mother saw this fast girl sitting with her legs spread apart on the stool with the imprints of her nipples during the band's garage rehearsals. They almost lost their friendship over this girl, and if bad blood remained between them, there would be no Irate. Noelle came up with the band's name because she knew Ramiro's life was full of shit. His father was a Jesus freak. There are Jesus freaks out in the world, but some are extremists to the point of no return. And now, Ramiro's lead singer/bassist of this band and has got the most beautiful girl in the world. Zack recalls Noelle strutting down the hallway in high school. He didn't have the guts to approach her because of the fear of rejection. Ramiro dared to pursue Noelle, making her an important part of his life. The Thrash Metal bassist and House Songstress embraced and kissed passionately. Zack stared as if he were watching a love story in the making. Perhaps a dark one with Ramiro's fucked-up life. Zack wondered if Noelle knew about Ramiro's life. She has to or maybe she knows something or nothing at all. Douglas crept up behind Zack.

"Zack, what are you doing?" his manager focused his eyes on Zack and then on Ramiro and Noelle kissing.

"Nothing," Zack blinked his eyes.

"Those two seemed to be happy. They've got my blessing. Come and test your drum kit out," Douglas clapped his hands. After hearing his manager give his blessing to Ramiro and Noelle's happiness, Zack turned blazing red. He darted to his Tama kit, drumming wildly like "Animal" from the Muppets trying to annoy the loving couple.

"What the fuck!" Ramiro shouted while holding Noelle closer to him.

He could tell that his so-called best friend/bandmate showed him no respect and kept on playing.

"Let's get out of here," he grabbed Noelle's hand, leaving the stage.

ABOUT AN HOUR LATER, Zack stepped out of the rear of the concert arena for a smoke. He puffed circles of the smoke into the air. He wished he could create different shapes and designs with the smoke that he released from his mouth. The almost empty parking lot had two trucks that held the band's instruments, equipment, etc. Irate's trailer stood further in the lot's distance. He wondered if the two lovebirds were in the RV. He took the last puff of his cigarette, mashing it with his foot on the concrete. Zack gazed at the windows of the band's trailer. As he got closer and closer, Zack heard moaning. A devilish smile surfaced on his face. He crept alongside the trailer, ducking to make sure no one would see him. The feminine moans turned Zack on, causing a rush of blood and tissue that gave him a bulge in his pants. The rear window of the trailer had a crack in it. Zack cautiously rose his head up to the window, seeing live porn before his eyes. Ramiro had Noelle's legs over his shoulders as he gave her loving strokes. Their naked bodies engaged in every position imaginable to man and acted as if the trailer belonged to them. Zack noticed Noelle's juicy thighs wrapped around this lead singer/bassist's waist. Noelle became Zack's new fantasy, plus he didn't even have a steady girlfriend.

"Shit!" Zack murmured. Ramiro stopped, looking over his shoulder towards the rear window. He stopped, slipping on his boxers. He dashed to the window, seeing Zack scurrying away.

"Fuck!" Ramiro bellowed.

Noelle covered her breasts with a t-shirt.

THAT NIGHT, A CHANTING crowd filled the concert arena from top to bottom, anticipating an electrifying show. Irate fans prepared for the mosh pit in the middle of the audience. The admirers wore Irate t-shirts while accompanied by friends, meeting new friends and lovers in the crowd. A young couple kissed as they waited for the show to begin. On the balcony, fans pounded their fists on the railing. "Irate! Irate! Irate!"

Backstage security guarded the band's dressing room while inside, with more security. Ramiro leaned against the wall with his bass guitar, eyeing Zack. Instead of this bassist thinking about putting on a great show, Zack preoccupied his mind. He knew Zack eavesdropped on him and Noelle in the trailer. He glared at Zack, putting on his sneakers and not making eye contact. The height of the tension between these two musicians could set off a bomb. Danny's eyes shifted back and forth between his fellow bandmates, feeling the pressure. Stanley didn't sense any tension in the air; they focused on getting the band on stage. Douglas checked on the band members to make sure everything ran smoothly.

"Are you feeling okay, Ramiro?" Douglas patted Ramiro on the shoulder. He noticed his client aiming his vision in the other direction. "Are you feeling okay?"

"I'm cool," Ramiro shrugged and stormed away with his bass guitar. Noelle gave chase right behind him, and she continually glanced over her shoulders. Douglas followed this time. He didn't bother to stop Ramiro from going on stage. Hopefully, the owner doesn't bitch about this hot-headed rock star doing whatever the fuck. Ramiro swung the door opened and trotted down a couple of steps through a long dark corridor, which led backstage. He didn't give two shits about starting his show before it was time. Noelle held a grip on his t-shirt while heading to the stage. "Baby, when I hear the crowd shouting, that's when it's time to start!" Ramiro raised his voice as fans' cheers drowned out his voice.

"Yes, baby! Do your thing!" she encouraged and got every word Ramiro uttered to her, despite the bellowing audience. They lip-locked.

The fans went wild when Ramiro rushed on the stage. He stepped to the microphone.

"How the fuck are you fuckheads tonight!"

The fans' cheers elevated as if someone turned it up on the radio. They held the "Sign of the Horns" gesture in the air. Ramiro shifted his eyes from left to right, not seeing Danny heaving with his electric guitar to the stage. He avoided looking back at the drum platform, sensing that Zack wasn't there. He turned around to the crowd, who cheered like crazy. The admiration rushed through his body like fresh oxygen flowing through his lungs. He tweaked a couple of strings of his bass as the audience went wild. Ramiro leaned his head back, knowing the spotlight had his name on it, similar to a Star on the Hollywood Walk of Fame. He played "Everyone Sees Death" as the crowd hooted. Noelle stood on the sidelines, cheering Ramiro on as if she were in the audience. His management stepped backstage while this bassist entertained his fans with his bass solo of the band's popular song. The talented bassist played and played, holding down the fort. In his mind, the fans were his; he wrote most of the lyrics, produce the tunes, did most of the interviews, etc.

MEANWHILE, BACKSTAGE Noelle watched the one-person show along with his bandmates and management. Zack inched behind Noelle, close to her ear. She glanced over her shoulder, recognizing her boyfriend's best friend/bandmate. Zack released his breath on her neck. Noelle inched away from him as he moved closer. "Do you love Ramiro?"

"What kind of question is that?" Noelle sneered at him. She didn't turn around to face him.

"Answer the question, Noelle?"

"Yes, I do," she turned to him. "Where is this coming from?"

"Zack, get your ass up there!" Stanley shouted. Zack dashed on his drum kit platform and collaborated his instrument with the bass. Then Danny scrambled with his electric guitar in his hand and jammed with his bandmates. From there, the trio performed songs from the "Don't F*** Wit Me album to the tracks from the "For Fuck's Sake's" album. Ramiro kept spewing his disturbing lyrics into the microphone. The songs didn't bother Noelle this time. She hoped that none of the songs Ramiro bellowed didn't become a reality.

A FEW DAYS LATER, RAMIRO'S bass solo reverberated during his performance at the House of Blues in Boston, Massachusetts. The spotlight beamed on him while he played his bass guitar, headbanging with his long brunette hair flowing in the air. Fans went wild with applause, cheers, whistles, and lit cigarette lighters as they glistened like Christmas lights trimmed on the tree. His bandmates allowed this lead singer/bassist to shine. Of course, he'd be the center of attention, but Ramiro worked hard at his craft. He heaved his bass guitar from the moment he received it as a gift from his grandmother on Christmas morning. Yes, his mother and sister pitched in, but Ramiro gives more credit to his Abuela (grandmother). He thought of her every step of the way while he toured the world. The spotlight shined upon Ramiro, feeling a heavenly glow as a reminder she kept watching him. He knew why he sensed those pearly gates because of Abuela, even though he didn't believe in God.

CHEERING FROM THE SIDELINES, Noelle witnessed Ramiro showing off his bass techniques. Also, Danny, Stanley, and their management team cheered this talented player as well. "Alright, baby!" Noelle applauded. She seized her clapping as someone blew in her ear. She turned and noticed Zack grinning from ear to ear.

"What are you doing?" she asked.

"I'm not doing anything," he took a couple of steps back.

Noelle turned around and focused her attention on Ramiro's performance on stage. "Are you sure you love Ramiro?" Zack questioned in her ear. Noelle didn't bother to turn around, ignoring him. He could see she continued to root for Ramiro.

"You know about his abusive home life?" he whispered again.

"What!" she folded her arms.

"His father used to beat up his mother all the time," he dished the dirt on his best friend's family.

"I heard about the situation. Ramiro's not his father," she turned around.

Stanley placed his hand on Zack's shoulder, alerting him to get back on stage. Zack leaped on his drum kit platform with his drumsticks and played a mean drum solo with the bass solo battling for domination. The two instruments sounded like music at first but transformed into a bunch of noise. Then Danny dashed on stage with his electric guitar and joined the battle of the instruments. All three musicians got their tools in tune with one another.

"Polluted Politics!" Ramiro bellowed on the microphone as the fans roared.

"Get the fuck in that Mosh pit!" he demanded.

Irate performed the song "Polluted Politics" as the middle of the audience bounced in a circular motion to the beat's rhythms.

A FEW DAYS LATER, DARKNESS loomed as fog swept on a stage while Ramiro played his bass with a spotlight on him at a concert hall in Chicago. The concert hall held over three thousand people that sold out within a day. As usual, Noelle and Irate's management stood backstage watching Ramiro.

"Aren't you curious, Noelle?" Zack rose his voice in her ear. She didn't turn around and listened to the details of her lover's tragic childhood. Noelle's attention shifted from Ramiro's bass performance to a movie pictured in her mind of Ramiro and Maritza fleeing from their home in the middle of the night in their pajamas. Their mother's screams echoed throughout the neighborhood. She envisioned eight-year-old Ramiro dashing down the block with Maritza ahead of him. These two children were in distress, beating on a neighbor's door, trembling in fear. Neil thrust the front door open, seeing these two helpless kids at his door. He rushed the kids into his home. When the police came to confront the situation, Ramiro's mother refused to press charges.

Noelle turned to Zack, snapping out of the frightening ordeal.

"I heard enough," she pushed him away.

A COUPLE OF NIGHTS later, Irate played on an enormous stage at a concert venue in the Motor City that held about four thousand metalheads. Ramiro sweated out a performance of his bass solo. Fans cheered at his entertainment. Due to his electrifying presentation, he felt that his mouth was dry and inhaled mucus through his nostrils, releasing yellow saliva on the stage. The crowd went crazy, witnessing their hero "not giving a fuck" about the consequences. Backstage, Noelle's eyes widened seeing Ramiro show such disrespect. She hoped that he didn't get a fine or be reprimanded. Meanwhile, Zack wouldn't let up, continuing in Noelle's ear about her lover's past life. But Ramiro's loud bass playing drowned out Zack's voice and then the tales went in and out. So, Noelle only got bits and pieces of the story.

THE THRASH METAL BAND toured American big cities and small towns from the East to West coast. At every show, Irate thrilled devotees who came near and far to hear Ramiro's well-known bass sound, popular aggressive tunes, and mosh. Still, Zack exposed his best friend's ill-treated youth to Noelle's ear. She pictured Ramiro's father severely disciplining Ramiro and his sister as babies. She closed her eyes as she fought back tears.

"I'm going to have to tell Ramiro what's going on. If I do, Zack can deny it. And I don't want to bring up any terrible memories. Maybe, I should just keep my mouth shut," she envisioned Ramiro's father severely spanking him over something so petty. *"He was probably younger than eight years old."* She stormed away from Zack, moving to the other side of the stage. She wanted to avoid disturbing stories.

CHAPTER SEVENTEEN

During a two-month break, Irate remained in a Northern California rental home in which they shared. The big house had lots of spacious rooms, a swimming pool, and a large patio. Danny and his girlfriend, Kate, who he met in a bar in Sausalito a couple of days earlier, made noise all night long. Danny made weird noises and told stupid jokes that made little sense while she cackled like a Hyena. She had the most annoying laugh that pierced your eardrum. That night, Ramiro and Noelle had a master bedroom with a king-sized canopy bed, walk-in closet, dresser, and private bathroom. Almost every night, Ramiro couldn't get any shut-eye because of this strange woman. He tossed and turned, noticing Noelle couldn't sleep as well. He came face to face with her.

"You can't sleep either?" Ramiro rubbed Noelle's cheek.

"No," she whispered.

Then a high, piercing laugh echoed throughout the entire house. Noelle's body jerked when she heard it.

"That's fuckin it!" he threw the covers off himself, hopping out of bed, storming out of the bedroom. He stomped down the dark hallway in his boxers with nightlights on the wall. Kate's snickering proceeded while Ramiro pounded on the door. Danny swung it open, "What the fuck, dude!"

"What the fuck do you mean? Keep it the fuck down!" Ramiro waved his fists in the air. Kate only wore only panties with her jiggling exposed breasts. She cracked a smile at Ramiro.

"Put a muzzle on that dog!" Ramiro stomped away to his bedroom. Kate gasped.

"What the fuck crawled up your ass! Fuck you!" Danny slammed the door.

A breeze blew down the hallway as Ramiro headed back to his master bedroom. It intensified, blowing through his long brunette hair as he shut the door behind him. He noticed the sheer drapes flowing lightly because of the gust of wind. Noelle left her body imprint in the king-sized bed where she slept. The covers draped alongside the bed towards the foot. Ramiro noticed the double balcony door open. He crept on it with the views of the Golden Gate Bridge, Downtown San Francisco, and the San Francisco Bay right in front of him.

"Ramiro!" a gentle feminine voice called.

Noelle stretched on the lounge chair in her red rose, long, silk lingerie gown with her eyes closed. Ramiro lounged in a patio chair right next to her. He grabbed Noelle's hand and kissed it.

"What made you come out here, baby!" he rubbed her hair.

"I can't sleep when other people make a lot of noise," she replied.

"Hopefully, those two will go to sleep," Ramiro said.

"And then we'll go to sleep," Noelle smiled.

"Or maybe we'll stay up until sunrise," Ramiro kissed her on the lips. He clutched her hand and wouldn't let go. *I want to ask her to marry me, but I'm not sure of it yet. I guess I'll wait!*

Ramiro smiled at Noelle. She could tell that he had something on his mind and wanted to get it off his chest, but he hesitated.

"What's bothering you, Ramiro?"

"Nothing. I'm cool," he eyed the Golden Gate Bridge.

"It's so beautiful here. I would love for you and I to live here," she smiled at Ramiro.

"Holy shit! It's like she read my mind! I'm working on getting a house for us somewhere. Maybe, here in the Bay Area or New York.

Maybe we can have two homes?" he didn't bother to ask further questions. The horn tooted on the Bay Area ferry while it graced the body of water, sailing away. He glared at Noelle while she shut her eyes.

"Hey," Ramiro gently shook her hand.

"Yes, honey!"

"There's a music festival in mission Dolores Park tomorrow. Do you want to go?" Ramiro asked.

"What do you think my answer is going to be?" Noelle mumbled.

"Yes?" Ramiro laughed, kissing her on the lips. "I hope she'd say yes if I proposed. I can't worry about that now," he said in his mind. On a third-floor home balcony, Zack peered over the railing, eavesdropping on Ramiro and Noelle's conversation. He's still fully dressed from head to toe in the middle of the night. Zack paced the concrete balcony, frowning at his so-called best friend's happiness. He puffed on a cigarette, throwing the nicotine stick on the patio, mashing it with his sneaker.

"Mother fucker!" he murmured. Zack stormed into the house, sliding the glass patio door.

THE NEXT MORNING, RAMIRO, Zack, and Stanley browsed at the different shops in a shopping mall as a Zales jewelry store advertised in big letters with its glistening jewels drew Ramiro's eyes. "I want to go in here," he swaggered towards the establishment. "Why the fuck is he going in there? Ah, shit! Don't tell me it's not what I think it is!" Zack and Stanley followed. A jeweler presented some engagement rings to Ramiro a few moments later. Stanley leaned over his shoulder and patted him on the back. "Are you going to propose to Noelle?"

"Yeah," Ramiro checked out the rings.

"That's great, man! That's beautiful!" Stanley shook his hand.

Then some blue Tanzanite birthstone jewels glistened in the glass case on the other side that grabbed Ramiro's eyes. He swaggered to it, seeing nothing but an ocean of blue. He thought of Noelle's birthday, which was Christmas day. *"Maybe it'll be cool to slip the ring on her finger on that day. But I don't want to waste any time. I'm going to do it as soon as possible,"* he then set his eyes on the obscure jewels in the glass case across from him. Onyx jewelry drew Ramiro with rings, necklaces, bracelets, etc. He disregarded Noelle's birthstone, indulged in his immoral, irreligious ways. Ramiro's face hovered over the glass case as the dark engagement rings drew him like a ghost haunting a person sleeping. Two black mattes finished wedding rings with skeletal imagery enchanted him. A black Onyx rectangular stone fourteen karat gold ring would be suitable for Noelle. A large heart-shaped Onyx stone diamond cut eighteen karat gold ring seduced him like the first time he made love to Noelle.

Zack peered over Ramiro's shoulder, noticing the murky engagement ring. "You're wasting your time," Zack murmured and stormed away.

"What the fuck!" Ramiro was wide-eyed because of his best friend's remark. He saw Zack dashing out of the shop.

"What happened, Ramiro!" Stanley wondered.

"Nothing," Ramiro focused his attention on the jeweler. "Can I see the heart-shaped Onyx eighteen karat ring?"

The jeweler presented it to Ramiro as he held the fancy ring on his finger. "I think this will fit Noelle's finger. She's got skinny ones!"

"Make sure it's the right size, Ramiro? You never know," his manager advised.

"How much?" Ramiro eyed the jeweler.

"Six-thousand, seven-hundred," the jeweler smiled.

Ramiro pulled his Discover credit card from his wallet. He still used the credit card that he got in college and used it during his career. He handed it to the sales associate. The jeweler swiped Ramiro's credit card as the machine beeped and then the machine read: declined.

"I'm sorry, sir. Your transaction failed," the sales associate shook his head.

"What! What do you mean? Try it again!" Ramiro insisted.

The sales associate slid the credit card through the machine again. Stanley stood over his client's shoulder. Ramiro's eyes widened. *"Holy shit! Please let my card go through. If not, I'm fucked!"* then there was another beep from the credit card machine.

"Declined, I'm sorry, sir, "the jeweler gave Ramiro his Discover card. He glared at the sales associate for a second.

"What the fuck!" Ramiro pounded both fists on the glass counter of jewels, shattering the entire case. Glass fragments scattered all over the floor. Customers were frightened and astonished at the sudden outburst from this long-haired rocker who left a trail of his blood as he rushed out of the establishment.

"Ramiro! Don't worry, sir! I'll pay for the damages!" Stanley gave the sales associate his MasterCard from his wallet. The sales associate's boss rushed over.

"What the hell!" the jewelry manager smacked himself in the head. "What am I supposed to tell my boss?"

"I'll pay for the damages. Sincerely I apologize for my client's behavior and I'll purchase the ring as well," Stanley reassured the manager. "Fuck!" he held his head down in shame.

THAT NIGHT, A JAZZ trumpeter blared his horn in collaboration with the pianist, bassist, and drummer of his band. A mature crowd of spectators watched the entertainment at a music festival at Dolores Park. On the other side, a younger gathering of people danced to the thumping bass of House Music blasting through enormous speakers. In the distance, a rock band jammed out on an outdoor stage with a massive audience taking part in a mosh pit. The two guitarists, a bassist, and a drummer played cover songs from Jimi Hendrix to Slipknot. Ramiro clutched Noelle's hand, guiding her towards the enormous lawn where the rock band played. She noticed his bandaged hands. She asked him what happened and he told her a half-ass story. He told her that he cut his hands on a window at the mall. She glared at Ramiro because she could tell something wasn't right about his story. At the amateur rock show, they stood in the back so they wouldn't be in anyone's way. Ramiro leaned against a large tree watching the rockers play "Creeping Death" by Metallica. Noelle saw that he enjoyed the show and related to these guys who shared the same lifestyle. She looked at the singer on stage, who resembled Ramiro. Noelle leaned on his shoulder, clutching his hand once again glaring at the dry bloody bandages. He kissed her on the forehead, knowing he had her support.

LATER, BACKSTAGE, RAMIRO guided Noelle by the hand towards the amateur rockers while groupies flocked to them as if they were professionals. He released his grip from Noelle's hand and extended it to the band's vocalist. "What's up, dude!"

"Holy shit! Ramiro Espinoza!" the amateur lead singer/guitarist smiled. He rushed to Ramiro and shook his hand as the rest of the bandmates did as well.

"I attended your first show in San Jose, Ram!" the drummer patted him on the back.

Ramiro and this local band spoke about music, the rocker lifestyle, Irate's international tour in a couple of weeks. "This is my girlfriend, Noelle?"

"How are you?" the lead singer and the rest of the band greeted with a nod.

"Hello," she waved.

The amateur band, who were supposed to act like professional musicians, acted like crazed fans because of Ramiro's professional musicianship. They worshiped him like a god and ignored the female admirers who came to see them. Noelle took a couple of steps behind Ramiro, hearing the loud thumping bass line of House music playing across the way. She saw dancers on the lawn getting their groove on. A Dj stood on a platform, getting the crowd dancing. Noelle focused her attention back on Ramiro, chatting with these musicians in deep conversation. They discussed the subject matters that he wrote, bass lines, and subgenres of Heavy Metal.

MINUTES LATER, THE synthesizing keyboards drew Noelle like a spirit lurking in the shadows. She weaved in and out of people to get to the crowd. The bass line got louder as she moved closer to the dancers. She didn't bother to glance over her shoulder to see if Ramiro was behind. Then a masculine arm wrapped around her waist as she leaned her head on him and caught a whiff of nicotine. She abruptly turned as her jaw dropped. "What are you doing here?"

"Why are you wandering around alone, Noelle?" Zack took the last puff of his cigarette, throwing it to the ground and mashing it with his sneaker.

"Zack?" her eyes widened.

"In the flesh! Where's Ramiro?" he blew smoke into the air.

"He's back there somewhere," she bellowed.

"It's a shame he's not tolerant of you being a singer. You love House Music, and he should support you. That's very narrow-minded of him," Zack lit up another cigarette, blowing smoke into the air.

"Maybe, Zack isn't such a pain in the neck after all. He seems to be down to earth. I can't get Ramiro to listen to my music," Noelle thought.

She took a step away from Zack as he moved closer. While he kept yapping at the mouth about Ramiro, he continued to move closer. Noelle stepped away, looking around because she wanted to scream. But she kept her cool. Zack realized that their space showed to him she wanted him to leave her alone. He always had eyes for Noelle, but his best friend beat him to the punch. He stepped closer to Noelle again, and he wouldn't allow her to move from his sight. And she did that, Noelle inched away from her boyfriend's best friend, cracking a smile now and then.

"Why do you keep moving away from me, Noelle? I will not bite," he kept moving towards her even more.

"Ramiro will be here in a minute," Noelle cowered as Zack wrapped his arms around her waist.

"Zack, please. Don't do that."

"I see the way you look at me. I know you could tell the way I look at you. So, let's stop fuckin' around," Zack kissed her on the neck. Noelle pushed Zack away as she marched away from him. She got a taste of unwanted touching and comments from this drummer. For God's sake, Zack was her boyfriend's best friend who he's known for years. And she sure in hell didn't want to be caught between Ramiro, Zack, and their careers. *Ramiro's going to be on touring internationally in two months, and I don't want to screw things up for him. Let me keep walking and find Ramiro. I hope Zack's not following me. I will not look back to see,* her heart raced in her chest. Noelle noticed Ramiro heading straight towards her. She had to compose herself and slow down her racing heart because Ramiro will sense something's up.

"Hey, baby! I was listening to the music," she inhaled, wrapping her arms around Ramiro's waist. They kissed on the lips.

"I hope you weren't dancing with any other guys," Ramiro clenched his teeth.

"I only dance with you!" Noelle swayed to the music.

"You know I don't dance," Ramiro kissed Noelle.

"Missing You" Remix by Larry Heard blasted from the speakers. Noelle swung her hips around her lover, who didn't dig this musical genre. She attempted to pull Ramiro into the crowd of dancers as they played tug of war, pulling him in and out of the group. And of course, Ramiro won, pressing his body close to her and laying a kiss on Noelle. Kiss after kiss, hug after hug, and lovemaking repeatedly at this moment if he had the chance, but right now, Ramiro guided Noelle by the hand to an empty bench where there was a small gathering of people.

"Baby, sit!" Ramiro commanded.

His assorted thoughts about his parent's marriage boggled in his head. Ramiro couldn't utter any words without getting mixed up with events that occurred. He wanted no contradictions in his story so that Noelle would believe him. Ramiro had to do this if he wanted her to be at the altar when they exchange their vows. Noelle saw Ramiro's puzzled expression and wasn't sure what he was going to say.

"Noelle, I didn't get into detail about my life. It wasn't peaches and cream. But I want to make our life peaches and cream," Ramiro had a flashback.

AT THE KITCHEN TABLE on a late autumn Sunday evening, five-year-old Ramiro, six-year-old Maritza, their parents Anna Maria and Jorge bowed their heads, giving the blessing.

"Heavenly Father, we would like to thank you for this food, for the nourishment of our bodies, for good health, and many blessings. Amen," Jorge crossed himself. Anna Maria did the sign of the cross, and so did the kids. Ramiro stuck his fork into the slice of chicken on his plate, shoving it in his mouth. He smacked his food, making a noise. His father glared at him because of the disruptive sound.

"Ramiro! Chew with your mouth closed!" his father pounded his fist on the table, which shook and got the family's attention. Jorge's thick, ashy fingers created a monstrous hand when he balled it up. Ramiro held the chewed pieces of chicken in his mouth, afraid to eat because he might pound his fist again. The kindergartener cautiously chewed and picked up his veggies with a fork with ease. Anna Maria and Maritza ate quietly, where you could hear a pin drop. Ramiro placed the veggies in his mouth and gulped it down. He then released an enormous burp that he couldn't help. Ramiro covered his mouth, afraid to glare up at his father. He peered up, seeing the evil in his father's eye. Jorge towered over Ramiro's body like the monster that gave kids nightmares. Then his father's grotesque fist punched in the middle of Ramiro's plate.

"What the hell! You little pig! That's disgusting!" Jorge threw Ramiro's plate, flipping the entire table over with dinner plates of food scattered on the floor. Anna Maria and Maritza huddled in fear. Ramiro cringed in the kitchen chair, flinching as his father took off his belt. Jorge grabbed his son's small framed body. Ramiro wrestled his way out of his father's arms.

"Let me go!" Ramiro pleaded, continuing to get away from this creature from the unknown.

"I'm going to show you some respect!" his father struck Ramiro with the first lash of his belt. Ramiro screamed at the top of his lungs and then made it his business not to get that second lash. He kicked his father.

"Oh, Christ!" Jorge hopped on one leg in agony. "Bring yourself over here!"

Ramiro dashed up the staircase, his father right on his tail. Before Ramiro could get to his bedroom, Jorge grabbed him by the collar. He threw Ramiro to the floor as he backed away from his father. Anna Maria attempted to stop her husband from hurting this small-framed child who weighed only eighty pounds. Maritza plugged her fingers in her ears to prevent her from hearing the nightmare that was her family's reality.

"Stop!" Maritza bellowed with tears flowing down her cheeks.

While Anna Maria struggled to get Jorge off her son, she received a backhand slap causing her to plummet to the wooden floor. Anna Maria lay on there in tears while Jorge hovered over her body. She saw this menacing giant who once was a loving soul who charged at her like a bull. Jorge hauled Anna Maria across the floor by her long brunette hair, picking her body and slapping her across the face. She flew across the living room, almost hitting her head on the coffee table.

RAMIRO BLINKED HIS eyes and came back to reality. He didn't want to give any more details about what his father did next. He fought his tears as best he could and looked at Noelle. He hoped she didn't think less of him or wonder about his behavior towards her in the future. Noelle gently wiped a tear that streamed down his face with her finger.

"You still got me," Noelle said.

Ramiro kneeled before Noelle and presented the ring box. Her heart raced in her chest and she couldn't believe what occurred before her eyes. "Is this what I think it is?"

He opened the ring box, presenting the heart-shaped Onyx stone diamond cut eighteen karat gold ring.

"I know this may be sudden, but I want you to be my wife," Ramiro slipped the ring on her finger.

Noelle teary-eyed wrapped her arms around Ramiro. They kissed as if they were actually at the altar. Ramiro and Noelle didn't know whether to have a big or a small wedding. Most likely, he would want to go to city hall to tie the knot or something else that's small. Noelle, like most women, wanted more of a traditional Wedding Saturday in

June or July with family, friends, and food to celebrate their new lives together. From behind a tree, Zack puffed on a cigarette, eyeing the couple like a spy gathering information. He took the last puff of the nicotine stick, mashing the light on it with his foot, and crept off into the night.

CHAPTER EIGHTEEN

Two months later, boisterous fans packed the Manchester Arena in England as they signaled the "Sign Of The Horns" in the air along with their cellphones snapping photos and videos of the show. The stage darkened with blue lighting beamed on the drum set platform with the band's tarantula logo. The crowd pumped their hands in the air, demanding for this concert to be worth their while. "Irate! Irate! Irate!" Suddenly, the venue darkened, then a drum solo played as a spotlight beamed on Ramiro's front and center, playing his bass guitar. The band's devotees applauded, whistled, flicked cigarette lights, and continued to use their cellphones to capture a glimpse of the event.

Ramiro headbanged with his bass, giving fans the best of him. He had more showmanship than his other bandmates and indirectly threw it up in their faces, especially Zack. Ramiro knew of his best friend/bandmate glaring at Noelle, he knew of Zack spying on them in the middle of their heated passion. If Ramiro didn't sense Zack eavesdropping, he would've watched until they reached their climaxes. And he also knew of Zack listening to their conversations. Danny strummed his electric lead guitar, making his way to Ramiro's side. They played their guitar fiercely and headbanged with their hair flowing all over. The trio played the instrumental of "Six Feet Under." At this moment, Ramiro wasn't up to singing, so their instruments sang. A mosh pit circulated with fans joining in the rowdy dance to the unruly music. Ramiro maneuvered with his bass guitar to the drum platform. He played wildly and eyeing Zack.

"You think I'm stupid! I know you saw me fucking Noelle!" Ramiro played his bass.

"What the fuck are you talking about!" Zack kept drumming.

"I saw you when Noelle and I were in the trailer! You ass!" Ramiro bellowed.

"You're imagining things!" Zack's drumming alternated from the beat of the song they performed to a bunch of noise.

"And you've been eavesdropping whatever we talk about!" Ramiro turned red in the face.

"Yeah, you're cursing her out. You're prone to put your hands on her too!" Zack insulted.

Ramiro removed his bass guitar from around his shoulder, leaping on Zack, knocking him off his drum set platform. They crashed to the floor.

"Ramiro!" Noelle screamed in shock. Stanley, Douglas, and their management rushed towards the two men, pulling them apart.

Some audience members witnessed the scene from the front rows and the big screen. Their jaws dropped, noticing the lead singer and drummer going toe to toe. But they couldn't see because the rest of the fight occurred backstage. Other fans in the mosh pit stopped bouncing around and noticed something was wrong.

The two musicians hurled punches at each other while their management attempted to break up the fight.

"Ramiro! What the fuck are you doing!" Stanley pulled Ramiro off Zack.

"You fuckin' asshole!" Ramiro touched his face to see if he was bleeding. No blood.

Stanley pulled Ramiro to the side, giving him a tongue lashing. Noelle crept to Ramiro's side and gently touched his shoulder. He flinched, realizing it was Noelle's touch. He wrapped his arms around her.

"Ramiro, your t-shirt ripped! You can't go on stage like that!" she bellowed.

"Yes, I can. I don't have to look flashy for anyone," he kissed Noelle. Ramiro headed back to that stage like the born musician he was and knew his role.

"Get back on those drums, Zack!" Stanley waved his fist in the air.

Zack drummed, "Six Feet Under."

"Struck over the head with a metal bat, your body collapses to the floor for dead. But, the air you breathe from your lungs after the plunge. The shit you put me through for being individual, I could never appease you. God hates me, and so do you. As his messenger, you made my life a living hell," Ramiro sang with aggression in his voice. He aimed his anger at Zack because he's acting like an asshole. As Ramiro proceeded with his performance, he and Danny stood by each other playing their guitars. The fans took part in the mosh pit, while others went back to enjoying the concert. Ramiro had to put on a show for his fans, his music, not a fight. Luckily, the physical altercation didn't disappoint fans. After Ramiro concluded the song, he engaged with his audience.

"How are you fuckers doing tonight! I would like to apologize for the bullshit that you witnessed. But we're here to fuckin' bang our heads off! Am I fuckin' right!"

The crowd cheered in response.

"Everyone Sees Death!" Ramiro announced as the fans roared. He quickly turned to Zack and gave him the finger. Zack returned the favor, drummed "Everyone Sees Death." Ramiro spewed lyrics, trying to focus his mind on other things besides the meaning of the content. Instead, he pictured Noelle and himself exchanging their vows at the altar or breaking off their engagement because of outside interference. Zack stuck his fuckin' nose where it didn't belong. He doesn't have a girlfriend, nor did he bother to bring a girl along with him. Stanley kept watching over Ramiro and Zack. He shook his head in disappointment and couldn't figure out the problem with these guys. But Noelle knew. She had the info on Zack exposing Ramiro's personal life. The green-eyed monster played drums for the most popular band in the world. She leaned against the wall backstage, where four groupies stood directly behind the drum kit platform. These females had an interest in Zack, so what's the problem? All the sex he wanted, drinking and partying like a rock star. But he wanted more than just all-night orgies.

"Why the hell was he so fixed on Ramiro and Noelle's relationship? Because they had a musical connection, even though Ramiro wasn't crazy about her type of music. Her beautiful singing captured him. And it sure grabbed Zack's attention as well. While he drummed on his Tama kit, he could see her from the corner of his eye. Noelle juggled the bottled water in her hands as a lemony-tress, rocker chick, mid-twenties, wearing a short black skirt, cut-off Irate band t-shirt, fishnet stockings, and high-heeled boots glanced at her leaning against the wall. The blond, rocker groupie whispered to the other girls as they glanced at Noelle. Noelle felt these loose women watching her as she continued to ignore them. She applauded and cheered on her lover. The blond rocker girl strutted towards her, grabbing Noelle's name tag. "Noelle?" she sneered.

"Yes, and who are you?" Noelle's eyes widened.

"It's not important of who I am. Do you work for the band?" the rocker chick threw Noelle's name tag.

"Yeah. I'm the band's secretary and Ramiro Espinoza's fiance," she flashed her engagement ring.

"That's very nice and all. But you're not the only woman he fantasizes about," this groupie chick exposed her breasts, licking her lips. A security guard hauled her away from Noelle.

"Are you alright, Noelle?" Stanley patted her on the shoulder.

"I'm fine," she shook her head.

"What a whore! She probably came to give it up to Ramiro, Zack, and Danny. I don't have time for this bull crap from these tramps who have to throw themselves on men. The American tour went fine, but I'm getting deeper into Ramiro's lifestyle. I see the dirt," she focused back on Ramiro's performance.

After the concert, backstage, Irate, fans with passes, took pictures with Ramiro, Zack, and Danny while Noelle stood in the background, watching the entire thing take place. A forty-something, short-haired, fine-lined face female admirer, grabbed Ramiro's waist, trying to kiss him on the lips. But before this old-looking groupie could do so, he pushed her away "What the fuck are you doing!"

"You fuckin' pussy! You're a weak bastard!" the forty-something groupie stormed away.

"Groupie troll!" Douglas insulted.

Then a porcelain-skinned, jet-black, straight hair groupie lifted her t-shirt, exposing her breasts with her almost white nipples. "You would love to suck these!"

Noelle turned away, quick and shocked at this crazed woman.

"I'm sorry, fans. I've got to go! Stanley, let's go. I want to get the fuck out of here!" Ramiro wrapped his arms around Noelle.

Zack loved the groupies hugging him, but a pink-colored, slender female fan, late-teens, wrapped her legs around his waist and constantly kissing him.

"Take me with you, Zack!" Please!"

"I wish I could. I can't!" he tried to pull away from the young woman who had a good grip on him.

"Zack, let's go! Holy shit!" Stanley rushed over, seeing that Zack couldn't get away from this adorning fan.

"Take me, Zack! Take me, Zack! Take me on tour! I'll be your Thrash Metal whore!" the pink-colored hair fan breathed in his ear. She still wouldn't let go of Zack.

"Stanley, get her off me! Holy fuck!" Zack desperately wrestled out of the woman's arms. Douglas, the management team, and at least eight security guards struggled to free Zack. The bubble-gum-colored- haired fan who loved Zack, it took an army, the navy, and the marines to free him.

TWO NIGHTS LATER, AT the Resort World, fans screamed their heads off as Ramiro performed his bass solo. Noelle, Stanley, and the management team watched him entertain the crowd as he usual-ly did. Zack and Danny stood backstage, eyeing Ramiro to light up the stage with darkness surrounding the glowing spotlight on him. As the performance proceeded, Noelle glanced over her shoulder to see if Zack was going to sneak up and whisper nonsense in her ear. She kept her mind focused on Ramiro and forgot about the drama that occurred in Manchester. Noelle closed her eyes and indulged in Ramiro's playing. He always struck his cords with low tones, which she loved because it reminded her of House music with lots of bass touches. *"One day, I'm going to make Ramiro respect my creativity. He never listened to what I do. Ramiro's stuck in his ways. I'm his girl-friend. Oh, I almost forgot. I'm his fiancé, so he needs to respect me,"* Noelle shook her head.

ON THE TOUR BUS, NOELLE sang on a high note while she danced to House music that blared from the speakers. The band's management loved this young lady's fantastic voice. Ramiro resided in the lounge chair as his face turned fiery red. He placed his head down in his hand. He peeked up, seeing that Danny enjoyed Noelle's singing. He and Zack haven't spoken for almost a week and avoided each other. Ramiro didn't want this tour to fuck up, so he kept his cool. He didn't like Noelle showing off. With her voice, she could charm the pants off any man. That certainly worked on Ramiro. He eased his way from the living room area while she proceeded with her one-woman show. He didn't bother to glance back to see if Noelle noticed that he was gone. He swaggered towards the back, pulling the curtain that separated the bunk area from the bus's front. Ramiro expected Zack to come through to hear Noelle sing. Nope. No sign of Zack. *Does he hear this angelic voice echoing through the RV?* Right now, Ramiro believed this drummer was low-key and had a plan. Whatever his plan, Ramiro hoped to beat him to the chase. For now, he had to keep a close eye on his future wife. He glared at Noelle from the bunk area to the living room where she proceeded to sing.

"Noelle's angelic voice is a magnet. There's a part of me who believes she's faithful and then another side tells that she could be another Kim. I never saw Noelle look at Zack, she doesn't say Hello to him. I worry too fuckin' much. I should be worried about our show in London tomorrow night," he disregarded his negative thoughts and smirked. He pictured Noelle's songstress performance in his mind. She concluded her song with a high note as the tour bus erupted into applause from everyone.

"Ramiro, you've got a real winner here," Stanley clapped. He looked around, noticing that Ramiro was nowhere to be found.

"She's good," Danny whistled. "Where the fuck is Ramiro?"

Stanley marched towards the back of the RV. He snatched the curtains back, noticing Ramiro leaning against the bunk beds.

"Ramiro, why aren't you up there! Noelle's great!" his manager patted him on the back.

"Yeah, Noelle's something else alright," Ramiro snickered, holding his head down, concealing the hellish red in his face.

"Ramiro! Baby, where were you," Noelle rushed into Ramiro's arms. He embraced her, playing it off. Ramiro bitched about migraines from the last show. The love of his life offered to get him some aspirin, but he rejected the idea. When Stanley went back up front, Ramiro wanted to let Noelle have it. Instead, he allowed the pain in the middle of his head to throb. He got used to it and tolerated the misery in his temple until it subsided.

A FEW HOURS LATER, Big Ben stood elevated in the heart of London for all to see; the pigeons flew around in search of food as they did every day. That day, Ramiro and Noelle had some time to spend alone, so they strolled through Saint James Park. The landscape had a Central Park feel to it, but it was London. The sun beamed in the sky with a cool breeze that caused the hairs to stand up on anyone's skin. Noelle wore the latest long-sleeve Irate t-shirt for their international tour with the dates, jeans, and sneakers. Underneath the top, she still shivered. Ramiro sported his black denim, a black skull t-shirt, sneakers, and leather jacket. Noelle didn't realize that it would be so cold. Her teeth chattered as the goosebumps on her neck surfaced. She crossed her arms around her body as she shivered from the UK temperature.

"Put this on, babe," Ramiro placed his jacket on Noelle. He side-eyed Noelle as she felt snug in his heavy leather jacket. Of course, Ramiro didn't want her freezing her ass off even though he was salty about her putting on a show.

"Thanks," she clutched Ramiro's hand as he gave a smile and then focused his eyes in the other direction. Her face dropped because she could tell something vexed him. "Was it something I did? Should I ask him? Or maybe I'll leave him alone because Ramiro's under some stress from this tour. I'll allow him to talk to me about it when he's ready," she rubbed his arm. They stopped at the bridge, seeing Big Ben with its clock made of roman numbers, British time.

"Ramiro, what's wrong?" she caressed his hand.

"What's wrong? I'll tell you what's wrong? What's up with the singing for everyone!"

"Singing! What's wrong with that?" Noelle trembled.

"There's no need to do anything. Just sit pretty," he glared at Noelle.

"Why, Ramiro!" Noelle stomped her foot on the ground. Ramiro turned away without responding. "Where is this coming from, baby? Okay, you don't like my style of music. Fine. Do you want me to sing Thrash Metal?"

"Fuck no! Don't think about or even fuckin' attempt to step into my territory!" he elevated his voice.

"Am I embarrassing you?" she shouted.

"Fuck, no! You have a beautiful voice," he looked her in the eye.

"Beautiful voice? But you want to shut me down!" she scoffed.

"Focus on your shit later!" Ramiro threw his hands up in the air.

"My shit! Do you want me here?" Noelle clenched her teeth.

"Yes!" he shouted.

"I'm going home," Noelle stormed away. Ramiro turned fiery red, balling his hands into fists, and followed Noelle. He blocked her path.

"Where are you going, Noelle?" he restrained Noelle's wrists.

"Home!" she attempted to wrestle from Ramiro's grip. No luck. Ramiro didn't want his fiance leaving him in the middle of his tour.

"Your home is with me. You're not going anywhere," he pushed Noelle. She stumbled, but she stood correctly on her feet.

"Stop, Ramiro!" she stormed in the other direction. Ramiro grabbed her by the arm, pinning her body close to him. "You fuckin' said, yes! You're going to be my wife? Yes?"

"No!" her yelling echoed throughout the park. Then she released an ear-piercing scream that grabbed everyone's parkgoer's attention. A man walking his dog, a woman jogging, and other park-goers witnessed the friction between the couple. Ramiro noticed all eyes were on him and Noelle. *Holy shit! I've got to calm the fuck down before I land my ass in the London slammer!*

"Don't scream!" Ramiro crept towards Noelle.

"Don't come any closer and I will," she backed away as Ramiro extended his hands to her.

"Don't fuckin' scream, Noelle," Ramiro grabbed her. Again, she released another ear-piercing bellow.

"Come here. I'm sorry," he wrapped his arms around her. Tears flowed from her eyes with fire in them.

"What's wrong with you!" she sobbed.

"Are you going to be my wife?"

She glared at him with no response. "What do you think? Do you want me to be your wife?"

"I do," Ramiro leaned his head close to Noelle's while she wept. He grabbed Noelle by the hand, guiding her away. "Let's go!"

Noelle snatched her hand from Ramiro while they walked side by side.

"Mosh!" a spiky green-haired Irate fan leaped in with other fans, crashing into one another that night. Ramiro, Danny, and Zack played the song "Sickness Of The Mind." The band's music had the entire venue vibrating and quivering because of the dominant sound. Noelle stood backstage along with the management team. She didn't seem too happy at this point. She watched Ramiro played his bass guitar wildly and headbanged. Noelle wanted to jump for joy seeing him perform, but she was upset. She tossed the bottled water in her hands to give to her future husband so he could quench his thirst. Noelle's body trembled while goosebumps surfaced on her bare arms from wearing the Irate short-sleeved t-shirt. She dreaded the cold that overwhelmed her body, plus being upset with Ramiro. She never discussed Ramiro's childhood, the abuse that his father projected on him, Maritza, and his mother. All she could think about was herself for now. Noelle wanted to storm to the trailer and be alone. Then she thought, maybe she should do that because that'll show him. If he wants Noelle to be his wife, start supporting her as she supports him.

That's what a relationship is about spousal support. But, in some relationships or marriages, it's one way or no way at all.

"I'm out of here!" she slammed the bottled water down on the table and stormed away. She had to get back at Ramiro and maybe he'll change his ways. In reality, Noelle knew she couldn't change this man. *Is there any way to make Ramiro act right? I hope things don't get worse or deadly. There are horror stories of abusive relationships where someone got seriously hurt or worse. I hope to God not,*" she took long strides, getting closer to the RV. She strolled past security guards and noticed groupie girls who died to bang Ramiro or Zack or someone. I'm going to have to face reality. Ramiro could easily fall into the arms of another woman," her vision blurred because of her eyes watering as tears cascaded down her cheeks. She swung open the door of the trailer. Creeping up the RV steps, she looked around and hoped no one was around. Noelle pulled the lever, closing the door. She navigated through the living, dining, and kitchen area, and through the long corridor where the bunk beds laid on each side, and to the recreation room in the rear—no one in sight. Noelle looked around, not knowing if she wanted to sit in the back and cry her eyes out or go in the bathroom. Ramiro's lounge chair sat upfront, so she made her way to the front. She felt as if the piece of furniture was a therapist that counseled her on all of her pain. The leather recliner certainly did that for Ramiro because he sat in it constantly. The chair understood whatever he experienced in his past and present life. So, Noelle plopped her body into the cushiony chair, hoping it would understand her pain as well. Noelle's tears flowed down her cheeks like a running faucet. She kept wiping every teardrop with her hands. A box of Kleenex sat on the side table; Noelle snatched a piece to dry her eyes. She didn't give a damn about throwing every soaked, balled-up paper on the floor. Noelle didn't bother to clean it until she got out her feelings. Then Noelle grabbed the last sheet of tissue, wiping her last tear.

"How does a person talk to a chair? It's not a person who you can confine in. But you can't trust people in your situation. I can't go to my parents, telling them about Ramiro's aggression and past life. They'll never forgive him. My parents are very fond of him and so am I," Noelle stopped thinking. Ramiro's voice echoed throughout the arena. *"Maybe, I better go backstage because Ramiro will have a shit fit. Whatever, I'm comfortable in the recliner and not moving my rear end. I deserve a break. I worked my ass off for Ramiro and his band. I answer phones, make travel arrangements, get his coffee, cook for him and his band, and of course, give him sex whenever he wants it. Well, I'm in here. I might as well do some work so that Ramiro won't get suspicious,"* Noelle played her House music from the radio. She kept the volume down, just in case. Noelle opened the laptop, scrolling through the business files. She had to get some work done to be early. Noelle then noticed the file for Ramiro's bass solo. She smiled, hearing the deep throbbing of the four-stringed electric bass. As great as Ramiro played, Noelle believed with his talent that he could branch out into other musical genres. She grabbed a USB portal, inserting it into the laptop. Noelle dragged and dropped Ramiro's bass file into the icon of the USB. The music file was downloaded, and Noelle snatched the flash drive from the computer. She sashayed to her bunk, dropped the small device in her handbag.

MEANWHILE, ON STAGE, Ramiro and his bandmates concluded, "Sickness Of The Mind."

"Are you guys ready for a fierce drum solo!" Ramiro bellowed into the microphone. Zack struck the tom-toms, working his foot pedals for the floor bass drums and splashing the cymbals with his drumsticks. Ramiro didn't make eye contact with Zack because he still had it in for him. Ramiro rushed backstage, looking around as Stanley gave Ramiro the bottled water.

"Where's Noelle?" he took his bass guitar off his body. He wanted to patch things up. But, since Noelle wasn't around, his heart pounded heavily in his chest as his eyes enlarged. Stanley shrugged his shoulders. Ramiro handed his instrument to the sound technician. He swaggered down a corridor while roadies minded the equipment along with the management team and some groupies expecting a meet and greet with one musician. A ginger-tressed, thin-framed young woman, early twenties, grabbed his arm. "Hey! Ramiro, it's you!" she blocked his path as he tried to move. This Auburn-head groupie prevented this sexy rocker from getting away. "How about you and I getting more acquainted after the show?" she pressed her body close to Ramiro.

"Excuse me, I have a fiancé," he nuzzled her to the side.

"Don't you believe in open marriages? Asshole!" the red-tress groupie stormed away.

BACK ON THE TOUR BUS, Noelle sat back down in front of the laptop and shut it off. She then blared House music throughout the RV from the stereo. She envisioned a club of dancers grooving as she sang, dressed in a fabulous gown. In reality, Noelle swung her hips towards the rear of the RV, having a ball. Outside, Ramiro stomped towards the tour bus, hearing the deep bass vibrating. "Noelle!" he opened the RV's front door, rushing up the steps. He cut off the music.

"Why the fuck aren't you by my fuckin' side!" he charged at Noelle.

"Oh my God!" Noelle trembled as Ramiro grabbed her, shaking her like a rag doll. "Why aren't you backstage! Fuck! What are you doing in here!" he wanted to strangle the shit out of Noelle. He threw Noelle down on the sofa. Ramiro scrambled to her bunk, gathering her garments and shoving them into a duffel bag.

"Ramiro, what are you doing!" she tried to prevent Ramiro from packing her belongings.

"You can't make up your fuckin' mind! Noelle, you don't know what the fuck you want!" he continued to gather her things, shoving them into the duffel bag.

"I know what I want!"

"What do you want!"

"I want you!" tears flowed from her eyes.

"Bull fuckin' shit! Go home! Work on your House music and fuck the shit out of Jeremy!" The couple's argument attracted the attention of everyone in the parking lot.

"Shit! You're wasting my fuckin' time!" he opened the entrance door of the bus. He threw out her duffel bag and purse.

"Okay, Ramiro! Stop!" Noelle stomped her foot on the floor.

"Get out!" he stood at the entrance, waiting for Noelle to obey his command. Noelle trembled, exiting the bus and sobbing profusely. The fans chanted Ramiro's name. Stanley dashed through the parking lot, waving his fist in the air.

"Ramiro, what the fuck are you doing! The fans are going nuts!" he noticed Noelle leaning against the bus in tears. Stanley saw luggage with Noelle's things scattered on the ground. "What are these clothes doing all over the place?"

"Noelle's fired! I've got a show to do!" he swaggered back on stage.

Stanley whispered in her ear, giving her encouragement. Noelle wondered if Ramiro's manager was aware of his client's behavior. Noelle choked back her tears as she and Stanley gathered up her garments off of the concrete.

CHAPTER NINETEEN

Four-thousand, five hundred fans filled the Dome De Paris concert arena in France that night. Irate performed the song "Hell On Earth" as Ramiro bellowed the lyrics. As he sang for his audience, Noelle was surely on his mind. "I'm sorry that I had to toss Noelle's shit off the bus the way I did. But she disrespected me. She might have fucked up this tour for me. And she's getting under my fuckin' skin nowadays," he eyed the mosh pit. For a second, he realized his actions were like his father's. But he made up excuses and erased the notion from his head, concluding the song.

"Are you fuckin' enjoying yourselves, Paris!" he addressed the metalhead admirers moments later as they cheered. His heart raced in his chest, angry with Noelle and Zack for different reasons. Fans snapped shots from their camera phones and took video footage of this long-tressed, Metal god on stage cradling his bass guitar. Zack stood up from the drum kit, giving Ramiro the finger. The fans gasped as Ramiro turned to the drum platform, knowing Zack did something stupid. The audience captured Zack's fuckery on their devices. He swirled on his drum stool, drinking his bottled water and avoiding eye contact. Noelle witnessed Zack give her fiancé the finger as she sneered at him. Ramiro faced the fans, giving his undivided attention. "Are you ready to get your head bashed the fuck in!" The fans cheered. "For Fuck, Sakes!" his voice reverberated on the microphone.

Zack kept eyeing Noelle, hoping to make eye contact. And so she did; Zack blew a kiss at Noelle with a sinister smile. He played the fast, aggressive bass beat for the tune. She rolled her eyes, focusing her attention on Ramiro. As she kept Ramiro within her vision, Noelle's mind drifted off. *"I hope this doesn't turn into a love triangle. I'm just going to remain calm and try to keep my distance from him. I don't remember seeing Zack in high school. I was so busy studying and all. I only recall a few people from my junior year and senior. Anyway, I'm here for Ramiro, and Zack needs to find someone else. All these women backstage are dying to be with him,"* she looked at dozens of provocatively dressed young women lined up to get their turn to sleep with Zack. Anyway, Noelle and the band's management align backstage, cheering for the band. Noelle blocked out the argument that she and Ramiro had. She didn't want any tears nor to talk to someone about it. That was her and Ramiro's business, but Stanley witnessed the argument and might confront the situation. By Stanley managing Irate, anyone would assume that he only thought about his pockets.

Noelle hoped Ramiro's pockets benefited. Well, of course, he's the vocalist/bassist of this thrash metal band of the Millennium. During the drum solo, Ramiro swaggered backstage as Noelle wiped every drop of sweat from his face, gave him bottled water, and a kiss. He whispered in her ear, telling her "That he loved her," and returned a kiss upon her cheek. Ramiro put the argument that he and Noelle had behind him and wanted to move forward. He twisted off the cap, gulping down the water, and released an enormous burp. He always knew how to make Noelle laugh. She watched Ramiro swagger back to the stage, gesturing "The Sign of the Horns" in the air as the audience cheered. Noelle loved seeing him interact with his fans; it made her super proud. The fans held up "The Sign Of The Horns" in return. They did it because it was the popular thing to do, even though they didn't believe in the evildoer. Noelle knew about the motion representing Lucifer that influenced people to do. She did none of that stuff. Some people would call her a square because she doesn't live on the edge. Noelle's engaged to a heavy metal bassist. That's edgy enough.

THAT NIGHT, THE EIFFEL Tower lit up the night sky like a giant diamond ring on a woman's finger through the large picture window of a French hotel suite. Noelle's engagement ring glistened similar to the French structure that's known throughout the world. She and Ramiro tossed in the king-sized bed as her thighs wrapped tight around his waist with lots of thrusting, panting, and balls of sweat dripping down their nude bodies. *"So, after a long show, Ramiro wanted to fuck. What man doesn't? We're in the most romantic place in the world. Why didn't we have a candlelight dinner? What the hell am I complaining about? At least, Ramiro put a ring on it,"* she rolled on top of Ramiro, straddling him as they achieved their climaxes.

MINUTES LATER, RAMIRO popped the cap off a beer bottle from the kitchen. He guzzled down the sizzling alcoholic beverage. He released an enormous burp, shutting the refrigerator in the suite's kitchen. "Noelle, do you want something?"

"Candy!" she hollered from the bedroom suite.

"I gave you candy already!" Ramiro grabbed his pelvis and laughed.

"I want M&M's!" she hollered from the master bedroom.

He grabbed two packs of chocolate candies and bottled water from the snack bar, heading to the bedroom.

Noelle sat up in the bed with her breast covered. Ramiro placed his beer on the nightstand, giving her the water and candy. She opened the M&Ms and devoured them.

" Shit, honey! Why the fuck are you still hungry?"

"Yes. I'm dying for a chicken salad," she gobbled the candy.

"*Is she expecting? I know if she were, she'd tell me,*" Ramiro frowned.

AN HOUR LATER, A HOTEL server rolled a food cart with two plates, a bottled wine, two glasses, and a single fresh bloomed rose in a small vase down the hotel's hallway to Ramiro's suite. The server knocked on the door. "Room service!" he spoke English with his heavy French accent. Ramiro widened the door, moving out of the way, so the server could wheel in the food. Noelle was seated in the dining room as the server lifted the silver lid from her plate with a Chicken salad. Then he removed the next lid from Ramiro's plate with a rib-eye steak with French fries and broccoli. He poured some French wine in two tall glasses. Ramiro tipped the waiter twenty dollars as he smiled and left the suite. Ramiro slammed the door, noticing Noelle devouring her salad. She wasn't paying him any attention. The only thing that mattered was her food. Noelle carved a piece of Ramiro's steak with a knife, stuffing it in her mouth. Then she devoured some French fries.

"Noelle's pregnant for sure!" he watched Noelle stuff her face.

SUNLIGHT PEEKED IN and out of the cloudy sky the next morning as Irate's tour bus engine rumbled. Danny, Zack, and their management shuffled on it with the luxurious French hotel in the distance. The band spent a couple of nights in the hotel because they had such a gap between shows. Plus, the RV got too crowded for everyone to be on top of each other. Their management didn't want them to stress out and wanted them to relax before their next destination. Stanley stood by the entrance of the bus, constantly checking his watch. "Where the hell is Ramiro?"

Then Ramiro and Noelle exited the hotel, holding hands. They took their time and weren't in a hurry to get back on that bus.

"Ramiro! Let's go!" Stanley clapped his hands.

"We've got plenty of time! Stop!" Ramiro still took his time approaching the tour bus. Next to the hotel was a French florist with beautiful, vibrant flowers. He stopped, noticing the gorgeous bouquet of red roses. He gave Noelle one rose stem, kissing her on the lips.

"Ramiro! Come on!" Stanley shouted.

"Hold your fuckin' horses! Shit!" Ramiro responded. The French florist approached, speaking with his accent. Ramiro handed him a few dollars for the flower. Ramiro wrapped his arms around Noelle's waist as they made their way to the bus.

A FEW NIGHTS LATER, at a chapel-like concert venue in Florence, Italy, Ramiro played his bass guitar on the murky stage with the spotlight on him. His fans held up "The Sign Of The Horns" gesture. He worked his fingers along the neck of his bass, aggressively shaking his head at the music. Sweat never gave Ramiro a break; balls of the salty water from his body emerged from his hair, making it greasy. His fans saw this metal god's wet spotty t-shirt from the audience while the sweat made his skin glisten. He spilled his guts at every performance, making people happy. *'I hope Ramiro doesn't overdo it. My God. Ramiro's drenched,'* Noelle glanced up at the wobbling spotlight above the stage.

"Ramiro!" fans hollered. They noticed the stage light above their hero's head.

"Ramiro! Holy shit!" Stanley cried out to him.

Zack kept drumming, noticing the unsteady light as well. He kept playing the song and hoped someone would draw Ramiro's attention to the light in the ceiling.

"Ramiro!" Noelle screamed.

Then the floodlight swung on its cord. Danny pushed Ramiro out of the way as the spotlight crashed on the stage.

"What the fuck!" Ramiro plummeted to the wooden stage.

Zack then continued to switch his drumming from the song to wild drumming. He didn't care at this point. He snickered as he witnessed Ramiro flat on his ass. Stanley waved his hand to get Zack to stop playing.

"Are you alright! You would've been a goner!" Danny stood to his feet while extending his hand to Ramiro. The light shattered in the middle of the stage with glass all over. Luckily, the fixture didn't explode into flames as roadies rushed into action. The stage lights remained lit, giving fans hope that the show will continue.

"I've got a fuckin' show!" Ramiro bitched.

"Are you ok?" Noelle felt Ramiro's heart racing as she embraced him. His bass guitar still strapped around him; it didn't come between them.

"Honey, I'm fine! I'm fine, everyone! We've got a show to do, Stanley!" Ramiro rose his horn-hand gesture in the air as fans copied him.

"Ramiro! Ramiro!" the fans chanted. His management left the stage, so this bassist could get on with the show. Danny took a couple of steps, allowing him to have the limelight. Ramiro communicated as loud as he could to his fans without a microphone. A roadie grabbed the microphone, placing it in front of him. "I'm alright everybody!" his voice echoed throughout the arena.

"Are you alright, Ramiro?" a concerned fan shouted.

"I'm cool! Let's get this fuckin' show on the road! Get the fuck back in that mosh pit!" he hollered. Fans went berserk, bounced around, and crashing into one another.

"For Fuck's, Sakes!" Ramiro cursed. Zack stroked the tom-toms drums with his drumsticks and moving the foot pedals on the floor bass drum. Ramiro and Danny collaborated their guitars in the foundation of the song. They engaged fans with their guitars, battling it out instrumental- wise. Ramiro took the piece to a whole other level, which sounded different. It was still the same song, but fresh tunes were added. From "Fuck Sakes" to Migraine, to Klown, the band's favorite metal tunes captivated rockers.

TWO DAYS LATER, IRATE played at an arena in Rome, Italy, where thousands of energized fans engaged in an enormous mosh pit. Night after night, European city after city, Madrid, Munich, Berlin, Athens, Warsaw, Poland, Brussels, Belgium, and Scandinavia.

Three weeks later, in Copenhagen, Denmark, a tinted-windowed tour bus pulled into a parking space in the rear of a concert venue. The light-sounding engine kept running as the entrance door swung open. Stanley stepped off first, looking around and up at the enormous arena. He acted as if this was something new to him, but he had a job to do. Danny stepped off the RV, stretching his arms in the air. "Damn, we're in Denmark already?"

"Yes, we're in the capital," Stanley replied.

On the tour bus bunk beds, Ramiro had his drapes pulled back with his eyes closed. He seemed peaceful in his slumber, which was in the middle. Noelle's bunk was above Ramiro's bed; she heard low chattering and the maneuvering of Irate's management team exiting the bus. She sat up in her bed, climbing down, and drew back Ramiro's bunk drape, noticing he was still asleep. "Baby," she called his name in a gentle tone.

He widened his eyes as Noelle stood right before him. He then rubbed them to clear up his sight. He blinked to a clear vision of the love of his life. He laid bare-chested with his muscular build, so-so of a belly, and 3D tarantula tattoo in plain sight. Touring indeed caused

Ramiro to stuff his face, even though Noelle ate more than he did. Noelle caressed her fingers along his chest and his nipples.

"What's so funny?" Ramiro glared.

"I don't know," Noelle shrugged her shoulders and ran fingers along his abdominal area.

"You like it," Ramiro stared.

"What do you think?" she still ran her fingers on his chest.

"I'm getting fat. You're still going to be my wife. Remember?" he grabbed Noelle, force kissing her.

"How could I forget, Ramiro?" she flashed the engagement ring in his face. She strutted away. *I've got a show tonight and an interview with a rock reporter. I do so much—studio sessions, interviews, music videos, touring, which I love greeting my fans. But, I want to be home with Noelle and having a family. Speaking of that, Noelle consumed a lot of food. I'll get to that later,"* Ramiro hopped off his bunk and headed into the shower.

BEFORE IRATE TOOK THE stage, a Danish Heavy Metal reporter Sam Hanson interviewed them LIVE from the Royal Arena in Copenhagen. During the backstage interview, a cameraman focused the camera on the trio. Ramiro and Danny sat next to one another, while Zack sat in a chair on the end. Ramiro and Zack avoided as much visual contact as possible. Still, Ramiro wanted to beat the shit out of his drummer, but he had an interview to do. Sam asked Ramiro most of the questions since he led the group. Ramiro respected his bandmates for answering, but then he got selfish about it.

"How did you guys become a trio?" Sam held the microphone to Ramiro.

"Zack and I grew up in the same neighborhood as kids, and we've been playing together for years. We both decided that all we needed was a lead guitarist, and we found Danny here," Ramiro patted Danny hard on the back.

"Ah, shit, dude!" Danny choked.

Sam guffawed as Ramiro and Danny were like the two stooges. Zack didn't engage in the interview; he kept quiet. He wanted to avoid any type of physical altercation like their show in England. Just like Ramiro, they both had the same goal, which was to put on a great show.

Noelle hid behind some lockers, watching the interview. She hoped the camera didn't capture her shot. As she turned, the white cinderblock walls stared her right in the face as it confronted her relationship. *"Like the walls could talk. What if they could, they'd hound me with questions? Why do I feel this wall could talk? Shouldn't I be talking to the wall? Talking to a concrete wall is insane. I can't trust anyone to discuss my problems. I want to call my parents so badly, but I don't want to bother them with my issues. I've been feeling dizzy and overeating. I don't want to mess up Ramiro's goals,"* Noelle peered from behind the lockers. She then focused her eyes back on the cinderblock walls. She wondered if any other girl hid behind these lockers, where athletes or musical artists' girlfriends told their trials of their relationship with their celebrity lover. She subsided her despairing ideas and had to be optimistic about her and Ramiro's future.

"Noelle," a voice called her name. She peeked from behind the lockers as Ramiro saw her pretty Mahogany face glaring at him. He grasped both of Noelle's hands, pulling her body close to him. "Why are you hiding back here?"

"So, I won't be in your way. You were doing an interview," Noelle gently expressed.

"You're never in my way," Ramiro whispered. He licked Noelle's neck, moving it upward to her ear and then her lips. They pressed their bodies close together as Noelle wrapped her arms around his waist. She heard the roaring crowd chanting her lover's name. They subsided their kiss, gazing into each other's eyes.

"Your fans are waiting," Noelle kissed him on the cheek.

"Ramiro! Let's go!" Stanley clapped his hands, trying to alert Ramiro.

"I'm coming!" he stormed away from Noelle with a frown on his face. He grabbed his bass guitar from the sound technician, glancing behind him, noticing Noelle following him. She held a towel and two bottles of water in her hands. His nine-pound bass guitar weighed him down while he marched up to the stage. Ramiro's bass slipped through his hands as he hoped they wouldn't slice the tender skin of his fingers. Noelle tugged the back of Ramiro's black t-shirt as they got closer and closer to the stage. The boisterous crowd's roars got louder. Ramiro stopped, seeing a patch of the audience. Danny had his electric guitar strapped over his shoulder, Zack twirled his drumsticks as Stanley and management waited for the lead singer to make his appearance. Ramiro heaved his bass guitar towards his bandmates and management.

"Good Ramiro, you're here!" Stanley patted him on the back.

"It's about time," Zack smirked.

"What the fuck did you say!" Ramiro approached Zack aggressively.

"What the hell, you two! We've got a show! Get the fuck on the stage!" Stanley punched his hand into the palm of his hand. "Do you know what's going on with Ramiro, Noelle?"

"I don't know," she shrugged.

"Copenhagen!" Ramiro's voice bellowed through the microphone. As he spoke, the fans stood on opposite sides of each other, where the mosh pit would take place.

"Everyone Sees Death!" he hollered as the music started. The rockers collided with each other like cars on a highway going in the opposite lanes. Ramiro kept a straight face while seeing his fans act boisterously. While Ramiro spewed lyrics to the song, he envisioned his father falling ill. Something like cancer, where doctors couldn't help him. Or maybe Ramiro behind the wheel of his Black Dodge Durango and running him over. He slammed on the brakes, peering through the rearview mirror as his father laid on the street bleeding. No way in fuckin' hell was he going to help his father. Or some type of killing or suffering that would plaster a smile on his face. He didn't regret these feelings. "It is what it is."

"DARK ROMANCE!" RAMIRO'S voice echoed through the concert venue minutes later. He recited the lyrics for the song he wrote, describing a love affair with a woman whoever that was. Since Noelle was his fiancé. Then it was her. He never spoke to Noelle about the dark forces within him. he didn't have to because actions speak louder than words. Ramiro was evil, like his father, he'll admit that. He'll decide on how they'll live their lives. It sounds sexist, but Ramiro didn't give a fuck. Noelle's going to be his wife no matter what. And he dared Noelle to challenge him. While singing the dominating, murky lyrics, he pictured an occult dark chapel adorned with black flowers, tarantulas crawling on the walls, and ravens soaring above. A wicked priest stood with the evildoer's Bible in his hands. Ramiro wore an utterly black tuxedo. The guests dressed in black, from dark tuxedos to dresses, bearing vile expressions as if they stepped out of a horror film. A skinny, sixty-something gentleman dressed in a coal-black three-piece suit with a ghost-white, wrinkled face escorted Noelle down the aisle. She wore a black bridal gown, displaying a long train and a veil over her face, holding a bouquet of black roses. Ramiro snapped out of his dark fantasy, focusing his attention on his fans.

"You're not going anywhere!" Ramiro screamed in the microphone. The fans cheered and bumped into each other in the mosh pit. He belted out the lyrics for another domineering song about a rocky relationship between lovers. Ramiro drifted back into his dark wedding fantasy. The obscure rocker older gentleman finally walked Noelle to the altar. The dark priest grabbed a large blade as Ramiro held his hand out as it slit his palm. Blood dripped down his hand; he lifted Noelle's veil as she then held her palm out as the priest slit it. Ramiro snapped out of the sadist dream and back to reality. He set his mind on his fans, giving them the best show ever.

A COUPLE OF NIGHTS later, at the Oslo Spektrum Arena in Norway's capital, a spotlight beamed on Ramiro as he gave his bass solo. Perspiration drenched Ramiro's entire body from head to toe as if someone threw a bucket of water on him. He displayed his best performance ever with his bass as fans saw the fury in his eyes. *"Every hotel room that Noelle and I occupy, she's constantly eating junk food and even off my plate. If she's pregnant, then fuckin' tell me and stop fuckin around,"* he proceeded with his performance. Noelle claimed she's not, but Ramiro wanted her to go to the doctor, anyway. Just like most people, she hated going to the doctor. Ramiro went back and forth with concerns for Noelle and his fans right before his eyes.

Backstage, Noelle cheered like a cheerleader on the sideline at a Friday Night football game. She held the bottle of water and towel for him. Ramiro swaggered to Noelle, glaring at her. His bass guitar hung from his shoulders as he looked unpleased. He snatched the water from her hand, gulping it down. He gave Noelle his back.

"Ramiro, that's rude!" she stomped her foot. He chatted with Stanley. She knew Ramiro heard her words, and she didn't like him treating her like this. Stanley stepped away from Ramiro. Noelle got in Ramiro's sweaty face, "Why did you do that!"

Ramiro continued to gulp down the water, turning away from her. Noelle got up in Ramiro's face again. "Look at me, Ramiro!"

"Leave me alone, Noelle!" Ramiro warned. He turned his back on Noelle again. She then pushed him as he dropped the water on the floor. Noelle stormed away; Ramiro was right on her trail and grabbed her from behind. He pinned this five-foot, seven, weighing at only one hundred, twenty-one-pounded woman to the wall. Noelle screamed at the top of her lungs.

"Ramiro, no! What the hell are you doing?" Stanley sprung into action. His management witnessed Ramiro's abuse before their eyes as they widened.

"If you are pregnant. Get fuckin' rid of it!" Ramiro tossed Noelle as she fell to the floor, leaving her in tears. He swaggered to the stage. The fans chanted his name. "Ramiro! Ramiro! Ramiro!"

MEANWHILE, IN THE RV, Noelle shoved her clothes in a suitcase as tears flowed down her face, wiping them away. *"Ramiro doesn't have to worry about me anymore. He doesn't have to worry about me being pregnant if I am. I doubt it. The funny thing is. If I'm pregnant, why does it bother him? He wants me to marry him. Right? Oh, I forgot his career is first. And he's the one probably fucking around,"* she zipped her suitcase. Noelle took the red rose that Ramiro brought for her in France. She wheeled her luggage through the RV, holding the flower in her hand. Noelle noticed Ramiro's black matte bass guitar that his grandmother got for him for Christmas sat on an angle. She stuck the stem of the rose between the four strings of the instrument. Noelle stepped back and noticed that the rose was decaying. It's been a while since they were in France.

"Our love is dying. Just look at how the flower is deteriorating. I can't marry Ramiro. I can't help him and I'm not going to. It's not my job. Whatever's going on with him, he has to work it out. I'm gone," Noelle exited the RV.

CHAPTER TWENTY

On a commercial flight, Ramiro gazed out of the window while Stanley slept in an aisle seat next to him. Ramiro focused so hard on the clouds, they had shapes of a bear, a cat, or some chunky animal. He leaned his face against the plane window and wanted to go to sleep. Ramiro forced himself to keep his eyes open, wondering if Noelle got home safely. He didn't bother to call her, and neither did she pick up the phone to call him. So, they were even. Stanley cleared his throat, squirming in his chair, finding a comfortable position. Ramiro felt his manager's movement in the seat next to him. Ramiro then closed his eyes, leaning in the airplane seat. *"If Noelle is pregnant, I hope she doesn't do anything stupid like have an abortion. I didn't mean what I said. I was talking out of my ass! I want my baby, and I want her. Since Noelle's not here, she might go back to gigs at the House clubs. I'm stuck in my ways. Fuck, I love Noelle! Shit! Next stop, Mexico City, where I'll entertain fans and off to Panama City, Panama, and then shows for thousands of fans, probably millions in Colombia, Chile, Ecuador, Brazil, Venezuela, Peru, and Argentina. Is Stanely going to mention the fight I had with Noelle? He saw with his own eyes that I threw Noelle's things off the bus and I pushed her. Shit! That's the same thing my father did to my mother when she gave birth to me on October, thirtieth. And his push ended my grandmother's life. Luckily, Noelle didn't hit her head on anything. Instead, she landed on her ass, which was a good thing. I may have to talk to a therapist or something because I need to get help. Yes, I have a problem. My mother and*

sister believe that I might be a replica of my father," Ramiro leaned his head on the headrest, still with his eyes shut.

THE NEXT NIGHT, "WHAT the fuck is up, Mexico City!" Ramiro raved on the microphone. The crazed fans screamed, piled on top of one another like bricks of a house. "Are you ready to fuckin' mosh!" His voice echoed throughout the arena. Irate fans stood on opposite sides, ready for battle. "Everyone Sees Death!" Irate played the aggressive sound as the metalheads crashed into one another. Ramiro recited the lyrics for the song, noticing fans get hyped by the music. Through all the fans and shows in the beautiful cities and countries, Noelle resonated in his brain. After performing a few songs, Ramiro swaggered backstage with sweat pouring down the side of his face and soaked head. Stanley gave Ramiro a towel and bottled water. He took the items from his manager's hand. The backstage atmosphere felt strange without Noelle being by his side. She, of course, wasn't there to wipe the sweat from his temple, give him water, laying a kiss upon his lips, and tell him to "Keep it rockin'!"

Ramiro discussed his romantic dilemma with Stanley for a minute. His manager wanted to know everything about his situation. Stanley didn't want to put the band's career in jeopardy. Like a man, Ramiro admitted Noelle did nothing wrong. He told Stanley that his father abused him and his family when he was little, but he couldn't go into too much detail because the fans chanted his name.

"Ramiro! Ramiro! Ramiro!"

His manager patted Ramiro on the back, showing that they're going to work on his problems. Ramiro swaggered back to the stage with his bass guitar strapped on him. He held up the horn-hand gesture in the air. The audience cheered, whistled, made the evil gesture with their hands, and holding up cell cameras.

A WEEK LATER IN PANAMA City, the trio played before thousands of fans as the mosh pit was in full force with rockers going nuts. Like always, Ramiro spewed the ugly lyrics to the "Dark Romance" song. He envisioned Noelle waiting for him backstage and making up as most couples do. But not this time. Or will there be a next time? "I've got to call Noelle and apologize to her. I didn't buy her that ring for nothing," Ramiro violently threw his head up and down, feeling a sharp pain in the middle of his head. The migraine seemed to happen when he had too much on his mind. His headaches gave him ideas as well. "Migraine!" Ramiro's voice echoed on the microphone. The metalheads hollered, head-banging to the song. He felt extremely hot as his blood rushed up to his back and over his head. His legs wobbled as the weight of his bass pulled his body down. He collapsed to the hardwood stage floor with a sweaty head. Danny dashed to his side with his electric guitar strapped over his shoulders. Horrified fans gasped, noticing their Rockstar hero stretched out on stage.

"Ramiro! Can you hear me!" Danny cried out. Stanley, Zack, and his management team surrounded him. Ramiro recognized everyone around him, but they held his head up and made him drink the bottled water. As he sipped the H2O, Noelle popped into his mind and knew if she were there, he probably wouldn't have passed out. The blood in his body swished around like water. He hated that because it made him unbalanced. For a moment, he believed his life was coming to a close. He pictured his grandmother standing alongside Stanley. Rebecca placed her heavenly hands-on Ramiro's head. Her Godly energies strengthen his body as they swept through his veins like medication given to a sick child. This badass metal bassist stood to his feet like a champ. The fans cheered, whistled, applauded.

"Ramiro! Ramiro! Ramiro!"

"Are you okay, Ramiro!" Stanley asked. He embraced him.

"Drink more water!" Danny advised. Ramiro took a couple of more sips. He looked to the audience, strapping on his bass guitar, and gestured the horn hands to them.

"I'm cool!" he spoke to the audience. Deep down inside, he experienced some physical and emotional pain from his past and the present and wasn't so sure about the future. Ramiro expunged his dilemmas from his mindset and focused on the audience who spent money to see him play his bass. He took a couple of steps back from the microphone while the spotlight shined upon him. Ramiro wasn't going to let some floodlight prevent him from his performance. He allowed his fingers to do the work along the arm and strings of his guitar as the audience cheered. Zack automatically added the drums to the bass line. Danny stood back with the electric guitar silenced to allow this drummer and bassist to battle it out. *"What the fuck is he doing! This solo is mine, not his! He better sleep with one eye opened,"* Ramiro threatened in his mind. He expressed fury through his bass. Noelle not being there for him, Zack fucking with him, and he passed the fuck out right before thousands of fans was a kick in the fuckin' nuts.

LATER, A HURLING FIST knocked Zack to the floor on a tour bus on their way to Bogota, Colombia. He jumped to his feet as Ramiro charged at him, both musicians plummeted to the floor. Stanley, Douglas, and the roadies tried their best to separate them.

"That was my solo! You stupid fuck!"

Fuck you, Ram! That was my drum solo!" Zack tried to lunge at Ramiro, but Douglas held him back.

"Shit! Both of you stop acting like kids!" Stanley stomped his foot on the floor. He escorted Ramiro to the seating area of the tour bus, slamming the door.

Ramiro sat on the cushion seat. He placed his hands over his face.

"Do you want a beer?"

"Yeah," Ramiro shook his head. His manager grabbed two beer bottles from the refrigerator and gave one to him. Stanley sat opposite of his client, who popped the top off the beer bottle and guzzled down the alcoholic beverage. Ramiro aimed his eyes in the other direction.

"Ramiro, I saw what happened between you and Noelle. Would you like to tell me what's going on? Because I'm hearing that you're hitting her," Stanley tapped his fingers on the glass bottle.

"Who the fuck told you that shit! Zack! You fucking cocksucker!" Ramiro jumped out of his seat, rushing to the back of the tour bus. Stanley attempted to block Ramiro from getting into another altercation.

"Ramiro! Sit the fuck down!" Stanley restrained him.

"Who the fuck is calling my fuckin' name!" Zack stormed to the front as Douglas blocked him. Then this manager forced Zack to the bus's rear.

"Get your ass in the back, Zack!" Douglas constantly shoved him to the rear of the bus as the band's management team kept these two musicians apart.

"You better get your fuckin' facts straight! You fuck!" Ramiro pounded his fist on the table. He turned fiery red, as he always did. He plopped down in the chair and gazed out of the window. "Shit! Shit! What the fuck now! Zack better not fuck up this tour or I'll fuck him up! None of these rumors better get to my fans or I'll be fucked!" Ramiro turned, glaring at his manager. He couldn't stand him hovering over him.

"Would you mind getting counseling, Ramiro?" Stanley asked him with caution. Ramiro nodded his head. "How soon can I talk to someone?"

"As soon as possible," his manager gently smiled.

THE NEXT NIGHT, IRATE fans stormed into a massive arena in Bogota in a matter of no time; fourteen thousand metalheads jammed the venue. The darkened stage had the band's logo of Ramiro's pet tarantula. Then a spotlight brightened on Ramiro, playing his bass with Danny and Zack's collaborated instruments. He improvised his bass line, not caring about the sound. And his fans didn't complain as they moshed in the center aisles, some fans falling to the floor as they were helped to their feet.

"Everyone Sees Death!" Ramiro bellowed through the microphone. Irate performed all of their songs from the second album "For Fuck Sakes" and their first album. During the concert, Ramiro didn't make eye contact with Zack. He communicated with some fans in the front rows. A gorgeous brown-skinned Colombian girl, mid-twenties, kinky-curly hair, smiled at him. Ramiro returned the gesture, and she reminded him of Noelle. He couldn't take his eyes off her. Hooking up with a female wasn't the right time. Ramiro had to get this show on the road.

"Hell On Earth!" he proceeded with the show.

FROM THE MASSIVE ARENA in Bogota, Colombia to another grand arena in Quito, Ecuador, a few nights where sixteen thousand fans chanted the band's name. "Irate! Irate!"

Ramiro and Danny strutted to the stage, playing their guitars while Zack pounded his drum kit. The fans went nuts over the band's starting off the show. The two guitarists headbanged and played familiar songs that excited the audience. He moved about the stage, playing his bass and engaging with fans. Receiving counseling seemed humiliating, but Ramiro shut down the idea. His therapist would meet him in Peru, which should show a sign of blessings for his future.

AFTER THE CONCERT, Ramiro luxuriated in a recliner in the living room area of the tour bus. He didn't bother to sleep in his bunk as the darkened RV felt like his permanent home on wheels. Luckily, the tour bus encountered no bumps on the road, which would waken him from his sleep and would also piss him off. He squinted his eyes, where his vision had a blur of the spotlights in the ceiling. Ramiro slowly widened his eyes as his sight cleared. There was nothing but quiet. The low, relaxing engine was all he could hear. He heard someone snoring close to him. Ramiro turned, noticing Stanley stretched out on the couch with a book over his face.

"What the fuck," Ramiro murmured. He shook his head, aiming his eyes on the ceiling with nothing but lights. He looked forward to another show, exhibiting his musical skills to fans. He didn't think about Noelle at all. Nor his family. Stanley snored louder with bubbling mucus in his nostrils. Ramiro sneered, attempted to nudge his manager to shut the fuck up, but he plugged his fingers in his ears.

ON THE NIGHT OF IRATE'S concert at an enormous venue in Lima, Peru, Ramiro and Danny tuned the strings on their guitars backstage. The two guitarists practiced how they would battle it out with their instruments as they juddered their heads with their hair flying around. Zack slipped on a black rottweiler-faced t-shirt before an opened locker. He glanced at his bandmates with their instruments, headbanging. *What a fuckin' asshole! Ramiro's getting counseling. Why does he need that? Ramiro's a lost cause. No way on God's green earth anything or anyone could help this pathetic fuck! Hopefully, Noelle's through with his ass. When we were kids, I witnessed Mr.*

Espinoza's out of fuckin' control behavior," Zack pictured playing at Ramiro's house in the backyard. He witnessed Mr. Espinoza strike his wife, Mrs. Espinoza, across the face from their bedroom window. Zack recalled the shock of his life, of a man hurting a woman. He knew these events affected his so-called best friend tremendously. *"There was no reason for Ramiro to repeat this pattern towards Noelle. She doesn't deserve that. Maybe, she needs a man who is going to respect her and allowed her to express herself. I always knew that Ramiro hated House music. Not everyone likes Metal, Jazz, New Age, Classical, or any other genre of music. Despite that, show some respect. Noelle will probably never sing again to make Ramiro happy. That's fucked up,"* his heart raced in his chest as he slammed the locker door. The loud noise caught Ramiro's attention as he glared at this drummer who gave him his back.

"Fuckin' ass!" Ramiro murmured.

"It's showtime, guys!" Stanley clapped, getting the band's attention. Ramiro stormed out of the dressing room first with Danny right behind with their guitars ready to rock. Zack swaggered out with his drumsticks.

MOMENTS LATER, RAMIRO took the stage, holding the hand-horned gesture in the air, and greeted fans on the microphone, "Peru!" The audience cheered, applauded, and copied their metal god gesturing the hand-horns in the air. He and his band were ready to rock fans. During his performances, Ramiro didn't think about Noelle. But he thought of her every time he went backstage and when Stanley gave him bottled water and a towel. Ramiro always snatched it from Stanley's hands, turning his back. He gulped down the water and threw it against the wall. "Fuckin' shit!" Stanley knew what was bothering his client. Ramiro was lovesick because his fu-

ture wife wasn't there for him. He swaggered down the murky hallway as Zack's drum solo echoed throughout the arena.

FOUR AND A HALF HOURS later, Ramiro stood in the shower
while hot steamy water trickled down his nude body. He squeezed
the Dove Mens shower gel into the palm of his hand and lathered his
body. He then shampooed his long tress that draped to the middle
of his back. The lathery studs streamed down his face as he closed his
eyes. The shower gel burnt his eyes, Ramiro cupped his hands with
water, splashing it on his face. Out of nowhere, a bar of soap tossed
across the tile floor, hitting his feet. "What the fuck!" he jumped, not
knowing what scurried across his feet. He thought it was a mouse or
some rodent. Ramiro almost slipped on the tile but was able to stand
firm on his feet. A gold-colored soap sat in the shower's corner with
its perfumy scent. Ramiro knew it was Dial by the smell and shape. If
he had a nasty fall, it'll delay the tour. And he couldn't afford to have
any mishaps.

"Who the fuck threw this in here!" Ramiro rinsed the soap off
his body.

SECONDS LATER, RAMIRO stormed out of the shower
drenched, fully naked, and confronted Zack before everyone. "Did
you throw this soap in the shower!" Ramiro held the soap in his
hand. He didn't give a damn who saw his bare ass and nuts.

"Ramiro! My God!" Stanley grabbed a towel and threw it
around Ramiro's nude body.

"Put some clothes on, Ramiro! You're fuckin' losing it!" Zack
laughed as he stood back.

"Ramiro, what's up with you?" Stanley hollered.

"I almost tripped in the shower!" Ramiro wrapped the towel around his waist. Zack cackled.

"Fuck it!" Ramiro charged at Zack. Both men wrestled to the floor, Ramiro didn't care if he was in his birthday suit. They hurled punches at each other. Irate's management team had to separate the rockers. At least nine roadies, including Stanley, had to restrain Ramiro.

"Get dressed, Ramiro!" Stanley blew his top. He turned blood red in the face.

WITHIN A FEW HOURS, at a peaceful Peruvian cemetery, Ramiro maneuvered between the dead buried on these grounds. The air didn't feel right to him. He sensed death in his path; he glanced over his shoulders. He picked up his pace to get to his grandmother's tombstone. Her gravesite read REBECCA FLORA with her photo, date of birth, and time of death engraved on a large granite tombstone with angels. Ramiro kneeled, praying to her as if she were God. As good-hearted as Rebecca was, she could've been the next best thing to him. His eyes watered as tears flowed down his face. He sobbed like a baby. Ramiro's managers and a Caucasian male, mid-forties, Dr. Adrian Hopper, glass-clad, thin, average-looking, dressed in a casual shirt with slacks, stood in the background witnessing this young musician at his most vulnerable. Ramiro sensed some eyes gazing at him while at his grandmother's tombstone.

"This was murder. Simple! I don't care what anyone thinks. My father pushed her," Ramiro cried. Danny placed his hand on Ramiro's shoulder.

"Your grandmother would be proud of you, Ramiro. Look at what you've achieved. You're a badass bassist," Danny patted him on the shoulder. "You're going to be fine, dude."

"Ramiro, you've got a successful career and one of the world's most influential bassists," his manager embraced him.

"Abuela, I miss you so much. I know you're looking down on me. Please protect the family and me. I love you," Ramiro finished his prayer to his grandmother.

"Ramiro, I would like you to meet Dr. Hopper," Stanley introduced as Ramiro shook the hand of this soft-spoken gentleman with a genuine smile. Ramiro seemed nervous, not knowing what to say except "Hello."

"How are you, Ramiro?" the therapist extended his hand to him.

Ramiro still didn't say anything else, shaking this strange man's hand whose job was to dig into his psyche. He rose to his feet, towering over this five-foot, six-man. Ramiro took a step back, so he wouldn't intimidate him.

*"What the fuck do I say, Dr. whatever his fuckin' name is. I'm fuckin' lost for words right now. How much time do I have to spend talking to this therapist? Maybe, I should tell Stanley to tell him to leave because I'm not ready to spill out my fuckin' guts to a stranger even though I need to, "*he stormed to the tour bus. Stanley, Dr. Hopper, and Danny waltzed their way to the RV as well.

CHAPTER TWENTY-ONE

Thousands of Irate fans packed a huge arena in Brazil as they held up the horn hand gesture in the air. "Brazil!", Ramiro bellowed on the microphone while standing on a foggy darkened stage. The crowd cheered as soon as they saw their hero. He focused his eyes on the audience ready to put on a good show. A few hours earlier, he and Dr. Hopper spoke a bit about his past childhood. He got as far as telling him the first he witnessed his father pin his mother up against the wall. The slender therapist sat in a cushioned chair, drilling him about his father. Ramiro held his head down, covering his eyes and avoiding tears from flowing down his face. "This is hard for me. I don't think I can do this yet," he rose his head up and stormed out of the bus.

"Everyone Sees Death!" Ramiro's voice echoed through the venue. The headbangers bounced in a circular motion like an ocean whirlpool in the mosh pit. He spewed lyrics to the song, watching the audience headbanging. Ramiro took a couple of steps back, moving about the stage, and playing along with Danny. Utter silence occurred during the first couple of sessions, where Ramiro had a few hours before showtime. Dr. Hopper analyzed this talented young man perform while backstage with Stanley.

"How long has he been playing music?" Dr. Hopper asked.

"A long time. Ramiro will give you all the info," Stanley shouted. He refused to tell the therapist everything about Ramiro. He agreed Ramiro was the one to do that.

The loud, aggressive rock music struck a high note by Danny's screeching guitar and Ramiro maintaining the bass with the song. As usual, the backstage floor vibrated because of Irate playing their powerful instruments. Dr. Hopper had to sit in a chair because he felt the music would knock him off his feet. He dragged a folded chair from backstage and sat down. He unfolded the chair and watched Ramiro. Ramiro's anger reflected on his face while he spewed more lyrics to another vile, distasteful song that he wrote. The therapist gazed at his expression, the violent way he shook his head to the unruly music, and then he got it. He jotted down some notes on Ramiro's attitude as he strummed the strings of his bass and disgruntled voice echoing through the microphone.

"I can see the reason he plays this type of music, which is Heavy Metal, not because he enjoys it. There's anger within his lyrics and his sound. Ramiro's ill feelings towards his family explain why he does what he does. He started by telling me about his father, but he couldn't because it was too painful. It explains why the band's name is Irate," Dr. Hopper continued to write notes in his pad. He glanced at Ramiro while he performed.

THE NEXT MORNING, RAMIRO and Dr. Hopper occupied the living room where Ramiro lounged in the recliner in the bus's front. Ramiro's bandmates and management team resided in the recreation room, so they could have some privacy. The session gave Ramiro some comfort because of the smooth ride and low-engine sound of the RV. He slumped in the lounge chair, eyeing the therapist sitting across from him. Dr. Hopper wanted to engage in the conversation, but he wanted Ramiro to do the talking because his life depended on it. He turned away for a second, scratching his head, and looked back at the counselor.

"What kind of fuckin' session is this? Are we going to fuckin' sit here and not say a word," he combed his fingers through his long brunette hair. "What the fuck."

"Ramiro, this is your time to let your feelings out," Dr. Hopper added. He leaned in his chair.

"I don't know where to fuckin' start," Ramiro grabbed his cellphone, scanned through his photo gallery, and showed the therapist photos of Noelle. "This is the love of my life right there," Dr. Hopper noticed the photo of this beautiful African-American female.

"She's beautiful. And her name is?" the therapist asked.

"Noelle," Ramiro answered quickly. "You can scroll through it," he advised.

Dr. Hopper scrolled through the photo gallery, seeing the dozens of pictures of Ramiro and Noelle and individual photos as well. He then came across a photo of an older woman.

"Is this your mother, Ramiro?" Dr. Hopper flashed the cell to him.

"Yes," Ramiro shyly.

"She's a beautiful woman. You look like your mom," Dr. Hopper complimented and scrolled through the gallery. He came across his sister, Maritza, and grandmother on Christmas day.

The therapist flashed the cellphone again. "And this is,"

"My sister, Maritza, and Grandmother," Ramiro shied away because Dr. Hopper saw the photo of his grandmother who was now buried six feet under.

"Would you like to tell me about your mother, Ramiro?" Dr. Hopper questioned.

"What do you want me to say?" he shrugged.

"Maybe, you can tell how special she is to you. Maybe, you can tell how much you love her," the counselor responded.

"Of course, I love my mother. I'd do anything for her. I'll fuckin' die for her. My mother would've died for me and my sister when my father put his hands on her," the flashback played vividly in his mind. Anna Maria's husband backhanded her as she flew across the floor in the kitchen. Ramiro, age five, and Maritza age, six cringed in the corner, crying. The experience horrified these two kids, seeing their father hurting their mother. Jorge claimed to be a man of God but used the good book for his evil deeds.

"I am your husband, and you obey me!" Jorge waved the bible in her face. He smacked her with it. "You two get upstairs!" Ramiro dashed upstairs with Maritza behind him.

"Hide!" Ramiro glanced over both shoulders, trying to figure out where he and his sister could find a safe place.

"Ramiro, where!" Maritza looked over both of her shoulders. Her heart pounded heavily in her chest.

"In the bathroom," Ramiro dashed in with his sister behind, slamming the door and locking it.

RETURNING TO RAMIRO'S session, he bawled like a baby, having difficulty trying to continue with his pain. Dr. Hopper gave Ramiro a box of tissues to wipe his tears streaming down his red cherry face. He refused to use the wipes and instead used his hands.

"Ramiro, do you want to end the session?" Dr. Hopper gave Ramiro respect.

"We'll do this next time," Ramiro stood up from the lounge chair, storming from the living room to his bunk. There he took off his construction boots, pants, and drew back the drapes with a slight opening. He glared at Zack's bunk with drapes closed. He had a feeling that Zack probably eavesdropped on his session. Ramiro pulled the light blanket over him. He experienced pain in the middle of his head because of his crying like a bitch. Men aren't supposed to cry. Ramiro recalled his father telling him that repeatedly while growing up.

BACK TO THE HALF-TOLD story of his childhood, in the bathroom where Ramiro and Maritza hid, they heard their father bawling at the top of his lungs. "Ramiro, where are you! You're going to get the worst beating of your life! Maritza!" while Ramiro lied in his bunk, the flashbacks of his father visualized in his head.

Jorge kicked open the bathroom door; he threw back the shower curtain. Ramiro and Maritza huddled together and screaming. He grabbed Ramiro, throwing the small-framed, five-year-old child across the floor. Jorge snatched the belt from the waist of his pants and beat the child like a slave. The thick leather strap struck Ramiro on every part of his body.

BACK TO THE PRESENT, Ramiro turned on his stomach, pulling the blanket way over his head, hearing the lashes of the strap hitting his body as a child. He turned on the radio in his bunk with rock music playing at a low volume. It relaxed him as he continued to close his eyes.

THE NEXT NIGHT, TWELVE thousand Irate fans cheered for Ramiro as he gave his amazing bass solo at the Movistar Arena in Santiago, Chile. Dr. Hopper watched this young musician's showmanship, holding the audience in the palm of his hands. He could see Ramiro's passion and his attachment to his bass. The therapist observed his facial expressions as best he could. Ramiro's hair blocked his face while he headbanged. Dr. Hopper only could get bits and pieces of what Ramiro's face read. He took notes and believed if Ramiro didn't have his music that he'd be a washed-up rock star. He still refused to give details about his father's disapproval of his music tastes, talents, and goals. What did his mother want Ramiro to be? Was he treated differently from his sister? And how did Ramiro's Heavy Metal beginnings affect his relationship with his father? Did it become worse? That's all the notes that Dr. Hopper jotted down and watched Ramiro perform his ass off. His fans went berserk.

OUTSIDE OF THE CONCERT arena, Irate took pictures and signed autographs for fans. And of course, the beautiful brunette females, dressed in Irate t-shirts and miniskirts, hugged and kissed Ramiro like there was no tomorrow. Dr. Hopper observed the girls throwing themselves on this lead singer/bassist, who's very handsome. He could see these young ladies have good taste in this man.

ON THE ROAD AGAIN, the tour bus zoomed along the highway from Santiago, Chile, to Buenos Aires, Argentina, for the band's next show. The living room in the bus's front was where Ramiro and Dr. Hopper occupied for a couple of hours again. Danny and Zack's chilled out in the recreation room, but couldn't play their music loud. They had to show some respect. The two bandmates didn't say a word to each other due to them being in a world of their own. God only knows what was on Danny's mind, but gazing outside of the side with the passing of the Chilean rural roads. He was probably thinking of a girl or maybe nervous about another performance.

Zack, on the other hand, popping off the top of a beer, guzzling it down. He wished he could have a one on one with Dr. Hopper about his so-called best friend's past because Ramiro might not tell the therapist everything. Zack felt he would help Ramiro's situation or hurting it.

IN THE LIVING ROOM, Ramiro and Dr. Hopper didn't ex-change any words between them, only the low engine sound of the RV could be heard. The therapist held an empty pad in his hand, waiting for this troubled rocker to speak his peace. He needed Ramiro to tell him more about his childhood, and his love life that could be in jeopardy. The therapist glared at Ramiro, who glared at the floor. He sat his ass in the recliner, realizing the silence between them. Time waited for him to say the first words. He glared at Dr. Hopper, noticing the frail-looking man before him who seemed as if he needed some counseling himself. Counseling on eating habits. Ramiro then forgot about how puny this gentleman was for a mo-ment as he was there to help him. No crazy ideas ran through his head, but Noelle was the only notion he had.

"So, did you like the show?" Ramiro asked, breaking the silence.

"Yes, I did. I enjoyed your performance," Dr. Hopper smiled.

"Well, you'll get to see another show tomorrow," Ramiro added. He looked away.

"When did you discover you wanted to be a musician?"

"When Zack's father introduced me to his rock and Jazz music collection with all that good stuff," Ramiro looked away. He seemed shy about the entire session but wanted to get to the nitty-gritty. But he was scared as shit. Ramiro's never been so fearful, confronting his past, but he had to deal with it.

"Alright, Dr. Hopper, let's cut to the chase," Ramiro eyed the therapist.

"Go on, let it all out," Dr. Hopper encouraged him.

Ramiro held his head down, inhaled, and then held his head up, trying to fight the tears that streamed down his face. No success. The liquid drops slid down his cheeks, anyway. He wiped them away. Ramiro told the time when he played the "Ride The Lightning" al-bum by Metallica in the house. He had a vivid picture in his head about the incident.

IN THE LIVING ROOM of his childhood home, Ramiro inserted the CD into the player as the loud, blaring guitars and pounding drums erupted through the air. Maritza dashed halfway down the stairs. "Ramiro, don't let dad hear you playing that?"

Ramiro ignored his sister's warning about his father's disapproval of this so-called evil music. He imitated bass guitarist Cliff Burton from Metallica. And yes, Cliff Burton influenced this young boy to follow his dreams. Maritza made her way down the flight of steps and cut off the cd player.

"What the fuck!" Ramiro rose his voice and then lowered it with caution.

"You're not supposed to listen to this kind of music, Ramiro?"

"What kind of music?" Ramiro sucked his teeth.

"The devil's music," Maritza clicked on the Cd player, ejecting the CD. She grabbed the disc, placing it back in the Metallica case.

"What the hell! We're not living in the stone age," Ramiro stomped his feet on the floor.

"I suggest you give this back to Zack," Maritza handed the CD to her brother.

"Did your father ever find that CD?" Dr. Hopper asked.

"No. There's so much shit I can't recall right now," he shied away from the counselor. Dr. Hopper squirmed in his chair, allowing this young musician to get his feelings out. "Do you want to stop, and we'll continue tomorrow?"

"No!" Ramiro bellowed, closing his eyes for a moment. He could tell him stories for days, but he didn't feel like doing all the talking. But he was there to get help. Right? So, he discussed when he and the entire family sat at the kitchen table, reading the Bible. He recalled Maritza reading chapter 14:2, In my Father's house are "Many Mansions" and John 3:16, "For so God loved the world, he sent his one and only son Jesus Christ, that whoever believes in him shall not perish but have eternal life." His father glared at Ramiro who slouched in his chair, sensing his father's eyes hovering over his small body. He didn't know what to think about his father, who preached to him about God but practiced such extreme behavior towards his family.

"How many times do I have to tell you, Ramiro, to sit up straight," Jorge kept staring at him. Ramiro straightened his back and kept his eyes on the word. Maritza concluded the verses of the bible.

"Very good," this crazed holy man praised his daughter. He then looked to his son for the same performance. The verses of the bible Ramiro he didn't remember because it was so long ago. And Ramiro didn't have any faith in God. At this young tender age, Ramiro believed God was a fairytale. Adults used this invisible man in the sky to scare the wits out of children so they would behave. Zack's father, Neil, introduced me to music and if it weren't for him, I don't know where I'd be. Zack was already on his way because he played drums at a very young age. He's been playing drums before I started playing bass.

"Where do you think you'd be if you didn't have your music?" the doctor asked.

"I guess I'd probably have a fucked-up marriage with a kid, living in a dump somewhere," Ramiro said.

"Can you tell me a little about Noelle?" Dr. Hopper smiled.

"Is Dr. Hopper asking me this because he believes I'm referring to Noelle? I will not give him too much detail on my relationship!" Ramiro rubbed his eyes, hesitant to respond to the question.

"The only thing I can say is "I love her," he addressed the therapist.

"What do you love about Noelle?" Dr. Hopper smiled.

"She's beautiful, kind-hearted and she can sing her ass off," Ramiro salty.

"That's impressive. What kind of music does she sing?"

"House," Ramiro smirked.

"My daughter listens to House music," Dr. Hopper said.

"House! What the fuck is this world coming to," Ramiro scoffed, mumbling.

"Do you like House?" the counselor asked.

"No!" Ramiro answered abruptly.

"Okay. How do you feel about Noelle singing house music?"

"It's her choice. I don't care," he turned away, shrugging.

"Do you support what she does?"

Ramiro shrugged, glaring at the counselor, and scoffed. "I guess so."

"Is it because it's not your type of music?"

"Yeah. I don't mean to show any disrespect to anyone who likes it, but it's not my thing. My sister likes house music also," Ramiro sucked his teeth.

"How does Noelle feel about you and your thing?"

"She's proud of me," Ramiro braced his shoulders back with a smirk on his face.

"Have you ever thought about doing a duet?"

"No! I don't fuckin' think so," Ramiro turned fiery red in the face because he wanted to get off the subject. He knew it was his job. *"But shit! Fuckin' stop already!"*

Dr. Hopper noticed the fire in this rocker's eyes, but he had to dig deep into his soul to see what was going on.

"All I have to say is, I love Noelle to death! This fuckin' session is done!" this metal god stood to his feet, storming from the living room to the bunk area. He laid in his bed and took off his boots and jeans while on his back. No one better not dare say a word to him right now. Just leave this pissed rocker alone for now. He pulled the drapes back on his bunk bed, closed his eyes.

"DARK ROMANCE!" THIS bassist's voice echoed on the microphone the next night in Buenos Aires, Argentina. The arena held four-thousand, seven-hundred enthused fans. Ramiro and his bandmates played the fierce, belligerent tunes of the song. The mosh pit was in full swing, with rockers crashing into one another. While backstage, Dr. Hopper watched Ramiro's disgruntled expression on his face while he sang. The counselor grabbed his cell and did a google search for Irate's song lyrics. The band's two albums came up as he needed info on his client. He scrolled through the list of songs and came across "Dark Romance." But he wanted to see what Ramiro was trying to convey.

CHAPTER TWENTY-TWO

The unidentified flying object-shaped Mercedes-Benz Arena in Shanghai; China held a capacity of eighteen thousand enthused fans who traveled far to hear their favorite bassist and band play. They pumped their fist in the air, demanding Ramiro to take his place on stage. The tarantula logo appeared on the screen while the scene darkened. The rockers applauded and whistling. Then the bass line started the show as the spotlight beamed on Ramiro's headbanging with his long brunette hair flying all over the place. A drop of sweat streamed down the side of his face already while working the strings of his instrument. He hoped not to have another episode. Disappointing fans was a "No" in his eyes. The best thing Ramiro did was to keep himself playing his bass. He prayed to his grandmother, who watched over him and judged his every move. With his heart set on her, Ramiro entertained the audience with improvised tunes.

"Abuelita, please keep me grounded on my feet. I don't want any rumors about me passing out on stage during concerts in the media. It's embarrassing," Ramiro played as he could see the admirers loving the show. "Wow, my band and I have fans here in China. Thousands of loyal fans. I'm grateful for them. I noticed how I keep saying, "My fans." Abuelita, you're probably wondering why I seem so self-centered. I'll admit that. What am I going to do about Noelle? She probably hates me after I pushed her. And I know you're not too proud of me for doing that to her. That's why I'm getting help so that I can build a life for Noelle. So, can you please guide me in the right direction? I love you, Abuela," Zack added the drums to Ramiro's bass line and then the electric guitar, bringing a musical collaboration. The middle of the audience formed a mosh pit that moved in a circular motion. "Dark Romance!" he bellowed on the microphone. The music alternated into a fast pace rhythm, where fans moshed and body surfed. Ramiro's handsome face appeared on the enormous screens set on opposite sides of the stage. Dr. Hopper watched this talented musician do his thing once again in this massive country with over a billion people. If this arena held this many fans or they would reach to the heavens. Ramiro performed the same songs he sang during his South American tour. Dr. Hopper listened again to the "Dark Romance" lyrics. He already had his notes on the song and wanted to confront Ramiro.

"Everyone Sees Death," Ramiro announced on the microphone. The audience cheered, continued moshing. The titled song was clear as day. People die every day, and some see the shadow of death coming, and others don't. Dr. Hopper wanted to know what was going on in his head with this song when he wrote it. He heard Ramiro did a lot of the writing on the band's albums. His music reflected his past and issues in society. Dr. Hopper sat in a chair, watching the show as if he got the Irate concert on Pay Per View. An assistant tapped him on the shoulder, giving him bottled water. "Here you go, Dr. Hopper."

"Thank you," smiled the silver thin-framed glasses therapist. He wondered about Noelle and Ramiro's relationship. Did Noelle wear her hair in a particular style that turned him on? Does he know her favorite color? What was her favorite song from Irate? And all that good stuff. Ramiro's performance distracted Dr. Hopper from taking notes. For now, he enjoyed the show.

ON THE ROAD AGAIN, the band's tour bus zoomed on the G50 Shanghai-Chongqing Expressway to Hong Kong for another show.

Danny, Zack, and two roadies played cards with the radio blaring rock music. Stanley punched the keys on his laptop, taking care of business affairs for the band. He lounged on the leather sofa, sipping on his coffee. Douglas lounged on the small couch with his cellphone to his ear. He made calls to the management of the Hong Kong coliseum that Irate would be on time for their gig. In the recreation room, Ramiro's session was being held as he sat on the edge of the sofa with his head down. He didn't have the recliner this time where he usually lounged. Again, he didn't have the heart to start the conversation. The session was his life, and he'd better speak on it and not waste this therapist's time. Dr. Hopper stared, waiting for Ramiro. "Do you want to end the session, Ramiro?"

"Why?" he looked up at Dr. Hopper.

"You're not saying anything,"

"Fuck it! I'm going to get to the real deal of this shit! I'm an abuser and put my hands on Noelle!" Ramiro turned away, holding his head down.

"What have you been doing to your girlfriend? Abuse her how?" Dr. Hopper leaned forward in his chair. He was getting somewhere with this young man.

Ramiro stood to his feet, pacing the floor and focusing his eyes down. The guilt of throwing Noelle with all his strength to the floor. She could've hit her head. By the grace of GOD, she plummeted to her rear end. This badass rock musician sobbed like a baby. Dr. Hopper grabbed the box of Kleenex that sat on the table.

"Ramiro, here," he offered the tissues to him. Ramiro knocked the box out of the therapist's hand, wiping the salty water from his eyes with his hands.

"I can see Noelle plummeting to the floor. I would've gone crazy if I saw my grandmother pushed!"

"Do you believe you're repeating the same pattern?"

"Yes. I don't want to be like my father," Ramiro then sat on the edge of the leather sofa.

"Do you want to talk more about your father?" Dr. Hopper asked.

Ramiro didn't utter a word; he looked at Dr. Hopper and nodded. He reminisced about the time when he heard his mother's agonizing cries. He and Maritza couldn't do anything to get this giant monster off their mother. They were too little. His father wanted him to grow up quickly.

SPONGEBOB SQUARE PANTS cartoon played on Nickelodeon tv on a Saturday morning while Ramiro and Maritza devoured a bowl of Fruity Pebbles cereal in the kitchen. The kids did this routine as all American youth did. Maritza grabbed the remote, turning down the volume so the television wouldn't wake their parents, especially their father. Jorge wasn't too crazy about SpongeBob Square pants, and other animated shows because he believed they had demonic forces. The kids heard the hinges squeak on a bedroom door from the second floor. Maritza turned the volume off.

"Are you kids down there!" Jorge hollered.

Maritza and Ramiro glared at each other, not knowing what to do. Heavy footsteps pounded down the carpeted steps to the first floor, seeing his kids watching the television. The kids were frozen in their chairs, noticing their father's brown complexion turn cherry red. He crept towards the kitchen table, peering at the television. Their father's eyes widened, noticing the SpongeBob Square Pants cartoon playing. Jorge snatched the plug from its socket, throwing the small tv against the wall where it knocked the picture frame of Anna Maria. Jorge meant to do that, seeing his wife's beautiful photo on the floor with the shattered glass was telling of their marriage. Ramiro backed away from his father while his menacing shadow hovered over him. His father took his fist, punching this little boy in the stomach. Ramiro curled up in a fetal position, sobbing. Maritza dashed to her brother's side. Anna Maria hurried down the staircase and noticed her son on the floor in pain. She cradled Ramiro in her arms.

"Stop babying him!" Jorge pulled Ramiro from Anna Maria's arms.

"That's my son!" Anna Maria received a backhanded slap across the face where she fell to the floor.

"He could take a punch!" Jorge bellowed.

Ramiro stood to his feet, back to reality, glaring at Dr. Hopper. "Could we talk about this later?"

"No! Ramiro, we're going to face it now!" Dr. Hopper demanded. "I want to know how that affected you?

Ramiro sat on the leather sofa, looking in the other direction. He knew what he wanted to say but couldn't trust anyone.

"You're not going to let anyone know about this shit, right?" he glared out of the window.

"Everything is strictly confidential, Ramiro," Dr. Hopper said.

"I was jealous of Zack. He and his father had such a bond. Fuck! That's something my father and I never had," Ramiro still facing the window.

Standing outside of the closed recreation door, Zack pressed his ear on the wall. He picked up the conversation and crept away.

TWELVE-THOUSAND, FIVE-hundred metal heads jammed the Hong Kong Coliseum the next night, headbanging. Ramiro played his bass guitar while Dr. Hopper and his management observed from backstage. This counselor watched Ramiro while he played his solos. He didn't get into the discussion of his lyrics and their meaning. But, he got into his father doing shit and meaning to do it without any sympathy. While performing and engaging with the audience, these thoughts were in the back of Ramiro's mind. On the surface, he smiled, spoke to his fans, and performed, but behind the Heavy Metal glitz and glamour, he was a broken bassist.

A FEW NIGHTS LATER, in a hotel suite at the Tokyo Hilton, Ramiro and Dr. Hopper argued like crazy just a couple of hours before Irate's performance. Guests stayed on the same floor and upper floors where they heard the verbal fight. Ramiro paced the carpet of the living room, while his counselor sat in the fancy cushioned chair. Dr. Hopper had a pen and pad in his hand. Ramiro stopped as he came to the window before his eyes, getting a view of downtown Tokyo similar to Times Square. The virtual advertisements of American and Japanese products in enormous display. He couldn't enough this moment, getting the royal treatment.

In the hallway, two Japanese groupies dashed to Ramiro's hotel room. But they didn't succeed because three security guards blocked the door. They heard loud bickering coming from the hotel room, knowing it was Ramiro.

"Is this Ramiro Espinoza's room?" one of the female Japanese fans asked. She wore red and purple hair, with a short black skirt, Irate t-shirt, fishnet stockings, and combat boots.

The security guard brushed it off, so the girl wouldn't know that Ramiro was in a session at that moment.

"I can hear Ramiro's voice. Let me see him," the girly fan kicked the hotel door. The guard grabbed the girl, but she jumped away from him. "Don't do that. Mr. Espinoza doesn't want to be disturbed!"

"Ramiro! Ramiro! Ramiro, we know you're in there come out!" the Japanese fans chanted.

Ramiro heard the girls screaming his name from outside of his hotel suite, "What the fuck! Excuse me, Doc!"

"Can't keep your fans waiting!" Dr. Hopper gave him the okay.

"Mr. Espinoza, I'm sorry to disturb you, but you have some fans," the guard knocked on the door as Ramiro head towards it. "I'll sign some autographs and shit." Ramiro smiled from ear to ear, greeting his female admirers. "What's up, ladies!"

"Oh, my God! Ramiro!" the female fans embraced him, taking a photo with their cellphone camera.

RETURNING TO HIS SESSION with Dr. Hopper, Ramiro faked a smile for fans and the public turned to a frown behind the scenes. "Yes! I want to kill my father! The shit that mother fucker's put me through!" he glared at Dr. Hopper while proceeding to pace the carpeted floor. "Don't you have anything to say!"

"I want to help calm the storm inside you! I know you've been irate for a long time to where you and Noelle broke up!"

"We didn't break up!"

"Are you sure about that?" Dr. Hopper twirled his pen.

"Yes! She went home!" Ramiro threw his hands up, stopping at the window once again.

"Tell me about the song "Dark Romance", the therapist asked.

"Read the lyrics," Ramiro turned to his therapist.

"Are the words referring to Noelle?" he asked.

"Yes. She's my fiance," Ramiro replied.

"Would you love to scare Noelle?" Dr. Hopper asked.

"Scare Noelle? She's already afraid of my two tarantulas. And it's just a fuckin' song" he rose his voice and then lowered it.

"It's not just a fuckin' song? It shows that you want to afflict pain on the woman you supposedly love! A midnight candlelit dinner, tarantulas crawled on the walls, a python slithers on the table. You screamed your head off at the fuckin' creepy crawlies," Dr. Hopper read the lyrics from a music website on his cellphone. He continued to read the entire song, which made him guilty about writing the song.

"Fuckin' stop!" Ramiro threw a coffee pot against the wall.

"Ramiro! What the hell!" the counselor stood up from his chair. He witnessed his violent behavior.

"It's your job to help me!" Ramiro paced around, throwing his fists in the air. He turned fiery red.

"I'm trying to help you, Ramiro. You've got to figure out how you're going to do this!"

"That engagement ring was a pretty penny that I slipped on Noelle's finger," Ramiro stormed out of the hotel room without looking back. He didn't tell his counselor that Stanley had to cover his ass because his credit card declined and that he shattered the glass counter with his fists. He would not bring his lousy credit to Dr. Hopper because his childhood past and his fuck up relationship with Noelle was enough. The therapist tossed his pad and pen on the table and took a seat. He shook his head, not knowing how to deal with Ramiro.

SIMULTANEOUSLY, A JAPANESE rock reporter interviewed Zack in the hotel room across the hallway. A cameraman aimed the camera at him while he sat in a chair alone, answering questions about the band's concert, future music, and their lives period. He dished the dirt on how he and Ramiro's bond was broken over creative differences. Ramiro always wanted to take credit for songwriting and instrumentals. He had to let the world know this talented musician had a dark side. And the reason for the song "Dark Romance." Zack knew good and well what he said.

"So, you and Ramiro haven't been getting along?"

"What did I just tell you. It's all about Ramiro," Zack told the Japanese Heavy Metal reporter, cringing in his seat, hearing two best friends with their success and friendship possibly falling apart.

MINUTES LATER, RAMIRO sat before this Japanese reporter in the same hotel room. The rock journalist peppered questions about his music, career, bandmates, and Noelle. Ramiro snapped at the journalist with answers, making the atmosphere hostile. The reporter didn't allow this bassist's salty persona to stop him. The Japanese rock reporter kept coming with questions and returning the exact dreadful attitude. Ramiro's heart raced in his chest, hearing the rumor about an instrumental House song with his bass line incorporated into it. "What the fuck!" Ramiro hopped out of his seat and choked the interviewer. Stanley and Douglas pulled Ramiro off the music reporter. Ramiro stormed out of the hotel room.

"Are you okay? Get him some water!" Stanley patted the reporter on the back. The interviewer held his hand around his neck, gasping for air.

THAT NIGHT A BLUISH spotlight beamed on the stage while Ramiro was in silhouette at the Saitama Super Arena. The roar of fans erupted throughout the venue as they lit cigarette lighters that made the audience resemble holiday lights. The rockers brought every seat in the house of thirty-seven thousand capacity. The band's last show had arrived, and Ramiro wanted to make the best of it. He wanted it to go as smoothly as possible, so he could get home. "Fuck! I miss the shit out of Noelle! I love her!" Ramiro juddered his head around, playing his aggressive bass. And then after the tour is over, Ramiro would make his way back to the states.

CHAPTER TWENTY-THREE

Ramiro widened his eyes as they followed the twirling ceiling fan above his head. He slumbered in his king-sized bed with the black satin sheets covering him from the waist down. The fourteen-hour flight from Tokyo to New York caused jet lag, where he took catnaps. His plane landed in the Big Apple at six in the evening, which was pretty good because it allowed Ramiro to get home and rest. As the fan rotated cold air, Ramiro dosed off and on lying in his comfortable bed. He turned, realizing Noelle wasn't there on the other side to slumber next to him. Ramiro heard about the House song that had his bass solo sampled into it. *"Noelle's responsible for this shit. She swiped the file of my bass solo from the management laptop. What the fuck! Is this her way of getting back at me?"* Ramiro sat on the edge of his bed, feeling a heaviness in his chest. A severe sadness because of this embarrassment. He wanted to see if the rumor was true about this House song. He worried that his fans would look at him fuckin' differently! They'll fuckin' lose respect for him. He didn't have the balls to turn on his desktop computer or check the internet on his cellphone. Ramiro ignored the devices that harbored the gossip. His enormous glass tank where his tarantulas occupied was empty. Neil took care of Ramiro's spiders while he toured the globe until he came back home. He'll get to his pets later.

RAMIRO THEN DRAGGED his bare feet along the icy floor in the dark corridor. A long drawstring of the ceiling fan in the hallway hung right before his eyes. He pulled it, turning on the light. He marched in the kitchen where a digital clock read five, forty-seven a.m. He swung open the refrigerator as a foul smell hit him like a punch in the face. The gallon of milk had a sour stench, including orange juice, cheese, and other foods that he should've gotten rid of before he went on tour. Ramiro poured the spoiled milk down the drain in the sink. Then he poured the orange juice down as well. He tossed the cheese and outdated food in the trash. He saw the half-opened Chips Ahoy cookies on the counter. The last time he ate one was a year and a half ago. Ramiro tossed that in the trash. He violently opened the cabinets of canned goods, throwing them into the can, and didn't care if the food was still good. He grabbed a trash bag, throwing more canned goods, boxes of cereal, crackers, and whatever else he got his hands on. *"What the fuck! Noelle's not fuckin' here! So, why the fuck should I even keep this food. She's not here to cook even if it was good,"* Ramiro proceeded to shove the food in the garbage. He threw it across the kitchen, leaning his body against the wall. He slid down against it until his rear end hit the floor. *"Should I call Noelle and curse her out? She probably won't fuckin' answer my calls. Fuck!"*

AN HOUR LATER, IN A steamy bathroom, Ramiro wiped the fogged cabinet mirror with his hand. He glared at his reflection with water dripping from his wet hair as he did not know what he would do for the day. He dreaded checking out the internet about this House song that's got him fucked up. Ramiro already wrote songs for the band's third album. It's a good thing that's out of the way. He wanted to lounge and not do a fuckin' thing but wallow in his misery. *"Noelle's somewhere getting her fuck on with some fuck! Dr. Hopper's practice is in Midtown. He arranged more sessions for me. I'm a fuck-up,"* he spat at his reflection in the mirror. Then his cellphone rang with the "Dark Romance" ringtone. He turned, hearing the call coming from his bedroom.

MOMENTS LATER, RAMIRO paced the floor wearing his boxers on and bare-chested with his hair partially dried. He held his cellphone to his ear as the ring tone buzzed in his ear. He hoped Noelle would answer. He allowed the phone to ring until it went to her voice message. "Hello, this is Noelle. Leave your name and number and I'll get back to you. Have a blessed day," then the voice message beeped as the recording allowed Ramiro the opportunity to speak.

"Noelle! I don't know if this is true or not! Did you take my bass solo and sample it! What the fuck possessed you to do that shit! I dread looking at what my fans are probably saying! It's me. I don't expect you to pick up because I know you must hate the shit out of me. After you left, I felt like shit and I was going to make things right until you pulled this shit! Now, fuckin' what!" Ramiro ended his call. Then his cellphone rang again. It read: Stanley.

"What's up, Stanley," Ramiro answered the call while he paced his apartment.

"What's up, Ramiro? Noelle's responsible for this. Did you check out the internet?" Stanley inhaled.

LATER, RAMIRO TURNED on his computer and googled Ramiro Espinoza does House music. A musical track appeared on the screen with a play button. He clicked on it as the House song began. Noelle's voice emerged over the track, harmonizing with it. Ramiro sneered because he did not know what Noelle was saying or tried to convey.

Her singing sounded like shit. The artist of the track was "Noelle." The song received thousands of downloads and likes.

Ramiro went to YouTube, checking out the reaction videos for the untitled House track. Hundreds of rockers were pissed off with the rumor. A spiked-hair, white male, late-thirties, went on a rant about the Techno song. He cursed, waving his hands in the air, and pounding his fist on his desk. "Ramiro Espinoza is my fuckin' idol. I don't know about his girlfriend who sings House, but there's no way in fuckin' hell he co-signed for the pop song or House, mouse, or whatever the fuck you call that happy shit! Ramiro, I believe in you dude!" the Irate fan rocked in his chair, turning red in the face. Ramiro then clicked on the next YouTube video, a Strawberry-blond teen girl, sporting an Irate t-shirt who handled the hearsay, mildly, "I don't know. Maybe, Ramiro and Noelle have different musical tastes. Yes, his girlfriend's name is Noelle. From what I heard, they're engaged and they're hopefully going to patch things up. Ramiro will continue to rock the world with his bass." YouTube video after video, Irate fans didn't condemn Ramiro for the false of his fiancé. They still loved him and his band, looking forward to more music and concerts. Ramiro inhaled, relieved that his fans supported him on this incident that he had no control. The track played Zack's interview LIVE on YouTube. He clicked on the site, seeing Zack sitting alone, dishing the dirt on his former best friend's family issues and how their friendship has fallen apart. And the biggest shock of all, he's leaving the band.

"What the fuck!" he dialed Zack's number and paced the floor.

"What!" Zack answered calmly.

"I'll fuckin' tell you what! You're leaving!" Ramiro paced the floor faster than his cardiac muscle raced in his chest.

"Did you not see my interview," Zack spoke in a low tone.

"Good! Fuckin go! I'll find another drummer a zillion-times better than you! You're a piece of shit!" Zack guffawed from over the phone. Ramiro disconnected the call.

MOMENTS LATER, RAMIRO sported his dark denim, black hoodie, with black construction boots, ready to head to the studio to meet with his management. There was a knock on his apartment door; Ramiro opened it without asking to see who it was. A twenty-something young man, a postal carrier, held a stack of letters in his hands. The essential worker recognized Ramiro, greeting this metal god with a Good morning, and of course, asking for an autograph and that "For Fuck's Sake was his favorite album. Ramiro signed his name on scrap paper and taking a snapshot from the fan's cellphone. He shook hands with the admirer, closing the door. Ramiro shuffled through the stack of mail. His eyes widened, noticing the credit card bills coming up again. And then his heart dropped as he read the return address on a letter for court. He tore open the letter, reading it. Ramiro's blood boiled and tightened his hand into a fist.

"What! Court!" Ramiro immediately thought of Maritza. This time he would not keep his cool.

AT A MANHATTAN RECORDING studio, Danny rocked in a leather recliner with Stanley, Douglas, a studio engineer, and a few colleagues from the band's management team. "We can't work on anything until we have a drummer. How long are we going to audition?" Danny whined. "Until we find the right drummer! Dan, stop acting like a baby!" Douglas rocked his chair hard. Ramiro stormed into the studio, "What the fuck now?"

"We're going to hold auditions for a drummer as soon as possible!" Stanley and Ramiro made eye contact as if they wanted to go toe to toe. Ramiro didn't utter a word, turning his back. He plopped his body in a revolving chair. And of course, he gave his back as he faced the wall, turning on the very people who made him the person he is today. He eyed the picture of him on the Guitar magazine cover. "I've got no time to sit around waiting for these auditions to take place. I will not sit here and wait. There's nothing to do right now! I've got things to do!" Ramiro swerved his chair and stood to his feet.

"Stanley, I've got to appear in court because of my sister!"

"Your sister? What the hell happened?"

"Maritza used my social security number to open up credit cards that ran up to over sixty, three grand in bills!" Ramiro explained.

"Are you sure?" Stanley leaned forward in his chair.

"Who the fuck else would do this shit?"

"Let me contact my lawyers and have them look into the situation before you accuse your sister of identity theft!" Stanley patted Ramiro on the shoulder. "I've got something to show you".

MINUTES LATER, STANLEY removed an enormous white drape from a black matte Dodge Ram with shiny rims on its four wheels. Ramiro's eyes widened seeing the brand-new vehicle before him. The vehicle was a gift from Stanley and Douglas to Ramiro for a job well done on his international tour.

"Holy shit! She's a beauty," Ramiro opened the driver's side door and hopped in. He whiffed the aroma of the fresh truck. The black leather seats were huge and comforting. He checked out how large the dashboard was and the stereo in it. He immediately turned on the radio and then saw the logo for the Sirus XM satellite system.

"You downloaded Sirus, Stanley," Ramiro immediately turned to a rock station and increased the volume.

"You like it?" Stanley lightly slapped the driver's side door.

"I love it! Thanks, Stan!" Ramiro smile then turned to a frown, thinking about the drive to Syosset. "What the fuck am I going to do with two trucks?"

"Ramiro, you're a big name. You can do whatever you want. What do you mean?"

"Where am I going to keep my Durango?" he sighed.

"Don't worry I'll store it in my garage until you can find some room for both," Stanley smiled.

"Alright, cool! Like I said I've got to get to Long Island," Ramiro started up the engine and revved it.

"You'll be there in no time. Drive safely," his manager stepped away from the truck while Ramiro drove out of the garage.

WHILE RAMIRO OCCUPIED the driver's seat of his new black Dodge Ram, he zoomed along the FDR drive from Manhattan to Long Island. He hasn't seen his mother and wanted to surprise her. Boy, does he have a surprise in store for his sister, Maritza? Ramiro didn't like the idea of coming home to visit his mother only to upset her. He still hasn't eaten due to him dealing with Zack and Noelle's bullshit. Zack leaving the band is probably a good thing. Ramiro would have less stress. Chances are, his mother heard the news about her son's band having issues and his bass solo incorporated into Noelle's House music. Now, he's got more shit coming his way. Ramiro had some choice words for his sister who used his social security number for God only knows what.

LATER THAT DAY, RAMIRO picked his food at the kitchen table at his mother's home as she sat across from him. She had little to say to her son, but hello. Anna Maria asked about her son's tour because she knew Ramiro had a lot on his plate. There was nothing but silence between them. His mother felt the tension in the air. Something was about to jump off. She picked the carrots on the fork and ate the veggies. Ramiro's fork fell from his hand, clattering on the plate. Anna Maria glared at Ramiro, wondering why he dropped his utensil on his plate. His mother knew he wanted her attention. His mother continued eating her food.

"Mom, I've been away for a year and a half,"

"And!" his mother cut him off. Ramiro saw the glare in his mother's eye.

"Zack's leaving the band, Noelle sampled my bass solo and your daughter left me with sixty-three thousand in credit card bills! I have to go to court!" Anna Maria now dropped her fork on the plate. "It can't be! Maritza would never do a thing like that!" she grabbed her plate and stormed into the kitchen. Ramiro pushed his plate away from him. "What the fuck! My mother! My Mother's pissed!" Keys rattled at the front door, the locks clicked as the door pushed open with Maritza entering with some plastic bags in her hands. Ramiro rushed to his sister's side, taking the groceries from her hand. Maritza embraced her brother as he gave a slight smile. She wanted to know all about his tour, being one of the biggest rock stars in the world, his new Dodge Ram, and Noelle. She worshipped the ground that he walked on. But Ramiro wanted to curse Maritza out so severely while she did the opposite. Ramiro placed the grocery bags on the dining room table.

"What the fuck is this, Maritza!" Ramiro threw the batch of letters at his sister. She took the mail and looked through them. Maritza rose an eyebrow, not understanding what her brother was trying to convey.

"What is this, Ramiro?"

"You fuckin' know exactly what it is! You've been opening up credit cards using my social security number. Haven't you?" he confronted.

"Your social security number! What the fuck would I want with your SS number!"

"I've got an appearance in court!" he hollered.

"And? That's not my problem! You better take it up with a lawyer! I'm pretty sure you've got one!" Maritza threw the letters at Ramiro.

"What the hell, Ramiro!" Anna Maria strutted out of the kitchen.

"These are the notices from the credit card companies suing me for not paying the bills that I had nothing to do with!" he exclaimed.

Anna Maria took a deep breath, looking over the notices. She sat at the head of the table. "This can't be true! There's got to be some mistake!"

"Oh, my God! I don't believe this shit!" Maritza stomped her heel on the floor.

"Check out all the letters, mom," he showed his mother more of the credit card bills and the court summons. Her eyes shifted left to right and bulging because of the over sixty-thousand dollars in credit card bills. Then Anna Maria looked at the letter for Ramiro's court date.

"Like I said, Ramiro. There must be some mistake. Maritza wouldn't do this!" his mother shook her head.

"I don't know your social security number. I've got credit cards in my name opened up with my social security number," Maritza snatched credit cards from her wallet. She only showed two credit cards, a Visa and Mastercard. Maritza didn't own a Saks Fifth Avenue credit card, nor did she have a Discover card. Ramiro felt like a total ass. He grabbed the letters and stormed out of the house. "What the fuck is your problem, Ramiro!" his sister gave chase.

Outside, Ramiro rushed to his black Dodge Ram while Maritza pumped her fist in the air. He felt fuckin' stupid at this moment. Maybe he made a mistake. He shouldn't have jumped the gun and listened to his manager. "How the hell did you conjure up such bull-shit, Ramiro!" Maritza pounded her fist on the hood of his brand-new truck.

"Maritza, stop acting like a child!" Anna Maria pulled Maritza away from Ramiro's vehicle as he attempted to drive away.

"Get away before you get hurt!" Ramiro shouted as he rolled the window down.

"Maritza!" her mother shouted. Maritza continued to pound on the hood of her brother's vehicle.

"Please, you've got the neighbors looking at us!" Anna Maria pulled her daughter by the arm back into the house. "It's okay," she waved to the residence next door. Maritza rushed into the house as Anna Maria followed, slamming the front door.

LATER, DECAYING ROSES, Carnations, and Tulips laid in a dirt-filled wheelbarrow next to Mrs. Stein, now in her Golden years. She wore a sunbonnet, wallowing in her garden in front of her Mass-apequa home. No more noisy kids interrupting her family, but they did a job on her mother. Her mother transitioned a few years earlier. When Mrs. Stein's elderly mother died because of Alzheimer's disease. At first, she blamed Zack's drumming along with Ramiro's bass playing, but mainly that pounding Tama kit did it. Mrs. Stein stopped pointing the finger at these two musicians who have one of the biggest bands in the world. Mrs. Stein loves Ramiro's bass solos, but she can't take Zack's drumming. She never could. Sorry, but it is what it is. And a couple of songs that she might not know the name. If she hears the tune and knows that it's Irate, then okay. Mrs. Stein finished pulling out the old flowers and dug into the soil with a small shovel. She planted her new red tulips on the ground. A roaring car engine rumbled in the background. She heard it but pay no attention. The dedicated sixty-something floral fanatic kept inserting more flowers into the earth. Heavy footsteps pounded, approaching Mrs. Stein. She turned and stopped what she was doing. She squinted her eyes, standing to her feet, and noticed this long-haired, brunette gentleman with his black clothing getting closer. "How are you, Mrs. Stein?"

"Ramiro!" Mrs. Stein's face lit up like the groupies that hung out backstage at his concerts. "How are you, rock star?" this once grumpy old maid, embraced Ramiro.

"Wow, she's hugging me! This old bat always called the cops on Zack and I when we were kids. Now, she's a fan. Holy shit! What fame will do for you!" his eyes widened. "I'm cool."

"What brings you around to the old neighborhood? Homesick? It's a long way from Hollywood," Mrs. Stein nudged, winking her eye.

"I don't live in Hollywood. I live in the West Village with my fiancé," he smiled.

"Oh, wow! The West Village is ritzy," Mrs. Stein did a little dance. "What part?"

"West Seventh street," he smiled as he eyed the wheelbarrow with the decayed roses. He didn't want to come off fake towards her.

"Do you need those old flowers, Mrs. Stein?" Ramiro cut to the chase. He didn't even ask this old woman who lived alone how life has treated her. Ramiro didn't bother to ask about her deceased mother or anything else. He noticed a beetle that crawled amongst the dead flowers pulled from the soil. Without a doubt, Mrs. Stein gladly offered for Ramiro to have whatever he desired. She also invited him in for coffee she once shared with her husband. He noticed the smiled on this neighbor's face that seemed sneaky. Ramiro knew this old woman probably hasn't had good sex in a long time and wanted him to bang her. He immediately spoke about his fiancé, Noelle, and how they loved each other very much. But their relationship is dwindling because she disrespected him. The old neighbor's face dropped from a smile to a raise of an eyebrow. "What could the matter be?" Mrs. Stein tilted her head and couldn't believe this Thrash metal god had problems like everyone else. Ramiro didn't feel like getting into the matter. He gathered at least twelve dozen expired roses in his hand.

"What on earth do you want with deteriorating roses, Ramiro?"

"I'm showing my love to my fiancé. Thanks, Mrs. Stein, and thanks for listening," Ramiro kissed this older woman on the cheek, swaggered to his Dodge Ram, and sped away.

THAT SATURDAY NIGHT, the Paradise Club dancers shook their hips and moved their feet to the low bass line with screeching synthesizing keyboards of House music. Pink, Fushia, and red lights rotated, which made the dance floor sway. Noelle performed for eight weeks straight with some of her material, and the House track she produced sampling Ramiro's bass. She knew it was an evasion of copyright. She prayed Ramiro would let it go and they could move on. The messed-up thing would be if Ramiro sued her. Whenever Noelle had time to herself, she'd sit alone at a table with a glass of Pepsi. You can't go wrong with that.

"Hey, Noelle! How are you, babe?" Terry pulled out his chair and sat before Noelle.

"What's up, Terry?" she sipped on her glass of soda.

"Why are you sitting here? You should get your groove on!" Terry said.

"Not tonight! I'm tired and a little depressed," Noelle shook her head.

"Ramiro? Let me rephrase that "Is the engagement still on?" Terry asked.

"I don't know. I doubt after this stunt I pulled," Noelle glanced at the flashy heart-shaped onyx stoned diamond-cut eighteen karat ring.

"I told you not to use his bass solo. Ramiro's possibly going crazy!"

"It's too late for that," Noelle said.

"Why don't you get back in the studio and make some dance tracks that we could upload to social media. You've got the talent," he looked Noelle directly in the eye.

"Yeah, you're right," Noelle said.

"Alright. Call me if you need me," Terry walked away from the table.

Noelle watched the clubgoers down on the dance floor, enjoying themselves. *"I miss him so much. Ramiro didn't call me. Well, neither did I. I don't know how he's going to react to this House track I produced along with my colleagues. I sampled his work because I know he'd say no. So, I took it upon myself and used it,"* she gazed at the dancers. They were there, but then they weren't there. Worrisome about her relationship with this bassist who plays with passion and even makes love to her the same way.

"Noelle?" a skinny, pretty server approached her table with a long, narrow box with a fancy black ribbon on it.

"Yes," Noelle turned, smiling. The waitress placed the long box in her hands.

"These are for you," the server smiled.

"Oh, man. What's this?" Noelle's eyes popped.

"It's from Ramiro?" the server said, sashaying away.

"Oh, Ramiro. Baby," Noelle grabbed the card and read it. Her heart melted that her lover attempted to patch things up. *"Noelle, these roses are the symbol of our love,"* the small white card read. She smiled, opening the lid of the box as the smile on her face turned upside down. She pulled out the dozen decaying roses. Her eyes watered with tears of disappointment, anger, and sadness. "How the fuck could he?" she stormed away from the table with the expired flowers in her hands.

MOMENTS LATER, NOELLE stormed out of the rear of the Paradise club, looking around, trying to see if she could spot Ramiro. There were only club-goers who hung out, smoking, and socializing. She navigated through the long dark alleyway with a few dumpsters. Rats scurried alongside the foul-smelling garbage as Noelle noticed the rodents racing from piles of trash on the ground to the dumpsters. She turned back toward the Paradise Club rear, where she threw the dried roses on the ground. Noelle placed both her hands over her face, crying her eyes out. *"Is our love dead? I should've left his material alone. My fault. Ramiro must hate the shit out of me. What the hell was I thinking? I wanted Ramiro and I to have a connection. Not just with our love, but musically as well. But Ramiro's so caught up in his world. No other music will do. But Heavy Metal. That's fine. I'm not mad at him,"* Noelle wiped the tears from her eyes. She noticed the rock on that Ramiro slipped on her finger. "We're supposed to walk down the aisle!" Noelle continued to dry the droplets on her face. She looked around the rear of the club again, hoping that Ramiro would jump out. They kiss and have make-up sex, which most couples do. That would not happen, but you never know. The ring glistened on Noelle's finger with the diamonds and strong black onyx stone deep with its natural hues. "Maybe, we really may be over? Ramiro sent me dead flowers, so I'm dead in his eyes," she felt a depression in her chest. She wanted to hear from Ramiro's mouth if they were over. If then she could give him his ring.

CHAPTER TWENTY-FOUR

I n a recording studio, a couple of weeks later, Ramiro strummed his bass guitar as a new drummer played on the Tama drum kit to "Noise Pollution." This medium-built, black tank top, blue jeans, sneakers clad, drummer, early thirties, long-brunette hair similar to Ramiro's, competed with this pompous vocalist/bassist. These two artists played nicely together while both gave each other the evil eye. Ramiro's management watched while residing in some uncomfortable chairs. A stilled photographer from Rolling stone Magazine snapped pictures of Ramiro during the drummer audition. He wasn't nervous about his interview about the rumors amongst fans about this House song. He hoped this song would quickly die down. Ramiro still wanted to have some words with Noelle. Then his mind focused off the upcoming interview and alternated the tune from "Noise Pollution to Darkness." This bassist played faster, as the drummer couldn't keep up with this musician who switched themes. Ramiro tested this drummer to see what it took for him to make it in his band. Then he played "Klown" as this musician goofed with his drumming. He then caught up to Ramiro. Danny and Irate's management cackled while noticing Ramiro fuckin' around with the new hopeful musician. The drummer turned fiery red in the face while Ramiro alternated back to the song "Dark Romance." He did it again and again and again. The drummer played faster and faster, trying to track Ramiro playing around the band's songs. The drumming turned into a bunch of noise. The amateur drummer hopped off the drum seat, throwing the drumsticks down, and kicking over the floor drum.

"What the fuck! If you can't fuckin' keep up with my style, then fuck off!" Ramiro got up in the drummer's face with his bass in his hand.

"Fuck you, Ramiro! You fuckin' suck!" the drummer marched out of the recording studio as he swung the door opened.

"You fuckin' pussy! Go home!" Ramiro clutched his fists.

'Ramiro, you can't do that! You've got to be fair!"

"Be fair! For fuck, Sakes! Life isn't fuckin' fair! Is it fuckin' fair that my career could be on the line!! Is it fuckin' fair that I still have to go to counseling because I could still possibly lose the love of my fuckin' life! Fuck, I still love Noelle! Is it fuckin' fair that fuckhead Zack fucked some much shit up for me! And I'm due in fuckin' court!" Ramiro threw his bass guitar on the floor. He stormed out of the studio, kicking the door. His managers gave chase, trying to calm him down. Outside of the recording studio, a long line of drummers waited to get their chance at playing with Ramiro. These future Lars Ulrichs and Dave Lombardos witnessed their hero raging as his voice echoed throughout the building. Of course, they knew about the rumors about his sampled bass solo, his fiancé who causes this public humiliation, and his long-time friendship with Zack.

"He's fucked up over that House song. Poor dude," an auditioning drummer said.

"Do you believe she sampled his bass solo? I'd go fuckin' nuts if my girlfriend pulled some shit like that!" a second auditioning drummer twirling his drumsticks between his fingers.

"Fuckin' broads! She's trying to fuck up his career!" a third auditioning drummer shook his head.

WITHIN THE HOUR, RAMIRO played his bass guitar, testing out another drummer, an Asian musician who had no problem keeping up with every theme thrown his way. Ramiro played "Noise Pollution, Klown, Dark Romance, Everyone Sees Death, and so forth. This talented drummer was right on point when Ramiro changed tunes. The duo got into a competition with each other to where Ramiro couldn't keep up with this artist drumming along longer. He laughed it off because this musician had what it takes. Then drummer after drummer played alongside this Metal monster. After the musical tryouts, Ramiro shook hands with the drummers and would get back to them in the future.

A SPIKED-HAIRED, TATTOOED, body-pierced, Caucasian male, thirty-something Rolling Stone magazine reporter interviewed Ramiro while he sat in the recording studio. Ramiro gazed at this reporter, hoping that he asks nothing outrageous. Of course, he knows about his former drummer lying his ass off. "What's going on, Ramiro?" the rock reporter asked. He shook his hand.

"I'm cool," Ramiro took a deep breath. He expected something dumb to spew from this reporter's mouth.

"Word is that your band's looking for a new drummer?"

"That's right?"

"How have auditions been going?"

"The auditions went smoothly, and hopefully, Danny and I will decide as soon as possible," Ramiro responded.

"Where is Danny, by the way?"

"He doesn't want to be on camera right now?"

"Okay, that's cool. Ramiro, I don't mean to get off the subject, but is it true that your fiancé sampled your bass solo?" the Rolling Stone magazine reporter asked.

"Yes!" Ramiro inhaled.

"Do you think you guys will patch things up?" the music reporter asked.

Ramiro's heart raced in his chest, wanting to rip this reporter's throat out. "I don't care to fuckin' discuss my personal life right now! I'm here to talk about the music! Next question!"

"Your fans want to know about your new album," the Rolling Stone reporter rambled.

"The new album will be heavier and aggressive. You'll mosh to this one! I love you and appreciate all the Irate fans! This interview is over!" Ramiro stormed out of the recording studio.

TWO WEEKS LATER, ON a busy New York street, a newsstand displayed Ramiro on the front cover of the Rolling Stone Magazine with his bass guitar. A mid-twenties young man approached the vendor. "Give me a copy of Rolling Stone magazine," the young man at the same time placing two candies on the counter.

In a supermarket, a cashier placed the new Rolling Stone magazine in its right place. A seventeen-year-old young girl grabbed the periodical, seeing handsome Ramiro on the front cover with his bass. "Mom, look at Ramiro Espinoza," she gasped. Her mother pushed the shopping cart full of food to the register. "Do you have money to buy that?" the mother asked.

"No," the seventeen-year-old sighed.

"Well, put that trash back!" the mother snatched the magazine out of her daughter's hand, placing it back on the shelf.

THAT NIGHT ON A BLUE-lined, yellow writing tablet, Ramiro jotted "I'M NO F***IN' ANGEL" with a black ballpoint pen. Alone in his West Greenwich Village apartment, he didn't know what lyrics to write while in his recliner. The title was obvious to Ramiro's persona, he had no halo floating above his head with white wings spread from his back. The only thing Ramiro saw was horns sprouting out of his skull and talking in tongues. That's why he had to continue getting counseling, so maybe he could make things right. Everything right now is in limbo.

PACING THE FLOOR, RAMIRO gestured strangling Noelle due to him still infuriated with her the next morning in Dr. Hopper's office. His therapist sat right before him, wearing thin gold-framed glasses. As always, he allowed Ramiro to get his feelings out. He then simmered down and told that he sent Noelle some decaying roses. It was better than him doing something that would get him into deep shit. Dr. Hopper asked Ramiro what his next step would be? He and Noelle would have to meet face to face and sort things out. He struggled to find a new drummer for his band. And he dealt with writer's block when it came to writing songs. Dr. Hopper suggested he take it easy, maybe he should go for a walk around the city and maybe he'll come across something that would get his creative juices flowing again. Ramiro stopped pacing and then took a seat. He agreed that going out into the world and seeing different things would help.

"My mind is blank right now. I can't write any new material. I still have to struggle to find a new drummer. And Noelle and I have to talk," Ramiro stood up from the chair and paced as he usually did.

"How do you think Noelle felt about those roses?" Dr. Hopper asked.

"Fucked up! She might pawn the engagement ring," Ramiro halted his pacing, gazing out of the window.

"What are you going to do about it, Ramiro?" his counselor asked, tapping his pen on the arm of the chair.

"What can I do? I just have to hope for the best," he looked at his therapist and continued his gaze through the window. "I know one thing. I don't want to be my father," Ramiro then sat in the chair, placing his face in the palm of his hands. He then looked at Dr. Hopper again. "Dr. Hopper, am I my father?"

"That's a question you have to ask yourself?" he replied with a slight smile.

"I feel like my father physically and spiritually? Especially, spiritually. Maybe, someone has to perform an exorcism?"

"Do you think you've got an evil spirit within you?" Dr. Hopper pushed his glasses up on his nose.

"Yes. The demon is my father," Ramiro nodded.

AN HOUR LATER, RAMIRO strolled along the sidewalk of Saint Patrick's Cathedral on Fifth Avenue. The house of worship is known for its marble interior, religious artwork, detailed architecture, and events like the Christmas midnight mass. The double doors of the church were wide-opened, so anyone seeking spiritual guidance was welcome to do so. There weren't that many people sitting on the concrete steps of the Lord's house. Ramiro eyed the crucifix which sat on the tip-top of the cathedral. He acted like Damien in the movie "The Omen" when the little six-year-old child attacked his mother because of his fear of God. Ramiro inched his way up the stone stairs as the pigeons flew out of his way. He crept towards the entrance doors that welcomed the public. The incense aroma overwhelmed the house of worship as Ramiro got a strong whiff of it. He headed further and further inside without crossing himself; he glanced over his shoulders with the Christian imagery. A few people sat in rows at a distance from one another, some worshippers kneeled while others wallowed in the Lord's presence. Ramiro noticed a middle-aged, caucasian gentleman, Roman collared, black shirt, and slacks clad, whispering to a mother and daughter. No one occupied the middle rows; Ramiro eased his way between the wooden benches and sat down.

He gazed straight ahead of him with no thought. Ramiro looked over his shoulder, noticing this man of the cloth eyeing him.

"I'm going to sit here and try to get rid of this entity that dwells in me," from the corner of Ramiro's eye, the priest kept glancing at him. He didn't want to look at the priest again because this man of God could be in the closet. Or maybe the priest could cure demonic forces around him. Ramiro fought against the belief because his grandmother had a close and personal connection with God. If his grandmother were a God-fearing woman, then he would protect Ramiro from such evil forces. It's too late for that because the demon married her daughter, who is his father. So, the offspring carried the malevolent being throughout life and could pass down the behavior from generation to generation. Ramiro watched the mother and daughter praying, but the priest wasn't there. Ramiro's eyes googled around in its sockets as a soft-toned voice greeted him. "Ramiro Espinoza?"

Ramiro glanced over his shoulder, noticing the priest with his hand extended. "Can he feel that I have a disturbance in my life? This man of the cloth kept his eye on me and headed straight towards me. Is he going to splash some holy water on me and drive out my demons?"

"Irate, right?" The priest is an admirer of the band.

"Yes, it is," Ramiro reciprocated the handshake. "He's a fan. A priest listening to Metal? Wow!" he exclaimed.

The priest took a seat next to him, told him he watched their tour on YouTube and loved every moment of the show. Ramiro rose an eyebrow at this priest who gave details of Irate's tour, songs, and all. Then the priest was curious about Ramiro's rock-and-roll presence within the church. "What brings you here, my friend?"

"Do you believe in possession?" Ramiro cut to the chase. The priest kept his calm because he knew all about Ramiro's music.

"Not really? Why do you ask?" the priest questioned.

"You already know. Father, you know about my background. You're a fan. Right?" Ramiro said.

"I heard the stories," the priest said.

"And my rocky relationship with my fiance that I fu...," Ramiro stopped himself in time before he dropped the f-bomb in church. The priest placed his finger to his mouth.

"Ramiro, you don't believe in God?" the priest asked.

"No, I don't," Ramiro responded.

"So, what else are you doing to make things right with you and your fiance?"

"I'm seeking counseling," Ramiro shrugged.

"Okay. How is it working out for you?" the priest asked.

"My sessions are cool. I guess," he shrugged again.

"I'm Father Ryan," he extended his hand again to Ramiro. "Are you seeking God, Ramiro?"

"No. What has he done for me? Everything's just fu...," Ramiro halted his words before the f-bomb exploded again.

"You came to the right place. It's up to you not to repeat your father's sins so you can have a successful life," Father Ryan advised.

"I'm not sure about this God. Everyone brags about how great he is. Really?" Ramiro scoffed. He stood to his feet and didn't want to hear another word. He stormed by the priest and out of the church. As this angry rock musician rushed down the crowded Manhattan street, he maneuvered in between pedestrians. Still, he wasn't going to submit to God. He could only do so to his grandmother, who he saw as a god.

ON THAT YELLOW BLUE-lined paper that night, Ramiro jotted the word "Atheist" on the top of the page in black ink. He then wrote a list of song titles for the band's third album.

"ATHEIST"

1. "I'm No F**kin' Angel"
2. "The Angels Fell From Heaven"
3. "The Fault Of God,"
4. "The False Book"
5. "House Of Worship"
6. "Stuck In My Beliefs"
7. "Atheist"
8. "F**kin' Love Me Or F**kin Leave Me"
9. "My Fight With The Devil"
10. "Expired Rose"

Ramiro wrote the last title of that song; it was a way of him apologizing to Noelle. He had to make sure that the lyrics appealed to her and his female audience. They were the ones who downloaded Irate's music and attended the concerts along with his majority male fan base. He glared at the title of the last song he jotted on the notepad.

"I'M NO F**KIN' ANGEL"

"What the fuck do you expect, a choirboy who never did a daring thing in his life! I have! I became a musician and spewed ugly lyrics about how I hate everyone in my fuckin' path!" Ramiro wrote the hateful song towards anyone who disapproved. Then he wrote the lyrics for "The Angels Fell From Heaven" song. Most Christians would know what the song contained by the title. He flipped through the notepad as he became frustrated with some words not coming outright. He spent hours on end getting every word right. Ramiro never worried about offending anyone. He didn't care so that they could fuck off. He then wrote lyrics to the final song "Expired Rose."

CHAPTER TWENTY-FIVE

"I don't believe in religion, so I don't care about your opinion. I Believe in Me, not some man who walked on water, making the blind see, and the deaf hear, if this man was true, how come he doesn't make himself appear," Ramiro's voice echoed through the microphone to the song "Atheist" in a recording studio. He strummed his bass guitar with Danny by his side, playing lead guitar, and their new drummer, Eito Mori, a Japanese musician from the San Francisco Bay Area. He was born and raised in Yokohama, Japan, which is South of Tokyo, until age six. Eito's family moved to the San Francisco Bay Area, where he attended public school and learn about Jazz music in school. He enjoyed listening to drummers in that genre and then he turned to Rock/Heavy Metal music in High school, admiring those drummers as well. He had long black hair that reached his tailbone, similar to Ramiro's hair type. Eito had a medium-build, six-one, covered in tattoos and a few piercings. Ramiro and Eito hit it off right away, both musicians having a lot in common. They enjoyed the same music and had girlfriend issues. Eito's fiance got cold feet a day before the wedding, and he hasn't heard from her since then. But he's looking for someone new. Irate's sound was more aggressive because the new style of drumming had more bass. Eito didn't bother to mention Zack to Ramiro because of the band members falling out. So, he just went and playing and admired Zack's craft as an artist.

ABOUT AN HOUR LATER, a Rolling Stone magazine reporter sat before the trio with its new drummer, Eito Mori. Charlie Morton, a young woman, mid-twenties, who wore a baseball cap, Irate T-shirt, jeans, and sneakers, held a microphone in front of the guys.

"Were you nervous Eito about your audition?" Charlie asked.

"No. Not really. I just got on the Tama kit and drummed away," Eito responded.

"How do you feel about the recent addition to your band, Ramiro?"

"It's cool. His style is more upbeat," Ramiro answered.

I don't mean to go there. Have you guys heard from Zack?" the Rolling Stone reporter asked.

"I don't care to discuss that shit right now!" Ramiro exclaimed.

THEN THE BAND'S PHOTOGRAPHER snapped shots of the trio as they worked on new music. Eito drummed away like crazy on his eleven-piece drum set. The still cameraman took pictures of Irate's new drummer from the left and right angles, front and back views, bird's-eye view, etc. Ramiro and Danny tuned their guitars and trying out distinct sounds. The cameraman crept to the two guitarists, snapping pictures. Ramiro shifted his eyes on the cameraman, sneering. He glanced at the clock, reading eleven thirty-nine on the wall.

While Ramiro prepared for his session, he wondered what Noelle was doing. "I've got a feeling Noelle's at the club again. I'm still pissed about that fuckin' house song that she produced. I don't know How I'm going to let this shit go! Fuck! Earlier in our relationship, I fuckin' blew my top and hauled Noelle's ass out of the club. All of this back and forth between us has got to stop. I don't know if she's going to walk down that fuckin' aisle or not," Ramiro stood there still with a not-so-pleasant expression on his face. The photographer then scurried to Danny's side, snapping more shots. Ramiro placed his bass guitar on its stand, grabbing his cell, dialing Noelle's phone number. No answer. The cell rang and rang. Ramiro's face turned fiery red; he ended his call. He tapped the icon for FACE-BOOK, checking Noelle's page. On her status, it read that she was at the Paradise club. Exactly where she was going to be.

THAT NIGHT, NOELLE treated club goers, performing the new track entitled "To Love And To Cherish." The stage had a virtual background of wedding rings and white rose petals floating around as Noelle sported a white tight-fitting wedding gown that showed off her figure. The luxurious dress also had a long train behind it. She wore a white rose in her curly hair, pearl earrings, and lace wedding shoes. The audience danced as if Noelle was the DJ, but she put on a show. A low upbeat drumline, synthesizers that included Ramiro's sampled bass solo. Noelle loved the sound she created.

AFTER NOELLE'S PERFORMANCE, vivid colored flowers and gifts adorned her dressing room, where fans showered her with lots of love and support. The rosy bouquets perfumed the atmosphere with their natural fragrance. Noelle's white wedding outfit looked as if she stepped out of a fairytale, but her love life was far from it. The House song "To Love And To Cherish" gained attention from top producers and executives from the music industry. Terry wanted to produce a pop version of the song, but Noelle said no because Ramiro's already heated about it. One of Noelle's male admirers, a stunning bachelor, mid-forties, billionaire stockbroker, Maximus Farrington, snapped of shots with his cellphone. And of course, this high-value man spoiled Noelle with flowers, gifts and invited Noelle to sail away with him on his yacht. But Noelle declined the offer because she still sported the engagement ring on her finger. Maximus hoped to slip an even bigger ring on Noelle's finger. He understood and wished her all the best in the future. Noelle loved Ramiro and wanted to work on their relationship. Maximus pecked her on the cheek and went on his way.

A robust African-American bouncer guarded Noelle's dressing room; Maximus exited breezing past the guard. The bouncer peered inside, noticing there were no more fans in the dressing room with Noelle. He closed the door back.

"Where's Noelle?!" Ramiro confronted the muscular guard.

"She's not here!" he leaned his stocky body against the door, folding his arms.

"Don't bullshit me! Let me in!" Ramiro tried to reach for the doorknob.

"Get the fuck out of here!" the guard blocked Ramiro.

"Noelle, get out here! Now!" He shouted from the hallway. "Answer me! Fuck!" Ramiro threatened.

"And if I don't get the fuck out of here! What are you going to do?" Ramiro dared the guard to lay a finger on him. The bouncer shoved Ramiro. He then kicked the guard in the pelvis. The bouncer's face turned red and fell to the floor in a fetal position. Ramiro kicked the door opened, rushed in, and saw that Noelle sat alone in her vanity. She flinched because of the loud, pounding sound as Ramiro slammed the door and locked it. He swaggered inside, looking around. He blocked the door with a table. Noelle's heart raced in her chest as she panicked. Her eyes watered because she didn't know what Ramiro would do next.

"What's the problem, Ramiro?" Noelle backed into a corner. Ramiro grabbed two chairs to block the door. He kept his eyes fixed on Noelle. He snatched Noelle into his arms, giving her the most passionate kiss. Ramiro figured this would bring Noelle to her senses. Or maybe a good fuck would do the trick? Noelle pushed Ramiro away. "Don't think I didn't forget about the dead roses! What were you thinking!"

"And what were you thinking using my bass solo? You fuckin' embarrassed me in front of my fans! I was this close to cracking your fuckin' skull!"

"I'm sorry!" Noelle tapped her foot on the floor and looked in the other direction.

"It's too late for that! That corny song is all over the internet!" Ramiro insulted.

"Don't insult my music! I work hard on that, Ramiro!"

Ramiro scoffed "You worked hard? I worked fuckin' hard. I read and write music. You don't!"

"There's no need to put me down!"

"Well, you stole from me! What the fuck!" Ramiro noticed Noelle still wore the engagement ring. "You still love me? Right?"

"What do you think, Ramiro?" Noelle flashed the engagement ring to him. "I'm sorry for sampling your work," she cried.

"Don't worry about it. Forget about it," Ramiro laying a passionate kiss on Noelle.

AFTER THE COUPLE'S lovemaking that night, Noelle laid her head on the pillow with the skeletal night light beaming above the black headboard of the bed. She gazed at the ceiling, hearing Ramiro's lite snoring that kept her eyes wide open. Noelle cracked a smile. Ramiro laid on his back, bare-chested, resting his arm behind his head. His body piercings and 3D tarantula tattoo remained the same, nothing new. "I would love for Ramiro to get a tattoo of me on his body. Like on his shoulder blade, or on his chest where his heart pumped blood through his entire body," she couldn't keep her eyes off him. Then Ramiro slowly widened his eyes and turned to Noelle, seeing that she was awake.

"Why aren't you sleep?" Ramiro exhausted.

"You're snoring kept me up," Noelle snickered.

"I don't snore," Ramiro turned on his side, facing Noelle.

"Yes, you do. It's a low snore," she replied.

"A low snore? That's a first," Ramiro cleared his throat, shutting his eyes.

"It's not like it's disturbing," Noelle shrugged.

"What is it then? You missed me. Right?"

"Yes, I do," she kissed him on the lips. Noelle turned on her side as the couple faced one another and smiled. Ramiro felt at peace with his fiancé. He finally got over Noelle, incorporating his music into hers. But come to think about it. "To Love and To Cherish" is the song that Noelle produced is a unity of her and Ramiro. Even though it enraged him.

Ramiro clutched her hand. "I've got to tell you something. It's nothing bad, but it's a good thing for me. I'm talking to a counselor," Ramiro moved closer to Noelle.

She knew what it was for, but wanted more details. "Since when?" Noelle's eyes shifted from side to side because she knew Ramiro's situation.

"Since, you left. And then I knew I had to fight this shit," Ramiro wrapped his arms around her waist, pulling Noelle even closer to him.

"When is your next session?"

"Next week," he answered.

Noelle brought some wedding magazines, getting ideas on the type of gown she would wear. She purchased the periodical after she left Ramiro's tour. She flipped through the glossy pages, hoping they would reconcile their differences and move on. Ramiro asked Noelle if she ever thought of pawning the ring. Noelle shook her head because she loved him. She couldn't give up on him so easily. She continued to wear the ring and prayed to God that Ramiro would get help. And God answered her prayers. Noelle shared with Ramiro about God. And this invisible man Ramiro didn't believe in responding to Noelle's prayers. He sighed because he didn't want to hear it.

TWO WEEKS LATER, RAMIRO wore a three-piece suit, standing by his lawyer Elliot Foy, a glasses-clad, suit-wearing lawyer, who presented his client's case to the judge. Ramiro's band management sat in the front rows. Elliot Foy worked as an attorney for Irate whenever its members got into any trouble. The judge eyed Ramiro, noticing this long-haired, rock musician who he heard about. Ramiro's lawyer exhibited the credit card bills to this black-robed man on the bench. The judge wanted to hear this rocker's side of the story. Ramiro told the courtroom he did not know who used his social security number. The judge rose an eyebrow, not believing this nonsense.

"What is your social security number, Mr. Espinoza?"

Ramiro gave the judge his SS number.

"Do you have your social security card?

"I don't have it on me, your honor?"

"When did you train yourself to memorize your number?" the judge glared at Ramiro with his glasses hanging on the bridge of his nose.

"I'm not sure what age. It was easy to remember?" Ramiro said.

"I don't believe you, Mr. Espinoza! You've got credit card bills from Saks Fifth Avenue, Macy's, Mark's body spa, Bath and Body Works, etc."

"What the fuck do I look like shopping at Saks Fifth Avenue! This case is some fuckin' shit!" Ramiro pounded his fist on the table. "What the fuck!"

The judge banged his gavel on the wooden block. Stanley and Douglas had to calm Ramiro down before he receives additional fines for interruptions in the courtroom.

"Ramiro, relax! Please!" Douglas whispered in his client's ear. Stanley lifted his head, getting the attention of the judge.

"And who may you be?" the judge asked.

"Good morning, your honor. I'm Stanley Mitch, the manager of the Heavy Metal band Irate; of course, I manage Ramiro. I'll pay the funds for the credit card bills," Stanley promised.

"Are you kidding me, Stanley!"

"Shut the fuck up, Ramiro!" for the first time, Ramiro allowed his manager to take the fall.

ABOUT A DAY LATER, a studio engineer arranged the buttons on the mixing board while Ramiro bellowed "The Angels Fell from Heaven" through the microphone with his bass guitar in his hand. Eito kept the foundation for the song on his Tama drum set. He used his double bass technique on the floor bass drum while playing. Eito's talents caused Irate's sound to be even better as Danny head-banged with his electric guitar and their management team watched from behind the scenes.

"Disobedient and loyal angels battled amongst the clouds, God banished those with vile minds, falling beneath the earth to form their demonic congregation, then to influence nations to hate, steal, kill at will," Ramiro proceeded the sing the song. Danny moved his fingers along the neck of the guitar, playing a high screechy sound. During the band's session, Ramiro's cellphone was laid on the table along with his bandmates' valuables. Ramiro's cellphone vibrated with low buzzing as Noelle's picture surfaced. Then the vibration of his cellphone halted. Seconds later, the cellphone quivered again. Of course, Ramiro couldn't respond to the call and then the buzz subsided.

TWO HOURS LATER, AFTER the recording session, Ramiro picked up his cell and saw that he had voice messages and missed calls. "Stan, I'll be outside," Ramiro hurried away with his cell in his hand. He pressed the button to call home.

"Ramiro, hi. Can we go out to dinner or something? Or can you bring something?" Noelle said.

"Baby, I'm still in session. I don't know what time I'll be getting off tonight," Ramiro paced the ground outside of the building.

"I wanted to spend more time since you're so busy," Noelle's voice muffled over the phone.

"If I get off late, I'll try to bring something. Okay?" Ramiro stopped in his tracks.

LATER THAT NIGHT, AT the couple's Greenwich Village apartment, Noelle put on every light that made it more pleasant. Of course, Ramiro was the opposite; he loved the surrounding gloom. While in bed, Noelle watched a Christmas movie even though it wasn't that time of the year yet. She envisioned getting married on Christmas day, but that would be too many occasions wrapped up in one. Christmas day, her birthday, and their wedding. Getting married was a summer event, and where she wouldn't have so much on her plate. She grabbed the remote control for the television, turned the volume up. Noelle laid her head on two stacked pillows, thinking of Ramiro leaving her alone. She got an eerie sense in the apartment. And she wasn't watching a horror movie and couldn't figure it out. Noelle turned down the volume with the remote control. The floor in the corridor creaked as if someone were entering the master bedroom. She glimpsed a shadowy figure.

"Ramiro!" she sprung out of the king-sized slumber. She entered the doorway and caught another glimpse of a strange older man. Her eyes widened as her heart raced in her chest. Noelle looked around, trying to find an object to protect herself. A big umbrella standing in the corner was the best thing she could find. Noelle held it as if she were on the baseball field, ready to hit the ball out of the park.

"Who are you!" She cried out to the intruder again. Noelle crept down the corridor towards the living room. "If you don't get the hell out of my apartment, my fiancé's going to fuck you up!"

As Noelle got towards the end of the hallway, a fist struck her in the face. She plummeted to the wooden floor on her back. Blood streamed from her nose and mouth.

Jorge made his appearance known. "Fuck me up? I don't think so!" He brandished a saw-off shotgun at Noelle. She slid her backside along the floor, trying to get away from this sixty-something trespasser. "Who are you? Oh God, Ramiro!" Noelle cried as this man moved towards Noelle. He pointed the barrel of the gun to her neck.

"Please, please, please don't," she wept. She's meeting Ramiro's father under these deadly circumstances. The only thing she could think of was her life. She focused her mind on Ramiro because he made their love work. He still sought counseling in hopes of a successful marriage. Ramiro would lose his mind if Noelle wound up in a casket. He lost his grandmother already to this man, who was about to pull this trigger and end her life. Noelle's parents would lose their minds if something happened to their only daughter. God was the only one that could get her out of this situation.

"God, please help right now! Where's Ramiro! "Our Father Who Art In Heaven, Hallowed Be Thy Name, Thy Kingdom Come, Thy would be Done, On earth, as it is in Heaven," Noelle prayed.

"Are you sure you're going to be happy with Ramiro? You too have a possibility of having issues," Jorge still shoved the gun in Noelle's neck. "Is he hitting you?"

"No." Noelle shook her head. She didn't tell this mad man that their relationship had issues.

"Don't lie! Ramiro's like me. He hit you, but like most women, you want to cover up for his slaps and punches," Jorge cackled.

"Ramiro did none of that," Noelle shook her head quickly, whimpering.

"That's hard to believe" Jorge pulled back the hammer on top of the firearm. Then jingling keys and clicks unlocking the apartment door grabbed Jorge's attention.

"Noelle! Baby, I've got some Chinese food. I don't know if you want to eat," Ramiro's voice echoed from the front door. Noelle wanted to scream but couldn't because she had Jorge pointing this gun in her face. He immediately placed his hand over Noelle's mouth to prevent her from making a peep. Noelle wept as Jorge pressed the palm of his hand tighter against her mouth. "Shut up!" he whispered. He forced Noelle into the master bedroom with the gun pointed at her head. Jorge closed the door with his foot with ease. While this older gentleman covered Noelle's mouth, she smelt his mildewy aroma. His hands had a similar scent as well. This senior citizen who's about to end her life was the one who put Ramiro through hell as a child. Just thinking about a couple of Ramiro's horror stories made Noelle so Irate because now she's in this mess. Heavy footsteps pound towards the bedroom as Jorge clutched Noelle's body close to him. She felt this man's pelvis area against her buttocks that made her believe he could violate her. Teardrops trickled down the corner of Noelle's eyes as Ramiro's father pressed his hand against her mouth even harder. Jorge would crush her mouth because of the amount of pressure he used. They stood before the king-sized bed as Ramiro's footsteps became more aggressive approaching the door. "Noelle, where are you!" Ramiro pushed open the door with its squeaking hinges. "What the fuck!"

"Long time no see son!" Jorge brandished the firearm at his son.

Ramiro's jaw dropped, seeing the man who mocked, tortured, preached, and now putting his hands on his fiancé has come back to put him through some more shit. He noticed the fear in Noelle's eyes. Then Ramiro had no other choice than to plead with his father, even though he wanted to beat the living fuck out of him. Ramiro's heart throbbed in his rib cage because he didn't want Noelle going through this. They're already trying to put back the pieces of their love. It was like an absolute jigsaw puzzle, where it had pieces showing that Ramiro and Noelle were on the verge of falling apart.

"Let Noelle go. She has nothing to do with this!" Ramiro inched towards his father.

"Get the hell back!" Jorge then pointed the gun directly in his son's face while keeping Noelle close to him.

"Whatever you want or need, I'll give it to you," Ramiro raised his hands in the air. Then it hit Ramiro "What the fuck could I possibly give him. I'm in debt for reasons unknown?"

"Tell me what you want? Dad," Ramiro kept his hands up.

"Dad?" Jorge guffawed. "You have nothing! You may be some big hot shot rock star! You're a loser! God spoke to me and told me to finish you off!" he moved closer to Ramiro.

"Alright, if God told you that, then so be it! Just let Noelle go!" Ramiro spoke gently.

"You know damn well you want to rip my throat out! I heard the song "Everyone Sees Death! That's aimed towards me! And all the poison you spew into the world!"

"What the fuck do you expect when you constantly threw the Bible in my face! No friends! No candy! I wanted to do what other kids did! I had no fuckin' freedom!" Ramiro reminisced when his father accused him of stealing candy.

"Where did you get this!" Jorge held the handful of candy before seven-year-old, Ramiro. He didn't answer. "Who gave it to you!" his father bellowed. Still, Ramiro didn't answer because he got it from Zack during lunchtime at school. He remained quiet. Ramiro didn't want to see Zack get into trouble or lose their friendship. "Thief!" Jorge grabbed his son by the collar, dragging his small body up the steps to the second floor.

"You're choking me!" Ramiro's voice echoed throughout the house. His mother rushed out of the master bedroom. She saw her husband dragging Ramiro down the hallway. Anna Maria grabbed her son in her arms. Then her husband slapped her across the face where she collapsed to the floor. Jorge unbuckled his belt, slipping the leather from his pants, and released lashes to Ramiro's body. The child curled in a fetal position in agony.

"You fuckin' asshole!" Ramiro shouted at his father in reality. "Kill Me!"

"Killing is too easy! I'm going to make you suffer and your little sweetheart here!" Jorge kissed Noelle on the cheek. "Why don't you share her with me?" he then threw Noelle on the bed.

"What the fuck!" Ramiro charged at his father, which was a stupid move. Ramiro attempted to wrestle the gun out of his hand. The two men crashed into the dresser, breaking the mirror. Perfume, make-up, comb, hairbrushes, and other personal items belonging to the couple fell off the vanity. Noelle rolled off the bed, cowering in the corner and praying that none of those bullets came her way. Then BOOM! The first bullet fired into the ceiling. BOOM! Noelle quivered in the corner while covering her ears. The second firing struck in the wall. Ramiro and his father continued to scuffle over the shotgun. Then the third BOOM! Noelle held her hands over her head. Fourth BOOM! Fifth BOOM! A final bullet went off. Ramiro felt the force of the bullet. He felt no burning and warmth in his abdominal area. He looked his father in the eye, noticing the fear in his father's face. "Now you see death!" Ramiro stepped back from his father. "Holy fuck!" Ramiro mouthed. His father placed his hand over his stomach. Blood covered his hands and exposed them to Ramiro. Jorge inched towards Ramiro as if he were Christ-like. "Come with me and you shall be saved!" Ramiro's father fell before him. Jorge laid on his stomach in a pool of blood. Similar to his vision of his father dying right before, now it was a reality. Ramiro's heartbeat throb in his chest as he took a couple of steps to his father. "Is he dead?" then Ramiro stopped in his tracks with a frown. "Am I going to help this mother fucker! Or should I let him die if he is not already?" Ramiro noticed Noelle as she stood to her feet. She crept around the bed, witnessing an enormous pool of red on the floor. They looked at each other, trying to figure out what to do.

"I didn't kill him!" he said to Noelle with a straight face.

"Of course, you didn't!"

Red and blue lights flashed on the apartment window. "Holy shit!" Ramiro stepped to the windows as several Officers stormed out of their vehicles. He pounded his fist on the wall. "Shit!"

CHAPTER TWENTY-SIX

A black-robed judge banged his gavel on a wooden block that next morning in a packed vocal court with Ramiro and his family, Noelle's relatives, witnesses, first responding officers, and Irate fans lending their support to their favorite bassist. The News media covered this story with cameras and reporters getting coverage. "Order!" the judge banged his gavel on the block again. Then the courtroom settled down. "Will the defendant please rise!" the judge ordered. Jorge and his appointed lawyer stood from the seats, facing the judge. Ramiro sat on the first bench on the other side, glaring at his father. Ramiro's bandmates and management team were seated on the second bench right behind Ramiro. Stanley had both hands on Ramiro's shoulder, trying to keep his client from getting into any trouble. His manager felt the tension rising in Ramiro's body as his heart kept beating in his chest. He squirmed, murmuring to himself with his mother and sister on opposite sides of him. Maritza heard every word her brother said as she glared at him. She saw her brother's fiery red face and could feel his handshaking. "Ramiro!" Maritza whispered in his ear. He could hear his sister calling him, but he continued to fix his eyes on his father. "Calm down, please!"

"I am calm!" he whispered back.

"No, you're not! You're wriggling the bench! Relax!" his mother rubbed his back, whispering in his ear. Ramiro wanted to spring from his seat and beat the shit out of his father. The judge continued with the arraignment, but in Ramiro's eyes, jail time wasn't enough. He wanted his father dead. His father got off the hook for his grandmother's death, and there was no way in fuckin' hell he was going to get away with trying to kill him and his fiancé. "Your God will not save your ass now!" he stood to his feet as his mother and sister tried pulling him back into his seat. Stanley also eased Ramiro down in his seat from behind him. He continued to squirm on the bench. The judge addressed Jorge in the horrendous crime. Ramiro leaned forward, hollering where his voice echoed through the courtroom. He was about to break free from his family and manager's grip. Jorge turned to Ramiro, glaring at him with a smile.

"You think this is a fuckin' joke! You mother fucker!" Ramiro leaped from his seat. His family and manager continued to hold him down.

"Mr. Espinoza, calm yourself!" the judge banged his gavel on the block. The judge continued to address Jorge Espinoza. Jorge ignored the judge's words and kept smiling at his son, devilishly. Ramiro couldn't take it anymore and broke free from his manager. He husked on his father as they both plummeted to the floor. While on top of his father, Ramiro hurled multiple punches to his face. Jorge guffawed at every punch, supposedly not feeling the pain. Ramiro continued to throw punches as the courtroom erupted into chaos, screaming, crying, and cheering. Court Officers snatched Ramiro off his father. Irate fans cheered their hero on, fighting with additional court officers. Several Officers dragged Ramiro out of the chaotic courtroom with fans screaming.

"Ramiro! Ramiro! Let go of my son!" his mother cried. Maritza comforted her mother.

Hundreds of Irate fans, along with the media, waited outside. The officers rushed Ramiro to the NYPD patrol car. Metal fans went crazy and fought with dozens of police as well.

"Get the fuck in there!" the officer threw Ramiro in the back of the police car. He slammed the door.

"Fuck you!" Ramiro kicked the glass with his foot. The police car sped off as fans chased behind the vehicle.

"Ramiro! Ramiro!" his fans chanted, running behind the cop car pumping their fists in the air.

A WEEK AND A HALF LATER, Ramiro lounged in a chair in Dr. Hopper's office in a daze. The court didn't bother to hold Ramiro in contempt for his outbursts. But Officers charged Ramiro with kicking the window of the patrol car. God blessed Ramiro, but he failed to acknowledge it. While lounging in the recliner, he had nothing to say. Dr. Hopper stared at him, hoping he'd express his feelings. He wondered how Ramiro felt about his father attempting to come into his life to create havoc.

"The only thing I can say is Noelle's alive. Thanks to me," Ramiro said with an attitude.

"How is that?" Dr. Hopper asked, raising an eyebrow.

"I came home right in the nick of time," Ramiro smirked.

"You're a hero," Dr. Hopper smiled.

"I wouldn't say that," Ramiro tittered. "Noelle and I are getting married! Fuck it! This session is over!" he stormed out of the door. Dr. Hopper gave chase.

Ramiro pressed the button for the elevator desperately in the hallway. "Fuckin' come on!"

"You're going to be ok," Dr. Hopper nodded.

"I know I fuckin' am! I'm debt-free now, so Noelle and I can be happy," Ramiro smiled. the elevator door opened as he stepped in. "Look for your invitation in the mail," he pressed the elevator button as the heavy steel door slid shut.

IN A HALF-PACKED CHURCH, two and a half months later, a flower girl dropped rose petals, taking her steps down the aisle in her pink dress. In this house of worship, where Ramiro sought God for answers, he didn't bother anymore. But Ramiro still stood at the altar, dressed in his black tuxedo. Danny and Eito were Ramiro's best men who supported the bandmate/friend. Zack and his new girlfriend were amongst the guests on this special occasion. Zack joined the band Turmoil after their drummer left. He played for the group in the nick of time which gave him the opportunity. Ramiro's eyes widened, seeing Zack and a ginger-haired, thin, female, mid-twenties, wearing a pink dress. "What is he doing here? Alright, Zack's coming to congratulate me on my marriage. All the difficulties we've had during our career because of our egos getting in the way," he focused his eyes off his former best friend, noticing his sister Maritza holding a floral bouquet, wearing a rose-red bridesmaid's gown waltzing down the aisle.

Eito's cheeks turned a soft red while eyeing Maritza making her way towards the front of the church. Father Ryan clutched the Bible as he stood by Ramiro's side. Ramiro and this man of the cloth became friends despite their views on God. And the grand entrance they had all been waiting for, Noelle took her steps down the aisle escorted by her cousin, Jamal, early thirties, good-looking guy. She wore a champagne-colored Eve of Milady gown with a long vial with matching bridal shoes. Noelle's make-up and hair were done professionally, looking like a million bucks. Ramiro smiled proudly, seeing his bride, making her way to him. "Noelle looks beautiful. Well, I mean. It's our wedding day, of course. She went all out. We went all out. I'm going to make this right, even if my life depends on it. Even if I have to continue to get more counseling. Ramiro glanced at the rows of guests, seeing Noelle's family. As Noelle approached the altar, her cousin left her side for Ramiro to take his place. The bride and groom gazed into each other's eyes as Father Ryan presided over their union.

ON THE NEWLYWED'S NIGHT, Ramiro and Noelle had no time for a honeymoon because he had to go on tour in a couple of weeks. Noelle's cousin brought her the "Hello Fresh" dinner kit as a wedding gift. She cooked sausage and peppered spaghetti meal over a hot stove in the kitchen of their home. Moments later, Ramiro shoved some spaghetti into his mouth, grunting like a pig while he lounged on the couch. Noelle ate from a plate on her lap by his side. She watched her new husband enjoy his food and knew she did her wifely duties. she sipped her canned soda, placing it hard on the table. Ramiro jerked as the sound got his attention. "What's up, babe?" he asked with his mouth full.

"Nothing," Noelle answered.

"It must be something. The way you slammed that can down on the table. What's going on?" Ramiro slowed down his eating.

Noelle had something to tell her new husband, but she wanted the right time to do so. She placed her plate on the table, wiping her mouth with her napkin.

Ramiro ate his last piece of sausage, wiping his mouth with his napkin. He stacked his plate on his wife's plate, piled it on the table. She shifted her eyes between the plates and Ramiro. He lifted an eyebrow, wondering what his new wife hinted to him.

"I know because you cooked the dinner, I've got to wash dishes," Ramiro burped.

"That's disgusting, Ramiro!" she sneered.

"You like it!" Ramiro laid a kiss on her lips. "You're my wife now, and I want you to tour with me."

She placed Ramiro's hand on her stomach. "I can't. Doctor's orders."

Ramiro's eyes widened. "Are you serious, babe?"

"Yes, I wanted to surprise you," she said.

"When did you find out?"

"I went to the doctor last week," a tear streamed down Noelle's face. the couple embraced as Ramiro constantly laid kisses on her. "Why the fuck was I so negative about my future with Noelle. She kept my engagement ring, my love, her faith, and mine. Despite all the bullshit from my past, I say we both fought for our future," he cradled Noelle in his arms as they engaged in a passionate kiss.

IRATE TOURED AGAIN, where they packed arenas from New York to San Francisco. Their fans crashed into one another in mosh pits and headbanged enjoying the show. And then later, Ramiro will have to tour internationally. He kept in touch with Noelle on their baby's progress by video chat. The babies were healthy and hopefully should have a successful delivery. Ramiro received the sonogram of his unborn children and the ultrasound of triple heartbeats in Noelle's womb. He swerved around in his chair with Stanley, Eito, Danny, and the management cheering. One roadie popped the cork off a champagne bottle and poured the first glass. He offered Ramiro the drink with the bubbly alcoholic beverage. Ramiro gulped it down. "Triplets!"

THREE MONTHS LATER, Irate performed in Copenhagen, Denmark, with an audience of over two thousand fans. Ramiro spewed the lyrics to "My Fight With The Devil" of the band's third album entitled "Atheist." He performed his bass solos as he usually did and played as if that House song "To Love Or To Cherish" never existed. Then he played more songs from the third album and even their earlier works. Between songs, Eito struck the drum sticks against the tom-tom snare, cymbals, and using his foot pedals for the floor bass drum. Ramiro swaggered backstage; his manager held his cellphone.

"Ramiro! Noelle's on the phone!" Stanley held the cellphone up. Ramiro rushed to his manager's side, grabbing the cellphone. "Hello!" Ramiro noticed Noelle on the screen, shuffling and can hardly walk. She held the cellphone in her hand. "Hello, baby! How are you?"

"I'm cool. How are you? How are the babies?" Ramiro laughed with his bass guitar in his hand.

"Your daughters are doing great!" Noelle aimed the video camera of the cellphone on her earth-shaped belly.

"Daughters?" Ramiro's eyes widened.

"Yes, Ramiro. You have three daughters!" Noelle sighed as she rubbed her tummy.

"I love you," Ramiro said.

"I love you too," Noelle added.

A WEEK LATER, RAMIRO did a video chat with the court case against his father while pacing the floor of a hotel in Finland. Stanley rocked in a chair in front of the laptop. He eyed his client back and forth. Stanley mouthed to him. "Ramiro, sit down!"

"Leave me alone!" Ramiro mouthed in return, continuing to pace. The judge banged his gavel on the wooden block. "Order!"

Ramiro took a seat quickly as soon as he heard the judge ready to start the case. He felt as if he was in that packed courtroom with his fans giving him support and not in that hotel suite. Ramiro saw the media scrambling for coverage. He hoped the judge would throw the fuckin' book at his father, but first, they had to go through witnesses, first Officers on the scene, and Noelle would have to take the stand. He didn't want Noelle to relive the nightmare again. He pleaded with his lawyer not to allow Noelle to testify. They had enough evidence to pin on Jorge Espinoza. And instead, Ramiro wanted to testify on his wife's behalf because she's expecting and didn't want to jeopardize his unborn children's health.

The judge held up Ramiro's social security card in his hand. He told him that his father used it to purchase the gun. Then it hit Ramiro, how all of those credit card bills came in his name. Jorge used Ramiro's social security number to put him in debt. The judge needed Ramiro to get a new social security number. And he allowed Ramiro to say some words to his father.

"You told me when I was a kid that I wasn't your son and that God made a mistake. You're right. And he made a mistake. I couldn't understand why you were so against me. I never did drugs or took part in criminal activity. The music I listened to bothered you. And since I played it, you gave me the boot. I still made it. And for that reason, you tried to ruin my music career, my finances, and relationship," he expressed on the video chat. His kin sat in the front row, hoping to see this monster put away. Jorge glared at Ramiro through the video chat. He smiled devilishly.

"You are me! You will never get rid of me, Ramiro! You are the flesh of my flesh, the blood of my blood," Jorge guffawed, rocking in his chair like a madman.

"Stop using Bible verses!" his ex-wife stood up from the first row as Maritza tried to hold her down. "You know good and well, you're no man of God. What man tries to murder his son's fiancé!" Tears streamed down her cheeks.

"Alright, Mom. Sit down," Maritza wrapped her arms around her mother.

"I hope you burn in hell!" Mrs. Ellis stood up, raising her voice to the high heavens. Noelle's mother's voice echoed into Ramiro's hotel suite from the video chat. Ramiro rested his back in the chair, hearing his mother-in-law expressed the pain that the entire family has experienced.

"Mrs. Ellis simmer down!" the judge banged his gavel. She obeyed the orders.

"It's going to be ok, Samantha," her nephew sat her down.

The judge banged his gavel an hour later, the clamoring in the courtroom silenced. "Will the defendant please rise!" the judge demanded.

Jorge and his defense attorney stood to their feet, facing the judge.

"Has the jury reached a verdict?"

"Yes, your honor," a male juror answered.

"Your verdict!" the judge said.

"We the jury find Jorge Espinoza guilty of trespassing, weapons possession, and identity theft," the juror announced.

Suddenly, Jorge's heart raced in his chest. He turned red in the face, placing his hand over his heart. He gasped for air as he plummeted to the floor. His lawyer attempted to assist his client. Ramiro's eyes widened as his face glued to the computer screen. He witnessed his father getting a taste of his own medicine. Ramiro gazed and gazed at the laptop while the lawyer, court officers tried to revive him. This bassist wanted to smile because the demon was about to meet his maker. Then he heard the court gasping. Ramiro could hear people screaming that "He's dead!" And yes, Jorge was dead.

"Shit," Ramiro leaned back in his chair.

"I'm sorry," Stanley patted his client. Danny, Eito, and the management team entered the hotel room. They patted Ramiro on the back, giving their condolences.

"Are you alright, Ram!" Eito asked.

"I'm cool," Ramiro responded.

RIGHT IN THE NICK OF time, three months later, Ramiro sprinted through the hospital's double doors, rushing to the information desk. "I'm Ramiro Espinoza. My wife Noelle Espinoza is in labor.

"Mr. Espinoza! Come quickly!" a nurse cried to him. He followed the nurse through the enormous automatic doors. Ramiro heard Noelle's screams of pain as he got closer and closer. He washed his hands and then Ramiro put on the scrubs.

"Where's my husband!" she cried.

Ramiro dashed in behind Noelle, kissing her on the cheek and holding her hand. She pushed these three new lives into the world with all her might. Then the doctor held up the bloody newborn to the surgical light as the baby girl bawled. Then the second baby girl and then the third child.

FOUR YEARS LATER, PINK painted walls of a girl's bedroom, adorned with floral wall décor, dolls, teddies, and the girls' names spelled in capital letters on the walls, F-E-R-O-Z-A, on the other side E-L-I-Z-A-B-E-T-H, and other S-T-E-P-H-A-N-I-E for all to see. A tall stuffed giraffe in the room's corner with other stuffed animals. The bedroom had a cream-colored dresser/mirror, nightstand, and three full-sized beds with pink floral bedding. In these enlarged slumbers laid the four-year-old girls, pink pajama-clad.

"Oh my God, Ramiro! Don't!" a feminine voice cried.

Feroza sat upright in bed with her eyes bulging. She clutched the blankets, glancing at Stephanie. She glanced over her shoulders to Elizabeth as they noticing shadowy feet appearing from under the door cracks. "Is that a monster?" she clutched her doll.

"I'm going to handle this shit my way!" a male voice bellowed.

"That's daddy," Feroza held a tight grip on her blanket.

"I want to go see him," Stephanie added.

"I hope there are no monsters in the hallway," Elizabeth said.

The little girls sprung out of their plush beds, holding hands, and rushed out of the bedroom. They dashed through the dark hallway with a photo of a scary man and another obscure décor along the walls. Feroza led the way, seeing the glow from under the master bedroom door. Stephanie covered her eyes, running, and trying not to bump into anything. Elizabeth kept looking over her shoulders at the creepy pictures in the corridor. She screamed as she believed that something was going to grab her. "Daddy!" Feroza reached her hand to the doorknob of the master bedroom. The toddlers opened the door, only to find their parents, tossing and turning in the king-sized bed. Ramiro was on top of Noelle, with her legs wrapped around his waist.

"Mommy! Daddy! I'm scared!" the triplets hopped in the bed with their parents. Ramiro got off Noelle and grabbed his daughters in his arms.

"What was that screaming!"

"I'm sorry that was me. Acting crazy," Ramiro clutched his kids.

"We're sorry," Noelle apologized to Feroza. She stroked her daughter's long ebony hair.

"Girls, guess what? The Music awards Nominated daddy and his band," Noelle said.

"Yeah," the triplets cheered for their guitar hero father. They laid dozens of kisses on him.

"That means you're going to be on tv again, daddy?" Feroza sat up in bed.

"Yep," Ramiro pulled the covers over him.

"Can I play heavy metal when I grow up?" Stephanie smiled from ear to ear.

"No," Noelle answered abruptly.

"Why not?" Stephanie sucked her teeth.

"Heavy Metal isn't for little girls," her mother shook her head.

"You can do anything you want Stephanie. You can go on tour with me," Ramiro encouraged.

"Yeah," Stephanie cheered.

"I want to sing House music like you, mommy," Feroza caressed her mother's wedding ring.

"You do," Noelle kissed her daughter.

Ramiro laid down, kissing his wife and daughters. The family of five nestled in the king-sized bed. The girls huddled between their parents as all fell into a peaceful snooze.

THE END

About the Author

Alexis Soleil has been writing for thirty years, first starting with screenplays and then later adapting them into novels. She loves writing from her experiences and her massive imagination. She attended Bronx Community College studying Audiiovisual Technology and then to New York Film Academy. She hopes to continue writing stories that will captivate readers everywhere.

About the Publisher

Printed in Great Britain
by Amazon